SEP 0 6 2022

PRAISE FOR BRIAN FREEMAN

"It is so rare to have a psychological thriller that not only completely succeeds . . . but also plays with your heartstrings, leaving behind an incredibly memorable reading experience. *Infinite* is something special, and I cannot recommend it highly enough."

—Bookreporter on *Infinite*

"Even fans used to the wild inventions of Freeman's thrillers had better buckle their seat belts . . . A dizzying delight."

—Kirkus Reviews on *Infinite* (Best Fiction Books of 2021)

"Reads like a whirlwind . . . brilliantly crafted . . . highly recommended for those who enjoy their psychological thrillers infused with plenty of smarts and nonstop action."

—Bookreporter on *Thief River Falls*

"Freeman does a masterful job creating a nightmare scenario of never-ending darkness, roads that go nowhere with bogeymen at every intersection. A disturbing yet compelling thriller."

—*Booklist* on *Thief River Falls*

"This book is a delight to read . . . *The Deep, Deep Snow* is one to share with friends, to recommend for book clubs, or to stash away for a second reading down the road. It's just that good."

—*Star Tribune* on *The Deep, Deep Snow*

"This is a thriller that will keep you up all night. And even the most perceptive crime novel fan will be stunned by the cliff-hanger conclusion."

—*Pioneer Press* on *The Crooked Street*

"Excellent . . . A cleverly constructed, page-turning plot and fleshed-out primary and secondary characters make this a winner."
— *Publishers Weekly* on *Alter Ego* (Starred Review)

"Freeman's latest psychological thriller is sure to seize readers and not let go . . . Gripping, intense, and thoughtful, *The Night Bird* is a must-read."
— *Romantic Times* on *The Night Bird* (Top Pick)

"If there is a way to say 'higher' than 'highly recommended,' I wish I knew it. Because this is one of those thrillers that goes above and beyond."
— *Suspense Magazine* on *Goodbye to the Dead*

"Writing and storytelling don't get much stronger . . . and thriller fiction doesn't get much better than *The Cold Nowhere*."
— Bookreporter on *The Cold Nowhere*

"Brian Freeman proves once again he's a master of psychological suspense."
— Lisa Gardner, #1 *New York Times* bestselling author, on *Spilled Blood*

"Brian Freeman is a first-rate storyteller. *Stalked* is scary, fast paced, and refreshingly well written. The characters are so sharply drawn and interesting we can't wait to meet the next one in the story."
— Nelson DeMille, #1 *New York Times* bestselling author, on *Stalked*

"Breathtakingly real and utterly compelling, *Immoral* dishes up page-turning psychological suspense while treating us lucky readers to some of the most literate and stylish writing you'll find anywhere today."
— Jeffery Deaver, #1 *New York Times* bestselling author, on *Immoral*

I REMEMBER YOU

THE CAB BOLTON SERIES

Season of Fear
The Bone House
*Cab Bolton also appears in *Alter Ego*

ROBERT LUDLUM'S JASON BOURNE SERIES

The Bourne Sacrifice
The Bourne Treachery
The Bourne Evolution

I REMEMBER YOU

YOU

A THRILLER

BRIAN FREEMAN

THOMAS & MERCER

Text copyright © 2022 by Brian Freeman
All rights reserved.

Published by Thomas & Mercer, Seattle

www.apub.com

Amazon, the Amazon logo, and Thomas & Mercer are trademarks of Amazon.com, Inc., or its affiliates.

ISBN-13: 9781542035088 (hardcover)
ISBN-10: 1542035082 (hardcover)

ISBN-13: 9781542035101 (paperback)
ISBN-10: 1542035104 (paperback)

Cover design by Leah Jacobs-Gordon

Printed in the United States of America

First edition

For Marcia,
and in loving memory of Eileen Freeman

Two souls with but a single thought . . .
—John Keats

PART I

1

How bad was that July 4? Let me count the ways.

First, I got fired from my job that morning. Admittedly, this happens to me a lot. My headhunter tells me that I don't know how to play the corporate political games or make nice with people who offer up bad ideas. In other words, I'm not exactly diplomatic when I open my mouth. Guilty as charged. But hey, if you're writing web copy for an implantable prosthesis to treat impotence, expect me to mock you for the headline "Our Pump Will Get You Pumping."

I assumed my boss was kidding about that, but he wasn't. Unfortunately, by the time I realized that, I'd unleashed ten minutes of jokes in front of the entire marketing staff. When I was done, he looked like he needed that implant for himself. So I wasn't altogether surprised that he took time out of his holiday to call and tell me not to bother coming in to work the next day.

Once again, I was between jobs. If you're keeping count, that's three times in the past year. I'd like to pretend that I had enough savings to tide me over for a few months, but in fact, I was dead broke.

That was the beginning of my July 4 from hell.

Next, my boyfriend of two years broke up with me. Two years, and he dumped me cold, not in person but with a text: **You're great, Hallie, but here's the thing.**

What was the thing? Well, it turned out that Nico had been sleeping with my roommate, who was also my best girlfriend, and now he was moving in with her. That's bad enough, but if you read between the lines, you'll see that I lost my lover, my best friend, *and my apartment* in the space of one message thread.

Hallie's score for Independence Day: I was jobless, moneyless, friendless, sexless, and homeless.

And then, like the rocket's red glare to cap off my night, I died.

I'm not kidding. Literally, I died. My heart went into atrial fibrillation, and then it stopped altogether. RIP Hallie Evers, twenty-nine years old.

You'd think that once you die, things can't really get much worse, but oh no, you'd be wrong.

That was when my nightmare began.

I'd spent that July 4 evening at a rooftop party at one of the casinos on the Las Vegas Strip. The atmosphere up there was lush and dreamy, but most of all, it was hot. By ten o'clock at night, the temperature outside was still about a thousand degrees. When you live in Nevada, you feel a little closer to the sun than other places. That was the first of the problems that led to my cardiac arrest. The heat. Even when you think you're used to it, you're not, and you need to be careful. That's particularly true if you have a weak heart, which I do.

The party was sponsored by a New York venture capital firm named Temple Funds that pours millions of dollars into promising medical device start-ups. They were always on the hunt for the next big thing. Technically, the annual MedX convention had wrapped up the previous evening, but almost everyone stayed around for another day of gambling and a last night of free booze courtesy of Paul Temple and his partners. Plus, it was the Fourth, so we all had a great place on the roof to watch the fireworks. I'd planned to go to the party anyway, but now that I was back in the job market, I definitely wasn't going to miss the chance to hang out with a few hundred drunk doctors and engineers who might want to hire me.

Despite the heat, the garden felt like a magical desert. From the roof, the glimmering towers of the other casinos floated around us, as if we were high in the clouds. Orange light bathed rows of palm trees, and the swimming pools gleamed turquoise, making me want to jump in. The late-evening darkness gave the faces a kind of shadowy mystery, like zombies bumping and stumbling around me in a dead man's shuffle. There were private oases surrounding the pools, sheltered by curtains, so people back there could do whatever private things they wanted. A DJ played loud, bass-thumping dance music. Dua Lipa was levitating, and so was I.

That was my second problem. I was drinking way too much. I'm an introvert around strangers, and alcohol loosens me up. However, instead of nursing a little white wine while I networked, I downed psychedelic cocktails that gave off dry ice smoke and switched colors as the LED ice cubes flashed. No, it wasn't a smart strategy, but the booze did its thing for me. I grinned, laughed, joked, winked, flirted, and gathered up a couple dozen business cards from recruiters who were as drunk as I was. Meanwhile, I wondered for the millionth time if the universe was sending me a signal to do something different with my life.

Yeah, that was my real problem. I needed a job, I needed money, but I hated what I was doing to get it. Sound familiar? I had a journalism degree, but nobody hired reporters anymore. Instead, I'd spent seven years since college writing promotional copy and press releases for medical device companies. Most of the time, that meant translating a lot of science-y language written by MDs and PhDs into English and then running it all by the lawyers to make sure I hadn't made any promises that our products actually work. I was good at it. Super good, which was why places kept on hiring me despite my tendency to say out loud the things I was supposed to keep to myself.

Even so, I was having a hard time pretending to be someone I wasn't and to care about things that I didn't. Actually, I was unhappy with pretty much everything about my life and saw no way to change it.

Let's face it, I was having a really bad day.

This wasn't my first bad day, as the scars on my wrist will attest.

"Well, good evening," an accented male voice said while I stared off the rooftop at the lights of the nearby casinos. Then, as the man read the name tag on my lanyard, he added: "Hallie."

"Hi to you, too," I said. Smiles on. Be nice.

The voice belonged to a man in his thirties. He was about five ten, which is my height, but my heels gave me a couple of inches on him. He had short bristle-brush black hair and incredibly thick dark eyebrows. He wore tan slacks, an open-collared white shirt that revealed dense chest hair (sorry—ick), and an olive-colored sport coat. He sipped whiskey from a lowball glass.

According to the MedX badge clipped to his coat pocket, his name was Dov. He was a research scientist with a device company based in Tel Aviv. I hadn't heard of it before.

"Did you enjoy the convention, Hallie?" Dov asked.

"It was fine."

"What do you do in the industry?" he went on.

"Marketing," I said.

"Ah. Marketing."

Doctors and scientists all said that word with the same condescending smirk, not that I could really blame them.

"I'm a writer," I added.

"Oh, I see. Well, I admire writers. That's a real gift, putting thoughts together so people can understand them."

Having softened me up with an insincere compliment, Dov assumed he was free to admire the rest of me, as drunk convention goers usually do. I'd worn my sexiest club dress for this occasion, short and sequined, in shimmery layers of red and purple. I'm tall and bird-skinny, but in this dress, it works for me. I'd gone all out on my face, too, with flecks of gold on my lips and cheeks to hide the pallor. I'd swirled a couple of streaks of burgundy highlights into my swept-back shoulder-length black hair, and I'd done up my short fingernails to match.

"So where do you live, Hallie?" Dov asked me. "Where is home for you?"

"Here."

"In Las Vegas? Really? I thought only Mormons and showgirls lived here."

"Well, I work part time as a Mormon showgirl," I told him.

His eyes narrowed with surprise until he realized I was kidding. "Ah, you're funny. Very funny. Clever, too."

"Right on both counts."

"Have you ever been to Israel?" Dov asked.

"No, I haven't."

"You should go. If you like the desert, you'd love it there."

I was about to ask if he had any jobs available when Dov glanced down at his feet and smacked his lips with disgust. "Another one! They're everywhere, the little monsters. I hate the things. They creep me out."

When I looked down, I saw one of the tiny omnipresent desert lizards that call Las Vegas home. This one was obviously confused about where he was and scared to be in a land of giants. I was about to kneel down and pick him up when Dov stomped down on the reptile with his boot. The scientist slapped his hands together, grunted with satisfaction, and then lifted his foot and kicked the dead little lizard toward the wall.

I lost it. I completely lost it.

"What the fuck did you do that for?" I shouted at him. I mean, I *shouted*.

"Huh? It was a lizard."

"You killed it, you son of a bitch!"

Dov stared at me. "Are you kidding?"

"He wasn't doing anything to you. He was harmless. He had one chance at life, and you took it away. Jesus, who does something like that?"

Dov held up his hands in surrender and began to back away from me, the way you would from a rabid animal. I helped him by shoving hard on his chest, making him stumble and nearly fall.

"Fucker!" I screamed.

That was loud. That was very loud. People heard me all around the party and looked our way. Dov recovered his balance and couldn't get away from me fast enough, and I heard him muttering so that others could hear him: "Crazy bitch."

Okay, that was not my best career move.

Silence fell in a wave across the crowd, and my cheeks flushed red as everyone continued to stare at Drunk Swearing Girl. I even saw the man himself, Paul Temple of Temple Funds, give me a curious look and lean over to whisper something to the man next to him. I really didn't think he was saying, "That girl over there, see if she needs a job."

Fortunately, the Paris casino chose that moment to launch holiday fireworks across the street, which distracted the crowd. Most of them looked up to ooh and aah at the display, so I was able to slink away in a discreet retreat. I made my way back to the open bar because my hurricane glass was empty. I felt like an idiot and wanted to keep drowning my sorrows.

"Hey, could I get another drink?" I called out at the bar. "Hello?"

I spotted a tuxedo-clad bartender chatting up one of the waitresses as they watched the fireworks. He didn't notice me, or if he did, he didn't think I looked like a big tipper. I shrugged and reached over the bar and grabbed a bottle of cabernet that was two-thirds full. I yanked out the cork and took a long swig, not bothering to find a glass. Some of it spilled down my chin. I probably looked like a vampire, dripping blood from my mouth.

Not far away, I heard somebody call my name.

"That's not a good idea, Hallie."

I glanced at a nearby cocktail table, where an attractive young woman stood off by herself. She gave me a familiar look of disappointment, either because she didn't approve of me drinking the wine, or because she didn't approve of me stealing the wine. Or both. Either way, this woman wasn't a stranger to me. In fact, I knew her only too well, and she knew me even better. She was—I shit you not—my shrink.

God sends some people their guardian angels. Me, he sends my therapist.

I still had the bottle as I joined her at the table, and I tilted it toward her own wineglass in case she wanted more. She shook her head, so I took another swig. Mixing wine with the hard stuff—that was another bad idea.

"Tori," I said. "Of all the gin joints, et cetera, et cetera."

"Hello, Hallie."

"What are you doing here?"

Tori's eyes blinked in surprise. She probably wanted to roll them but figured she couldn't do that with a patient. "Um, the MedX convention?"

She could have added *Duh*, but she didn't need to.

"Yeah, sure, sorry," I said.

"How are you, Hallie?"

"I'm having a bad day."

"I can see that."

She sipped her wine as fireworks exploded over our heads. In the multicolored glow, she studied me with a shrink's directness over the rim of the wineglass. Most people look at you quickly and then look away, but Tori's large dark eyes were like the ones in a painting that follow you wherever you go without moving or blinking.

Even on a hot Vegas night, Tori had a cool look about her. She was attractive without working hard at it, which is a quality I envy. She had reddish-brown hair, falling to her shoulders in a shower of kinky curls. Her skin had a gorgeous tawny quality, with a few freckles across her nose and cheeks, and she wore pale lipstick. She was shorter than me but more curvy, with the kind of body that men noticed. Her little purple dress showed it off to full effect. Her ears and fingers glittered with expensive jewelry, and a little hint of lavender perfume hung in the air between us.

"It's been a while," Tori continued. "Four months?"

"I think so."

"You missed your last appointment."

"Yeah, something came up."

What came up was me chickening out. It wasn't Tori's fault. She was the latest in a string of therapists I'd jettisoned since I was a teenager. I liked Tori because she was young, unlike most of the dreary old men I'd seen in the past. She specialized in patients with violent trauma in their childhood—me again—and those patients are often sought after as guinea pigs by medical device and pharma companies. Hence her presence at MedX, where we'd met the previous year.

"What happened over there?" she asked, nodding toward where I'd had my altercation with Dov.

"Nothing."

"It didn't look like nothing."

"Some asshole did something I didn't like."

"Namely?"

"He stepped on a lizard."

Tori, to her credit, didn't treat that as a minor thing. "You like lizards."

Mom, look! Look what I found outside! Isn't he cute? Can I keep him?

"Yes, I do."

"Well, that was cruel of him," Tori said. "He shouldn't have done that."

"No."

She knew what buttons Dov had pushed because of our sessions together, but really, she'd figured me out as soon as she met me. When

I'd first chatted to her after a MedX panel the previous year, her enigmatic dark eyes had shifted to my left wrist, then back up to stare at me again. It happened so fast, in the space of a blink, that I could have missed it, but I didn't. She didn't say anything, but she didn't need to. I got the message.

Yes, I noticed the scars.

So what the hell, I gave her a shot as my therapist. For eight months, I went to see her every couple of weeks, and she peeled me like an onion. But four months ago, we'd finally gotten down to the heart of the matter—my mother's death—and she'd asked if I was willing to try hypnosis to see what my brain had been hiding from me all these years.

I said yes.

I said I was finally ready. Then I didn't show up for the appointment, and I never went back to see her again.

"May I ask you a question, Hallie?"

"Why not?"

"Are you seeing another therapist?"

"Jealous, are we?" I joked.

"Just concerned."

"I'm fine," I said. "That's why I quit. No problems."

"Until today?"

"Right. Today's not a good day, but it is what it is."

"Have you been purging?" she asked with that same startling directness.

"No."

"Really?"

"No, I don't do that anymore."

"Okay," she said, but those pale lips and way-too-smart eyes said she didn't believe me. And she was right not to believe me. I was lying through my teeth. I'd cut way back on my purging, but I still did it when I felt stressed. Like, you know, after being fired and dumped and fucked around by an asshole stepping on a lizard.

11

"I'd be happy to schedule an appointment for you," Tori told me. "If you're interested."

"Thanks, but no thanks."

"No offense, but I think you still could use some help."

"The 'no offense' part makes that sound a lot better," I said.

"Well, it's only my gut reaction, but I trust my gut."

"I need to go," I said impatiently. What I meant was, I needed to pee, but I didn't say that.

"Okay. It was a pleasure seeing you again, Hallie."

"Yeah, it was a real Rice Krispie treat."

"Take care of yourself."

"You too."

I took the wine bottle, tilted it back, and finished what was left. More of it spilled down my face and dress than went down my throat. I turned my back on Tori, and I tried not to fall down and completely embarrass myself as I wobbled toward the bathroom. I was angry that she'd seen through me so readily, but that was a convenient excuse to avoid being angry at myself. Because the real problem was me. At that particular moment, I hated myself, the world, and everyone and everything in it.

The elegant casino restroom was cold and dimly lit. I staggered into the nearest stall and locked the door. First I peed. Then I turned around and got down on my knees. I shoved a finger into my throat until I vomited. After that, I cried at what I'd done and beat my hands against the toilet seat in humiliation. Finally, I got out and went to the sink and rinsed out my mouth. When I looked at my reflection, I saw mascara and gold dust running in streaks down my cheeks. Tears leaked from my brown eyes, and the bright whites were shot through with red. I have a narrow face, and the shadows brought out the bones in my sunken cheeks. My lips were parted, as if asking myself questions that I couldn't answer.

Questions like *What are you sticking around for, Hallie?*

Yes, I was at the end of a bad day. A really, really bad day. The only thing I could think to do was make it worse. And so I did. Much worse.

I opened my purse, where I had a little plastic bag of cocaine I'd purchased earlier in the day with the last hundred dollars that I could get from an ATM. It had seemed like a good investment at the time. I laid it all out on the counter in a neat line, and then I leaned over.

No, this was not my first rodeo with coke, but it had been months since I'd done any. I'd been trying to quit cold turkey. I swear it had been months, but I told you, I told you, *I was having a really bad day!*

Anyway, it all went up my nose. It didn't take long for the coke to do what coke does. By the time I left the bathroom, my bad day had blown away with the Las Vegas winds. I marched back to the party, feeling invincible. I was Hallie the Great, Conqueror of Worlds. Take that and shove it, Tori. I knew, I just knew, everything was going to be fine. What the hell was I worried about? Someone would hire me. I would find an apartment. I would get a new boyfriend. And the fireworks! They were bright and beautiful, those roses in the sky, those white streaks cascading like shooting stars. I could stare at them forever. I could conduct them like an orchestra. I could take my fingers and paint the whole sky in colors.

The only tiny thing I didn't like, the only thing that felt even a little bit wrong, was the thunder vibrating in my chest. I kept waiting for it to thump in time with the rhythm of the fireworks, but the pounding under my breasts seemed off, like a dancer losing a step.

My heart was pushing to get out of my chest, beating a mile a minute.

Ten miles a minute.

One hundred miles a minute.

How could it go so fast?

But that seemed like such a tiny, tiny thing to worry about when the rest of the world was so fine.

2

That night at the casino was not the first time I died. I was a very competent fifteen-year-old, so when I slashed my wrist at that age (vertically, not horizontally, to maximize the blood loss), I arrested in the emergency room while they were in the middle of transfusing me. The doctors had to jolt my heart back to life, which they did. God must not be too anxious to meet Hallie Evers, because he keeps sending me back despite my best efforts to join him.

Just as I had fourteen years earlier, I woke up, alive, in a hospital bed. I had the warm drab room to myself. I didn't know how long I'd been unconscious, but the hot Las Vegas sun was beating in through the window. It looked like afternoon. I was hooked up to a variety of fluids and machines, and I heard a calm beep-beep-beep telling me that my heart was beating normally again. Even so, my chest hurt like hell, as if someone had punched me repeatedly in the ribs.

"You were dead," someone told me.

A grandmotherly Hispanic nurse bustled into the hospital room. She began to check my vitals, which still seemed pretty vital for a dead woman. She went about her work efficiently, but as she did, she shot me a smile that was made up of a spoonful of sympathy mixed with a generous dose of *tsk, tsk*.

"Your heart stopped," she went on. "You're lucky you were at a party full of doctors. One of them saved you with an AED. Otherwise, you wouldn't be with us. You'd be with God."

"I guess so."

That wasn't a very deep thing to say, but I was still processing the idea of dying and coming back to life.

"Pretty young thing like you, what a waste that would have been."

"Yeah."

"You shouldn't do drugs," she added, using her index finger to punctuate the point.

"I know that."

"How do you feel?"

How did I feel? That was a good question. I thought about it and said the first thing that popped into my head. "Crowded."

"What?"

"I feel crowded."

"I don't understand."

"Me neither."

I really didn't know how to explain it, but *crowded* was the only word that seemed to fit. I felt as if I'd wandered onto the I-15 at five o'clock, with cars crawling and honking all around me. But the Las Vegas rush hour was completely inside my head. The sensation produced a sharp, throbbing ache behind my eyes.

"Do you remember anything from when you died?" the nurse asked me. "I always ask the ones we revive. Sometimes they see things, you know?"

"Like what?"

"Oh, relatives that passed. Or angels."

In fact, I did remember something, but it wasn't an angel or a relative. Instead, it was a well-muscled naked guy with a beard. He occupied the middle ground of my brain while the rest of my thoughts and memories raced around him.

"Who's the guy with the trident?" I asked.

"What?"

15

"The sea god with the trident."

"I have no idea," the nurse replied.

"Poseidon," I suddenly said, snapping my fingers. "I remember Poseidon. I saw him while I was dead. What do you think that means?"

"I have no idea."

The nurse gave me an expression of concern, as if maybe the cocaine hadn't completely departed my system. She was also wearing a cross and probably didn't want to hear any loose talk about polytheism. Admittedly, I didn't believe in gods, either, and I couldn't recall thinking about Poseidon since I'd taken a mythology class in high school. But there he was in my head, twice my size, looming over me with his trident raised high in the air.

"I'll tell the doctor you're awake," the nurse said. She hurried out of the room as if she wanted to get away from the crazy girl.

When she was gone, I spent a long time staring at the ceiling. My headache got worse whenever I closed my eyes, so I tried to keep them open. I could have used a few Advil, but I didn't think they'd give me any. I wondered who knew I was here. Probably nobody, because I'd never filled out any emergency contact forms. Even if I had, I would have put Nico's name as my boyfriend, and he wasn't my boyfriend anymore. I also wondered how much this little hospital vacation was going to cost me. I wasn't sure if I still had any health insurance, since I'd been fired.

My mouth was so dry I could barely work up any spit on my tongue. There was a plastic pitcher of water on the table near my bed, so I assumed they didn't care if I drank something. I grabbed the pitcher and filled a foam cup, and after I drank the whole thing, I sank back on the pillow. Despite my best efforts to stay awake, my eyes blinked shut. I felt a whoosh as my brain sped up, so I opened my eyes again, not liking the sensation. Maybe somewhere in the middle, I slept for a couple of minutes, because I started in surprise to see an Indian doctor standing over the bed. I hadn't been aware of him entering the room. He was short and honey skinned, with a shaved head and wire-rimmed glasses.

"Ms. Evers," he said in a low polite voice. "Welcome back to the world. How are you feeling?"

"Like I was hit by a train."

"Yes, that's understandable. Your body has been through a lot. I'm sure the nurse told you that you had a very close call."

"She did. So what's the outlook? Am I going to live?"

He looked like he didn't want to make promises. "In all likelihood, you're out of immediate danger, but I want to keep you here for at least another day or two to monitor your progress."

More time in the hospital. *Ka-ching!*

"How long have I been here?" I asked.

"Since last night."

"And what exactly happened to me?"

"You went into cardiac arrest," the doctor explained. "No doubt as a result of excessive alcohol use combined with significant quantities of cocaine. Although I suspect there were other complicating factors, too. I found your name in our clinic records, and I talked to your primary care physician. She mentioned issues with bulimia stretching over a period of years. That probably weakened your heart."

"Yes, she warned me about that, too."

"You need to make some life changes, Ms. Evers," he told me with a fatherly frown. "I'd rather not see you back here. Being twenty-nine years old doesn't make you invincible."

"I understand."

"Do you?"

"I know I need to clean up my act."

"Good. Because if I conclude that you're a danger to yourself, I can bring in the county authorities, but I'd rather not do that."

"I'd rather you not do that, too. I screwed up, Doctor. I get that. And really, I'm very grateful. Which reminds me, who saved my life?"

"What?"

"At the party. The nurse said a doctor restarted my heart. Do you know who it was?"

"Yes, I met him briefly. I'm pretty sure he said his name was Dr. Reed Smith. He works at Johns Hopkins, and he was in town for the MedX convention. He's the one who revived you. He stopped in at the hospital to check on you a couple of hours ago, but you were still asleep. I think he's already on a plane back to the East Coast."

"Well, I'll have to send him flowers or something." Then I added, "By the way, I have a splitting headache. It's awful, like a spike through my forehead. Could I get something for it?"

"Eventually, I may be able to give you a low dose of acetaminophen, but it's too soon for that. In the meantime, I can have the nurse bring some damp towels and put on some soft music. Relaxation should ease the headache."

He turned to leave the room, but I called after him. "I feel crowded, too. Is that normal?"

The doctor smiled at me but obviously had no idea what I was talking about. "I'm sorry, what?"

"Crowded. Like there's too much in my head. Like my brain doesn't fit in there anymore. It's weird."

He pursed his lips, looking puzzled. "We did a CT scan. It's normal. There is no evidence of stroke or other anomalies."

"Oh. Okay. Well, I guess that's good."

"Try to get some sleep, Ms. Evers," he said in his best reassuring voice. "Your body and mind are both trying to recover from trauma. Sleep is the best medicine for you right now."

So I slept.

That was when I had the first dream.

I don't usually remember my dreams, but this one was different. I had never experienced a dream that was so vivid.

It was a starry night, a clear dark sky over my head. There was Poseidon, the man from my dead memories. He was a statue atop a marble base, at least twelve feet tall, golden bronze. He was naked, his muscles chiseled and genitals exposed, the male perfection of a god. His hair and beard were curly and full. He stared off toward some unseen horizon. With his left arm straight out, he pointed a threatening finger, and with his right arm, he gripped his trident, poised to hurl it into battle.

Beyond Poseidon, the angry sea roared. I stood on a high cliff, with the ocean hurling waves against the rocks below me. The wind howled. It made me shudder, and it swirled my long hair across my face. My body shivered with cold. My skin was damp, and my clothes were wet. I smelled and tasted salty brine blasting over me from the sea spray.

I had never been to this place before; it was foreign to me. And yet I remembered every detail, every color, every sensation. The lush green grass, sodden under my bare feet. The glint of starlight on the metal of the god's statue. The trees bending and tossing wildly with the frigid gales. And beyond the cliff, the vast black water erupting with foam.

None of it felt like a dream.

I was *here*. This was *happening*. This was *real*.

I glided to the cliff's edge, no longer feeling the ground beneath my feet. My summer dress blew behind me. The land ended in a fraying ribbon of grass and mud, and I stared down at the whirlpools whipping among the sharp rocks.

Jump, I thought. *Death is what you deserve.*

I shouted out loud to the ocean, to Poseidon, to the stars. But the wild night made my voice sound pitifully weak.

"Oh my God, what did I do?"

Tears poured down my face, and I could barely catch my breath. My arms trembled in spasms that I couldn't control. I lifted my hands and stared at them, and I saw with horror that my hands were bathed in a rich ruby color that the spray was slowly washing clean.

Blood.

My hands were covered in blood.

3

"Do you remember me?" someone asked.

I sat in a chair by the hospital window, where I could see the craggy cliffs of the western mountains. My chin leaned on my palm, and my foot tapped impatiently, because I was ready to leave. It was two days later. Checkout day. They'd be coming with the wheelchair soon to take me away. The Indian doctor had told me I was fine, but I had to remember that my heart was still weak.

"No more drugs," he said.

The nurse wagged her finger and told me the same thing. "No more drugs."

I promised both of them that I was ready to start a new life.

As I waited for the attendant to collect me, I spotted my shrink, Tori, standing in the doorway.

"Do you remember me?" she said again. "Do you know who I am?"

"All I did was die, Tori. Jeez."

That won a smile from her. "Well, good."

She flowed into the hospital room the way honey would, slowly and sweetly. Her reddish hair reminded me of a sunset, and the freckles on her mocha skin were like a constellation of stars. She was dressed in faded jeans and wore a casual green top with half sleeves. She came to the window and stared at the mountains, as I'd been doing. Her lavender perfume couldn't hide the lingering whiff of cigarette smoke. That was at least one vice I'd avoided in my life. I didn't smoke and never had.

She turned her cool dark eyes down to me, and her eyebrows arched curiously. "How are you, Hallie?"

"Recovering nicely, thank you," I said, although I didn't mention the crowded sensation inside my head.

"You'll be released soon?"

"In a few minutes."

"I'm glad to hear it."

"So what are you doing here, Tori?"

She gave me another *duh* look at that question. "You gave everyone quite the scare. I thought I would stop in here and see if you wanted to talk."

"Talk about what? The Raiders? The odds on keno? Which are really sucky, by the way."

She exhaled a long quiet sigh. "Denial isn't funny, you know."

"You think I'm in denial?"

"Hallie, you *died*," she reminded me with quiet firmness. "Call it whatever you want, but this was obviously a suicide attempt, and it wasn't your first. Unless you start dealing with your past, your self-destructive behavior is likely to continue. And on your next attempt, you might get it right. So my offer stands, if you're interested."

"What offer is that?"

"Going back into therapy."

"Yeah, I don't think so. But thanks."

"You need to talk to someone. I'm serious. If it's not me, then find someone else. I can give you names."

"Look, Tori, it's nice of you to come see me. That's going above and beyond. I appreciate your concern, too, but I don't need your help or anybody else's help. I have plenty of people to talk to."

"I'm relieved to hear that," she replied. Then she added, "Name two."

Shit. I couldn't even name one.

"What exactly do you want me to talk about?" I asked, not hiding my exasperation.

Tori chose her words carefully. "The issue with you hasn't changed, Hallie. Not since you were a girl. Blocked memories start out by protecting you, but later they can become a kind of cancer."

"I'm fine," I insisted.

"You still don't remember that day? You don't remember going into your mother's room?"

"No. I don't. And I don't know how it will help to remember it, anyway. I remember everything else. The whole long Book of Hallie, okay? My sister was murdered. My aunt and uncle took me in, but they made sure I knew that I was a pain in the ass. I started purging when I was twelve. A boy made me go down on him when I was fourteen because I wanted to use his swimming pool. A year later, that all led me to do this."

I held up my wrist, scars and all.

"So how much will you charge to fix all of that?" I asked sourly.

"Therapy isn't about fixing people," Tori replied. "You know that. It's about living with things you can't change."

"Yeah, you've said that before."

Tori hesitated, then spoke softly. "Hallie, I'm trying to get you to connect the dots. Your mother shot herself when you were ten years old. You were there, you saw it, and you ran away. And your brain won't let you back into her bedroom. I'm telling you there's a direct link between that day and what happened on the roof of that casino. What's more, I don't need to tell you that at all because you're wicked smart, and you already know it's true. But you're afraid of dealing with it, and you'd rather fuck up your whole life than do something about it."

If she figured I'd admit she was right, then she didn't know me as well as she thought. "Hey, Tori? I'm not trying to be a bitch or anything, but can you leave me alone?"

She shrugged in resignation. "Of course."

"Thank you."

Tori took a pink notepad out of her purse and used a Cross pen to write something down. Then she tore off the paper, folded it, and pushed it into my limp hand. "I don't know if you kept my number, so here it is again. Truly, if you ever want to talk, call me. Or text me if you prefer. Don't worry about the time. You don't have to live with this by yourself, Hallie. You really don't."

"Yeah. Right."

Tori stared out the window again. "The mountains really are beautiful, aren't they?"

"Yes, they are."

"One last thing, Hallie. Tell me about your sister."

I shook my head. "My sister? What are you talking about?"

"You said your sister was murdered. You've never mentioned anything about that before."

"I never said that."

The expression on her face didn't change. "Okay."

"I never said that," I repeated firmly. "I'm an only child. I don't have a sister."

"I see. Well, I must have misheard you."

Tori left the room without saying goodbye.

An hour later, I took a cab to retrieve my car from the parking garage at the casino. Just to add insult to injury, my credit card was declined when I tried to pay the bill for parking. The attendant wanted me to come up with cash, which I didn't have. I told him that I was the girl who'd died here a couple of days ago and asked him to give me a break. I don't know if he thought I was crazy, but he finally let me go without paying.

I drove away without any destination in mind. I had no job and no apartment, so there was no place for me to be. I also felt agitated, restless, keyed up, like a remote control car that a kid keeps shooting off in new directions. That was partly because of the things Tori had said— she really had a way of nailing my weaknesses—but partly because my brain simply felt *off*.

That sensation manifested itself in odd ways, but mostly with a suffocating sense of paranoia. As I drove, I noticed that my mirror wasn't adjusted right. My seat seemed to have been moved, too.

My first thought was, *Did someone break into my car?*

When a black Ford SUV stayed behind me for six blocks, I was sure that he was watching me. Following me.

Then he turned away. No, he wasn't.

I kept driving. Eventually, I merged onto the 215 Beltway at Decatur and headed west. I followed the highway to the northwest part of the city, and then I got off at Charleston Boulevard and made my way toward Red Rock Canyon. I had an annual pass to the park, and I came here to hike and write almost every week. The one-way thirteen-mile loop road climbed into the hills, and I followed a parade of tourists until I reached a turnoff near the highest elevation. There, I parked and found a bench where I could sit by myself, with a view over the desert valley.

It was another summer day on the surface of the sun, 105 degrees before noon, the kind of ferocious heat that makes you feel as if your skin is peeling off. Most people didn't last long outside their air-conditioned cars. I looked down across the flat plain, which was strewn with yucca, greasewood, and cacti. The bone-dry creek beds looked like moonscapes, littered with loose rock spread in the flash floods of the monsoons. Where the plains ended on the far side of the canyon, rocky hills rose in geological layers of cream, beige, and rust-colored stone.

This was one of my favorite places. My mother used to take me to this spot when I was a little girl. She'd tell me that the hills had been in this place for millions of years and would be here for millions more after the two of us were gone. I had no concept of what that meant, but it sounded like a very long time. I also had no idea that my mother would be gone very soon herself.

My mother.

I was young enough when she left me that she didn't feel entirely real to me anymore. She was a person I knew mostly from photographs. I had a few blurry memories of her in my head, and that was all. But at Red Rock, she felt alive. I could hear the echo of her voice as she sang me a song and feel the smoothness of her hand holding mine. I could watch her close her eyes and lift her chin to savor the warm gusts of wind.

She was a very smart, very private, very troubled woman. She'd worked as a professor of romance languages at UNLV, and she looked a lot like me, tall, dark haired, dangerously thin. She was a Rhodes scholar who saw devils and winged aliens in restaurants and thought the dishwasher was spying on her and sometimes stayed in her bedroom with the lights off for days at a time. Before her condition worsened, she'd gone to an academic conference in Rome and had a one-night stand with an older married man from Cambridge. The result of that tryst was me. She never told him about the baby, and she never told me who he was. I only learned the story from my uncle a few years after my mother died.

It took me a long time to stop blaming her for taking her own life. She didn't ask for schizophrenia, and she didn't leave me alone because she wanted to. No, it wasn't her fault that the voices in her head were stronger than she was. But ever since, I'd lived in fear that I would follow the same road sooner or later.

That the day would come when *I'd* start hearing voices, too.

That was what terrified me about this strange, crowded feeling in my head.

It wasn't voices I heard. Not really. But I seemed to be *remembering* things I'd never experienced. As I stared down at the canyon, people came and went. They got out of their cars, admired the view, talked, laughed. They were strangers to me, and yet their faces triggered flashes of memory. Seeing them, I had visions of people I'd met and places I'd been. I could picture all of those things as sharply as if I were watching a 4K television screen, but the trouble was, I didn't actually know any of them. Not who the people were. Not where I was.

It was as if that vivid dream by the cliffside were chasing me into real life.

What was happening to me?

I'd thought—I'd hoped—that my mind would begin to feel calmer and slower among the tranquil peace of the hills. In fact, it only seemed to get worse. My mental traffic sped up, intensifying my headache. I needed to get out of here. I needed to keep moving, even if I had nowhere to go.

So in one quick, jerky motion, I got up from the bench and spun around. As I did, I saw a man standing next to a black Ford SUV on the far side of the parking area. He got back into his vehicle as soon as I saw him, and I didn't have time to focus on his features. He was young. Tall. Muscular. Long blond hair. That was all I noticed about him. Once he was inside, the Ford roared to life and drove away on the curving canyon road.

A black SUV.

My thoughts went crazy again.

Was that the same vehicle that had been behind me for several blocks as I drove through the city?

Was I really being followed?

I no longer knew whether I could trust what my brain was telling me. I didn't know what was real and what was illusion.

Paranoia.

That was how it had started with my mother, too.

4

Just about the last person I wanted to go to for help was Nico Tosis. He was my Greek ex-boyfriend, the one who'd dumped me with a few text messages on July 4. I really did not want to see his face again. On the other hand, he worked behind the registration desk at the Red Rock Casino, so I figured he could comp me a room for a couple of days while I figured out what to do next.

In the lobby there was a long line of people checking in and out of the hotel. Nico looked hassled, and seeing me obviously didn't help his mood. I caught his eye, then gestured toward the bar for him to meet me when he could break away for a couple of minutes. I took a seat in the central atrium, underneath a rocket-shaped white chandelier.

From where I was sitting, I could see Nico dealing with the guests. He was pretty enough to be a model, no doubt about that. Actually, he'd tried to break through as a model when he lived in LA, but that's a tough sell even for beautiful people. He had wild black hair, thick and curly, and an angular face. He was a couple of inches shorter than me and a couple of years younger than me, but I'd never minded that. His vulnerable brown eyes and Athenian accent had me melting from the moment we met. The sex was decent—not that I'd had a lot of experience for comparison. I didn't go for hookups, and I didn't fall for guys easily, so I could count on one hand the number of men who'd ever made it into my bed.

We'd met because of my work. I was doing brochure copy on a new type of hearing aid, and Nico had lost most of the hearing in one ear when he was a boy. The device had done wonders for him, and I was assigned to write his profile. The interview had led to dinner, and dinner had led to sex, and the result was the longest relationship of my life. Two years. Definitely a new record.

Of course, the thing with our names should have been a red flag. Celebrities got cute nicknames like Brangelina. I got HallieTosis.

I waited in the lobby for almost an hour before Nico came to see me. I can't blame him for not wanting to talk to me. He probably thought I was there to beg him to come back, or to pitch a fit and start beating on that beautiful face. To his credit, his eyes were sad when he looked at me. Yes, he'd been screwing my roommate for three months behind my back, but hey, he felt bad about it.

"Hallie, I am really sorry," he said. I hadn't heard that accent in a few days, and I was annoyed that it still made me kind of weak in the knees.

"Yeah. Me too."

I waited for his next attempt at sincerity, which I assumed would be *I never meant for this to happen.*

"I never meant for this to happen," Nico continued, right on schedule. "Me and Mishawn, we never expected these feelings for each other."

"Sure."

Nico was probably being honest. He was beautiful, but in many ways he was still just a little boy. I'd always found him to be pretty naive. My ex-roommate, on the other hand, was a cowbird just waiting to drop her eggs in somebody else's nest. Mishawn was a Cirque dancer with an absurdly flexible body, and I should have been on high alert as soon as I saw the hungry look in her eyes when she met Nico. But I guess I was a little naive, too.

"Are you okay?" Nico asked. "How are you?"

I felt no need to bring him up to speed. Drinking, drugs, dying.

"Look, I didn't come over here to rehash you and me," I said. "You want Mishawn, you can have her. Just watch your back, Nic. She likes the getting more than the having."

He wore a confused look, as if he didn't know what I meant. I gave their relationship four months tops.

"Then why are you here?" he asked.

"I need a place to crash. Just for a couple of days until I can find someplace new. I was hoping you could set me up here at the hotel."

Nico frowned. "We're very busy. Couldn't you stay with your aunt and uncle?"

"You know how it is with them," I said. "Every dinner is a chance for my aunt to tell me what I'm doing wrong with my life."

"Can you pay for the room?"

I rolled my eyes and said a little prayer that the rocket chandelier would fall on his head. "If I had any money, I could pay, but I cleaned out my checking account for the July rent on the place with Mishawn. So technically, I could move back there for the rest of the month, but I don't think any of the three of us want that, right? Come on, Nic. I'm not asking you to put me in a high roller suite. Give me a room with a bed and a shower for a few days. You must have something. As soon as I land a freelance gig, I'll have a few bucks, and I'll be gone."

"You lost your job again?"

"I lost my job again."

"You don't play nice with people."

"Yes, I know. I'm working on it. Look, you owe me. You were a bastard for cheating on me, and you didn't even have the balls to confront me in person when you dumped me. Now I'm homeless, all right? So get me a room. I'll pay you back as soon as I can."

That would be when hell froze over, which wasn't very likely in Las Vegas.

Nico breathed out an exaggerated sigh. "Yes, yes, all right."

"And give me some cash, too."

"Are you kidding?"

"No. What do you have on you? You always have money. I know you. You like flashing it around."

He gave me sigh number two and extracted his wallet from his tight hotel pants. He plucked out four hundred-dollar bills and handed them over to me. That's another weird thing about Las Vegas. Men compete over how many hundreds they have on them at any given time.

"That's all I have," Nico said.

I was sure he had more, but I decided not to be greedy. "Thank you."

"I'll get you a key."

"Great. Make the room high up. I like the view."

He was about to complain, but he shut his mouth with a scowl. I watched him go back to the desk, and he worked his magic at the keyboard. A couple of minutes later, he returned and shoved a plastic key card into my hand. "Here."

"Thanks."

I danced on my feet, trying to decide what to do next. I was pissed about things ending this way, because he'd been a colossal jerk. But two years was two years. So I leaned in and kissed him, with enough pressure to make him miss me, but not so much that he thought I wanted him back.

"See ya," I told him.

"Yeah, see ya."

I had a little roller bag with me that contained most of my clothes. It had been sitting in the trunk of my car for two days. I pulled it behind me as I headed into the casino, which gave me a headache with all of its bells and whistles and the stale smell of cigarettes. Chris Martin and Coldplay sang on speakers overhead to keep the millennial gamblers happy. The song was "Don't Panic." That was good advice. I was actually feeling a little better, because now I had a place to sleep and some money in my pocket again. I went to the service window and broke the hundreds into twenties, and I took one of the twenties and dropped it into a Zodiac Lion slot machine. I played eight dollars, and a couple of minutes later I won ninety.

Things were looking up.

I decided to go to my room for a shower, which I badly needed. When I headed for the elevators, I checked the sticky note where Nico had written my room number and saw that he'd put me on the fifteenth floor. High up, as I'd asked him. After the doors opened, I rolled my bag inside and pushed the button marked **15**. The doors began to close, but then an arm sliced between them and they opened again.

A man got inside with me.

He had no luggage. He didn't say anything or look at me, but he reached for the elevator panel, then pulled his hand back when he saw that the button for the fifteenth floor was already illuminated. He was going where I was going. As the elevator rose, he leaned against the wall of the car and played with his phone.

It happened again. My fears ran out of control.

I studied him from the back of the elevator. He was young, around my age, and taller than me, with a strong physique. He wore an untucked button-down shirt and dark jeans and had longish, unkempt blond hair.

Something about him looked oddly familiar. Staring at him, I found myself gripped by panic. Was he the man I saw in Red Rock? The one standing by the black SUV?

I tried to remember if the look matched the man I'd seen, but it had all happened so fast that I couldn't be sure. His shoes were leather slip-ons. When I glanced down, I saw a layer of dust on them and on the cuffs of his pants.

As if he'd been outside? In the desert?

Oh, my God.

I waited for him to flick his eyes toward the mirrored door to see what I was doing. One look would give away the game. But he acted as if I wasn't even there. We were nothing but two strangers riding the same elevator. Weren't we? It took only a few seconds for the car to reach the upper floor, and when the doors opened, I had to decide what to do.

He got off. I got off, too.

My plan was to hang out by the elevator and see where he went. Instead, he lingered by the doors himself and pretended to make a phone call. Or maybe he *was* making a phone call. Was this all in my head? I used the opportunity to hurry down the hallway toward my room, dragging my wobbling roller bag behind me. When I got there, I took a quick, pretend-casual look over my shoulder. The man was still by the elevators, and now he was checking his hair in the mirror as he talked on the phone. He didn't look my way.

Quickly, I slid in the key card that Nico had given me. It didn't work. I tried it two more times, but the lock gave an annoyed buzz and wouldn't open. Was I doing it too fast? Down the hall, the man put his phone back in his pocket. He strolled toward me from the elevators. As he got closer, I inserted the card again, very slowly this time, but the door refused to budge.

Shit, Nico!

Then I glanced at the number posted by the door and realized that I'd stopped at the wrong room. My own room was across the hall. With a stupid, nervous laugh, I switched to the room behind me, and the door opened on the first try. The man was barely ten feet away from me now. I hurried inside and pushed hard on the door to close it, but the hydraulics moved slowly. When the lock eventually clicked back into place, I turned the deadbolt. I put my eye to the peephole, and as I did, the man from the elevator passed my door.

He didn't stop or pause or look my way. Instead, he kept on going down the hallway.

I exhaled, loud and long, and my body slumped with relief, tension draining away. What was I doing to myself? I was being a fool. None of this was real. This suspicion was all in my head.

I put my bag on the bed and was going to unpack when I heard another noise from the hallway. I ran to the peephole again, and when I looked out, I stifled a gasp of horror with a hand over my mouth. The same man passed my room, heading back the opposite way. He hadn't had time to go to his own room, and yet he was already returning to the elevators.

Why?

It meant nothing. This was a normal man doing normal things. He'd forgotten something. Or, like me, he'd tried his key and it didn't work. Or he'd gotten off on the wrong floor.

Except my brain screamed at me that there was also another possibility.

He wanted to know where I was staying.

5

Taking a shower eased a little bit of my stress. I stayed under the hot water for half an hour, and by the time I got out and wrapped myself up in a plush towel, I'd decided that my imagination was getting carried away with me. I had more practical things to worry about than strangers who might or might not be following me. I needed to find work and make some money.

I called my headhunter, Jill Oliver. Jill had been with me through my career ups and downs ever since college. She was actually based in Minneapolis, not Las Vegas, but she recruited for the med-tech field all over the country. I knew that she was frustrated with me because I could never seem to get along with my bosses, but she also admitted that I was a better writer than any of her other clients. So she kept trying to find the right fit for me.

Of course, in my mind the right fit had nothing to do with medical devices and marketing strategies. I wanted to write articles for the *Atlantic* and the *New Yorker*. Plus nonfiction books that would take me to exotic places around the world. Maybe novels, too. But thousands of other writers had the same dream, and they all had better contacts than me. So for the time being, I had to make ends meet by writing sales copy about bone densitometers and endocavity ultrasound probes.

"Hallie," Jill said when I reached her. Her voice had a tone of weary inevitability. "Let me guess. You got fired."

"Yeah. Sorry."

"Well, I knew I was taking a chance having you work for a company that makes penis pumps. There was no way that would end well."

"They gave me the shaft," I said.

"Funny."

"Look, I know I'm a pain in your ass, but do you have anything for me? Freelance is fine. Preferably something with part of the contract paid up front."

"Money's tight?"

"Very tight. Nico was cheating on me. I had to move out of my apartment. I could use some quick cash while I look for a new place. I'm comped at a casino for a few days, but that won't last long."

Jill took a long time to say anything, which usually meant she was going to tell me something I didn't want to hear. "You know, it's getting hard to land jobs for you, Hallie. Your reputation is starting to spread, and not in a good way. The word on you is that you're difficult to work with."

"Oh, come on, Jill. A male writer pushes back on stupid shit, and he's 'not afraid to challenge the status quo.' I do it, and I'm just a bitch."

"I didn't say it was fair. It is what it is. Research is still a male-dominated field, and doctors and engineers don't like it when a pretty young thing points out that they're wrong. Which sucks, because you're really good. But you need to find a way to put your tongue on a leash."

"You must have something," I said. "I'll play nice, I promise."

I heard the tapping of keys on the phone.

"I do have a short-term assignment," Jill replied. "Actually, I was going to call you about it before you got fired, just to see if you could take it on in your spare time. It's for a biotech company, and they're actually located in Las Vegas. The money's good, half up front. They figure it should take a couple of weeks, but I bet you'll bang it out faster than that. In the meantime, I'll hunt for something more permanent."

"What's the project?"

"You won't like it. They need their website rewritten. New copy, new interviews, new product descriptions, et cetera."

I groaned, because web overhauls were the dullest of the dull. "Seriously?"

"It's five thousand dollars for a few days' work. If they like you, they'll cut you a check for twenty-five hundred after the interview. The rest when you're done with the job."

There was no way I could turn that down.

"Yeah, okay. Sold."

She heard the reluctance in my voice. "Try to ramp up your enthusiasm when you meet them, okay? I know you'll do a good job even on a crummy project, but you need to make sure that they know it, too."

"I will. Thanks, Jill."

"When can you get over there?"

"Are you kidding? For five grand, I'll be there in an hour. Half an hour if they don't mind me being naked. I just got out of the shower."

She gave me the address, which was on Rainbow Boulevard north of 95. The company was called BioEfx, and the contact was a senior researcher named Sean Howard. I was true to my word and rolled into the company parking lot, fully dressed, exactly one hour after I hung up with Jill.

It was a generic corporate building, sided with mirrored blue glass. A few lonely palm trees guarded the entrance. I could hear the noise of the freeway not far away. The blacktop radiated heat like the fire of a crematorium, and I walked quickly to make sure my heels didn't melt into the asphalt. There was a strip mall across the street featuring a dry cleaner, a UPS Store, and a pizza restaurant. Otherwise, the area looked like the concrete jungle that made up most of the Las Vegas valley.

Inside, I asked for Sean Howard and was led to a large office on the top floor that looked eastward toward the Strip. Dr. Howard wasn't there yet, so I checked out what he kept on his wall to get a better sense of the man. I'd already read his bio online, and I knew that Dr. Howard was a graduate of Harvard Medical School. He had a Harvard PhD in bioinformatics and integrative genomics, too. He was also a family man and had a dozen framed pictures on the wall of himself and his wife and five kids in locations around Boston.

For some reason, I couldn't take my eyes off the pictures.

Not Sean Howard or his children, but the Boston locations. I squinted to study the streets, the buildings, the signs, the restaurants, and the people. Some of the locations were famous and easy to identify. Faneuil Hall. The Isabella Stewart Gardner Museum. Boston Common. But there were other, less recognizable places, too. I spotted an oxidized old statue of General Joseph Warren near the green grass of the Roxbury Latin School. Another picture showed a stone arch that looked like the gateway to a castle but that I knew was located in Franklin Park. Another had been taken near a row of four-story redbrick condominiums that smelled of money, obviously on Beacon Street. I became so caught up in the photographs that I didn't even hear the office door open behind me.

"Ms. Evers?"

I turned around. Sean Howard stood there, looking smart and formal in a suit and tie. I recognized him from his picture on the website. He was in his forties, with neat brown hair and gold glasses. He had a younger Asian woman with him who was wearing a white lab coat.

"Yes, I'm Hallie Evers. Dr. Howard?"

"That's right. This is my colleague, Dr. Ellen Yamoto."

"Pleased to meet you."

Dr. Howard sat down behind his desk, and Dr. Yamoto took one of the two chairs on the opposite side. I took the other. Dr. Howard was all business. He launched into a description of the company's mission, which involved the production of transfection reagents. He asked me if I knew what that was, and I smoothly told him that they were mechanisms for delivering genetic material into cells using vehicles such as liposomes and calcium phosphate. I asked if their work included messenger RNA and whether they'd done any work to support COVID-19 vaccine development. They had.

From that point, we got along fine. They both knew that I knew my shit. An hour later, Dr. Yamoto went off to talk to the business folks to cut me a check for $2,500. I stayed behind with Dr. Howard, who was now all smiles.

"I really didn't know what to expect from you," he told me. "Honestly, my experience has been that marketing people are all expense and no revenue, if you know what I mean. It takes more time to correct what they do than it would for me to sit down and write the whole thing myself. But Jill Oliver said you were smart, and she was right."

"Well, I have a good memory, and I've worked with a number of biosciences companies," I said, with my best let's-get-along smile. I was trying not to yawn at the idea of rewriting yet another website, but I was thinking about the money and staying on my best behavior.

"Can you start on the project soon?" he asked.

"Sure, I can begin immediately. Right now if you like."

"Excellent."

My gaze drifted back to the photographs on the wall. "So did you and your family move here from Boston?"

"Actually, my wife and kids are still out there," Dr. Howard replied. "I shuttle back and forth between here and the coast a couple times a month. No offense, but the cultural attractions of Penn & Teller and Shania Twain weren't quite enough to convince Suzanne to leave Boston behind."

I got up from the chair and returned to the pictures, which gripped me with a strange fascination. I resisted the urge to run my fingers along the frames. The next words came out of my mouth without my even thinking about them, as if they'd come from someone else. "You live in Back Bay?"

"Yes, we do."

"There's a seafood bar on Dartmouth that does an amazing ginger-miso lobster," I commented. "Have you been there?"

"Do you mean Saltie Girl?" he asked.

"That's it."

"Well, you have good taste. It's one of our favorite spots."

Saltie Girl.

Yes, I remembered having dinner there. I could taste the lobster in my mouth, hot and succulent. If I inhaled, I could smell the Asian fragrance of the marinade. I'd had a grapefruit cocktail with it. The drink went down cold and smooth. When I closed my eyes, I could hear voices around me, the chatter of the restaurant. Looking across the booth, I saw a man's blurry face across from me. The features weren't clear enough for me to recognize him.

Who was it?

I shook myself, then pointed at another of the photographs, the one with Sean Howard standing with one of his sons near the statue of Joseph Warren.

"That's the Roxbury Latin School, isn't it?" I asked.

"It is."

"Did you go there?"

"I did, and my oldest son goes there now, too. That's him in the picture. Jason."

"So you grew up in that area?"

"Yes indeed, born and raised. You sound like you know Boston very well, Hallie. You must have lived there yourself at some point."

I shook my head. "No, I'm a Vegas girl, always have been."

"So how is it you're so familiar with Boston?"

At that moment, I felt as if I'd awakened from a dream. My voice stuttered. "Well, I—I took a long vacation out there a couple of summers ago. When I go to new places, I like to do my research."

"Apparently so. That bodes well for your working on our website."
Dr. Howard got up from his chair. "Anyway, let me go check on what's
keeping Ellen. I want you to get started right away."

"Thank you."

He left me alone in the office.

I stayed where I was, by the wall where the doctor kept his family
photographs. When I looked at them, I felt as if I could climb inside
the pictures and follow them down the different streets and know what
I would find around every corner. That was how well I knew Boston.

And yet I'd lied to Dr. Howard. I hadn't taken a summer vacation
there two years ago.

I'd never been to Boston in my life.

6

I worked on copy for the BioEfx website until almost nine o'clock that evening. When I'm on a new project, I typically put in long hours to get it all started. Plus, Jill was right. What the company thought would take a couple of weeks would likely only take me a few days to complete. I'd already mapped out a proposed format and gotten it approved by Dr. Howard by the time I left for the day.

Outside, the sun was gone, but the heat hadn't broken. Hot wind blew dry dusty air into my face. The parking lot was almost empty, but needles of unease pricked the little hairs of my neck. As I drove back to the casino, I kept checking my mirrors obsessively—I was sure I'd see a black SUV following me. But I didn't. Even so, I avoided the freeway and used the city streets, where it was easier to check whether someone was behind me. I made dozens of sharp turns just to see if anyone else turned where I did, but I was alone.

When I got back to Red Rock, I thought about taking the stairs rather than using the elevator again. But I didn't think I had the stamina to make the climb. Instead, as soon as I got out of the elevator, I checked the hallway, which was empty, and then ran to my room. I closed the door and swung the extra lock shut. I also pulled the desk chair to the door and wedged it under the handle.

Then I walked back and forth, gripped by a formless panic, and tried to make sense of what was happening to me.

How could I know so much about a city I'd never visited?

Why did I feel like I was being watched?

But I was too tired to come up with any rational explanations. I was exhausted. Worn down. Usually I read or watched TV for a while before going to sleep, but not that night. Without even taking off my clothes, I sprawled on the bed, and as soon as I closed my eyes, I was gone.

Just like that, the next dream came.

It washed over me like the ocean. Every detail was crisp and sharp in my mind.

I was by the sea again, but this time it was a perfect summer day. A light breeze cooled the sunshine. Staring out from the clifftop, I saw blue water dotted with the white sails of dozens of boats. Some of the boats were close enough that I could hear music from their radios and see girls in bikinis tanning on the decks. Below me, lazy waves broke on the rocks. A tree-capped island nestled in the bay between me and the land on the horizon. Nearby, the silver span of a high suspension bridge arced gracefully across the water.

When I looked down, I saw that I was wearing a knee-length white summer dress. It was embroidered with a few stylized sunflowers and had a shirred waist that hugged my hips. Instead of my own wavy black hair, my hair was pure blond, long and straight, blowing in wisps across my face. I wore open leather sandals, and my toes had been painted to match the yellow flowers on my dress. When I did a pirouette by the cliff, I heard laughter, and I realized I was the one laughing. I was happy. Free. Filled with joy. Truly, I couldn't remember feeling so good in my whole life. This was a perfect me in a perfect place on a perfect day.

Trimmed green grass stretched along the clifftop for hundreds of yards. I saw low stone walls marking off property lines, and the rooftops, gables, and chimneys peeking above the trees hinted at grand estates tucked away from view. Dozens of young people—twenty-somethings, like me—stretched out on blankets. Some smoked, some drank wine, some kissed. One boy played a flute. A girl danced ballet moves. I felt as if I'd wandered into a garden party, but I was among friends. I recognized all their faces. I could recite their names. We'd grown up together.

In front of me, a handsome black man leaned on a golf club. He was older than me, in his thirties, but built like an athlete. He wore a navy-blue polo shirt that accented his torso, plus khakis and cleated golf shoes. He had a white baseball cap pulled low on his forehead, and his eyes hid behind reflective sunglasses. He had milk chocolate skin and a goatee. As I watched, he took the golf driver by its leather grip and swung the silver shaft in an easy pendulum. It made a whipping noise as it cut the air. The head of the club was bulbous and black.

He extended the club to me. I came and took the thick head in my hand, and he pulled me toward him. He positioned me in the grass, kneeling to spread my legs and point my feet. I slid my two hands over the leather grip, my fingers overlapping slightly as I waggled the club. He came around behind me, his waist pressing against my back. I felt his heaviness. Looking down, I saw his arms encircle me and his hands fold over mine on the grip of the club. He whispered something in my ear, but I couldn't hear what it was. All I sensed was his warm breath and the physical closeness of his body against mine.

Together, we swung the driver slowly. The club head went back, then swished through the grass. Again. And again. Finally, he let go. He came around in front of me and squatted, and he grabbed the shaft and eased it back and forth across the soft grass. Then it was my turn. I swung the club, arms bending, back twisting, and drove the head awkwardly down into the soft earth. The impact shuddered through my body. Dirt and grass flew into the air and left a huge divot in the field.

The black man laughed.

I laughed, too, although I'd injured my arms with the swing. I could feel a tingling like pins and needles in my wrists, and it didn't go away.

I dropped the club. It lay there in the grass, long and silver, glinting in the sunlight. My tutor still squatted in front of me, and I took two steps and pushed both of his shoulders hard. He spilled backward with a shout. I stood over him as he lay in the field, and his mouth opened into a wide, white grin.

I laughed again, so hard that I could barely breathe. I covered my face with both my hands, blotting out the summer day.

Then, when I took away my hands, the day was gone.

In a dreamlike instant, I was now in the midst of a cool, clear, dazzling night. Moonlight glowed on my skin, wind howled from the sea, and violent waves assaulted the cliff with the roars of a lion. I was in the same field, wearing the same white dress, but the happy yellow sunflowers were now spattered with red.

A body lay at my feet.

I stood over a young woman on her back. She had long blond hair like me, but the color was barely distinguishable. Her face looked untouched, blue eyes open. I knew this girl. I'd known her my whole life.

She was my sister.

And now she was dead. Above her slim eyebrows, her skull had been beaten into a pulp by multiple blows. Her forehead had been crushed, brain showing where the bone had shattered.

In the grass next to her was the golf club.

Its black head and silver shaft were now the deep red color of blood. Like the blood on my dress. Like the blood on my hands.

I heard words in my head, almost like a voice.

It was me.

I bolted upright as I awoke, my mouth open in a scream. My cheeks were wet with tears.

I leaped out of bed, reminding myself where I was. I was in a casino hotel, not in a field by the sea, not standing at the cliff's edge with a dead body at my feet. My heart raced like a spinning top, and I worried that it would keep thumping faster and faster until it stopped again. I paced frantically, tearing at my hair. I wore down the carpet, going back and forth from the locked door to the window that looked out on the valley's fiery ribbon of lights.

I'd killed my sister.

Me.

But I don't have a sister.

The hotel phone rang while I was by the window, and the noise of it made me jump. I thought about letting it ring, but then I ran to the desk and grabbed it. "Yes, hello?"

"Ms. Evers?"

"Yes, what is it? What do you want?"

"This is hotel security, ma'am. We got a call about a disturbance in your room. A woman screaming. Is everything all right?"

"I'm fine. Sorry. I had a nightmare."

"Is anyone with you?"

"No, I'm alone. But really, I'm fine. I have night terrors sometimes. That's all it is."

"Do you need a doctor?"

"No. No doctor."

"Well, we have a security guard on the way. It's standard procedure. We need to make sure you're okay."

"I understand. You don't have to do that, but it's okay."

I hung up the phone.

What was happening to me?

A nightmare. That was all it was. I'd had bad dreams before. But this dream clung to me and refused to fade away, because it didn't *feel* like a dream at all. I'd lived it. I'd been there. It was real.

A body at my feet. A bloody golf club in the grass. A woman beaten to death.

My sister.

I looked at the hotel phone, and suddenly I began to panic all over again. *Jesus!* Was that really hotel security who'd called me? Or was it someone else? How did I know?

I'd told them I was alone! I would open the door for the guard, and he'd come in and check my room. He'd be inside with me. He could wrap his hands around my throat, and I wouldn't be able to stop him.

Would it be him?

The one who was following me?

The man in the black SUV.

Paranoia!

I couldn't stay here.

I grabbed my purse and dashed out of the room. Behind me, the soft ding told me the elevator was arriving. That would be him. He'd see me if I didn't hurry. I couldn't let him see me! I ran down the hallway away from the elevators and bolted through the exit door to the stairs.

7

The cameras found me anyway. I couldn't hide. This was Las Vegas, and there were cameras everywhere. I sat in a deserted corner of the Lucky Penny, which was the casino's twenty-four-hour café, and I ordered a cobb salad. Not long after I arrived, Nico joined me. His name must have been on my hotel reservation, so they'd sent him to check on the crazy lady who'd been screaming in the night.

He was dressed in casual clothes, which meant his shift was done. He slid into the booth and signaled for the waitress to bring him an IPA. He had a sad, serious, I-care-about-you look on his face. A thick lock of his black hair dangled across his forehead, and I resisted the urge to reach over and smooth it back into place.

"Security called me," Nico said. "They said something about you screaming in your room. Is everything okay?"

"I had a nightmare. It happens sometimes."

"You never had nightmares like that with me."

"Well, I'm not with you anymore, am I? But don't worry. It had nothing to do with you."

"What was the dream?"

"It doesn't matter. I can't remember."

But that wasn't true. I remembered every detail.

The waitress brought his beer, and Nico sipped it. He was a beer sipper, not a beer drinker, which was one of those little habits you overlook when you're together but that annoy you after you split up. I took big bites of my salad, which probably annoyed him, too. We didn't talk for a while. Nico used his phone to let the anxious security department know that I was fine.

"Look, you don't need to babysit me," I said when we'd set a record for awkward silence. "Go home to Mishawn."

Nico shrugged. "I texted her and said I had to work overtime. I told her I'd stay at my place tonight."

"I hope you didn't mention me. She wouldn't like that."

"No, I didn't."

He was already lying to her. One day together, and the bloom was off the rose.

"Why didn't you tell me?" Nico went on, sounding unhappy.

"Tell you what?"

"About the hospital."

"How did you find out about that?" I asked.

"A doctor called. My number must still be in your records. He said he couldn't reach you."

"I mute my phone at work. I must have forgotten to turn it back on."

"He was following up to see if you were okay. It sounded serious."

"It was. My heart stopped."

"Your heart!" Nico exclaimed.

"They started it again. I'm alive. I'm okay now."

"What happened?"

I didn't feel the need to sugarcoat things for Nico. Frankly, I wanted him to feel like a shit. "I overdid it on coke. I was feeling sorry for myself. July 4 sort of sucked for me, you know?"

Guilt deepened the blush on his face. He knew what I meant.

"Hallie, how could you not tell me?"

"Why would I?"

"Because I deserve to know. We were together for a long time. Do you think I don't still love you?"

"You dumped me, so yeah, that's usually what that means."

"Well, I didn't stop caring for you overnight."

"If you cared for me, you wouldn't be screwing Mishawn," I snapped. Then I sighed, because being snarky wasn't helping the situation. He was genuinely concerned about me. I could see it in his face. His feelings hadn't gone away, and honestly, neither had mine. "Sorry, Nic."

"No, you're right, I treated you badly. But this thing with your heart, it scares me. You could have died."

"I could have, but I didn't."

"Do you need anything? What can I do?"

I didn't answer him. At that moment, two middle-aged white men took seats at a table on the other side of the restaurant. It wasn't clear to me if they were checking in or checking out, but they had luggage with them, including two sets of golf clubs zipped inside travel bags.

Golf clubs.

Just like that, I zoomed back into the world of my dream. I had another vision of the bloody golf club lying in the grass at my feet. Of a young woman, dead, with a broken skull. I saw myself kneeling down to pick up the club, its leather grip still warm where a killer had swung it.

Me.

I was the killer.

"Hallie?" Nico said, breaking into my thoughts. "What is it? What's wrong?"

I blinked. The images washed away like a wave retreating on the sand. I was back in the restaurant again. But it bothered me that the dreams had begun to invade my waking hours, not just my sleep.

"Nothing. I'm fine."

"You're lying. Something is going on with you."

Nico reached across the table and took my hands. I didn't pull away. I stared at my ex-boyfriend, whose face was as beautiful as it had always been, whose lips were incredibly kissable, whose eyes still made me weak. He was a jerk, but being with him made me feel less alone, and at that moment, I didn't want to be alone.

"Weird things are going on in my head," I told him.

"I don't understand."

"Neither do I. I'm seeing things. I'm remembering people and places, but I don't actually recognize any of them. And the dreams I'm having are bad. They're so real they don't even feel like dreams."

"Is this because of what happened to you? Your heart?"

"I don't know. I assume so. But there's more. I'm pretty sure I—"

I stopped, because I didn't know if I could say it out loud. It would sound absurd that way.

"I'm pretty sure I'm being followed," I went on. "There was a black Ford SUV behind me for a long time yesterday. I saw it again at Red Rock. I think the driver was here at the casino, too."

Nico didn't come out and say that I was nuts, but it was obvious that he didn't believe me. "Hallie, why would someone be following you?"

"I have no idea."

"You went through a terrible experience. It's natural you might be shaken up."

"No, it's more than that. This is real."

But was it?

Was it really?

Nico stroked my cheek with the back of his hand. "You know, I'm not saying this is what's happening, but I can't help but remember the stories you told me about your mother."

I erupted with anger, but only because he was right. My fists clenched. I bit hard on my tongue and tasted blood.

My mother.

Was I my mother now?

As a girl, I'd watched her descend into madness. She'd screamed about hordes of scorpions in her bed. She'd covered our windows with duct tape so the aliens and satellites couldn't see us. She'd locked me out of our house when she saw horns growing out of my head. She'd told me she was the reincarnation of the goddess Andromeda.

And the lizard. My pretty little lizard.

Mom, look! Look what I found outside! Isn't he cute? Can I keep him?

I offered it up to her, and she grabbed the lizard out of my hand. She said it was radioactive and had been sent by the ghost of President Lincoln, and then she took a knife and sliced off its head right in front of me.

I screamed and screamed and screamed.

My mother.

In the end, she couldn't live with who she'd become.

That day. That last day of her life. I did remember some things about it. I could still hear the music she played at a deafening volume and the awful, horrible, terrible noises from the other side of the bedroom door. The wailing. The moaning. The beating on the walls. And me, calling to her, walking to the bedroom, my hand on the doorknob. I could still see it, my scared ten-year-old hand poised on the brass doorknob, wondering what I would find when I went inside.

But after that—nothing.

Hours later, a park ranger found me sitting on the valley floor at Red Rock among the yuccas and cacti. The police concluded that I'd walked ten miles in the summer heat to get there. I remembered none of it.

"You understand what I'm saying, don't you?" Nico went on, like a buzz of white noise in my head. "I'm sorry, but how can I not wonder? The way you're talking—about people following you—it all sounds crazy."

"I realize that, but I'm *not* my mother," I insisted, hoping that was true. "I'm not losing my mind."

◆ ◆ ◆

As if to reassure me with a dose of sanity, I had no more dreams that night. But maybe that was because I didn't sleep alone. When I opened my eyes in the hotel bed the next morning, I saw Nico beside me. We were both naked. Neither one of us had planned it, but Nico had walked me back to my hotel room from the Lucky Penny, and then he'd kissed me good night at my door. The kiss led to him coming inside with me and then to other things.

Sleeping with him felt normal, the way it had for two years, even though I had no intention of getting back together with him. I won't deny that I also enjoyed having a little taste of revenge against Mishawn. After all, two can play at the screw-your-boyfriend game.

It was almost eleven o'clock when we finally woke up. I'd told Sean Howard at BioEfx that I kept strange hours, and he had no problem with that. However, Nico realized he was late for work, and he scrambled to get his clothes on and rush downstairs. Honestly, I was pretty sure he was scrambling to get away from me, too. He felt guilty, and he left without giving me another kiss. I didn't think he'd tell Mishawn what he'd done, but I assumed she'd figure it out soon enough. Let's just say I left a few clues on Nico's back with my fingernails.

When he was gone, I went into the bathroom and took a long hot shower, which woke me up. When I got out, dripping wet, I heard my phone ringing in the other room. I ran to get it and didn't recognize the number or the area code on the caller ID, but I answered anyway.

"Hello?"

"Is this Hallie Evers?"

The deep male voice had an upper-crust feel to it. If he'd told me his name was Biff or Chet, I wouldn't have been surprised. I've worked with a lot of doctors who have that kind of cultured smarter-than-thou quality you can only get through years of expensive private school.

"Yes, this is Hallie."

"Hallie, I'm Dr. Reed Smith."

"Oh! Dr. Smith. Sure. It was you who—"

I tried to bring myself to say it.

"You're the one who saved my life," I went on.

"Well, you picked the right place to have trouble," Smith replied, as if playing God and saving lives was no big deal. "There were doctors everywhere. I was simply the first one to get to you."

"I really don't know what to say. Thank you. That sounds pretty lame under the circumstances."

"No, it's fine, and you're welcome. I'm sorry I had to leave town before you woke up in the hospital. I had a flight to catch, so I didn't get a chance to talk to you."

When Dr. Smith said that, I remembered that I'd never actually met him.

So why did he feel *familiar* to me?

I knew his voice, but more than that, I could picture his face clearly in my head, too. I saw a handsome man in his midthirties with short spiky blond hair, intelligent blue eyes, and a mouth that was serious and rarely smiled. He had a high forehead and narrow jaw. His pale skin had a burnt flush, as you might get from too much time skippering a catamaran on the Atlantic.

If I met him on the street, I'd know who he was. I'd *recognize* him.

But I didn't know how that could be true.

"At the hospital, they said you practice at Johns Hopkins," I said. "Are you a cardiac specialist?"

"No, but I've spent plenty of time in the emergency room, so when I saw you collapse, I jumped in."

"I'm very glad you did."

"Well, I don't mean to take up much of your time, but I did want to follow up and make sure you're doing okay. Have you been released from the hospital?"

"Yes, I got out yesterday."

"Are you feeling all right? Any lingering pain or shortness of breath?"

"No, I mostly feel fine. A little tired, maybe."

"Good, I'm glad to hear it. The doctors at the hospital probably advised you to take it easy for a while. You're young, but you need to get your strength back. Also, you probably don't need another reminder, but drug use and bulimia can have long-term ramifications. You should look into rehab and counseling."

"I will. It's nice of you to check on me."

"Of course." Then the smooth young doctor began to sound tongue tied. Or at least that was how it sounded to me. "So are you experiencing any other symptoms or issues? Anything odd you want to tell me about?"

Anything odd?

Well, yes—that question, Dr. Smith. That's a little odd.

"Like what?" I asked.

"Oh, patients who have been resuscitated after a cardiac event often report some degree of psychological trauma," he replied, but I got the strange feeling he was waiting for me to tell him about the visions I was having.

As if he expected it. As if he *knew*.

"Would that include weird dreams?" I asked.

He was quiet for much longer than he should have been. "Yes, it certainly could. Have you been having strange dreams?"

"Very."

"Do you . . . remember any details about them?"

This time I lied. "No. I don't."

"Well, you shouldn't be concerned. What you went through was traumatic. As I mentioned, some degree of mental stress is perfectly normal in these circumstances. I believe you'll find it will get better with time."

"That's a relief. There's something else, though."

"What is it?"

"I'm not sure how to describe it. It's like I'm remembering things that didn't happen."

"That didn't happen? What do you mean?"

"I remember faces, but they're not people I've met. And I remember places that I've never been."

There was another long pause on the line.

"A certain amount of disorientation could linger from the shock of the heart treatment. Cancer patients experience something similar after radiation treatments. They call it 'cancer brain.' Odds are these are perfectly normal memories, but you've temporarily lost their connection to your past. I'm sure it will all start to come back to you soon."

"I guess that makes sense."

"As I say, don't be too concerned," Dr. Smith went on. "Anyway, I hate to rush our call, but I do have another appointment. I just wanted to make sure you were on the mend."

"I am. And thank you again."

"I'm glad everything turned out okay for you, Hallie."

"Yes, goodbye, Dr. Smith," I said.

I hung up the phone and thought, *You're lying to me.*

8

For the next several days, I did nothing but work. I went to BioEfx, stayed late, slept a few hours, and then returned as the sun came up. When I get in the zone on a project, I don't think about much else. The weekend came and went while I wrote and rewrote web copy, both at the office and in my hotel room. I was still staying at Red Rock. Nico hadn't made any effort to get me to move out or to suggest that I start paying for the room. Actually, he seemed to be avoiding me altogether after spending the night in my hotel bed. That was fine. I was definitely not interested in an off-Broadway revival of *Hallie Tosis: The Musical*.

By the time the following Tuesday night rolled around, I'd wrapped up the first draft of the project and put the file in Dr. Howard's hands. He promised that their team would review it and get back to me with editorial feedback in a couple of days. I called Jill Oliver to let her know, and she sounded thrilled and a little relieved that I'd completed the first phase of the job without incident.

So it was nearly midnight when I left BioEfx that Tuesday. I decided to relax for a while. I'd gone more than a week without a drink, and I didn't think a glass of wine (or two) would kill me. Partly, I was glad to get the project done, but most of all I was relieved because I was feeling more like myself again. I'd been hitting the bed exhausted when I got back to my room each night, and I'd had no more disturbing dreams. I felt as if I'd turned a corner. Maybe Dr. Smith was right that I'd just needed some time for my stress to go away.

There was a small casino located in a strip mall within a couple of blocks of the company, so I left my car in the parking lot and walked over there. There were only a dozen or so other people inside, most of them night shift workers. A layer of cigarette smoke hung under the low ceiling, and rap music blared from speakers. This was definitely not the Bellagio, but I didn't need anything but a few free drinks and a couple of hours of video poker play.

I sat down at a Game King machine that had to be twenty years old. I liked the vintage machines, although I never seemed to win anything at them. The waitress came over after I plugged in twenty dollars. She had enough tattoos to give a marine a run for his money, plus multiple lip rings. When she asked what I wanted, I started to order wine, but instead I heard myself say, "Rum and Coke."

That was strange. I couldn't remember ever ordering rum and Coke in my life, but at that moment I couldn't imagine drinking anything else. When she brought it, the juice-size drink was watered down with lots of ice, but it tasted sweet and fizzy on my lips. I sipped the cocktail and lost a few hands of Double Bonus Poker. Half an hour later, the waitress wandered my way again, and I ordered another rum and Coke. The second one went down as smoothly as the first.

By two in the morning, I was one hundred dollars down, and I'd drunk a fair amount of cheap rum. The caffeine of the Coke was keeping me awake. I felt good and was in no hurry to leave.

That was when I noticed the man sitting at the bar. And I could tell that he had definitely noticed me.

I hadn't seen him come in, which surprised me. When you're a twenty-something single girl in Las Vegas, you develop a kind of radar for the men around you. It's like having eyes in the back of your head. This guy was alone and drinking beer, and he'd swung around in his seat to watch the action in the tiny casino. Not that there was much action on a weekday in the middle of the night. The fact is, he was mostly looking at me. I'm young and pretty, and other than the waitresses,

I didn't have much female competition. So it wasn't odd that he was checking me out.

Even so, my radar told me that I had trouble right here in Sin City.

He was a big guy, probably in his late thirties. He had thinning dark hair and a full beard, with an earring in one ear. He wore a gray hoodie, partially unzipped to show chest hair and no shirt underneath. His jeans were frayed and tight. So far, that made him look like a thousand other Vegas guys you meet in a casino at two in the morning, but what bothered me were his eyes. They had a fishlike quality, the kind of dead stare that looked right through you. He'd study me from across the bar, and as soon as he saw me looking back, he'd blink and turn away.

A few seconds later, I'd catch him staring again.

Time to go, Hallie.

But the bar was next to the casino door. That meant I'd have to walk right by the man in order to leave. And my car was parked several blocks away.

I checked my watch. Nico would be wrapping up his shift soon, if he hadn't already. I decided to play the ex-girlfriend card and see if he would swing by the casino and pick me up.

However, when I dialed Nico's number, he didn't answer. Mishawn did. This was not a good thing.

"What the hell do *you* want?" she demanded.

Actually, I'm cleaning up what she said, but you get the idea.

Here's the thing about Mishawn. I really thought we were best friends. In my life, I've never had many friends, male or female. I'm a loner, and most of the time I'm happier with a book or a computer than with other people. But sometimes I push myself out of my comfort zone, and I'll end up at a bar. I met Mishawn on one of those nights, at a karaoke joint on Koval about five years ago. She was unwinding after her Cirque show with some of the other dancers, and she howled at my drunken take on "Me and Bobby McGee." Afterward, she sat down with me. She was sharp, crass, and funny, and I liked her a lot.

We began to hang out together. Three years ago, when her roommate moved out, she asked me if I wanted to move in. I did.

All of that was pre-Nico. I should have known what would happen after she met him. I'd seen Mishawn take away boyfriends from other girls, but honestly, I never thought she'd do it to me. Like I said, I was naive, and I really thought she'd put friendship over sex. Oh well. The frog didn't think the scorpion would sting him in the river, but that's what scorpions do.

"Is Nico there?" I asked her. "Can I talk to him?"

"No."

"It will just take a minute."

"No."

"Mishawn, come on."

"I'm not letting you talk to him. Are you kidding? I'm not letting you anywhere near him. You slept with him. You begged him to put you up in the hotel, and then you screwed him."

"That's not what happened."

"Don't give me that shit. You were getting even with me. I stole him away from you, and this was payback."

"No, it wasn't," I told her, although that was only partially true. "Him and me the other night, it didn't mean anything. I was just in a bad place, and he was there for me. It'll never happen again."

"You're right. It won't. In the morning, you're checking out of the hotel. Got it? I don't care where you go, but I don't want you anywhere near Nico."

"Sure. Fine. In the morning, I'm gone. I'll go tonight if you want. But I need somebody to pick me up. There's this creep checking me out at a bar, and I need a ride back to my car."

"Call an Uber."

"Mishawn, it's fifteen minutes away. You can come along, too. Nothing's going to happen."

"Don't call this number again," she snapped, and then she hung up.

I swore under my breath. Nico would not be riding to my rescue.

I shot another glance at the bar. The man was still there, drinking beer and pretending to look everywhere except at me. I kept hoping all that beer would work its way through his system and he'd have to pee, and I could slip out of the casino while he was at the urinal. But he must have had a huge bladder because he ordered another beer and gave no indication that he'd be relieving himself soon.

The casino wasn't large, so it wasn't like there was anywhere for me to hide. Wherever I was, he could see me. There was a glass door near the bar that led out to the parking lot, and then there was an employee exit at the back that led to an alley behind the strip mall. But if I headed that way, he'd see me go.

I didn't have a gun or Taser or pepper spray with me, but I wasn't completely defenseless. In my purse, I had a steak knife that I'd swiped from a casino restaurant. It was better than nothing, but I'd have to be up close to use it, and I really didn't like the idea of trying to stab anybody.

Not far from the rear door were the casino bathrooms. I saw my tattooed waitress duck inside the women's room, and I took that opportunity to follow her to the toilet. I didn't look back, but I was sure the man at the bar was keeping an eye on me. I went in the bathroom and saw the waitress at the sink. She lurched up with a guilty start when I came inside, because she was doing what I'd done the previous week. Snorting up a line of cocaine.

Yeah, I won't lie—a part of me wanted to ask if she'd sell me some. I still felt the need. But after what happened July 4, I was on my third life, and I didn't know how many more I had left.

The young woman wiped her nose with a surly expression. "You gonna rat me out? Tell my boss?"

"No. It's none of my business. But I need your help."

She gave me a suspicious look. "What kind of help?"

"There's a guy at the bar. Beard, gray hoodie. Do you know him?"

"No. He's not a regular."

"I don't like the way he's looking at me. I need to get out of here without him seeing me."

She shrugged. "What do you want me to do?"

I dug in my purse and pulled out a hundred-dollar bill. "When you get your next tray of drinks at the bar, spill it on the guy. Make it a big mess. Okay?"

Her lip rings quivered as her mouth scrunched into a frown. She snatched the bill out of my hand. "Yeah. Okay."

I let her leave the bathroom first. After a couple of minutes, I reemerged into the casino and wasn't surprised to see that the bearded man had his eyes glued to the restroom door. As soon as he saw me, he glanced away. I wandered down a row of slot machines, as if hunting for one that spoke to me, but I kept an eye on the waitress and on the rear door, which was a few feet away from the machines.

I put in money and started to play, and I signaled the waitress to bring me another drink. She gave me a nod and a wink. I watched her gathering up orders, and I kept playing, as if I was planning to stay for a while. When she went to the bar, she made small talk with the bartender as he got the drinks ready. There were a lot of them on the tray. Maybe a dozen. The waitress was standing right next to the bearded man, who was watching me and not paying any attention to her.

She picked up the tray, turned, and then tripped. The tray and the drinks cascaded over the man's body and made him leap to his feet with a curse. She apologized loudly and began wiping him off with a towel, and he pushed her away.

He was distracted. That was my moment.

I slid off the stool, shot to the exit, and slipped out the back door. I was through it in a moment, and I swung it shut behind me. As I'd expected, I was in a narrow alley between two buildings. On my left was Rainbow Boulevard. On my right, the alley continued along the concrete wall of the strip mall. I headed for Rainbow, but then I stopped dead.

At the curb at Rainbow was a black Ford SUV.

A man stood by the passenger door, smoking. He was tall, muscular, with long blond hair, dressed all in black. It was the man I'd seen in the canyon. The man who'd gone up in the elevator with me at the casino.

I wasn't dreaming. He was *here*.

Immediately, I shoved a hand inside my purse and drew out the casino steak knife. With the knife clutched in my hand, I backed away slowly, hoping he wouldn't see me in the shadows.

But he did.

The man sprang off the chassis of the SUV and came my way. I yanked on the door to get back into the casino, but it was locked from the inside. I heard footsteps getting closer behind me. On my right were the locked doors of the strip mall shops, and on my left was the fenced rear wall of the adjacent building, topped with barbed wire. All I could do was run straight down the alley.

I was fast, but he was faster. Ahead of me, the alley turned in an L-shape, and a low concrete wall separated the strip mall from a residential development below it. I saw the caps of palm trees rising above the height of the wall. If I reached it, if I jumped, I would land in someone's backyard, and maybe I could lose myself among the houses. But I was running out of time to escape.

The man was right behind me. He gained with each step, and when I looked back, I saw his face in shadow, expressionless and violent. With nowhere to run, I jerked to a stop and spun to confront him, slashing with the knife. He held up his hands and stayed warily out of my reach, and I jabbed at him, driving him backward. As we faced each other, I drew in a breath and screamed.

"Help! Somebody call—"

My voice cut off.

From behind me, from around the corner of the alley, someone threw me against the wall. My head slammed into the building, dizzying me. A huge hand twisted my wrist, forcing my fingers open, and the knife spilled to the pavement. The new man hiked me off the ground. He was huge, his forearms like tree trunks, and he held me with one thick arm around my waist. With his other arm, he blocked my nose and mouth so tightly that I couldn't breathe.

The other man, the one who'd been chasing me, walked calmly toward me. He wore tight nylon gloves. He squatted and picked up the knife I'd dropped and secured it in his belt. Then he reached into the pocket of his black pants and removed a small plastic case.

From inside, he withdrew a hypodermic needle.

I squirmed and kicked, because I knew what was going to happen next.

He came for me with the syringe. I lashed out furiously with my feet, trying to drive him away, but he grabbed one of my ankles and pushed closer to me. He held the needle at my arm, the point of the hypodermic near the inside of my elbow, his finger on the plunger.

Then someone bellowed from a few feet away. "Hey! What are you guys doing? Hey, let her go!"

It was the bearded man from the bar. The man who'd been watching me. The man I'd been trying to escape. He charged at the two men like a kind of crazed bull. The diversion gave me a chance to land my knee hard against the groin of the man with the needle. He howled and staggered backward, and I lashed out with my foot. The kick connected with his wrist, and the syringe spun away.

My savior, the man I'd thought had been stalking me, dived at the giant who had me in his grasp. The big man had no choice but to let go of me. I gulped air into my lungs and staggered toward the low wall at the back of the alley. The man from the bar swung wildly with his fists, but the big man shot a hard blow to his chest, which made him bend over and choke. Meanwhile, the man I'd kicked had recovered now, and he yanked my knife from his belt back into his hand.

Still gasping for air, the bearded man tried to run, but the man from the black SUV slashed the blade in a wide arc. It cut straight across the bearded man's throat, opening up a deep gash that erupted in a geyser of blood. I screamed, seeing the spray. The man backed up, colliding with the building wall, his hands clutching his neck. He fell to his knees, blood pouring from between his fingers.

The other two focused on me again. I tensed, ready to leap the wall and escape, but they were too far away to come after me now. Instead, the one man dropped the knife, and the other collected the syringe where it had fallen. They bolted down the alley toward the SUV, leaving the body of the man they'd attacked on the ground behind them.

When they were gone, I ran forward and knelt beside him. He'd already lost an incredible amount of blood. His breathing rattled, but when I grabbed my phone to call for help, he took my wrist and stopped me. With his other hand, he gestured for me to run.

I didn't know what to say or do.

What was happening?

Who was this man?

I stayed with him a few more seconds, but then he stopped breathing with a last sickening gurgle. I got to my feet and looked at my hands and saw that they were covered in blood.

It was just like my dream.

And on the ground beside me was the murder weapon. The casino knife. With my fingerprints all over it.

I dashed to the low wall at the end of the alley. I grabbed the top, pulled myself up, and hurled myself to the other side, landing hard in the desert landscape of a small residential backyard. Then I pushed myself to my feet and escaped through the empty streets.

9

I found a water hose in someone's backyard and used it to wash away as much of the blood as I could. My head throbbed. When I gingerly touched the back of my skull, I felt the damp sticky goo of blood in my hair, too. I'd bled from the impact with the wall. I was still dizzy, and whenever I turned too fast, waves of nausea rolled through me. I needed to see a doctor.

There was a hospital less than two miles from where I was. I didn't know whether it was safe to go back to my car, so I stayed off the main streets and walked to the emergency room. Along the way, I stopped at a gas station to use the bathroom and clean myself up enough to make sure my appearance didn't immediately make the ER doctors call the police.

It was a busy night for trauma. My excuse for the check-in nurse was that I'd slipped in the shower and bumped my head, but apparently a possible concussion didn't rise to the top of their priority list. They told me to wait, and I sat in a corner of the room and watched the minutes tick by slowly. Being there made me nervous. Every few minutes, police arrived with EMS ambulances, and they usually lingered for a while, talking to the hospital security personnel. I heard them mention a murder behind a strip mall on Rainbow, and I was afraid they would look at me in the corner of the waiting room and somehow put two and two together.

Did they have my picture from the casino video yet?

Did they know who I was?

I thought about calling the cops over and admitting that *I'd* been the girl in that alley with the dead man. I was sure they'd identify me sooner or later and come knocking on my door. But what would I tell them? Yes, I'd been afraid that man was stalking me in the casino. Yes, it was my knife. Yes, my prints were on it. Yes, I'd died of an overdose and then been brought back to life, and ever since I'd been having strange dreams of murder and seeing people following me.

Yes, there was a history of schizophrenia in my family.

None of that would end well for me.

Ninety minutes later, a nurse finally called my name. She showed me to a room and had me undress and switch into a hospital gown. I wasn't crazy about doing that, because there were fresh bruises all over my body from the fight. That was hard to explain away as an accident in the shower. But I changed anyway and sat on the bed with my bare legs sticking out below the gown. The nurse came back and took a sample of blood. She said it was to check for infection, but I figured they'd be running a drug test.

The doctor arrived to see me a few minutes later. She was in her forties, with curly brown hair and heavy black glasses. Her face showed the frazzled, overworked strain of the ER shift, but she wasn't unfriendly. She studied my check-in form, reviewed my medical history on her computer screen, then put down the clipboard and made sure the door to the room was closed.

"Ms. Evers? May I call you Hallie?"

"Sure."

"Hallie, I'm Dr. Fanning. You slipped in the shower and hit your head? Is that what happened?"

"Yes."

"How long ago was this?"

"About three hours."

"Did you lose consciousness at all?"

"No."

"Did you throw up?"

"I thought I was going to, but I didn't."

"Are you still feeling dizzy? Nauseous?"

"A little. My neck is really stiff, too."

"Okay, let's take a look."

She checked my head. Her fingers had a soft touch, but I winced as she explored the injury to my skull. Then she ran me through some neurological tests, including having me follow a pen in her hand with my eyes. When she was done, she went to the small desk and tapped on the computer keyboard.

"I'll have the nurse clean the wound and apply a bandage," she told me. "You'll be achy for a while, and you'll want to take it easy. Avoid sudden moves, or you might find the dizziness return. Just to be safe, I'm going to order an MRI to make sure we don't see any bleeding in your brain. That's the kind of thing we like to check after a head injury. Assuming that's all clear, we'll let you go."

"Thank you."

Dr. Fanning tapped her pen on the desk. "So what really happened to you, Hallie?"

"I told you."

She shook her head. "You didn't slip in the shower. There's dirt and paint in the wound, so it looks to me like you were outside when this happened. Plus, I see bruises on your back and legs, and the joint on your toe is purple, like you've been kicking something. Were you involved in a fight?"

"If I tell you, are you required to notify the police?"

"That depends on what you tell me. My primary concern is your well-being and safety. If you're in an abusive situation, I don't want to send you back there, and I can point you to resources that can give you help and support."

I shook my head. "It's not that. There's no abuse."

"Okay."

The doctor waited to see if I would tell her anything more, but I didn't. She frowned and then glanced at her computer screen. "I see that you were treated in one of our other facilities for a serious heart issue recently and that cocaine was involved. Did you use any drugs this evening?"

"No. I wasn't doing drugs. Didn't you already check for that?"

She shrugged. "Yes, you're right, we did. There was no indication of drugs in your system, but your blood alcohol was slightly elevated. You should probably avoid drinking altogether, given your heart issues."

"It was just a few watered-down casino freebies. That's all."

"Casino?"

I realized I'd already said too much. It wouldn't take much for the doctor to make a link between a dead body behind a casino and a woman showing up bruised and bloody in the emergency room.

"Yes, I was at a casino for a while. Then I went home and slipped in the shower."

"Final answer?" she said.

"Final answer."

Dr. Fanning sighed. I wasn't the first ER patient to lie to her. "I can't help but notice the scars on your wrist, Hallie. When did you try to kill yourself?"

"A long time ago. I was fifteen."

"Fifteen is a tough age for girls," she said.

"Yeah."

"Did you get counseling?"

"Actually, I'm running out of shrinks in Las Vegas that I haven't seen. I may have to go to Reno."

The doctor didn't laugh. "The most recent incident. The cocaine overdose. Was that a suicide attempt also?"

"I don't know. I guess you could say that. I was having a bad day, and I didn't care if I lived or died. They say the second time's the charm, but not in my case. My heart stopped, but here I am. Close but no cigar."

Still no laugh.

"Humor is fine as a defense mechanism," she pointed out, "but nearly dying is a serious thing."

"It happens to me a lot. I'm getting used to it."

Dr. Fanning shot another look at the computer screen. "What's your IQ, Hallie? Have you ever been tested? Your primary doc made a special note that she considered you extremely intelligent."

"One fifty-seven," I said.

Her eyebrows arched. "That's very high. Almost genius level."

"My mother's was one sixty-nine. But don't be impressed. I was only eight when she had me tested. I'm pretty sure I've gotten more stupid over time."

This time I got a smile, but it didn't last long.

"Bulimia?" the doctor asked.

"Yeah. Every now and then. Stress triggers it, but I'm better than I was."

She wheeled her chair closer to me. "Suicide attempts. Bulimia. Those are usually indicators of some kind of underlying dysfunction. Often it's abuse or some other childhood trauma. This has obviously been going on with you for a long time, Hallie. Do you remember when you first purged?"

Did I remember?

Yes, I remembered. I knew the very day.

"I was twelve years old," I said.

Aunt Phoebe was getting impatient with me. We'd been sitting in the driveway for ten minutes, and I refused to get out of the car.

"I don't want to go inside," I said again.

She made an annoyed huff. "Oh, for heaven's sake, all of her stuff is gone. The house is empty. You're going to have to see it sooner or later."

"No! You go. I'll stay here."

"You can't sit in the car," she snapped. "I'm not doing this by myself. You haven't been in the house in two years. It's time for you to grow up."

When I squeezed my eyes shut and shook my head, she stamped around to the passenger side of the old Camry. She pulled open the door and yanked me outside, where I fell to the pavement and skinned my knees. Phoebe slammed the car door shut.

"Let's *go*."

But I didn't want to go. Still on my knees, I moaned, cried, and squirmed. I begged her not to make me see it. My aunt didn't care. She took hold of my wrist and dragged me toward the front door of the house.

Phoebe was my mother's sister. Mom had been thirty-nine years old when she died, and Phoebe was eight years older at forty-seven. Her husband, Jim, was another five years older than her. They'd never had kids. A year before I moved in with them, they'd retired, thanks to a disability settlement Jim received for a workplace injury in a postal facility. Their life plan had been to buy a motor home and travel around the country. Instead, they became instant parents to a grieving, angry, lonely little girl, and their travel plans got permanently shelved. Phoebe didn't take it well.

"We need to clean the place up, and you're going to help," she told me as she unlocked the door. "I'm sick of dealing with renters. It's time to unload this white elephant."

She gave me a shove through the doorway.

Just like that, I was inside. Two years had passed since that last day, and now I was back.

Yes, the house was empty, but not in my head. I could still see everything the way it had been. It wasn't a big house, with the living room, dining room, and kitchen all connected in one open space. The walls were painted white, with just some holes and a few nails where the renters had put up artwork, but I still saw what it used to look like. The strange monsters my mother had drawn all over the walls with crayon. The plastic runners across the floor because she thought the carpet was made of quicksand. The cans of Campbell's chicken noodle soup stacked on the kitchen counters and behind the sofa and in front of the patio doors. Hundreds of them. Whenever she went shopping, she bought a dozen more.

The house had a fragile, almost ghostly silence about it, but I could still hear ABBA's "The Visitors." That last week, she'd played it twenty-four seven, that one song on repeat all day and all night. She'd sung the part out loud about waiting for the visitors to arrive. Like she knew they were coming for her soon.

"We'll do the bedroom first," Phoebe said. "I'll get the vacuum cleaner and the supplies out of the car. You stay here."

She left, and I was alone.

My head pounded. I felt dizzy, and my knees knocked together. I stared at the hallway that led to my mother's bedroom door. Just like that day, the door was closed. A brass knob, polished and shiny, was the only glow in the shadows. I remembered walking down that hallway like a pirate walking the plank. The ABBA song was in my head, and my mother was wailing from the other side of the door. What was happening in there?

But I already knew. The visitors had arrived.

As I stood frozen in the hallway, Phoebe swept past me, vacuum cleaner in hand. "Come on, I don't want this to take all day."

She bustled to the door and turned the brass knob and began to sweep it open.

As she did, I screamed and ran the other way. Back in the main part of the house, I bolted to the closet and hid inside. I slammed the door behind me and tried to hold it shut, but a few seconds later, Phoebe came and ripped it open. The light from the back windows framed her in silhouette. I pushed against the closet wall, and tears poured down my face.

"I can't go in there."

"You'll do what I tell you to do, you ugly little crybaby."

"Please don't make me."

Phoebe stepped into the tiny closet with me. We were face to face, eye to eye. "Look at you. You're just like *her*. She used to hide in closets as a girl, too. Whenever the world overwhelmed her, she ran away. Our parents indulged her, and look how that turned out. She was weak and stupid and crazy. If you think I'll let you grow up the same way, you've got another thing coming, young lady. Now get your lazy, sorry ass into that bedroom."

I didn't even make it out of the closet. I didn't even try. My knees buckled beneath me, and I shoved two fingers down my throat and vomited that morning's Pop-Tarts and milk all over my aunt's legs.

10

By the time they checked me out of the emergency room, the gift shop was open. I bought a change of clothes—new T-shirt and shorts, floppy sun hat, sunglasses—and I changed in one of the bathrooms. Outside, it was another burning July day despite the early hour. I was exhausted because I'd been up all night, and the long walk in the heat back to BioEfx didn't help. But I needed to get to my car and then to the hotel to retrieve my things. I didn't know where I would go next, but I couldn't stay at the casino.

I didn't trust anyone now. People were following me. Trying to kill me.

Or maybe I was just drawing monsters on the wall in crayon.

When I got to the company parking lot, I waited across the street and bought myself a drink at the 7-Eleven. I wanted to make sure no one was watching out for me, but I didn't notice anyone keeping an eye on the lot. Eventually, I hurried to my car and got inside. I was about to start up the engine when I remembered something. That very first day, when I was driving to Red Rock, I'd had the sense that someone had been in my car while I was recovering in the hospital. My mirror was off. My seat had been adjusted.

I'd written it off to paranoia, but now I didn't know what to believe.

I threw open the driver's door and got out. I bent down and ran my hand under the dashboard. When I didn't find anything, I tried again, stretching forward to lean as far as I could under the seat. My fingers grazed across the metal frame of the car, but I found nothing unusual.

I bent down to look under the wheel wells, too, although I didn't know what I was looking for or whether I'd know it if I saw it.

Still nothing.

When I straightened up again, I let out a yelp of surprise. Two cars away, Dr. Sean Howard was staring at me.

"Hallie," he called. "Is everything okay?"

"Oh! Oh, yes, I dropped something."

"I haven't had a chance to go over your draft in detail yet. I will soon, I promise. On a first pass, though, it all looks terrific."

"Thank you," I replied. "Take your time getting back to me."

"Do you need anything from the office?" he asked. The question of why I was back in their corporate parking lot remained unspoken.

I gave him an innocent smile and a thumbs-up. "No, I stayed with a girlfriend last night. She just dropped me off at my car."

"Ah, of course."

It was amazing how, once you started telling lies, it got easier with each one.

"Well, I'll e-mail you feedback on the project," Dr. Howard went on. "If you want to do the edits here, that's fine. Otherwise, you can make any changes remotely if you prefer."

"I appreciate that."

"You do great work, Hallie. I'll make sure Jill Oliver knows that."

"Thank you."

He turned toward the building, then stopped and looked back. "Oh, and I talked to my wife last night. She had dinner at Saltie Girl. I told her I'd met another fan of the restaurant."

It took me a moment, but then I recalled our conversation about the restaurant in the Back Bay neighborhood of Boston. A restaurant I'd never been to in a city I'd never visited—and yet I *remembered* eating there.

"I hope she had a good time," I said.

"She did. Goodbye, Hallie. And thank you again."

I waited while Dr. Howard continued into the building. Then I got in my car and headed out of the parking lot.

When I got back to Red Rock twenty minutes later, my nerves grew edgy again. I wondered if there were spies waiting to see if I'd returned to the casino. I wanted to get in and out as quickly as I could, and I wanted to avoid the hotel lobby. I took the back entrance to the complex and turned into the parking garage that was reserved for team members. I'd parked there with Nico many times. Leaving the garage, wearing my sun hat and sunglasses, I crossed to the employee service entrance on the south side of the hotel tower.

I didn't have a key card to get inside, so I drummed my fingers on the glass door. A man in a maintenance uniform opened it a few seconds later.

"Hi," I told him, using a flirty voice. I waved my room key in front of him and said, "Can I ask you a big favor? I'm staying on the fifteenth floor. Do you mind if I take the service elevator? My husband is waiting in the lobby, and I'd rather he not realize I was out and about. Know what I mean?"

Another lie that came too easily.

I also slipped a hundred-dollar bill into the man's hand.

"Sure, why not," he replied with a shrug, pocketing the money. He led me to the elevator, and I winked at him as the doors closed. Fifteen floors up, I stared at the carpet as I walked down the hallway, with my hat and sunglasses protecting my face from the hotel cameras. When I got to my room, I went inside, hoping no one at the front desk had been alerted to watch for my key card being used.

I packed quickly. I didn't have much, and the rest of my life was still in the trunk of my car. Of course, I didn't know where I was going or how to find any answers for the madness in my head.

When I was ready to leave, I did one last survey of the room. My mind must have been attuned to anything that looked out of place, because I noticed that one of the double outlets in the room didn't seem to match the others. It was a different color, and it didn't fit quite right in the wall. When I went over to look more closely, I noticed a few flecks of plaster dust on the carpet below the outlet, as if the screws had recently been removed and reinstalled.

I bent down and studied the outlet. It didn't look like an ordinary plug. There was a small opaque window in the middle of the device where a screw would normally have gone.

What was it?

A camera?

That was the only explanation. The hotel outlet had been replaced with a spy camera. They'd been watching me. Watching me as I dressed and undressed. Watching me sleep. Watching me have sex with Nico. Most likely, they were watching me right now.

They knew I was back.

I stumbled from the wall in a panic and grabbed my bag and ran to the hotel room door. If they'd seen me, the visitors would be coming for me soon. I put on my hat and sunglasses, and I dragged my bag down the hallway. There was no time to take the stairs. I headed for the main elevators and rode to the lobby, and I wondered what to expect when the doors opened.

Would someone be waiting?

But the area near the casino was quiet. No one was around. I got out and headed for the hotel exit, but as I reached the atrium, I glanced toward the front desk and froze. Not even thirty feet away, I saw Nico talking to four Las Vegas police officers. I didn't have to wonder who or what they were talking about.

They were looking for me.

Nico hadn't spotted me yet, and I turned around before he looked in my direction. I hoped he wouldn't recognize me from the back. I headed toward the rear of the tower and used the door that led out to the pool. It was busy and hot, with children splashing and men and women lounging in swimsuits under the ferocious sun. I pretended to be calm, so I didn't hurry as I pulled my bag among the palm trees and then to the stairs that led to the outdoor parking lot. I continued to the employee parking garage, where I found my car. I hadn't been inside the hotel more than ten minutes.

The police were looking for me.

Strangers were looking for me, too. Watching my every move.

Why?

As I drove my car out of the garage, I waited for the traffic to clear before I turned off the ramp. When I saw a gap among the cars, I tapped the accelerator, but just as quickly I jammed the brake again.

Right in front of me, a black SUV sped toward the hotel's porte cochere. The windows were smoked, and I couldn't see inside, but I knew who the driver had to be. It was the man with the long blond hair. The man who'd come after me with a hypodermic in the alley behind the casino.

I gripped the wheel hard. My eyes blinked shut.

I was so, so tired. I didn't think I'd ever been so tired. I must have fallen asleep for a second or two, because suddenly the blare of a horn from a car behind me jolted me out of my trance. In the road ahead of me, the SUV was already gone. I glanced both ways and didn't see it.

Jesus.

Had it really been there at all?

I didn't even know.

11

The first thing I needed was sleep. God, I needed sleep, but the Las Vegas temperature was 113 degrees outside, so I couldn't stay in my car. I thought about going to another casino, but I was wary of cameras, and I didn't want to check in at a hotel where I would have to use a credit card. For one thing, I was worried that they'd cut up my card. For another, I didn't know if my account would be flagged for a desk clerk to make a discreet call to the police.

The only thing I could do was the one thing I really, really didn't want to do. I went to my aunt and uncle's house in Summerlin.

Aunt Phoebe and Uncle Jim owned a small rambler in one of the older neighborhoods of the Pueblo, near Lake Mead Boulevard. They'd lived there since before I moved in with them when I was ten years old. The house looked like every other house in the neighborhood, with the same beige stucco, red clay roof, and dirty beige walls marking off the postage-stamp backyard. When I was a kid, it had felt like living in a prison compound.

Some of the neighbors had swimming pools, but a luxury like that was too frivolous for Phoebe. I loved loved loved to swim, and I would have done it every day if I could. I remember asking her when I was about eleven whether we could move to a house with a pool. My aunt didn't simply say no. She ranted at me that a pool was a stupid idea, because only pretty girls had pools and I was ugly and should never show off my body in a swimsuit.

Ugly.

She liked to use that word.

All these years later, I'm not a kid anymore, but Phoebe's criticisms have stayed with me. Whenever I'm feeling bad about myself, I can hear her voice in my head. She hated me, and I hated her.

I parked in their driveway and rang the doorbell. My aunt, who was now gray haired and in her late sixties, answered the door. She had shrunk in on herself like a withering grape. We hadn't seen each other in more than a year, but somehow she didn't look surprised to see me on their doorstep. She waved me inside without a word or a greeting. The house was as gloomy as a tomb, because all the plantation shutters had been closed to keep out the heat. It was warm anyway because Phoebe never set the air conditioner lower than eighty degrees. The place smelled as it had my whole life—like the fake, sweet aroma of dryer sheets.

In the living room, her husband, Jim, watched television from his wheelchair. His leg had stiffened up in the years since his injury at the postal facility, and he couldn't walk anymore.

"Hello, Uncle Jim," I called to him.

Jim, unlike his wife, had always done his best with me, even when I didn't make it easy for him. He was a genuinely nice man, living with a woman who thought life had treated her unfairly and wanted the whole world to know it. I think he'd learned how to tune out Phoebe over the years.

"Hallie," he said, giving me a warm smile. "You want to watch the *Wheel* with me?"

I glanced at the TV screen and solved the puzzle in my head. Movie, four words, last word starting with N. *Jewel of the Nile.*

"No, thanks."

Phoebe put her hands on her narrow hips. She was tall and thin like me and my mother, even though her skin was sagging into ill-fitting wrinkles. "So why are you here? What do you want?"

"Nothing."

"Well, that's a first," she snorted.

My aunt always talked as if I'd been some kind of endless burden on them. In fact, I'd only lived in this house through my graduation from UNLV. While I was in college, I'd paid rent. Through the ups and downs of the last few years, one thing I'd never done was come to them for help. I wanted to prove I was independent, even if it meant crashing on a friend's couch between apartments or living on Kraft Macaroni & Cheese until I collected my next paycheck. But it didn't matter. In my aunt's eyes, I was still the little girl draining their retirement security.

"I just need a place to sleep for a few hours," I told her.

"Why? What trouble are you in now?"

I had no interest in sharing my story of the last few days. "I was up all night working on a project," I lied, "and I'm too tired to drive home. Can I crash on my old bed for a few hours? Then I'll be gone, I promise."

"You look like shit," Phoebe said.

"Thanks."

"Still doing drugs, I bet."

"I'm trying to quit."

"What about the disgusting vomiting? I can see it in your face. You're doing that, too. Don't you dare do that in my house. I don't need to clean up any more of your puke."

"Please, I just need to sleep. I'm exhausted."

Just being with my aunt made me feel like a lost, desperate girl again. The nasal pitch of her voice was like fingernails on a chalkboard. My insides twisted, and I felt all the grief of being alone again, but I wasn't going to give her the satisfaction of seeing me break down.

"Oh, let her go, Pheebs," my uncle called from the living room.

"Fine, whatever, you know the way," Phoebe told me with a scowl. Then she managed to stab me with one last remark. "More like her worthless mother every day."

With a shuffling walk, I headed to the little bedroom that looked out on the wall of the neighboring house. There was a concrete walkway below the window, lined with trap rock. When I was a teenager, I'd spent hours lying on the bed, reading books, listening to Linkin Park on my headphones, and writing in my diary. One of my therapists had suggested I keep a journal because I'd told her that I liked to write. But when I moved out of this house, I burned it. There was nothing I wanted to remember from the years I'd spent here. To tell you the truth, I wished I could erase my childhood altogether, not just the one day I'd blocked out.

Nothing had changed. The room was exactly the same as it had been when I was in school. It was neat and dust-free—Aunt Phoebe was good about things like that—and if I closed my eyes, I could still have been ten or fourteen or eighteen or twenty-one.

I went to the window and opened the plantation shutters. Immediately, the burn of the outside heat radiated through the glass. The warmth made me even more tired. I stood there and stared at the drab wall of the neighbor's house a few feet away. The Kasims lived there. Aron and Julia, and their two sons, Harold and Aron Jr., who went by the nickname Ronny. They'd moved in when our previous neighbors sold the house and moved to Wyoming. The Kasim house had a swimming pool, and I couldn't get enough of the water. The other neighbors had let me swim there whenever I wanted, because they were old and liked seeing a child playing in the water. When they left and Ronny Kasim moved into the room across from my bedroom, I was fourteen years old. I'd asked Ronny if I could still come over and swim in their pool.

He said sure. Then he pulled down his swim trunks and told me what the price was going to be.

This house. Jesus, I hated this house.

I closed the plantation shutters and barely even made it to the twin bed before I collapsed and slept.

The next dream came as soon as my eyes were closed.

A long, angry, vivid dream.

This time I wasn't outside by the cliff. I was inside a house that was really more like a mansion. My bedroom was spacious and elegant, decorated down to every detail. A thick handmade quilt covered a queen bed, with plush individual squares depicting fruits and vegetables. Eggplant. Artichoke. Strawberry. Pineapple. One corner of the quilt had been peeled back by the maid to make a perfect triangle, showing peach-colored sheets. Vintage wallpaper made the room look as if it were enclosed by a weathered beach fence, with multicolored roses growing along the beams and butterflies in the air that matched the flowers. The other furnishings of the room were cherrywood antiques.

It was beautiful, but it was also the kind of sterile, forbidding room where you didn't dare touch anything or sit down. I decided that I hated it here. I wanted to escape, run away, live a completely different life. I was a fish out of water.

A wide set of bay windows looked out on the darkness. I stood by the glass and saw that my bedroom was on the top floor of the estate. A huge yard, dozens of acres, sprawled below me, and beyond the yard were the cliffs and the sea. The moon gave the world a silver glow. I could see the black outline of the statue of Poseidon, the one constant in my dream world.

I held out my hands to study them. My fingers were long and slim, my nails perfectly manicured. I twisted strands of my long blond hair around my fingers, and I hummed nervously. I was wearing the same dress with a few embroidered sunflowers that I'd been wearing earlier, under the sunshine, when Elijah had his hands around mine as he taught me how to swing a golf club.

Elijah.

I knew his name. It popped into my head.

Joyous emotions flooded through me, changing second by second. Restlessness. Excitement. Anticipation. I glanced at a walnut writing desk near my bureau and saw an old leather suitcase there, half-packed with clothes. I would take only the things I needed. The rest I'd leave behind. Just a few more days, and I'd be gone. A new life, a new beginning.

I left my bedroom to go downstairs. My feet practically floated as I ran down the spiral staircase, past the family paintings, past the shiny brass and crystal teardrops of the chandelier. The massive front door led outside. I was too excited to sleep; I needed fresh ocean air and starlight. But before I could leave, I heard raised voices, angry shouts nearby. With an unhappy little wrinkle in my forehead, I followed the shadows of a long, long hallway, where the lights were off. One side of the hallway was built of windows. The other side led to a ballroom, flush with gold leaf and a glossy oak floor for dancing. The loud voices came from inside.

Ahead of me, I saw that a spy was already watching the action. A teenage girl stood near one of the doors. Her face was pressed to the crack to look inside. She had the gangly prettiness of a fifteen-year-old—part girl, but part woman, too. She wore a revealing bikini, covered up only by a sheer wrap tied around her waist. When she saw me coming, she backed away from the ballroom door and gave me a strange smirk.

"They're really going at it this time."

Then she ran toward the house's rear terrace like a fairy in her bare feet.

I took her place and peered into the ballroom with one eye around the doorframe. I didn't want them to see me. Inside, in the space where we held elaborate Christmas parties and summer dances, I saw the decorations for a wedding reception: tables with tablecloths and tall candles waiting to be lit, swaths of heavy white fabric on the walls, a stage decorated with lace curtains and arrays of fresh flowers, and sconces glowing with dim romantic light.

A man and a woman confronted each other near the stage. The man stood stiff and immobile while the woman paced back and forth, her high heels clicking like gunfire on the varnished oak floor. Her long hair was golden like mine, but her face was less than the sum of its parts, eyes slightly too big, nose hooked and too long, mouth a little too wide. And now her face was streaked with tears and twisted with anger as she screamed at the man. She punctuated her accusations by jabbing a long slim finger at his face, and her cheeks had a flush that was as hot and fiery as the summer sun. She'd always been a girl of hard edges.

"You son of a bitch! How could you do this to me? How? You don't give a shit about me, do you? You never have. I've loved you my whole life, and this is how you treat me?"

Her fury washed over the man like nothing more than a calm ocean wave that barely moved the sand. He let her cry herself out, and when she took a breath, he said, "Do we really have to do this now?"

He even checked his watch, which turned up the boil on her rage.

"Oh, so we should do it later? After we're married? How about we discuss it on our honeymoon? That sounds like the perfect time for me to hear about your affairs. Don't you get it? The wedding's off!"

"Don't be ridiculous," the man replied, completely unruffled. "Nothing's off."

He was handsome and young, in his midtwenties. He was tall, built with the preppy grace and sturdy frame of an athlete. His hair was blond, mussed into casual spikes. He wore a zipped blue hoodie, khaki shorts, and boat shoes with no socks, like a kind of rich boy's summer uniform.

"I'm not going to marry you!" the woman insisted. "Don't you get it? Not now, not when I know who you really are. We're through! We're done!"

He gave her a sigh, as if she were nothing but a child in need of a lecture. "The rules are different for families like ours. Do I really need to spell it out for you?"

"Oh, yes, yes, we need to keep the money where it belongs, don't we? This is a merger as much as a marriage. But I also had the strange idea that you should actually love me. Because *I've* never loved anyone else in my life."

"I do love you, Savannah."

"What the hell does that even mean to you?"

He shrugged. "It means I promise to keep you in the style in which you grew up. It means we'll go to Europe and have children and own dogs and eat wonderful meals with wealthy, important people. In our circle, that's the definition of love. Don't pretend to be shocked by it."

"And meanwhile, you screw other women behind my back." She pushed her face so close to his that they were almost touching. "Who is it? Tell me."

"It's not relevant."

"Is it Cara? You wouldn't care about sleeping with my best friend. That's part of the game."

"Enough."

"Tell me."

"I don't think that's a good idea. In fact, I don't think any of this is your business."

"Not my *business*? Are you kidding?"

The woman turned toward the ballroom door, where I was standing. Her blue eyes burned into the shadows. Her face, normally as rigid as a corset laced too tightly, seethed with bitterness and jealousy.

"It's *her*, isn't it?" she hissed. "It's always *her*."

I wondered if she could see me, so I backed away into the darkness of the hallway.

The man's smooth voice didn't change at all. "Who?"

"You know who. My sister. Everyone wants her, everyone loves her. She's the angel, the good girl. What a little liar. Do you think I haven't seen her sneaking out at night? Do you think I don't know where she was going? Tell me the truth. *Are you fucking my sister?*"

◆ ◆ ◆

My eyes flew open. My heart raced.

I was still in the tiny twin bed in my tiny Summerlin bedroom. The air was stifling. I stared at the drab, dull furniture, but I could still see the lavish ballroom in front of my eyes. Just like the other dreams, this one didn't drift away like steam in the air. I remembered every detail. I remembered the emotions wrenching my gut. I was living someone else's life in my head, but now it was *my* life, too. Those people were part of me.

The woman in the ballroom. I'd seen her before.

She was my sister, and she was dead. She'd been lying at my feet, her skull crushed by a golf club. *Savannah.*

And the man. I knew the man, too. I'd seen his face, and I knew his voice, not just from dreams or hallucinations, but from a phone call only days earlier. There was no doubt in my mind. He was younger—much younger—but it was him. He'd saved my life by restarting my heart, and now he was showing up in my dreams.

The man in the ballroom was Dr. Reed Smith.

I got up from the bed and went to the window. I peered through the shutters. On the other side of the wall, I saw the window of Ronny Kasim's room in the neighboring house. He'd moved away years ago and never come back to Nevada, but I still expected to see him there. That had been our midnight tradition, him watching me *perform* in my bedroom.

Somehow I knew Reed Smith was the same kind of man.

The rules are different for families like ours.

I grabbed my phone from my pocket. It didn't take me long to find Smith's number in my call log, and I tapped the button to dial him. I remembered that patrician tone in his voice, devoid of emotion, exactly the way he'd been with the woman in the ballroom.

As the phone rang, I wondered what I would say to him.

Who are you?

But more than that: *What's happening to me?*

Because I was sure he knew the answer.

However, the call didn't go through. After only a couple of rings, I got a carrier error. I tried again and got the same message. This was the number that Dr. Smith had used to call me, but now it was no longer in service.

He'd jettisoned his phone.

Somehow I knew it was because of me.

I sat back down on the bed and used the Safari browser on my phone to navigate to the website for Johns Hopkins University. In the site's search box, I typed in "Reed Smith." The resulting list showed me lacrosse box scores for a player named Scott Smith, baseball scores for a player named Reed Thompson, and an alumni news article about an ophthalmic surgeon named William Reed.

But there were no listings for a doctor named Reed Smith.

Next I went to the page for the medical school. I called up a roster of faculty and found Armine Smith, Wanli Smith, Douglas Smith, Hermon Smith, Kellie Smith, and half a dozen other Smiths, but Reed Smith wasn't among them.

There was no such man teaching, practicing, or doing research at Johns Hopkins.

Dr. Reed Smith didn't exist.

12

As night fell, I sat alone in the small backyard of the house in Summerlin. There was no desert landscaping inside the walls other than a couple of prickly pear cacti looking lonely among the barren rocks. The cacti were weathered and sharp, which was also a fair way of describing my aunt. Sitting in an old wicker chair on the paver patio, I listened to the noise of traffic not far away. The silhouettes of the western mountains rose above the horizon. It was a clear night, and the heat had receded into the eighties, which felt cool compared to the day.

"Mind if I join you?"

My uncle Jim rolled his wheelchair up beside me. I glanced at the patio door to confirm that my aunt wasn't with him. The last thing I needed in my current mood was another guilt trip from her.

"Phoebe's already in bed," he added with a smile, as if reading my thoughts.

"Oh. Okay."

"Mind if I smoke? She won't allow it in the house, and this is one of my last remaining pleasures."

I shrugged. "Go ahead."

Jim produced a cigar from his pants pocket. He lit it and took a couple of puffs, then exhaled smoke that hung like a slow-moving cloud in the still air. "You want to try it, too?"

"We did that once," I reminded him. "It didn't go well."

He'd let me try his cigar when I was thirteen years old, and I'd promptly thrown up.

"Oh, yes," he said with a smile. "I forgot."

We sat in silence for a while. Jim smoked, and I stared at the handful of stars that were bright enough to outshine the Las Vegas lights. My uncle was a heavy man, and he'd gotten even heavier since he'd been restricted to the wheelchair. His skin had a sallow paleness, and his hair had gotten gray and thin. He didn't look well. But Jim had an easy come, easy go attitude about life.

"Anything on your mind, Hallie?" he asked, with a casual tone that wasn't casual at all.

I thought about where I was. This house. It didn't matter how much time passed; when I returned here, I was always a child again. I'd stayed away for a year, but nothing had changed, and nothing ever would. I didn't think there would be a next time, and I think Jim knew it, too. I was never coming back.

"Why does she hate me so much?" I asked.

"Who . . . Phoebe?"

"Yeah."

"Phoebe doesn't hate you."

"It sure feels that way."

Jim patted my wrist in a fatherly way.

"You're a smart girl, Hallie. Just like your mother. You should be doing great things, and someday I'm sure you will. Phoebe realizes that, too. She doesn't hate you. She's jealous of you. She was jealous of your mother for the same reason. Phoebe and I are both ordinary, and when you're ordinary, it can be tough to be around not-so-ordinary people." He sucked on his cigar and grinned. "Mind you, I will deny ever saying that about my wife."

I smiled, too. "It's our secret."

Jim eyed the stars, then looked back at the patio door. He blew out a cloud of smoke, and his voice went down to a whisper. "Are you in some kind of trouble, Hallie?"

"What makes you say that?"

"Because the police called a little while ago, looking for you."

I bolted up in the chair. "The police? What did you tell them?"

"Take it easy. I told them that you hadn't been here in months. I assumed that was what you'd want me to say. And don't worry, I took the call, not your aunt."

"I should go," I told him. "I need to leave."

"Did something happen?"

"Yes. Someone died. Someone—was killed. But I didn't do anything wrong."

"Can I help?"

"I don't want to make it your problem."

"Well, you can, you know," my uncle said. "We're family. That's my job."

"I appreciate that, but there's nothing you can do."

"Do you need money? I don't have much, but I can give you what I've got."

"No, I'm okay for now."

I began to get up, but Jim gently nudged me back into the chair. "There's no rush, Hallie. I know you need to go, but the truth is, I miss you when you're not here. And something tells me I won't be around the next time you stop by. Assuming you ever do. So give me a few more minutes, okay?"

His gentle tone calmed me a little. "Yes, okay."

"Good."

"I miss you, too, you know," I added.

"That's nice to hear. I know life hasn't been easy for you, Hallie. I'm sure it's been lonely, and I wish I could have done more. But no one can replace a mother for a little girl. Deep down, you're probably still angry at her for what she did, and I don't blame you. But I'll tell you something. She loved you. She loved you way more than she cared about her own life. She would have done absolutely anything to protect you. That thing inside her, that wasn't who she was. That was definitely not her."

I didn't say anything for a while. Then I finally admitted the truth.

"I'm scared that I'm becoming just like her, Uncle Jim. You heard Phoebe. I'm getting more like my mother every day."

Jim took his cigar out of his mouth, and his eyes narrowed. "What's going on with you, Hallie?"

"I don't know. Things are happening to me. Things I can't explain, things that make no sense. I'm not even sure what's real anymore. I saw Mom go down the same road, and it kept getting worse and worse. Until—"

He nodded. "Until that terrible day."

"I don't want to go through that myself."

"Yes, I understand."

I took his hand and squeezed it tightly. "Tell me something. Did I really go into her bedroom? Did I really see it happen?"

"I'm sorry. Believe me, I wish you hadn't seen that. But yes, you did."

"Are you sure? I don't remember it. I see myself walking up to the door, but I can't open it. All I can feel is the brass doorknob under my fingers. Maybe I heard the shot inside, and I just ran."

He sighed. He wasn't telling me anything I hadn't heard a hundred times before. "Hallie, when they found you at Red Rock, you had her blood on your hands. You were there. You went inside. The therapists think you saw her do it. It was too much for you. It would have been too much for anyone, but a ten-year-old girl? And yes, after that, you ran away."

I looked at my hands. They were my hands, not part of any dream. And they were covered in blood. I shivered.

Jim noticed my discomfort and pulled my head to his shoulder, the way he'd done when I was just a girl. I liked the feel of him and the smell of him, and I tried to lock that sensation into my memory so that I would never forget it. He whispered into my ear.

"You've been running ever since," he told me. "Someday, Hallie, it would be nice if you could let yourself stop running."

◆ ◆ ◆

My therapist, Tori, worked in a high-rise on Third Street a few blocks south of the Fremont Street casinos. In the early morning, I parked near a bail bondsman's office across the street and waited for her. It was quiet downtown right after sunrise—the gamblers and drunks were finally in bed—but even so, I was nervous about being in public. This part of downtown was ground zero for many of the Clark County buildings, so I saw a handful of police cars passing near me. I kept out of sight when they did, and I hoped they didn't run the license plate on my car.

I didn't have to wait long for Tori to arrive. I knew she liked to get to the office before her appointments to study patient files for the day. Her rust-colored curls bounced, and she checked her phone as she walked. She wore a gorgeous black pencil dress that looked as if it had come from a designer boutique, plus sky-high heels. Her ruby anklet probably cost more than my whole BioEfx payment. I felt pretty downscale in my T-shirt and shorts as I ran across the street to intercept her.

"Hallie," she said with surprise, looking up from her phone to see me on the sidewalk.

"You said not to worry about the time."

Her eyes traveled up and down my body with their usual sharpness. She knew I was in trouble. "No, of course. I'm glad you came."

"Do you have some time? I really need to talk."

"That's good. Yes, I have time. Come on up."

We were the only ones in the office lobby at that hour, and we took the elevator to one of the upper floors of the building. Tori's suite wasn't large—just an exterior waiting room and then her clinical office on the other side of a walnut door—but it was elegantly decorated and had a great location looking northward toward the Strip casinos. She led me through the waiting room directly into her office, and she shut the door behind us. With the push of a few buttons, she started coffee brewing.

I fidgeted on a leather sofa by the window, and Tori turned her swivel chair around and pulled it closer.

"Do you want something to drink?" she asked.

"No."

"When's the last time you ate something?"

"I don't know. Yesterday sometime. But I'm not hungry."

"What's going on?"

I took a deep breath. How could I even say it?

"Last night two men tried to kill me."

Tori blinked with surprise. "I'm sorry, what?"

"It was in an alley behind a casino on Rainbow. They had a needle. They were going to make it look like I overdosed again. Nobody would have had any trouble believing that after what happened on the rooftop. Before they could do it, someone else intervened to stop them, but then they killed *him*. The thing is, I'm virtually sure *he* was watching me, too. Plus, I'm—I'm pretty sure there was a camera in my hotel room."

Her face took on a dark cast, and her lips pressed into a frown. She grabbed a pen from her desk and twirled it in her fingers. "Go on. You don't look like you're done. What else?"

There was no point in holding back the rest.

"I'm having dreams, too. But they don't feel like dreams. They feel real. They feel more like *memories*. Except they're someone else's memories, not mine."

"Someone else's memories?"

"Yes. It's like I'm seeing someone else's life through my eyes. Plus, I know things. Things I couldn't possibly know. I can recognize places I've never been. How is that possible?"

Tori didn't say anything. She sat there twiddling her pen and studying me so closely I wanted to cover up my face with my hands. Her legs were crossed at the ankles, and a few curls dipped onto her forehead.

"You want some coffee?" she asked.

"Coffee? No."

"I need some coffee."

She went to retrieve a cup from the wet bar behind her desk. Her mug was gray-and-white handmade ceramic. She sat down again and still didn't respond to anything I'd said. She just sipped her coffee.

She was waiting for me. It was still my turn.

"Tori, none of this makes sense. What's happening to me?"

This time she put her mug down on a glass table beside her. She steepled her fingers in front of her chin. "Well, that's a very good question, Hallie. I'd like to give you answers, but I don't know. Let's take it one step at a time, okay? First the people who tried to kill you. There *was* a murder near Rainbow a couple of nights ago. I saw it on the news. I have no idea whether you were really involved or whether you heard about it and made it a part of your story."

"Tori, I'm not lying."

"I didn't say you were lying. It's not a lie if you think it's the truth."

"I'm being followed. People are *spying* on me. And the police are looking for me, too."

"Okay."

I shook my head bitterly at her reaction. "You don't believe me."

"I believe you believe it. Right now, that's all that matters."

"Don't fucking patronize me! Yes, I know it sounds crazy. I know I may *be* crazy. Believe me, I know that better than most people. Genetics aren't exactly working in my favor, you know? But something is happening to me."

The calm didn't change in Tori's voice. "I'm not patronizing you, and yes, I can see that something is happening to you. The question is what."

I sighed. I didn't know how to convince her, because I didn't know how to convince myself. "The doctor who saved my life? He doesn't exist."

"What do you mean?"

"He told the ER doc his name was Reed Smith from Johns Hopkins. There's no such person."

"Okay. That's odd, but not necessarily impossible. The ER doc probably got it wrong. Or maybe this guy was afraid you'd sue him, so he used a false name. It happens."

"Yeah, but Reed Smith called *me*, too. Why would he do that? He said he wanted to follow up and see if I was okay. But the whole thing was weird. I didn't trust him."

"Hallie—"

"Look, tell me what happened on the roof," I interrupted her.

"The roof?"

"You were there during the party at the casino. You saw me, right? I went to the bathroom, and I came out, and I collapsed. You saw everything."

"Of course."

"Tell me what happened."

Tori was silent for another long stretch.

"Well, I saw you fall. After that, it was chaos. People screaming for help, dialing 911. One of the doctors started CPR and called out to ask if the hotel had any emergency equipment on the rooftop."

"Did they?"

Tori paused. "Yes, but that's not how it went down."

"What are you talking about? What do you mean that's not how it went down?"

"I mean, yes, someone ran to grab a defibrillator, but before they got back, another doctor had already set up a portable unit."

"A portable unit? What is that?"

"One of the doctors had a pocket-size AED that integrated with his cell phone. He had it set up in seconds, and he used it to stabilize your heartbeat. The fact that he acted so quickly is probably what saved your life."

"The doctor who did that—did you hear anyone talking about who he was? Did you hear the name Reed Smith? Or some other name?"

"I didn't. I'm sorry. Everything happened very quickly, Hallie. Then the paramedics came and took you away not long after. The fact is, there was nothing particularly unusual about it from a medical standpoint, but I'm not trying to minimize the emotional effects of what you went through."

I got up and went to the window. All of Las Vegas was spread out in front of me. The drab beige houses and strip malls. The surreal glass towers of the casinos. The dry, dusty, beautiful mountains ringing the valley. The barren desert where I'd lived my whole life. My hometown.

I hated my hometown.

"Tori, do you think this is schizophrenia?" I asked quietly. "Are these all delusions? Am I making it up in my head? I saw what happened to my mother. I don't want that to happen to me."

Her voice was quiet, like mine. "I wish I could give you a yes-or-no answer, Hallie. I can't. But am I concerned? Yes, of course."

"At least that's honest. Thank you. Except how do you explain the things I know? I remember people I've never met, places I've never been. But they're *real*. I had a conversation with a man from Boston about restaurants and schools and neighborhoods there. But I've never been to Boston in my life."

"I can give you a clinical explanation," Tori said, "but it may or may not be what's really happening."

"What is it?"

"Well, you could be experiencing some kind of personality disorder. Maybe even split personalities. You could be meeting people and going places and not remembering any of it when you're Hallie."

I shook my head. "Jesus."

"Remember, I'm not saying that's the answer. Simply that it's possible."

"So what do I do?" I asked.

Tori took her coffee mug in her hand again. "You know what to do. You know where this all comes from."

I closed my eyes. "My mother."

"That's right. You've blocked out the most important memory of your life. Until you find it, you'll never move on."

I saw my fingers on the brass doorknob.

I heard ABBA singing "The Visitors."

My mother wailed from the other side of the door. My name. *Hallie, oh God, Hallie, help me!*

"No," I said.

"I can hypnotize you. I can take you back there."

"No."

"I know it's painful. I know you're scared. But sooner or later, you're going to have to confront it."

Even louder now. *"No!"*

I didn't give Tori a chance to say anything more. I didn't want to be convinced. I wasn't ready to face that part of my past.

I ran from her office without another word. In the hallway, I pushed the button for the elevator, but it was too slow, too slow, so I bolted to the stairs and took them two at a time. I needed to get away. It was like the building was on fire. It was like my mind was on fire.

In the lobby, I hurled myself through the outer door, gulping in the hot morning air. I was crying.

Then I looked across the street toward my car. There were squad cars surrounding it.

The police were waiting for me.

13

"I didn't kill anyone," I told the detective. "There were two men in that alley, and they were trying to kill *me*."

"Uh-huh."

The detective chewed gum and didn't seem to be paying attention to what I was saying. He'd introduced himself as Cordy Angel, but Detective Angel had said almost nothing to me since the street cops brought me in. Instead, he played with his phone as we sat on opposite sides of the interview room in a police station on Cheyenne. The longer the silence dragged on, the more I felt a need to fill it with words. Then I realized that was the whole point of what he was doing, so I shut up.

Eventually, after I stopped playing his game, he reached into a box on the floor beside him. He removed a plastic bag with a knife inside and put it on the table. "This knife belong to you?"

"Sort of. I took it from a restaurant at the hotel where I was staying."

"Why'd you do that?"

"I wanted it for self-defense."

"Your prints are on it."

"I know. I just told you, I took it with me. It was in my purse."

"You a spy or something? CIA? Shit like that?"

"No."

"Witness protection?"

"No."

"Then why are people trying to kill you?" he asked.

"I don't know."

The detective put the knife back in the box. Casually, he put his hands behind his head. He was a small man, several inches shorter than I was, and probably in his late thirties. He had a slick Vegas look about him, wearing a flowered summer shirt and tight black pants. His hair was greased back over his head, and he exuded a dense smell of cologne. His skin was the color of extra-virgin olive oil. He had hawkish brown eyes and obviously thought of himself as a lady-killer. You couldn't walk through a Strip casino without tripping over men just like him.

"Mind if I call you Hallie?" he asked, giving me a smile that could have been an advertisement for teeth-whitening gel.

"Go ahead."

"Okay, Hallie. You can call me Cordy."

"I'll call you Detective," I told him.

"Whatever. Listen, Hallie, here's the thing. You ain't under arrest. You want to leave right now, then go. I know you didn't kill anybody."

I was wary. "Really?"

"Yeah. There was a security camera in the alley behind the casino. It's not great, but we could see enough on the video to figure out what happened. Two guys attacked you, another guy showed up to break it up. He got his throat cut for being a Good Samaritan. The killers ran, and so did you. Nobody's calling you a murderer, but right now, you're our only witness. So I'm hoping you can help us figure out what the hell's going on."

"I wish I could help, but I have no idea."

Cordy chewed his gum for a while, then took it out of his mouth. He used his index finger to flick it off his thumb into the trash basket. "These guys who came after you, do you know who they were?"

"No."

"Ever seen them before?"

I hesitated. "Well, I'm pretty sure one of them had been following me for a few days. I saw the vehicle he was driving—a black Ford SUV—at Red Rock Canyon. And then the same man was in the hotel with me. At least I think it was him. The black SUV was at the curb outside the casino, so if there were any street cameras around, you could probably get a license plate."

"We did. The SUV was stolen a few days ago. We found it abandoned this afternoon."

"Well, that's all I know."

He pushed a photograph across the desk, and I grimaced as I saw a man's dead body on a slab. Only his face and shoulders were visible, but he seemed to be an Asian man with a huge physique.

"Recognize this guy?" the detective asked.

"I'm not sure. I think it could be the second man who attacked me. The one who came from the other side of the building."

He nodded. "Yeah, we think so, too. We found him in the SUV. He'd been shot in the back of the head."

"Jesus."

"But you don't know him?"

"No, I've never seen him before. Do you know who killed him?"

"Not yet, but since we found him in the truck, my guess is that his partner—the one you say was following you—decided to get rid of him. No need to leave somebody else around for the police to find."

"Oh."

"The big question is this: *Why* would this man be following you?" Cordy asked.

"I told you, I don't know."

"What do you do for a living, Hallie?"

"I write marketing copy for medical devices."

"Pretty glamorous, huh?"

"Oh, yeah."

"Lotta people get killed in that line of work?" Cordy asked.

"Not that I know of."

"What do you do when you're not working?"

"The usual stuff. I go to shows sometimes. Play the slots."

"The slots? You got a gambling problem, Hallie? No shame in admitting it. This is Sin City. Lotsa people get into debt. I been there myself."

"I'm not a high roller, Detective. If I put in twenty or thirty bucks, that's a lot for me. The only debts I have are my student loans and my credit cards, but I don't think Visa and Bank of America have started sending hit men after their customers. Not yet, anyway."

The detective drummed his manicured fingernails on the table. "What about drugs?"

"You think I'm going to admit anything to you about drugs?"

"Hey, I'm homicide, not vice. I'm not looking to bust you for what you put up your nose. But let me explain something to you. When people call 911 about medical emergencies, most of the time the cops show up, too, not just the EMTs. So let's say a young woman collapses at a casino, and an ambulance gets called. Chances are there's going to be a police report about it. You understand what I'm saying, Hallie?"

Oh, yes. I did.

"Okay. I had a problem last week."

"Big problem, it looks like," Cordy said.

"You're right. My heart stopped. A doctor had to restart it."

"Yeah, and the ambulance guys told my guys that they thought cocaine was involved. Cops found an empty envelope with traces of cocaine in the women's bathroom, which was where you were right before you collapsed. And before you get your panties bunched up and start calling a lawyer, let me tell you why this matters. The guy who tried to kill you—we don't know who he is, but odds are somebody paid him to follow you and whack you. Got it? Nine times out of ten, when that happens, drugs are involved."

"Well, I'm sorry, Detective. This is the one time out of ten."

"Do you deny taking cocaine?"

"I'm not perfect, and I don't claim to be. Yes, I've used occasionally since college, but I've been clean for months. The fact is, I had a shitty

July 4, and I slipped. I bought some coke from a nobody on the street, and I took too much."

"You don't sell?"

"Never."

"You ever been a mule? You carry? Make deliveries?"

"Never."

Cordy shook his head. He buried his nose in a file again and then looked back up at me. "Hallie Evers. Pretty name. Pretty girl, too, if you don't mind my saying. I got your record here, you know. You've had some problems with the law over the years, haven't you, Hallie?"

"A few times. Nothing serious."

"Drunk and disorderly once near the UNLV campus. Lotta college kids can say that. Shoplifting once, too, looks like. Over at the Forum Shops."

"It was a stupid mistake when I was broke and had a job interview. I made restitution."

"Yup, it's all here." Then his lips formed a wolfish grin. "How about attempted murder? You think that's nothing serious?"

My stomach churned. "I was fifteen. That record was supposed to be sealed."

"Hey, this is Vegas, mama. Nothing's ever sealed unless you bury it in the desert. Says here you tried to drown the boy who lived next door to you."

Ronny Kasim.

I twitched. Instinctively, I covered the scars on my wrist.

"You almost did it, too," Cordy went on. "Bashed the kid's head on the concrete and held him under the water. If the boy's dad hadn't seen you and dived in to break it up, Ronny would have been a goner."

"Yes, you're right."

"Why'd you do it?"

"I was tired of him raping me."

Cordy frowned. "Oh."

"That's why his parents agreed to let me do community service. They knew."

"And nothing like that since then?"

"No."

He leaned across the table, his cologne wafting my way. "Well, mama, that gets us back to square one. Why the hell would anybody want you dead? Because I saw that video, and there's no two ways about it. They came after *you*. This wasn't random."

"Like I've told you eighteen times, I have no idea."

"You swear you're not a mule? I mean, desperate people do twisted shit for money. They swallow balloons full of drugs. They shove shit up their asses. If you've got a couple million dollars' worth of heroin or coke inside that pretty body of yours, then whoever owns it is not going to stop until they get it back. Better to tell me now, and we can get it out before it bursts and sends you into orbit."

"There's nothing inside me," I insisted.

The detective sighed loudly. He reached back into the box and retrieved a large manila envelope. "Tell you what, let's switch gears. We're not getting anywhere with the killers, so how about we take a look at the victim?"

"I didn't know him, either."

"Yeah, but you thought he was following you, too, right? You told the waitress at the casino you didn't like the way he was looking at you. You paid her to dump some drinks on him so you could sneak out the back."

"Yes."

"Did you know who he was? Had you seen him before?"

I shook my head. "No. That was the first time."

"His name was Todd Kivel. He was a private detective. That name ring any bells with you?"

"No."

Cordy reached inside the manila envelope and spread out a series of photographs. I glanced at them, and then I gasped in disbelief. The pictures were all of *me*. Me at the Red Rock Hotel. Me in the parking lot at BioEfx. Me eating dinner in a twenty-four-hour café. Me in the downscale casino where Todd Kivel had been watching me from the bar while he drank his beer.

"Jesus! Kivel took these?"

"Yeah, we found the pictures on his phone. You were right about him. The last few days, he was all over your ass."

My head spun. This wasn't a delusion. This was real.

I tried to make sense of it, and I couldn't. I looked around the police conference room as if I were an actor on a movie set. As if the wall would slide away and I'd see the cameras, and the director would yell, "Cut." Maybe I was dreaming again and I could jolt myself awake, and I'd be back in my apartment, and Nico would be with me. Maybe July 4 never happened. Maybe I never died.

But no. I was where I was.

"So Kivel intervened when these guys tried to kill you," Cordy went on in a kind of drone, "and they thanked him for it by cutting his throat. That means we've got *two* different sets of people looking for you. A private detective and a couple of hired thugs. You're really popular, Hallie. It just seems pretty hard for me to believe that you have no idea why this would be happening to you."

I stuttered. I didn't know what to say.

"I'm sorry, Detective, but I've told you everything I know."

Except the dreams.

There was no way I was going to tell him about the dreams.

Cordy frowned. He was obviously convinced I was still hiding something. "One more thing. You said you work in the medical device biz, right?"

"That's right."

"You ever hear of a company called . . ." Cordy checked his notes. "Hyppolex. Hyppolex Corporation."

"No. I haven't. There are thousands of device companies in the US and around the world."

"Hyppolex. Sounds like a place that teaches hippos to read or something."

I smiled. "Device companies pay a lot of money to come up with stupid names for things. They want something distinctive when they're marketing their products to doctors and investors."

"Yeah, but Hyppolex? What's that about?"

"Well, odds are, Hyppo references the hippocampus in the brain," I told him. "That's the kind of game we marketers play."

Then I thought about the hippocampus.

That was where *memories* were stored.

"What's this all about, Detective?" I asked. "What does this company have to do with anything?"

"Well, I looked it up on the web, and Hyppolex is a medical device company out of Boston. The thing is, our dead private eye, Todd Kivel, scribbled a note in his apartment about them. Just a sticky note that said 'Hyppolex, five thousand.' He put a bunch of dollar signs after it, too. Sounds to me like they were paying him for something. Given what we found on his camera, I'm thinking that was the price for keeping an eye on you, know what I'm saying?"

I did.

But my mind was already in a whirl. I'd begun to fall down the rabbit hole as soon as the detective mentioned the name of the city.

Boston.

14

That day, I packed up my life in my car, and I hit the road.

As I drove away from Las Vegas, a part of me understood that I would never come back. Maybe I should have realized long ago, when I was spending every waking hour in a swimming pool, that I didn't really belong in the desert. I was a water girl, and that meant going where the water was. In this case, I was heading for the East Coast.

My route out of town took me southeast into Arizona. I kept an eye on my mirrors to look for anyone following me through the flat scrubland, but for the time being, I was alone. Just me and the dusty highway.

But I knew where I was going.

With my phone hooked into the speakers of my car, I called my headhunter, Jill Oliver.

"Hallie," Jill said when she answered, with more enthusiasm than she usually showed for my calls. "I'm glad to hear from you. I got a call from Sean Howard at BioEfx. He was thrilled with the work you did for them. In fact, he said the edits on the copy were so light he didn't even feel the need to have you do a second round. He said he was putting through the rest of the contract for payment. It'll go straight into your bank account."

"Terrific," I replied.

"I've got a couple of other assignments I could send your way," she told me. "Want me to forward the details?"

"Actually, let's hold off on that for now."

Jill sounded puzzled. "Okay. What's up?"

"I've got a question for you. Are you familiar with a Boston-based device firm called Hyppolex?"

"Sure. Lots of big venture capital money behind them."

"What's their focus?"

"They've had promising results with a neuroprosthesis for translating brain wave activity directly into speech. The idea is to restore voice functions for people after strokes or TBIs."

"Anything else?"

"I've heard rumors that they're engineering a new treatment for Alzheimer's patients, but the details are hush-hush. Even the money men don't know anything about it, and everyone who works there is locked up behind nondisclosure agreements."

"Do you know anyone who works there?"

"Yes, I've met their CEO several times. He founded the company about ten years ago, when he was only in his midtwenties. His name is Tyler Reyes."

Hearing that name, my whole body jerked.

It was an instinctive reaction that I couldn't control. The steering wheel slipped under my fingers, and the car lurched into the next lane and across the rumble strips onto the median. Fortunately, there was no other traffic nearby. My tires bumped over hard rutted dirt, throwing up clouds of dust, and I slammed on the brakes. As the car crept over shrubs and rocks, I slowly made my way back onto the highway.

Tyler Reyes.

His nasal eastern accent echoed in my head, and his face loomed in front of me as vividly as a photograph.

I shot into one of my waking dreams, far from where I was.

Tyler was sitting at a table across from me. His hands covered mine. We were at the Boston restaurant—Saltie Girl. His was the blurred face that had failed to come into focus in my head, but now I saw him clearly. He had curly dark hair, long sideburns, and circular black glasses. He was a small man and not particularly attractive, with a long crooked nose, sunken chin, and distracted brown eyes. They were a scientist's eyes, always somewhere else even when they were looking right at you.

As I stared at him, I felt something roll through my heart.

What was it? What did I feel? Affection, warmth, but not love, not desire. And also regret. Deep regret.

I'm sorry, Tyler.

I dragged myself back into the present moment. I was still on the highway, heading east. Heading toward Boston. But I remembered what Tori had told me. *You could be meeting people and going places and not remembering any of it when you're Hallie.*

"What can you tell me about Tyler Reyes?" I asked Jill.

"Well, he's brilliant. Harvard, MIT. What is this about, Hallie? Why are you so interested in Hyppolex?"

I couldn't tell her the truth, because I didn't know what the truth was. So I came up with a lie.

"I met a couple of their people at MedX. It sounds like a cool company. I want to talk to them."

Jill was quiet for a beat. "You're thinking about relocating out of Las Vegas? I never thought you'd leave."

"In fact, I'm already gone," I said.

"You left? Why?"

"It doesn't matter. Do you think you can get me an interview at Hyppolex?"

"By phone? Zoom?"

"No, in person. I'm driving to Boston."

Jill spoke slowly, as if trying to get me to understand the facts of life. "Hallie, that's not how it works. You know that. I have no idea whether they have any openings in your area. I mean, if you just want a chance to meet the people there, I'll see what I can do. I can talk you up with the head of personnel. I've placed a couple of people there in the past, so we have a relationship. But if they're not anticipating any marketing openings, she probably won't be willing to take the time."

"Make the call," I repeated. "It's important."

Jill sighed. "Look, Hallie, I like you. We go back a long way, and I've stayed with you when a lot of other recruiters would have kicked you to the curb. But I can't simply go to the head of HR and tell her that a writer with a checkered employment history is on her way to Boston and wants an interview."

"Don't go to HR," I said, taking a leap of faith. "Call Tyler Reyes. Talk to him directly. Use my name, and tell him—" I hesitated as I thought about what to say. "Tell him I love the lobster at Saltie Girl."

"I'm sorry, you *know* Tyler?" Jill asked.

"Please, Jill. Just make the call."

I hung up the phone without letting her make any more protests. Jill wasn't happy, but I was pretty sure she'd call Tyler Reyes.

I opened the car windows despite the hot desert air. Then I turned on the radio to help the miles pass. There weren't many radio stations out here at all. What I found was a scratchy public radio station playing classical music, and I never listen to classical music. And yet I turned the volume up loud. Through the static, I heard a piano, its notes climbing higher and then swooping back down. The music gripped me like hands around my throat.

Rachmaninoff.

How did I know that?

But it was definitely Rachmaninoff. Piano Concerto no. 3. I not only knew the name of the piece, but I knew the notes. The keys. Holy hell, I could *play the piano*. As I drove, I tapped my fingers on the steering wheel, keeping pace with the soloist, my body twitching as if I were sitting at the piano myself. I pounded the steering wheel harder. The music thumped in my chest—so beautiful, so achingly beautiful that I wanted to cry. Up and down, up and down went the concerto, and there I was, playing every note from memory. The strings swelled, the horns marched, the rhythm dimmed to near silence, and then my fingers led the way up again, playful, like the chirrup of birds, like a choir of angels.

My head flicked my blond hair back in concentration. My hands flew, each finger possessed of its own mind, working independently. I felt the hushed anticipation of an audience in the darkness as the final chords swelled. The end was near. We came together as one—me, the piano, the orchestra, the conductor. We hurtled through the finale with a relentless charging beat, a thunder that stripped the breath from my chest, until the piano stampeded above every other instrument and the last notes died away in a fury.

A roar of applause erupted. Wild cheers. Whistles. I was covered in sweat. Standing. Bowing. Soaking up their approval.

Then I awakened.

The radio played nothing but static. I was still on the highway, driving in the middle of the lane, alone in the desert.

My phone rang.

I jumped at the noise, like a buzzing alarm in my head. I felt disoriented as I answered the phone. It was Jill. She sounded formal and oddly annoyed, as if she'd arrived at a costume party to find that she was the only person wearing street clothes.

"Well, you have an interview at Hyppolex on Monday morning at nine o'clock."

"Thank you, Jill. That's great work."

"You'll meet with the senior vice president of product marketing. I told them you were driving in. They're wiring two thousand dollars to your account to cover your travel expenses, and they're putting you up in a suite at the Copley Plaza."

"Wonderful."

"I truly don't understand this, Hallie."

"What's to understand? Obviously they need a marketer, and you know these start-ups are always flush with cash."

"What are you not telling me?" she asked. "Do you have some kind of relationship with Tyler Reyes?"

"No, I've never met him."

I heard an unhappy little hiss on the phone. "This whole thing makes me extremely uncomfortable, Hallie. I feel like I'm in the middle of something unethical, and I don't like it. I don't appreciate being set up as the go-between on a deal that feels all wrong."

"I understand. I'm sorry. That's all I can say."

"Find another recruiter," Jill snapped at me. "We're done."

She hung up. The call was over.

I felt bad about Jill, but what could I do? I couldn't explain to her things I couldn't explain to myself. I was flying on instinct now. All I knew was that the answers were in Boston, with Tyler Reyes and Hyppolex. That was where I had to go, so I shoved my foot down hard on the accelerator, and the car growled and shot along I-40. I was in a hurry to get there.

The life that I was looking for was waiting for me on the other side of the country.

I just didn't know whose life I was going to find.

PART II

15

I arrived in Boston on Sunday morning, the day before my interview at Hyppolex, and checked in at the Copley Plaza. The elegance of the hotel made me self-conscious. An arched skylight let in the July sunshine. My shoes squeaked on the white-and-gray marble floor, and I grazed my fingernails against Corinthian columns. The desk clerk put me in a suite that was bigger than the entire apartment I'd shared with Mishawn. It was high up and gave me views of Copley Square and the glass skyscrapers of downtown Boston.

Hyppolex had provided a gift for me. A huge bouquet of flowers sat on the coffee table in front of a gas fireplace, along with an oversize basket of goodies. When I unwrapped the plastic and ribbons, I found a Boston-themed selection of cookies, pretzels, tea, and chocolates, along with a map of the city. Included with the flowers was a handwritten card.

Hallie,

All of us at Hyppolex are looking forward to meeting you on Monday. In the meantime, enjoy the city.

Tyler Reyes

This was definitely over the top for a marketing position. Oh yes, I'd pushed some buttons.

After I showered and changed clothes, I decided to explore the city. Outside, I crossed Saint James Avenue to the green lawn of Copley Square, which was dominated by the stone arches and conical orange roof of Trinity Church. I hung out in the square near the statue of John Singleton Copley and eyed the crowds for a while. It was a weekend afternoon, and the city bustled with people. Eventually, I bought a hot dog from a street vendor and walked north along the cobblestone sidewalk on Dartmouth Street.

How did I feel?

I felt *at home*. But that feeling was scary in and of itself. I didn't understand what was happening to me, or what was going on inside my head. It seemed impossible that I could have been to Boston before and not remember it, or that I'd somehow lived a second life that my real life knew nothing about. And yet I felt as if I'd been walking these streets for most of my life. I knew where everything was. Wherever I looked, I had vivid recollections of things I'd done and places I'd gone.

There was the Copley light rail station. Symphony Hall was two stops away on the E line. I'd played Rachmaninoff there. Me, a girl who had never taken a music lesson in her life.

There was the Old South Church. I could picture its stained glass windows and hear its gospel choir. I'd sat in the church coffeehouse many times, listening to soft jazz on Thursdays.

There was the elegant bath store called Lush. I'd bought Dream Cream body lotion and Dragon's Egg bath bombs there.

But, of course, I'd never actually done any of those things. So how could I *remember* them so clearly?

Two blocks away, I found the black-trimmed bay windows of the seafood bar called Saltie Girl. I could picture the interior, could see the booths and the long counter in my mind, and when I went up to the restaurant window, I looked inside and saw that my memory of those details was dead on. I'd eaten in that restaurant—not once, but many times. I'd last been there during the winter, the cold Christmas season, with snow flurries drifting in the air. I'd sipped my cocktail and enjoyed my lobster—that was what I always had.

But I could also look at my phone calendar and remember what I'd done on every day of that same season *in Las Vegas*. I couldn't be in two places at the same time. There was simply no way I'd been in Boston.

My walk took me toward the river, past the Commonwealth Avenue greenway, and then to Beacon Street, where I could see the water of the Charles between the buildings. Dr. Howard of BioEfx lived nearby, but *so did I*. Or I'd lived here once. That was the impossible message that my brain was sending me. My condo overlooked the river, top floor, with a piano near the window where I could stare at the water while I played.

Who was I?

Because at that moment, I didn't feel like Hallie Evers.

I kept walking until I reached the park and then wandered eastward near the esplanade, past leafy trees and the calm lagoon. Ahead of me, a string quartet played in the band shell. I stretched out on my back on the green grass with my eyes closed. A hundred other people surrounded me, all of us warmed by the sun and the river breeze. For a few minutes, I was at peace, caught up in the music.

But the peace didn't last. I began to see other visions rushing darkly through my mind like Tolkien's Black Riders. There was the girl dead at my feet, her skull crushed. My sister. There was the golf club lying in the grass. There was the statue of Poseidon by the cliff.

Fierce winds blew around me. My hands were soaked in blood.

It was me.

Or was it? I didn't know. I realized now, seeing these visions again, that there was something missing in my head. A memory I couldn't grasp. A memory I needed to find.

And this one had nothing to do with my mother.

I got up in the park with a stab of fear and hurried away, taking the footbridge over Storrow back to the city.

There was somewhere I had to go, but I couldn't even explain why I felt that way. My feet picked the route without my even thinking about it. From the parkway, I headed to Charles Street and turned past the old meeting house. I walked quickly, and my breath started coming faster. My heartbeat sounded like a roar in my head. I was close to *something*. Something amazing, something terrible. It drew me like a magnet with an irresistible force.

When the traffic cleared, I dashed across the street toward a Beacon Hill pub that advertised Irish brews. Next to the pub was a small gallery squeezed into a narrow storefront, painted bone white against the redbrick building. That was it. That was where I'd been going since I left the hotel.

She'd been leading me here to this place.

She.

Do you want to meet me?

The question arose in my head as if someone were whispering in my ear. Not me. Someone else. A stranger.

I'm inside.

A revelation was waiting for me inside this gallery. I knew that. I had to see what it was, and yet my feet stayed rooted to the cobblestones. I was scared. Terrified of what I would find. I did not, did not, did not want to open that door. But I had no choice. *She* gave me no choice. Another customer came out, and before the door closed again, I slipped inside.

The interior was cool to the point of being cold. The beams on the floor looked weathered and dark, as if they'd been stripped from an old pirate ship. It was a narrow space, no more than ten or twelve feet across, and the walls were painted white, like the exterior. A row of paintings hung on wires on both walls. Somehow I knew each portrait, knew each artist. There was a snowy landscape in oil by Pastore. There, a still life of lemons by Avidor. There, a garden in the city by Bartlett.

I'd met the painters. Talked to them. Gotten drunk with them in the pub next door, where my own drink was always rum and Coke.

I was so sure that I'd been there before that I assumed they would know me, too. When I passed the gallery desk, I spotted a woman in a loose red blouse, with brunette hair piled on top of her head and lime-green glasses slipping down her nose. Her name popped into my mind. *Abigail.*

When I got close enough to read her manager's badge, I saw that I was right. I knew her name.

Abigail, it's me. How are you, darling?

A voice said that in my head. This wasn't Hallie talking.

The woman looked up, and our eyes met. I waited for her face to break into a smile as she recognized me. But all she did was give me a neutral look and ask if I needed help. When I shook my head, she went back to her work, humming softly and twiddling a pencil between her fingers. I was a stranger to her. She'd never seen me before in her life.

So why did I know her?

Why did I know the name of her husband—Nathan—and know that she had two kids and lived in Needham and had gotten a degree in visual arts from Boston University?

I continued to the far end of the gallery. There, one short set of stairs went up, and another set went down. At the top of the steps above me, I saw an easel holding a colorful oil portrait, rich with heavy swirls of pink, blue, black, and yellow. The painting drew my eyes. It was abstract enough that I didn't immediately realize I was looking at . . . *Poseidon.*

Poseidon.

The statue by the cliff overlooking the sea. The bearded myth-god with his trident. He was here. This was no dream.

Lured by a sense of anticipation and horror, I climbed the stairs. When I got there, I stood in front of the painting and found myself lost in its layers of color. It wasn't just a portrait of the statue. The longer I looked, the more I began to see other shapes woven into the sky. Maybe they were real; maybe they were my imagination. A woman drowning in the sea. Snakes wriggling in the long grass. A demon emerging from the clouds.

I glanced at the name of the artist.

Myron Glass.

Once again, my breath caught in my chest. I felt the most intense wave of emotion rippling through me. *Myron.*

All of the paintings hung up here had been done by Myron Glass, all of them made in the same wildly colorful, surreal style. I saw animals. Sea creatures. Angels. Gods. Each portrait was set against kaleidoscope skies, and the landscapes behind them looked foreboding and frightening. I loved them. I felt them deep in my chest. I could have stared at these portraits for hours, but then I glanced at the farthest wall of the gallery, and what I saw made me stiffen in shock.

There was only one painting hung on that wall. One portrait all by itself. It was huge, ten feet high, six feet wide. A nude by the sea at night.

My knees weakened.

I approached it, my mind lost in a fog.

A nude woman stretched gracefully, like a cat, her arms behind her head. Her lithe body looked like red-and-orange flames set against a vibrant black-and-blue sky, with huge Van Gogh–like stars twinkling behind her. Long blond hair swirled down her torso, with multicolored breasts peeking between the tresses. There was a yellow patch between her legs. Swirls of color outlined the curves of her body. The sky behind her looked ready to rain down with lightning and floods, but the woman seemed blissful, unaware of the gathering storm. Her eyes were open, staring right at me. I could feel a hypnotic power in her gaze. I couldn't look away. Her blue eyes matched the blue chaos in the background, as if the growing storm was also inside her.

Strange images took shape in the background. Was I making them up? Or were they really there? I saw dots of red that looked like blood. A shooting star arched across the sky, curved like the span of a high bridge. A silver horizon line bulged in a thick blob of black paint at the end. If I thought about it hard enough, I could imagine that it was a golf club.

I studied the label next to the painting. The artist was the same man who had done all the other works here. Myron Glass. But the model in the portrait, the woman who had inspired the nude, was unidentified. The only description of her was the title of the painting itself.

GIRL OF MY DREAMS

16

The next morning, I parked in front of Hyppolex.

The company headquarters was located a half hour outside the city in the suburb of Waltham, in a two-story building built along the Charles River. The area felt like another world compared to downtown Boston. There were schools nearby, and I could hear the noise of children playing. The facility looked across the calm water toward a row of modest riverfront houses nestled in the trees. In front of the building, a jogging trail followed the bending shoreline to the green grass of a large cemetery.

My car, which was dusty from its cross-country journey, looked decidedly second class in a gleaming row of Teslas and Jaguars. Even without the windfall of an IPO, the top execs here had lots of money. I was glad I'd dressed to make an impression. On the road, I'd bought a knee-length Ann Taylor dress in aubergine, with high heels and a necklace of fake pearls. If this had been an interview at a California start-up, I could have worn cutoffs, but this was the East Coast. I didn't know what to expect, and I wanted to send the message that I wasn't to be messed with.

When I walked through the entrance door, I got a taste of the company's buttoned-down culture. The security guard wore a suit and tie. There was no overhead music, just a kind of buzzy white noise. Colonial-era paintings—probably originals—adorned the walls. This was not a place for Silicon Valley meditation rooms, dog parks, and in-house sushi bars. I told the guard I had an interview with the senior vice president of marketing, and he asked for my ID and for my phone and watch, which he put into a box. He gave me a ticket so that I could reclaim them when I was leaving. Then he made me sign a form about not doing photography or video recording within the facility, and he gave me an electronic visitors' pass and told me to wear it at all times.

They definitely didn't want their secrets getting out into the world.

After I made it through the check-in process, a woman about my age arrived to greet me. She told me her name was Kimberly, and she wore a severe black pantsuit. She was friendly enough, but she deflected my questions about the company and the interview. Kimberly took me one level up in an elevator, then led me to a conference room with floor-to-ceiling windows looking out on the river. The long, sleek marble table could have seated forty. She asked me to wait, pointed to a coffee machine and selection of pastries if I wanted anything, and then left me alone.

I sipped coffee and watched the calm flow of the river. Without my watch, I didn't know how much time had passed, but it seemed as if I was waiting a long time. The conference room had a camera mounted in one corner, and I wiggled my fingers at it in a little wave. I assumed someone was watching me the whole time.

Finally, the door opened, and a man came inside. It was not the senior vice president of product marketing.

It was Tyler Reyes, CEO of Hyppolex.

I'd never met this man, and yet he was exactly as I remembered him in my head: curly, untamed black hair, owlish glasses, and a scientist's distracted intensity. He was a couple of inches shorter than me and several years older, probably in his midthirties. He wasn't the kind of man who would turn women's heads. He was lean but not athletic, handsome but not memorable. Even so, I was glad I'd worn my new dress, because Tyler wore a suit that fit too perfectly to have come off the rack.

"Hallie," he said, coming forward to shake my hand. "I'm Tyler Reyes."

He held my hand just a beat longer than he should have.

"Won't you sit down?" he added, pointing at one of the leather conference room chairs.

I took a seat, and Tyler took the nearest chair and pushed back from the table. He was trying to look the part of the CEO—completely in control—but I felt tension radiating from him like heat rising from the Las Vegas blacktops. This man was *scared* of me, which I found hard to explain. But he was also extremely curious at the same time. He kept squinting at me through his glasses, as if hunting for some secret hidden behind my eyes.

"I thought I'd be talking with your senior vice president of marketing," I said.

"Oh, there's plenty of time for that," Tyler replied. "I've scheduled other interviews for you throughout the day, but all of the key hiring decisions need my approval. So I like to talk to top candidates personally. Hyppolex is my baby. I started the company almost a decade ago."

"I suppose you thought it was odd that I asked Jill Oliver to arrange an introduction."

"No, not at all. You get points for enthusiasm. I like people who go after what they want, particularly if they're interested in my company. I've read samples of your work, and it's obvious how talented you are. Jill also sent me your résumé, warts and all. I was impressed."

I cocked an eyebrow. "Warts and all?"

"Well, I know you've burned through several jobs. You're strong minded. You say what you think. A lot of companies can't handle that. This industry can still be a rough road for smart women. Whereas I think you'd be a good fit for the culture at Hyppolex."

"What kind of culture is that?" I asked.

"We're risk takers. Rule breakers. We think big. I'd rather my people fly too close to the sun than stay stuck on the ground."

"Icarus drowned when he did that," I pointed out.

Tyler shrugged. "Yes, but eventually, we got the Wright brothers. That comes from dreaming about great things."

"So do you have any jobs available?" I asked.

"It doesn't matter. For the right person, I'm happy to create a job. You seem like the right person." He got up and went to the windows, and he watched the river with his arms folded across his chest. With his back to me, he said, "I am curious about one thing, Hallie."

I felt us tiptoeing toward the real reason I was here.

"Oh? What's that?"

"How did you hear about us?"

Because you paid a private detective to follow me.

Because that man was murdered right in front of me.

"The MedX convention was in Las Vegas last week," I said. "I always do a lot of networking there."

"Yes, of course."

"Were you there?" I asked.

He turned around to face me again. "No, but several of my people attended."

"Yes, it seems to me I met one of your researchers," I replied, holding his stare. "A doctor named Reed Smith."

He gave away nothing. "Reed Smith? No, not one of mine."

"What about Todd Kivel? Does that name ring a bell?"

"I'm afraid not," Tyler said, still a study in cool.

"Sorry. My mistake. I was sure they worked for you. Anyway, I heard a lot of buzz about Hyppolex throughout the convention. They say you've made great progress in treatments for people with strokes and traumatic brain injuries. I've always been fascinated with the mysteries of the brain. There's so much we still don't know about what it can do."

Tyler nodded. "You're right. We've been to the moon, but we haven't unlocked all the secrets of what's going on inside our own heads."

"Exactly. I love your focus on that. There are also rumors that you're in the midst of pioneering research on Alzheimer's. That you're on the edge of some amazing breakthroughs."

"Well, of course, I can't comment on that."

"Sure. I understand. You need to guard your intellectual property. But I want to be part of something like that. That's why I'm here."

"I'm glad you share our passion."

"Plus, something happened to me recently," I went on. "It was sort of a life-changing event."

"And what was that?"

"I died."

Tyler tried but failed to look surprised. I was sure that I wasn't telling him anything he didn't already know. "My goodness. What happened?"

"My heart stopped. Fortunately, a doctor was there to save me. But that's the kind of close call that makes you reevaluate your priorities."

"Yes, I'm sure."

"As you say, I decided after that experience to go after what I want. If you're looking for a risk taker, a rule breaker, that's me. Once I focus on something, I don't give up. Honestly, you'll find that I won't quit until I know everything there is to know about Hyppolex." I added with a smile, "Warts and all."

Tyler came and sat down next to me again. We didn't talk for a while, me looking at him, him looking at me. I thought about saying it out loud: *What's going on inside my head?*

Do you know?

Do you have the answers?

But at this point, all I would get from him was a lie.

"So are you enjoying Boston?" he asked.

"I am. In fact, it almost feels like home to me. Everywhere I go, things seem so familiar. It must be déjà vu, because I've never been here before. That's strange, don't you think? Feeling like you've been somewhere when you really haven't?"

Now he looked uncomfortable. "Yes, I guess it is."

"Even you," I added.

"What about me?"

"Well, you seem familiar, too. It's like we've met before."

He studied me with that searching look again. I tried to figure out what I saw in his face. Sadness. Longing. And desire, too. Definitely desire, the kind of raw hunger you can smell in the air. The intensity of it made me uncomfortable. I mean, men typically like me, and I get my share of come-ons and attention. But this was on a level way beyond ordinary attraction.

"I must have that look," he said, not taking his eyes off me.

"I guess so."

"I'm curious, though," Tyler went on. "You say you've never been to Boston, but when Jill called me, she mentioned a restaurant in Back Bay. Saltie Girl. She seemed to think you'd been there before."

The tension between us suddenly felt as dense and choking as smoke. He tried to keep a casual manner, but I sensed that our entire conversation had led to this one moment. *This* was the question he wanted answered. This was why I was here, why he'd agreed to see me, why he'd been lost in my face ever since he entered the room. More than anything else, Tyler Reyes was desperate to know what I remembered about Saltie Girl.

"Jill must have misunderstood. I read about that restaurant in a magazine somewhere."

"Oh. I see." He deflated in the chair with disappointment. Then I struck back while he was still vulnerable.

"Have *you* ever been there, Tyler?"

Because I knew he had. I'd seen him there. *I'd* been with him. And yet I hadn't.

"Just once," he admitted. Then he went on, and what he said took my breath away. "With my wife."

"Your *wife*!" I blurted out more loudly than I intended.

"Her name was Skye."

Skye . . .

Oh, my God.

I tried to control my reaction, but I couldn't. The impact of her name landed on me like a bomb. Skye. That was her. It was all her. Everything I remembered, everything inside me, was *Skye*. The girl in the painting. The girl of my dreams. I had no idea who this woman was, or how we were connected, and yet I knew with a rush of certainty that her life had somehow become enmeshed with mine.

I stared at Tyler. I felt as if we'd both taken off the masks we were hiding behind. Then my mind caught up to the implication of what he'd said.

"Was? Her name *was* Skye?"

"That's right," Tyler replied in a dark voice. "I lost my wife. Skye died six months ago."

◆　◆　◆

In the hotel that night, I had another dream.

I sat naked in a chair, my body angled. My legs were crossed at the ankles, my hands laced behind my head. My long blond hair fell across my chest. The artist had positioned the tresses exactly the way he wanted them, grazing his fingers across my breasts as he did.

The studio was huge and dark, like a kind of warehouse. Canvases hung on the walls. Easels surrounded me, containing half-finished paintings, alive with bold colors. Through a window, I could see charcoal clouds and the deep blue water of the channel. Boats were tied up to a pier. It was a cold, dreary December day, and Christmas was coming.

This painting was to be a gift for Tyler.

I was the gift. A way to say goodbye. A way to remember me. An apology for all of my lies.

"We're almost done," Myron told me.

I didn't speak or move in response. This was our fourth session, and I knew the rules. He could talk, but not me. The model must be silent in the studio until the artist is done.

The cold air puckered my skin. Myron kept looking between the canvas and me as he made his brushstrokes. His frank stare didn't bother me. He saw me nude, with my nipples erect, with my knees wide enough to display the pinkness between my legs, and yet I felt no self-consciousness and no embarrassment. My mind and body were disconnected. But I knew he could look right through me and see who I was.

"I call this *Blue Skye*," he said.

Skye.

Me. I was Skye.

Finally, he turned the easel around. I slid off the chair and stretched my limbs with a purr, catlike. There was a robe nearby, but I didn't bother putting it on. I walked naked to the portrait and studied it: the fire in my body, the splash of yellow between my legs, the threatening clouds and stars behind me.

No one would know it was me unless I told them. The face of the model reflected none of my true features. And yet it *was* me, more exposed than I'd ever been in my life. I couldn't have been more naked if I'd walked out of this warehouse without putting on any of my clothes.

This wasn't a painting of my body. It was my soul. My anguish. My sins. This was the real woman I'd kept from my husband for years.

"Will he like it?" Myron asked.

I brushed away tears from my face. "No. No, I'm sorry. You need to burn it. Tyler must never see this."

17

Now I could put a name to my dreams. Skye.

Skye was the mystery I had to solve. A fascination with this woman took root inside me and quickly began to grow into obsession. I needed to know everything about her—who she was, where she'd come from, what she'd done with her life, why she died. What I'd seen in my sleep told me that the place to start was with the man who'd painted her. Myron Glass.

So early the next morning, after a quick search online to find him, I drove to the Boston Fish Pier in the Seaport District.

The century-old twin buildings jutted into the channel, and the inlet was alive with the clang of boats and the shouts and curses of men unloading their catch. On the other side of the water, jets came and went at Logan Airport, and I felt the thunder of their engines vibrating under my feet. It was a hot, sticky day. I walked down the pier next to the water, alongside vats of monkfish, mackerel, and pollack staring at me with wide, dead eyes from among mounds of ice. The eyes of the fishermen followed me with equal intensity. A few whistled; a few winked; a few waved me over. A light breeze filled my nose with the pungent stink of fish, and around me seagulls screeched and dived, eyeing prizes they could steal.

I wound my way around trucks and pallets on the wet, slippery pavement. Near the end of the pier, where choppy seawater slapped over the pavement, I found a white door labeled with the name of one of the local seafood companies.

There was also a second, handwritten sign taped to the door: **Myron Glass Studio.**

An arrow pointed up.

Inside, I took the stairs to the upper level of the building and found another door with the same sign. I knocked, but when there was no answer, I twisted the knob. The door was open. I let myself in and found an open dark warehouse space that I'd seen before.

That was in my dream, not in real life, but I was finding it hard to separate the two.

"Hello?" I called.

There was no answer.

The studio was located at the corner of the building. There were windows on two sides, but most of the windows were covered by canvas tarps, leaving the interior gloomy and mystical. I wandered among surreal paintings like the ones I'd seen in the Beacon Hill gallery. Men, women, animals, and other creatures posed in front of symbolic skies, with paint slapped thickly onto the canvases in a rainbow of colors that hinted at messages hidden in the swirls. Each one was unique, but a thread of chaos and danger seemed to be the common denominator. They were beautiful but frightening.

I saw an empty chair positioned in the middle of the open space. From overhead, a single spotlight illuminated it, as if a prisoner were being interrogated there.

That was where Skye had been seated.

That was where *I* had been seated.

"Who are you?" a voice asked me.

I jumped in the darkness. A young black man, about thirty years old, appeared next to me. I hadn't seen or heard him. His muscular chest was bare, and he wore loose white cargo pants. His hair was a nest of wild, messy dreadlocks. He was taller than me by several inches and had very broad shoulders. His skin was walnut-dark and perfectly smooth. He had a long, sharp nose, broad lips, and his eyes—well, his eyes were amazing. I didn't think I'd ever seen eyes quite like his. They were two cat's-eye gems, and staring at them felt like staring into a black hole with its own powerful gravity.

He was handsome, but I'd met plenty of handsome men in Las Vegas. This was more than that. I felt an attraction to him that was strong enough that I forgot to answer his question.

"I said . . . Who are you?"

"Sorry," I stammered. "My name's Hallie Evers."

The man held a plain glass cup of tea, with a tea bag draped over the side. I could see bits of tea floating in the reddish liquid. "And what can I do for you, Hallie Evers?"

"You're Myron Glass? The artist?"

"That's right."

I looked around at the studio and stalled as I figured out how to explain myself. "This is a cool place."

"Thank you."

Then I wrinkled my nose at the smell. "Why a studio on a fishing pier? Do you really like fish or something?"

"As a teenager, I worked on those boats outside every summer," he told me. "You need to stay connected to your past. Too many people forget where they came from."

"I like that."

"You haven't told me what you want. Are you here to commission a portrait? Because to be honest, you don't look like you could afford me."

I was annoyed that he thought I had no money, even though I didn't. "What makes you say that?"

"I've been around enough rich people to know the look. You ain't got it."

"Actually, I'm here because I have a question about one of your paintings."

Myron didn't say anything. He wandered to one of the few uncovered windows, gazed at the water of the channel, and then padded back to me on his bare feet. His body had a fluid grace whenever he moved, and he had a voice that made me think of an actor reciting Shakespeare.

"I'm not in the business of trying to explain my paintings to people. Everybody sees what they want to see in them. If you have a question, you should answer it for yourself."

"Well, it's not so much about the painting as it is about the model."

As Myron drank his tea, his eyes drilled through me like an oil rig. He nodded at the empty chair in the middle of the floor, and I understood. That was where he wanted me. I sat in the chair the way Skye had. I felt the way she'd felt, too—naked and exposed, but also completely at ease. Honestly, if I'd begun to take off my clothes, I don't think he would have been surprised in the least.

Myron stood behind one of the easels. He put down his tea and picked up a thick piece of charcoal and began scratching on a white canvas in light, quick strokes. "So which painting are you talking about?"

"Girl of My Dreams."

He didn't flinch. He kept drawing.

"And what's your question?" he asked finally.

"The woman in the portrait. That's Skye Reyes, isn't it?"

"Who told you that?"

She did. But I couldn't tell him that.

"Well, I heard that Skye posed for you," I said. "Actually, I heard that the painting—it was supposed to be a gift for her husband, Tyler, but she decided not to give it to him. You were going to call it . . . you were going to call the painting *Blue Skye.* Then, when she didn't keep the portrait, you changed the name."

Myron put down the charcoal. He came out from behind the easel and walked over to me. The force of his presence made me nervous. "You are unusually well informed, Hallie Evers."

"Am I right? Is that what happened?"

"Why do you care? How does any of this matter to you?"

"I'm trying to find out everything I can about Skye."

133

"Why? Are you writing a book or something?"

A book. It was as good an excuse as any.

"Yes, that's right," I told him.

"And why write about Skye?"

"It's sort of hard to explain. Sometimes I find people who . . . intrigue me. There's something about Skye that makes me feel close to her. I think she has a story to tell."

He snorted. "Everybody felt close to Skye. That was ironic, because she never let people see what was really inside her. She knew how to make people talk to her, but she never opened up about herself."

"What can you tell me about her?"

Myron went back behind the easel and picked up the charcoal again. His eyes focused on me, peeling away my secrets. He looked suspicious. "Why ask me? Talk to her husband. Talk to her friends. Or look her up on Google or Wikipedia. That's what counts for reality these days."

"I want someone who will be honest with me," I said. "The things you find online are two dimensional. Sterile. Flat. That's not what I need. I need to know who Skye really was."

He didn't say anything, but I got the feeling that I'd given him the right answer. After a long pause, he said, "How much do you already know about her?"

"Not a lot, but I know she died."

His stoic face cracked just a little. "Yeah."

"I know she was married to Tyler Reyes. He's the CEO of a company called Hyppolex." Then I made a guess, wondering if I was right. "And I know she was a pianist."

He scratched on the canvas with the charcoal.

"Did you ever hear her play?" he asked.

"No."

"Too bad. Now that she's gone, you never will. She played with the Boston Symphony, but she refused to be recorded. Every one of her performances was live, and that was that. She said you couldn't cage music. It would be like putting an animal in a zoo."

Yes.

I knew he was right. That was exactly how she felt about it. This wasn't like a memory or something I'd seen from her life. This was simply *her*. It was like each little thing I learned about Skye multiplied inside my head and led me to something new. And the more I knew about her, the more I needed to discover the rest. Like she was a painting I couldn't stop staring at.

"She sounds like a special person," I said awkwardly, because I couldn't confess what I really felt. How deep it went. How strange it was.

"She was definitely special, but you wouldn't know it until you unwrapped the package. She could have been a rich bitch, you know. Family money. When I first met her, that was what I figured she'd be like. I told you, I know rich folks. But there was something deep about Skye. I don't say that about many people, because most people are shallow. It's not their fault—that's life. But Skye was like a web of tunnels carved into a mountain. You could dig and dig and never get to the end, because you kept finding another trail. It was easy to get lost in her."

"How did the painting come about?" I asked.

Myron stopped sketching again. "Last fall, Skye approached me to do a portrait. I told her I would do it, but I had terms for my paintings, just like she had when she did her concerts. I would only paint her if she posed nude. As soon as a woman puts on clothes, she puts on artifice. It's like a mask. She turns into someone else, just a disguise she wants the world to see. My job is to look behind all that bullshit and find the real person."

"That's an interesting philosophy," I said.

"You understand what I'm talking about, don't you, Hallie Evers? Because you're wearing a mask right now."

"I don't know what you mean."

"Oh, yes, you do. We both know you're lying. I don't know why, and I don't know how the hell you know what you do about Skye, but you're not researching some stranger for a book."

"I am," I insisted weakly.

He shook his head. "Two people knew that painting was called *Blue Skye*. Me and her. That's all. No way she told anyone else, and I know I didn't. So for the life of me, I can't figure out how it came to be in your head."

"I wish I could tell you, but I can't."

Because I don't know.

Myron studied me. Artist and subject. "You ever had a portrait of yourself done?"

"No."

"Well, you should. I see something in you. Something that wants to come out."

"Like *Alien*?" I joked.

Myron didn't laugh. He turned the easel around, and I saw the charcoal sketch he'd made of me. I expected something surreal, like his other paintings, but this sketch was true to life, a perfect likeness of my hair, eyes, face, and shoulders, all made with what seemed to be only a few lines of charcoal.

"Wow. That's amazing."

He scoffed at my review. He tore off the page and crumpled it in his hands and threw it on the floor like trash. "No, that's just the disguise. That's the mask. I'd like to know what's going on behind the mask, Hallie Evers."

"You think you can figure that out by painting me?"

"I know I can."

"Nude?"

"That's the only way I paint people."

"Well, I'll think about it," I said nervously.

"Uh-huh." Myron didn't look convinced that I'd take him up on his offer. "Don't worry if you're scared. And don't lie and tell me it's about keeping your clothes on. Most people just don't like seeing the truth about themselves."

"What else can you tell me about Skye?" I asked, trying to get the subject off me, because the way he was looking at me made me uncomfortable. And, to be honest, a little turned on.

He shrugged. "You want to know more about Skye, go to Symphony Hall. That's the only place she let the real woman out. She was herself when she played, and that's about it. Otherwise she kept herself locked away."

"What about when she was with you?" I asked.

Myron looked a little cocky. "Well, yeah. She was herself with me, too. Now are we done?"

"Yes. Thank you."

I turned toward the gallery door to leave, but then I stopped as I remembered something else. "I'm sorry, there's one other thing I was curious about. Another painting you did."

"Poseidon?" he asked.

My face showed my surprise. "How did you know?"

"I did that one for her. After."

"After she died? Why?"

Myron's eyes turned dark and distant. "Skye grew up in an estate on the coast in Newport, Rhode Island. Out in back, on the cliff, there's a huge statue of Poseidon that dates back to when the house was built. Skye loved that statue. She told me that when she was a girl, she used to talk to it for hours, like it was some kind of oracle. So it always reminds me of her."

Poseidon.

I'd awakened in the hospital with Poseidon in my head. That was my first memory. My first dream.

Poseidon was Skye.

"Can I ask you one more question?" I said.

"What is it?"

"Why *Blue Skye*? Why call the painting that?"

He went back to the window that overlooked the water. "Because Skye's color was always blue. She was dragging around a lot of guilt with her. That came out in the painting. I didn't mean it that way, but the brush sees things I don't. She hated it so much that she wanted me to burn it, but I couldn't do that. I felt bad afterward, like seeing herself in the painting was partly what helped her make her decision."

"Decision? What do you mean?"

"Don't you know how she died?" he asked.

I shook my head. "No."

He glanced at me, his whole face in shadow. "Four days after I saw her for the last time, she went back to Newport. She threw herself off the cliff with that goddamn statue watching her."

18

My phone rang as I left Myron's studio. It was Tyler Reyes.

"Hallie, good morning," he said. "I hope you slept well? Sweet dreams?"

Well. Wasn't that the interesting question.

"Actually, my dreams were pretty strange," I told him.

"Oh, yes?"

"Yes. That's been happening to me a lot lately. Ever since my heart stopped, in fact. Very strange, very intense dreams. You do brain research. What do you think that means?"

"Freud said the craziest dreams are the most profound," Tyler replied.

"So they must mean something."

"I'm sure they do. You should write them down. Keep a dream journal."

"I'll have to try that."

Tyler hesitated, then changed the subject. "I wanted to follow up and let you know how pleased I was to talk to you yesterday. And it wasn't just me. Everyone you met with during the rest of the day was extremely impressed, too."

"I'm glad to hear that."

"There's definitely a place for you at Hyppolex if you're interested. In fact, if you're *not* interested, I'd like the opportunity to change your mind. I want you to appreciate the importance of the work we're doing. Our research will change a lot of lives."

"I have a lot to think about," I told him.

"Of course. I'm not pushing you. Take your time. In fact, enjoy Boston for a couple of days, and see whether this is a place you'd like to call home. All on the company dime, of course."

"Thank you."

I heard a change in his voice, a forced casualness. "No pressure, but perhaps you'd let me take you to dinner tonight."

"Dinner?"

"Yes, I'd like to continue our conversation. I'm prepared to put a number on the table, and I think you'll be pleased at what we'd be offering in salary and benefits. I can also answer any other questions you have about Hyppolex. I'm sure you have questions I haven't addressed yet."

"You're right. I still have a lot of questions."

"Should we say eight o'clock at Saltie Girl? I know you said you wanted to try it."

I hesitated. There was something in his voice that I didn't like, an interest in me that was more than professional. I still felt that hunger, that wave of sexual desire. He didn't say anything more about his wife, but I also felt Skye's ghost hovering between us in an uncomfortable way.

"Actually, I already made plans for dinner," I lied. "A college friend of mine lives in Brookline. We're getting together."

"That's okay. How about breakfast tomorrow?"

I didn't think I could put him off twice, and breakfast sounded less awkward than dinner. "Yes, sure. That's fine."

"Excellent," he said. "Put your dinner on your expense roster. My treat."

"That's very generous of you."

"Enjoy your day, Hallie. I'll see you soon."

"Yes, goodbye, Tyler."

I hung up the phone.

My next stop was at Symphony Hall. I walked there from the Copley Plaza without even needing to consult a map.

As soon as I saw the redbrick temple that housed the Boston Symphony Orchestra, I felt like a traveler back home from a long journey. I entered the building through the box office door and began to explore. There was no performance that night, so the interior was quiet, and almost no one was around. The soft red carpet hushed my footsteps.

When I found a row of photographs of the symphony musicians, I ran my fingers tenderly along the frames with a kind of wonder, because these people felt like my family. I recognized their faces—I realized that I knew personal stories about most of them—but I found no picture of Skye herself. She'd been gone for months, and her photograph had already been taken down. And yet, in my head, I felt her presence everywhere. It was strong enough to make me believe in ghosts and to wonder if I'd somehow been possessed.

Next I climbed to the building's upper level. I found that one of the doors to the concert hall had been left open, and I wandered inside and took a front-row balcony seat, underneath the coffered ceiling. Statues of Greek and Roman gods, bathed in white light, glowed in niches on the far wall. It made me think of Poseidon posing by the cliff. I studied the cavernous empty stage below me, and when I closed my eyes, I could feel piano keys under my fingers and hear the music of the orchestra.

"It's quite a place, isn't it?" a voice said behind me.

I turned and saw a young woman in a polka dot blouse and black slacks. She had long curly brown hair.

"Yes, it is," I replied. "Sorry, I guess I'm not supposed to be in here, but I couldn't resist taking a look."

The woman waved her hand dismissively. "Don't worry about it. I come in here to admire it all the time. I'm Robyn, by the way. I'm one of the publicity reps for the BSO."

"Hallie," I replied. "I'm just a fan from out of town."

"Well, good. We love to meet fans. Are you coming to the concert on Friday?"

"No, I don't think I'll be here that long."

"Too bad. We're doing Mahler's Fifth. That opening trumpet solo? Gives me chills."

"Sorry I'll miss it," I told her. Then I made up a new lie. "Actually, I was here once before. The orchestra was playing Rachmaninoff. You had a piano soloist who was incredible. Young, attractive, long blond hair. I don't remember her name."

"You must be talking about Skye," Robyn replied.

"Yes, that's it."

"Skye Selden. She was amazing. I loved watching her play. It wasn't just the music; she had so much energy when she performed. The way her fingers flew, the way she tossed her hair. God, what a terrible loss."

"Loss?"

"She passed away a few months ago."

"Oh, no. That's awful. What happened?"

Robyn's face darkened. "Suicide. None of us could believe it when we heard. Skye always seemed so full of life. But artists come from dark places, I guess."

"Nobody knew why she did it?"

"No, we were shocked. I really miss her. She made a point of knowing everyone on the staff, saying hello, remembering birthdays, that sort of thing. I mean, a lot of musicians sort of look down on those of us on the admin side. They're the talent, and don't you forget it. But not Skye. She was sweet to everybody."

"You said Skye Selden," I murmured. "I feel like I remember her having a different last name."

"Well, her married name was Reyes. Her husband was some hot-shot young CEO. Some kind of medical company, I think. But Skye performed under her family name, which was Selden."

"Oh, I see."

"As in Selden Machine Tools," the woman went on. "Turn-of-the-century robber barons, like the Rockefellers. Her family was loaded. But I guess money doesn't buy happiness, huh?"

"I guess not."

"Skye inherited a fortune after her father passed away a few years ago, but you'd never know it from how she behaved. Even though she was a big contributor, she never wanted her name on anything. She took the Selden seat on the symphony board, and that was enough."

Suddenly, I heard voices in my head. A man and a woman. It was so clear to me, so vivid, that they could have been standing right next to us.

Is it going to be awkward, both of us on the board?
Why would it be awkward?
You know why. Because of Savannah.

Hearing that name made me shiver. Savannah.

"Actually, there's a memorial poster to Skye up here," Robyn went on. "In case you want to see it."

"Really? Yes, I do. Where is it?"

"Next door down. It's on the wall. You can't miss it."

I got up and thanked Robyn, and I returned to the hallway. Somehow, the idea of seeing a poster about Skye gave me an odd sense of excitement and foreboding. I wanted to meet her, to see who she really was, to understand how it felt when I saw her—not just in Myron's surreal painting, but in an actual photograph.

I wasn't disappointed.

Her face enraptured me. The oversize picture in the memorial poster showed Skye at the piano, in the midst of one of her performances. She'd moved so quickly that it was partly out of focus. Her blond hair was straight and long, but it had grown tangled from the rapid movements of her head as she played, with a few wispy strands on her forehead and cheek. She had a slim straight nose and pale-pink lips that were slightly open, showing perfect white teeth. The line of her jaw made a gentle U, smooth and not sharp. Her golden eyebrows angled sharply toward her sea-blue eyes, and she stared straight at the camera, as if aware she was being photographed.

I stared at her, and she stared back at me.

And I thought to myself, *I remember you.*

The poster told me the dates of her birth and death. She'd been thirty-one years old when she killed herself. Dozens of members of the orchestra had signed their names and left messages on the borders of the poster, and I could see the love that she'd evoked in them.

I also read the brief description that accompanied the poster.

SKYE SELDEN-REYES

AT CHRISTMASTIME, THE BSO LOST ONE OF ITS OWN. SKYE SELDEN WAS A PIANO SOLOIST WHO PERFORMED WITH THE ORCHESTRA NUMEROUS TIMES IN THE PAST FIVE YEARS AND WAS ALWAYS A CROWD FAVORITE. SHE WAS PARTICULARLY KNOWN FOR HER INTERPRETATION OF RACHMANINOFF'S PIANO CONCERTO NO. 3, WHICH THE *GLOBE* COMPARED TO THE DEFINI-TIVE VLADIMIR ASHKENAZY PERFORMANCE WITH ANDRÉ PREVIN AND THE LONDON SYMPHONY ORCHESTRA.

SKYE WAS THE LAST SURVIVING MEMBER OF THE SELDEN FAMILY OF NEWPORT, RHODE ISLAND, WHO HAVE BEEN SYMPHONY SUPPORTERS FOR GENERATIONS. SHE WAS MARRIED TO TYLER REYES, FOUNDER AND CEO OF HYPPOLEX CORPORATION. MR. REYES HAS ANNOUNCED A LARGE ENDOWMENT GIFT IN MEMORY OF HIS WIFE.

IN ADDITION TO HER MUSICAL GIFTS, SKYE WAS A PERSON OF INCREDIBLE LOVE AND WARMTH, AND SHE WILL BE MISSED BY ALL HER FRIENDS HERE AT THE BSO.

As I read the poster, my mind was swarmed by confusion and grief. I found myself tearing up at her loss. I didn't know this woman, and yet I *did* know her in an incredibly intimate way. Somehow I was seeing the world through her eyes, remembering things that were part of her past.

How was that possible?

She and I also had something terrible in common. Suicide.

Instinctively, I rubbed my fingers along the scars on my wrist. Hallie Evers, fifteen years old, had tried to kill herself in the bathtub. And let's face it, I'd tried again in that casino bathroom. I'd failed, but Skye had succeeded. I didn't know how a woman like her could have done what she'd done. She was rich, beautiful, successful; she'd achieved her dreams in a way I never had.

Then she'd thrown it all away.

Why?

I took a last long look at Skye's photograph, but her face gave me no answers. However, in some strange irresistible way, she was still guiding me, the way she had at the Beacon Hill gallery. When I got back to the ground floor, I found myself powerfully drawn to a framed display of the symphony board of directors. I heard an echo of that same conversation in my head.

Is it going to be awkward, both of us on the board?

One by one, I studied the photographs of the symphony board members, not sure who or what I was trying to find.

Then I saw him.

He was in his thirties, with spiky blond hair and a ruddy, sunburnt face. His blue eyes looked smart, but there was a distance in them, as if they offered no window into his soul. His mouth wore a serious expression, his lips in a thin, solemn line. The label under his photograph told me that his name was Dr. Andrew Edam of the Massachusetts Institute of Technology.

I remembered his voice and his face, but I knew him under a completely different name.

A fake name.

This was Reed Smith. The doctor who'd saved my life.

19

Andrew Edam.

I found his bio on the MIT website, as well as on the website for the symphony foundation. Academically, he was a ridiculous overachiever, with a medical degree from Harvard and a master's in engineering and a doctorate in neuroscience from MIT. He was now a member of MIT's core faculty in the Department of Brain and Cognitive Sciences. His research focus was on neurological disorders of the brain.

All that from a man who was only thirty-six years old.

But what mattered to me most was his personal background. He'd grown up in Newport, Rhode Island, like Skye Selden. In fact, it took me only a few minutes of research to learn that the Selden family and the Edam family had been next-door neighbors on the western tip of the Newport peninsula, where the waters of the Atlantic flowed into Narragansett Bay. Andrew, also like Skye, came from generations of money. His father, John David Edam, had been a principal investor in a start-up medical device company launched ten years ago by Tyler Reyes.

Hyppolex Corporation.

Tyler Reyes. Andrew Edam. Skye Selden-Reyes.

They were all connected. That was no coincidence. I was beginning to see the pieces of a puzzle take shape, even if I didn't yet know how they all fit together.

Less than two hours later, I crossed the Longfellow Bridge from Boston to Cambridge and made my way around the sprawling MIT campus. According to the university website, Andrew Edam worked in

Building 46, an imposing geometric facility of white stone and glass built around a high atrium. I considered going directly to his faculty office, but I didn't want to give him a chance to have campus security simply haul me away. Instead, I found a coffee shop called Area Four and chose a table outside, where I had a vantage on his building. Then I found the phone number for the academic department in which he worked.

An administrative assistant answered my call. When I asked for Dr. Edam, I wasn't surprised when she told me he was in a laboratory and couldn't be disturbed. So I segued into my lie.

"This is Natalie in the Department of Neuroscience at Johns Hopkins," I told her. "I just got a call from one of my faculty members. He's up at MIT today, and he's supposed to be meeting Dr. Edam for coffee. The meeting was set for twenty minutes ago, but Dr. Edam is a no-show. Do you think you'd be able to get him a message?"

I heard the tapping of keys.

"I don't show any meeting on Dr. Edam's calendar," the assistant told me. Then she gave me a little sigh. "But it wouldn't be the first time he forgot to make a note of something he scheduled himself. You know how scientists are. I'll see if I can get him over there. Where are they supposed to be meeting?"

"Area Four," I said.

"And what's the name of your faculty member?"

"Dr. Reed Smith."

"Have they met? Will Dr. Edam know what Dr. Smith looks like?"

"Oh, I'm sure he will," I said.

I thanked her and hung up. Then I waited.

It didn't take long for my call to get results. Less than fifteen minutes later, I recognized Andrew Edam as he emerged from the doors of Building 46. He was wearing a white lab coat, his hands in his pockets. He was a tall man, at least six-foot-four, and broad shouldered. He took hurried strides across Main Street onto the green grass outside the coffee shop. Briefly, he studied the outside tables, and then his gaze landed on me.

He knew exactly who I was.

He came up to the table and sat down across from me in the warm afternoon sun. I was halfway through an iced latte, and he uncapped a bottle of water from his coat pocket and took a long drink.

"Hello, Hallie."

"Hello, Dr. Edam. Or do you prefer Dr. Smith?"

His handsome face registered no emotion. Not surprise that I was here and had found him out, not guilt about his disguise in Las Vegas. I may as well have been sitting across from a statue. Instead, he eyed my coffee drink. "You should probably lay off the caffeine. It's not good for your heart."

"Gosh, thanks for your concern."

"What about drugs? Have you steered clear of drugs since the incident?"

"Yes."

"Good. And are you experiencing any side effects?"

I leaned forward. "You mean like seeing the world through the eyes of a dead woman?"

His mouth tightened into a frown, but he plunged ahead as if this were an ordinary doctor-patient consultation. "I mean chest pains, fast or irregular heartbeat, anything like that."

"My heart is fine."

"Any dizziness or nausea?"

"No, nothing. Are you really going to ignore what I said?"

Dr. Edam shrugged. "I'm not ignoring you. A dead woman? That's what you think?"

"That's right."

"Well, you mentioned strange dreams when we talked on the phone. Is that what you're referencing? The fact is, drug abuse can result in a variety of cognitive issues. Memory loss, delusions, and hallucinations are all very common. Sometimes the effects can be quite extreme. I suggested you think about counseling and addiction rehab. Have you looked into that?"

"I'm not a drug addict."

"Maybe not, but an overdose is a red flag for underlying issues, either physical or mental or both."

"That's what you're going with? I'm crazy?"

"It's not crazy to have a sickness, Hallie. There's no shame in that. The best thing to do is get help before it gets any worse. If I remember your file correctly, you have a family history of mental illness, don't you?"

Jesus!

I wanted to slap him. He was so calm, so cool, poking and prodding at all my doubts with that unflappable voice of his. None of this was about him. It was all about me.

You're schizophrenic.

You have multiple personalities.

You're possessed by demons.

It would have been easy to believe that. Part of me *wanted* to believe it. I'd been chasing devils since I was ten years old. But none of that explained what was happening to me. No, no, no, no—somewhere, somehow, I had to believe in myself. I was not crazy. I was not inventing another world.

This is real. Skye is real.

"Dr. Edam, you're a fucking liar."

For the first time, I landed a blow against that turtle shell he hid inside. I'd opened up a crack, and I hit it again.

"Why the disguise?" I went on.

"What?"

"*Dr. Reed Smith.* You lied to me. You lied to the ER doc at the hospital. Why do you need a false identity? What kind of MIT researcher goes around handing out fake names?"

It took him a long beat to come up with a story. Long enough that I didn't believe a word of it.

"I—well, yes, I apologize for that. I go to Las Vegas a lot and, I confess, have a bit of a gambling problem. It wouldn't do well for my reputation if people knew about that. So I often travel under an alias."

"Fucking . . . *liar!*" I repeated. "Something happened to me. My heart stopped on that rooftop, and when I came back to life, everything was different. I think you know why, and I think you're desperate to keep me from finding out the truth."

"Hallie, please—"

"I know about Skye. I know it's her. I'm remembering things from *her* life. Tell me how that's possible."

His composure began to shred at the sound of Skye's name on my lips. He struggled to find a way to deny it, to say it was impossible, to call me crazy again, but he didn't. I thought he might reach across the table and grab my shoulders and shake me until I told him everything I remembered. His face gave it all away. This was not my imagination.

Forcing down another wave of fear and rage, I dragged the words out of my throat. *"What did you do to me?"*

His head slumped. "It was an accident."

"What was?"

But he looked stricken now and didn't say anything more. I reached across the table and grabbed his wrist. "Goddamn it, tell me what you did! You knew what happened to me right from the beginning. You hired a private detective to follow me. Hyppolex paid Todd Kivel to watch me. Why? What were you afraid of?"

The doctor sighed. "It was for your *safety*, Hallie."

"Yeah. Sure."

"When I called you in Las Vegas, you mentioned odd dreams. That was a red flag that the transfer had taken hold, although I didn't know to what extent."

"Transfer?" I asked.

He ignored my question. "After that, I decided we should keep a closer eye on you. That's why we hired Kivel. He was only supposed to follow you and make sure nothing bad happened."

"Well, something bad did happen."

"What do you mean?"

I stared at him. "Don't you know about Kivel?"

Dr. Edam wrinkled his brow. "No. He stopped returning my calls. Before I could pursue it, we heard that you were on your way to Boston. You knew about Hyppolex, and you reached out to Tyler through your recruiter. We didn't know how, but you'd obviously connected us to what happened. Since you were coming to us, we didn't need Kivel anymore."

"Kivel's dead," I told him.

"*Dead?* What are you talking about?"

"He was murdered. He got his throat slashed while saving my life. Two men came after me. They were going to shoot me up with drugs and let me die in the alley. Kivel intervened, and I got away, but they killed him."

"Jesus Christ," Dr. Edam hissed, his face flushed with shock. He bolted out of the chair and took me by the arm. "We need to go, Hallie. We need to get you out of here right now."

20

We took Andrew's Ferrari. It was a silver convertible, and he drove fast with the top down, the wind swirling our hair. We didn't talk much, but every now and then he shot a stare across the car at me from behind his Balenciaga sunglasses. I didn't know if he was really looking at me, or whether he was imagining Skye sitting next to him in the passenger seat.

He promised me answers when we got where we were going, but so far, he'd told me nothing more.

Nothing about the *transfer*.

We headed south on I-93, leaving Boston behind. Obviously, our destination wasn't close by. We left the freeway near South Quincy on a parkway that led toward the water, and eventually we began to pass in and out of seaside towns. His eyes kept drifting to the mirror to see if we were being followed. Apparently I wasn't the only one who was paranoid.

"Who do you think would be coming after us?" I asked. "Or rather *me*."

"Take your pick. The Chinese. The Russians. Hell, it could be the NSA, too. I don't understand how they found out about you—about what happened—but if they did, that makes you extremely valuable to any number of people."

"Are you kidding?"

"I wish I was."

More than an hour after we'd left the university, we finally reached a peninsula jutting into the Atlantic. The road bordered a wide flat beach dotted with sunbathers. The tide was out, and faraway waves lapped calmly over the sand.

"This is Nantasket Beach," Andrew murmured, as we stopped at a three-story Nantucket-style house located across from the water. "I have a place in Cambridge, but my wife and kids stay out here during the summer. My hours at the lab are unpredictable, so I visit them on the weekends when I can."

The house had a sprawling front porch and tall windows that took advantage of the ocean view. When we got out of the Ferrari, Andrew didn't even glance at the water. I wondered how jaded you had to be not to notice that you lived in a place like this. We went inside, where the interior was airy and bright, thanks to the open seaside windows and skylights overhead. There were hardwood floors and walls painted in seafoam green, and the furniture had a beach-casual look. I smelled seafood. I followed Andrew into a surprisingly small kitchen, where a brunette woman in a blouse and shorts was washing clams in the sink. She was neatly put together and attractive, but in the starchy way of a well-groomed dog that would win you the show ribbon and not roll around in the mud.

He gave her a formal peck on the cheek, which wasn't returned.

I thought about what I'd heard Andrew say to Savannah in my dream. *In our circle, that's the definition of love. Don't pretend to be shocked by it.*

"Hallie, this is my wife, Cara," Andrew said. Then to his wife, "Hallie's helping us out on a research project."

"Hello," Cara said politely as she scrubbed the clams.

She gave me a look that told me I was not in her social circle and we were not going to be friends. I also felt the chilly breeze of someone who wondered when meeting every new woman whether her husband was being unfaithful.

"Is he here?" Andrew asked.

"Yes, he's up in the loft."

"This way," Andrew told me.

I followed him up two sets of stairs to a converted attic occupying the upper level of the house. Modern art hung on the walls, but nothing by Myron Glass. There was comfortable leather furniture here, a wet bar, and a grand piano, which made me wonder if Skye had spent time in this house. The beams of the roof climbed in sharp angles, and the ocean-view windows were open, letting in cool salty air. The windows were designed to allow you to climb out to a large balcony facing the water.

Outside, a man stood at the balcony railing, a glass of whiskey in one hand. It was Tyler Reyes.

He glanced back at the two of us in the shadows of the loft.

"Hallie," he said. "I'm sorry, but I just couldn't wait for breakfast to see you again. Come out and join me, and Andrew and I can tell you what's going on inside your head."

The tide began to come in, and evening began to fall. Most of the beachgoers left for home, leaving the rocky stretch of sand below us desolate and shadowed, with only a handful of silhouettes lingering near the water. As the wind picked up, the pounding of the surf got louder.

The three of us pulled Adirondack chairs into a semicircle facing the ocean. I didn't drink, although I would have loved something for my shattered nerves. But I wanted to be stone sober for this conversation. Tyler, on the other hand, had gone through a lot of whiskey before we got there. The alcohol had loosened something inside him, because the attraction I'd felt in our interview grew more pronounced. I was sure I understood the source of it now.

Just as I was seeing the world through Skye's eyes, Tyler was looking for Skye in *my* eyes. I was his dead wife come back to life.

"These aren't dreams I'm having," I concluded. "Or delusions. Or hallucinations. I'm not crazy. What I'm seeing in my head are really memories. *Skye's* memories. Right?"

Tyler's lips pressed into a thin pale line. "Yes."

"She's inside me."

"Yes. She is."

I stared at these men, these two scientists studying me like an interesting new virus on the other end of a microscope. A tidal wave of bitterness consumed me. God, what they'd put me through. The fear. The panic. The thoughts of madness. I spat the question at them.

"How?"

Tyler ignored the resentment in my voice. "Well, first, let me tell you a little bit about our background. That way you'll understand why the research we're doing is so important."

"I'd rather you jump to the part where you fucked with my mind."

My profanity seemed to make Tyler uncomfortable. "Hallie, I know you're upset. And I can see you're already way ahead of us. I wasn't lying about you being a good fit for the company, you know. That wasn't just spin. You're quick and savvy, and I'd love to see you with us. The other thing—well, that's a separate matter."

The other thing.

The girl of my dreams was the other thing.

"Get on with it," I snapped.

"Of course. You have every reason to be impatient. But I also have to *explain*. You see, Andrew and I grew up in Newport. We've been best friends all the way back to our prep school days. We shared an interest in science and technology. We were also prodigies. I'm sorry, that sounds arrogant, but it is what it is. We had the talent to make a difference with our lives. And when I was a teenager, something happened that brought my future home in a very personal way."

"What?"

"I watched my grandparents suffer through Alzheimer's."

"I'm sorry," I said, trying to dredge up some sympathy for this man. "It's a terrible disease."

"Yes, it is. After watching them become shells of who they once were, I vowed that I was going to do something about it."

"Namely?"

"Namely, make sure no one ever loses their memories to disease. *Preserve* the experiences that define our lives and who we are. That's what Hyppolex is about, Hallie. I founded the company when I was only twenty-six years old, and Andrew has worked with me in a research partnership at MIT ever since. Fortunately, Andrew's father saw the potential in what we were doing. He provided the funding to get the entire project started."

I got up restlessly from the chair and went to the balcony railing. It was almost night, and an early moon glow fell across the ocean. The air had turned cool. Or maybe I was just shivering. "Tell me the rest. What does this have to do with me?"

"I'm getting there, Hallie. Truly, I am. But first let me ask you a simple question. What's the best way to make sure you never lose data on your computer?"

"Oh, for fuck's sake."

"No, hear me out. Computers are amazing things, but they're subject to many different failures. Viruses. Power surges. Components wearing out. How do you make sure you don't lose everything if your computer crashes?"

I shrugged. "You back it up."

"Exactly. You back it up. You save your data in case you need to restore it. *That* was my brainstorm, as it were. That's what Andrew and I have been working on for the past decade. We've been developing a way to record and store the electrical impulses of human memory out of the hippocampus, and then, ultimately, to find a way to put them back if someone loses their memory to disease or injury."

Finally, I began to see a glimmer of the truth.

"You backed up *Skye's* memories."

"That's right."

"How did she get involved? Did she even know what you were doing to her?"

"Of course she did," he replied. "We'd reached a critical turning point in our research. Andrew and I needed a test subject to work with us, but we had to be careful about who we chose. This whole area is enormously competitive, so we didn't want to use an outsider. Skye volunteered."

"Why? Why would she do that?"

"She believed in what we were doing."

I shook my head but said nothing. Tyler was wrong. I knew there was more to it than that. Skye's memories were specific and violent. One particular night on one particular summer. A night that ended in death.

She had her own agenda for being part of her husband's research. I could feel it welling out of her thoughts like a relentless quest, something that refused to let go of her. And now it wouldn't let go of me, either.

She was looking for a mystery hidden in the mist.

She was looking for the truth about Savannah.

"Skye worked with Andrew at MIT," Tyler went on in his bland, irritating voice. "They conducted several sessions in which she focused on specific incidents in her life while he recorded her brain wave activity. The result was a sort of backup drive of her memories."

"When was this?" I asked.

"Last fall. The holidays. November and December."

Yes. Christmastime.

That was the same time when Skye had asked Myron Glass to paint her portrait. The same time she'd had dinner with Tyler at Saltie Girl, a dinner filled with loss and unhappiness. The same time she'd gone back to her childhood home and thrown herself off the cliff.

Tyler glanced at Andrew, who came up next to me at the railing.

"Of course, having a backup drive isn't particularly useful," Andrew told me, "if we can't do a restore. After we download someone's memories, can we actually put them back? That's the real test."

I knew exactly where this was going.

"*Me*," I said. "You put Skye's memories in me."

Andrew's face creased with discomfort. "As I told you, it was an accident."

"How? How did it happen?"

He withdrew a black iPhone 12 from his pocket and put it on the balcony railing. Then he took a second phone from his other pocket and positioned it next to the first one. The other phone was identical except for color. It was gold instead of black.

"The black phone is mine," he said. "The gold phone is where I kept Skye's memory files stored. I've been working on computer techniques to visualize the electrical pulses, but without someone's brain to read and interpret them, the results have been primitive. However, transferring the files is another story. Electricity is electricity. It flows through a body very easily."

I felt another chill. "Like through a defibrillator."

"Yes, exactly. The phone-based AED is another of our Hyppolex products. I always have one with me, including on that rooftop in Las Vegas. You died. I was there, and I brought you back to life." He paused. "But in all the confusion, I ended up using the gold phone, not my own phone. That's how the transfer happened. I'm sorry, Hallie."

It was dark now, but I could still see Andrew's cool blue eyes.

"I don't believe you," I told him.

"What?"

"You're still lying to me."

"Hallie—"

I leaned closer to his face, and the ocean air blew between us. "I don't believe anything makes you panic, Dr. Edam, and I don't believe you make mistakes. You took one phone out of your pocket when you intended to take out a different one? No way. You needed to run your experiment on someone to see if it worked. You needed a guinea pig. When I died, you saw your chance."

Andrew didn't say a word. Neither did Tyler. But I knew I was right. I'd worked with a lot of researchers, and they all had the same blindness. They worked in a moral vacuum, where discovery never had a dark side. They never saw the dangers until it was too late.

The sheer horror of what they'd done swelled in my chest and made it hard to breathe. I was a freak. I was the monster strapped down on the mad scientist's table while he harnessed lightning to bring me back from the dead. But it wasn't just me they'd brought back to life.

It was Skye. We were two souls sharing one body and one brain.

I couldn't take it. I simply couldn't deal with any of this. Not with them. Not with the woman inside me. I had to get away. As tears streamed down my face, I shoved past Andrew and Tyler and ran for the stairs.

21

I took my shoes off as I walked in the Atlantic surf across from Andrew's house. The ocean waves lapped at my ankles. For the most part, I was alone under the moon, with only a handful of beachgoers lingering in the shadows. Every wave seemed to bring a different emotion washing over me. Anger and humiliation at what they'd done to me. Fear of what came next. Disbelief that any of this could be real. I felt assaulted. Violated.

I didn't know where to go or who to talk to. Right there, at that moment, I wished I could rip Skye out of my brain, but I couldn't. She was always there. I saw what she saw. I felt what she felt. It was more than memories. Somehow, in ways I couldn't understand, she was alive.

And she was getting stronger.

That was the really scary part. With every day, I felt as if there was more Skye and less Hallie in my mind. Maybe it was because I was here, in the places where she'd lived her life. This was her world. Or maybe it was simply because she was so beautiful. Talented. Successful. I envied all of that. I felt intimidated by this dead woman who was inside me.

But there was also a darkness in Skye, and that darkness was encroaching on *me*.

I retreated from the surf and sat down on the rocky beach. I wrapped my arms tightly around my knees. Out on the ocean, a few boats sailed the nighttime water. I saw a dead fish that had been thrown onto the sand by the waves. I felt out of control. Overwhelmed. I couldn't deal with this by myself.

So I grabbed my phone from my pocket and called Tori in Las Vegas.

"Hallie," she said in that infuriatingly level voice she always used. "I'm glad to hear from you. I was worried. Are you okay?"

"Not really," I said.

"Where are you?"

"Near Boston," I told her. "I'm at the ocean."

"Boston?" she said with surprise. "What are you doing there?"

I glanced around at the wide dark beach, but no one else was nearby. "I know what happened to me now. The dreams. The violence. It's real. It's all real."

"Hallie, tell me what's going on."

I inhaled a long slow breath, and then I told her. I told her everything. I took her through the whole story of what they'd done to me and what was going on inside my head. Tori didn't ask any questions, not at first. She just listened, but I could sense her doubts. Her disbelief. To her, I was still drowning in a well of schizophrenia like my mother.

She stayed quiet after I finished. The silence went on for a long time, and I grew impatient.

"Tori, say something."

"I'm—I'm sort of at a loss for what to say."

"I'm not making any of this up," I insisted.

"Well, I know you're convinced it's true," she replied slowly. "I can hear it in your voice."

"Don't give me your therapist bullshit. Not now. I believe it's true because it *is* true. They told me what they did."

"Hallie, listen, you need to understand—"

"Look up Hyppolex," I interrupted her.

"What?"

"Do a search. See what it says about them. Look up Andrew Edam at MIT."

Tori sighed. I could feel her humoring me. "Hang on."

Another long silence went by, and I found it hard not to leap out of my skin. I knew I wasn't crazy, but somehow it was important to me that *Tori* knew I wasn't crazy, too. Someone had to believe me. Finally, I heard her come back on the line, and I held my breath.

"Well," she said, and there was something different in her voice now. "I have to admit, everything you're saying fits with what I see online about the company's research direction. As amazing as that sounds."

I couldn't keep the relief out of my voice. "So you think it's possible? They really did everything they said?"

"Technologically, it's a big leap forward, but there are companies all over the world working on brain research like this. Sooner or later, I suppose one of them was bound to make a significant breakthrough. And I was there. I saw that doctor working on you. It was definitely this same man—Andrew Edam."

"He put someone else's memories inside *my* head," I said with a shiver of wonder.

"I confess, it does seem that way."

"Tori, what do I do now? What's going to happen to me?"

"I wish I could tell you, but I'm not a medical doctor or a neuroscientist. If this is really what happened, I don't know how this procedure actually affected the workings of your brain."

"At least talk to me. Talk me through this."

She grasped for something to say. "Well, what's going on in your mind right now? Let's start there. Try to describe what you're experiencing."

The question felt like a dam bursting.

"Honestly? I'm having trouble holding on to myself. Everything in my brain is Skye. She tells me where to go, she tells me what to do. It's like she's taking over, squeezing me out. I mean, is it possible for her memories to get stronger the more time goes on? Does that make any sense?"

"Theoretically, I suppose that could be true. As your brain builds new pathways from her memories, then you're likely to feel her presence become more 'real' to you, for lack of a better word. I imagine your memories and Skye's memories are likely to get a bit tangled up with each other."

I squeezed my eyes shut. "There's something else, too."

"What?"

"I feel like there may be a *missing* memory inside me."

"I don't understand. Are you talking about your mother's death?"

"No. This is Skye's memory. I think that's why she volunteered for this experiment. She was hoping it might unlock something she couldn't remember. She wanted to know the truth, but she was scared of it, too. And I'm pretty sure I know why."

Tori hesitated. "Why?"

"I think Skye killed someone."

"*Killed* someone? Who?"

"Her sister."

"Are you sure?"

"No. I'm not sure of anything. I have a vision of her sister lying dead at Skye's feet, and Skye's hands—*my* hands—covered in blood. But I don't see the killing itself. I can't remember what actually happened. I don't think she could, either."

"Well, that's definitely the kind of trauma that someone might block out."

"Yes, but I feel this urgency from her. She *wanted* to remember. Hell, she still wants to remember. She keeps replaying those events over and over in my head. It's like she needs me to see what happened."

"But you can't?"

"No. At least not yet."

"Not yet?" Tori asked. "What do you mean?"

"Well, even if Skye blocked it out, the memory has to be in me somewhere, right? I should be able to find it."

"Why would you want to do something like that? You're talking about Skye's life, not your own."

"I'm not sure there's a difference anymore."

Tori's voice turned darker when I said that. "Listen to me. I really don't like the way you're talking. This is not a good path for you, especially given your history. Do you want my advice? Get out of there. Come home."

"I don't have a home anymore. Vegas was never my home. The weird thing is, this area feels more like home to me now."

"Hallie, you're in a strange place, surrounded by people who do *not* have your best interests at heart. You're obsessing about a girl with a missing memory and a violent death in her past. Does that sound familiar? Skye's story is triggering all the pain you've locked up about your mother. The best thing you can do is walk away and go back to your own life."

"I'm not sure I can do that."

"Why not?"

"Because until I know what happened to Skye's sister, I feel like the pressure in my head is only going to get worse. She won't let go of me. She keeps pushing me to find out more."

Tori breathed faster and louder. When she spoke again, her voice no longer had that unshakable calm.

"Hallie, you told me that Skye killed herself."

"Yes. She threw herself off a cliff in Newport."

"Well, don't you see why this is such a terrible risk for you?" Tori asked. "You've tried to kill yourself twice. It's sheer luck that you're still alive. Now this woman is in your head, and she's heading down a path that led her to the bottom of a cliff. Dead. That's a dangerous road for you of all people to follow, Hallie. A very dangerous road."

◆ ◆ ◆

After I hung up the phone, I was drained. Exhausted. I couldn't even get up. I stretched out under the stars, where the sand was still warm, but I tried not to sleep. If I slept, I knew Skye would show me more of her past, and I didn't want to see any more. I wanted it all to go away, to leave my mind altogether.

But soon my eyes blinked shut, blocking out the stars.

The next dream came.

I was in Andrew's lab. It was Christmastime.

I lay in a leather chair, with no sound around me but the hum of white noise. I wore a mesh cap that fit snugly over my skull, lined with a dense web of wires and electrodes. The red wires traveled down my body and joined at a cable that was connected to a computer.

Andrew typed rapidly, then came over to me and made adjustments on the electrodes. I could see electrical pathways streaming across his computer screen at a pace that was impossible to follow.

"Are those my brain waves on the screen?"

"That's right."

"So how will this work?" I asked.

"Well, for you, it's very easy. I'll start the recording process, and I'll leave the room so as not to distract you. The key is to focus on individual memories in as much detail as possible. Try to start at the beginning of an event, and work your way through it chronologically."

I stared at the screen again with anxious wonder. There was my life, distilled into a seemingly infinite number of pulses and waves. All the places I'd been, the people I'd loved.

The things I'd done.

Somewhere in there was a few minutes on the cliff that I'd forgotten.

"What if I don't remember something?" I asked. "What if there are gaps in my memory? Will it . . . fill them in?"

I hesitated, waiting to see what he said.

Andrew gave me a curious look. "The truth is, I don't know. Eventually, the idea is to pull the memories, not push them. As we perfect the technique, hopefully we'll be able to isolate thoughts and experiences that you've long since forgotten. But for now, the computer isn't really in charge. You are, Hallie. Your brain will feed data to us. Some of it may be conscious, and some of it may be unconscious."

Wait, what did he call me?

"Does it matter what I think about?"

"No, but the more vivid the memories are, the better."

"I had dinner with Tyler last week. I told him about wanting a divorce. God knows that was vivid."

Andrew stared at me. "It's better not to tell me what you're remembering. It could bias the results when we try to interpret what we've stored. Besides, what happens between you and Tyler doesn't involve me. He's my friend. So are you."

"I don't love him. I never did. I feel horrible about that, but it's the truth."

"Hallie, please. Enough."

Hallie?

"Should they be recent memories? Or from the past?"

"It doesn't matter. It's more important that the memories are powerful."

I debated whether to tell him the truth. "I need to think about Savannah. About . . . what happened to her."

His fingers froze over the keyboard. "Let's not talk about Savannah."

"Do you *not* want me to remember her?"

"What you remember is up to you, but it was ten years ago. We can't change the past. All we can do is live with it."

"Yes, but it's tearing me apart. An innocent man died because I didn't say anything. How do I live with that?"

"Innocent?" Andrew's forehead wrinkled with confusion. "What are you saying?"

"Elijah."

"Elijah wasn't innocent."

"He was. I'm sure he was."

"How can you possibly know that?"

"I was there."

He stared at me. What was in his eyes?

Fear, I thought.

"What are you saying?" he asked.

"I was there, Andrew. I was on the cliff that night. I was with Savannah when she was killed. But I can't remember what happened. It's like I've blocked out how she really died."

He leaned back in his chair and stared at the ceiling. He laced his fingers on top of his head, mussing his hair. "How come you've never said anything? How come you never told me this before now?"

"I didn't know for sure. Somehow I repressed that night, but lately . . . lately, parts of it are starting to come back."

His face darkened with concern. "Maybe doing this isn't such a good idea."

"*No.* Please. I need to know what happened to her. You can help me remember."

"It doesn't work like that. The technology can't simply unlock what your brain won't show you."

"Well, I want to try."

He frowned at me. "I think this is a bad idea, but ultimately it's your choice."

Andrew got up from the chair and prepared to leave me alone in the room, but I stopped him. "Wait. I have to know one thing."

"What is it?"

"What's my name?"

"I'm sorry?"

"Tell me my name," I said. "Tell me who I am."

"You're Hallie Evers."

He came around behind my chair, and he turned it toward the dark laboratory window, where I could see my reflection. There I was, under

168

the net cap, with the electrodes and red wires. I had shoulder-length black hair. Dark brown eyes. Pale lips, parted. Bony shoulders.

Yes, that was me. I was the girl from Las Vegas.

This was a dream. It wasn't real. Somewhere inside my head, I knew that I was still on the beach, and I could feel myself fighting back against the memories. Trying to hold on to myself.

My name is Hallie. I am not Skye.

22

"Are you all right, Hallie?" Tyler asked.

We sat at an outdoor table at a restaurant called Shipwreck'd, which was on Pemberton Point at the end of the peninsula. From there, ferries came and went to Boston. I'd be on one of those ferries soon. The two of us shared a table underneath an orange patio umbrella, and the stiff breeze made the canvas flap over our heads. To our left, a curved beach bent like a parenthesis around the calm harbor. I could see swimmers in the water.

"Hallie?" Tyler said again when I didn't answer him. He devoured a plate of corned beef hash while I picked at an egg white omelet.

"Am I *all right*? Is that what you're asking me?"

He heard the bitterness in my voice. "It's a lot to take in. I realize that. And I know we haven't given you much reason to trust us. But regardless, it's extremely important that we work together."

"You're right about one thing. I don't trust you. Not you and definitely not Andrew."

"Well, I still wish you'd stay here with Cara for a while, rather than go back to the city. If word has truly gotten out about what happened to you, I'm nervous about you being in Boston on your own. It's not safe."

"Do you not get that I don't want anything to do with you?" I asked, shaking my head in exasperation. "After what you people did to me?"

Tyler pursed his lips. "Is it a question of money? Naturally, we'll negotiate a generous settlement to compensate you for this incident.

We'll let the lawyers worry about the details, but you're going to be a rich woman, Hallie."

"Jesus. It's not about money. I don't even know who I am anymore."

He put down his fork. He reached out to take my hand, then pulled it back. "I won't pretend to know what that feels like. I'm sure it must be confusing and frightening. But you're an intelligent woman, Hallie. You know the research frontiers we're talking about. Even if none of us planned it this way, you're now part of something extraordinary. It would be a mistake to walk away from it."

"You mean it would be a mistake to walk away from *you*," I said.

"I don't understand."

"Yes, you do. You still love Skye. Whenever you look at me, it's like you're trying to find her inside me. Having me here with you is a fantasy of having your wife back, right? But I'm *not* her, Tyler."

"I know that."

"No, I'm not sure you do."

He glanced away at the beach, then back at me. "You're right that I still love her. Of course I do. I loved Skye since we were kids."

"But she didn't love you."

He winced as if I'd struck him. "That's not true."

"At Saltie Girl, she asked you for a divorce, didn't she? She said she was sorry, but she didn't love you, and she never had, and it wasn't right for either of you to keep pretending. I *remember* it, Tyler, so don't tell me it's not true."

"Skye was suffering from depression. She didn't know how she felt about anything."

"Yes, she did. I'm sorry, but yes, she knew how she felt about you."

Tyler got a pained look and pushed away his plate. "I suppose you're right. It's just hard to admit it to myself. Skye kept so much of herself hidden away from me. I thought it was because she was a private person, but she was never close to me, not in an emotional way. To be honest, not really in a physical way, either. She respected me, respected my work, but she kept a kind of distance from me. I tried to bridge it, I tried to reach out to her, but I never could."

"Tell me about her," I said.

"What?"

"Tell me about her. She's *inside* me, but all I know about her are fragments of memories. I want to know who she really was."

Tyler eased back in the patio chair. He slipped sunglasses over his face, as if that would cover his grief. He took a few bits of hash from his plate and tossed them onto the pier, where a flock of seagulls swooped down to fight over them in loud screeches. He watched them battle like gladiators.

"Skye was . . ." His voice drifted off.

I wondered what he would say.

"Skye was the golden child. Everybody loved her. That long blond hair. That perfect smile, that perfect face. The way she lost herself in the piano. She was the kind of girl who floated rather than walked."

"When did you meet her?"

"Oh, she was just a kid," Tyler replied. "Seven years old, I think? I was around twelve. I visited the house with Andrew. He and I became best friends in eighth grade, and we hung out together all the time. The Edams lived next door to the Seldens in Newport. Two incredible estates right on the cliff."

"The Seldens," I murmured, trying to remember her family.

"Yes, Terence and Alma Selden were Skye's parents. He was an investment banker in Manhattan."

"And Savannah," I said. "Skye's sister."

Tyler looked at me with a little wrinkle of surprise. "Yes. Savannah was two years older than Skye."

"The family had money?"

He laughed. "Many generations of money, thanks to Selden Machine Tools. The company helped launch the era of precision parts manufacturing. Her great-great-grandfather built their home in Newport when it was still just a summer getaway from New York. The Edams were the same way. But Skye actually resented her family's wealth. She saw people who had money as being mostly shallow. I think Skye would have run away from all that if she could."

I thought about Skye in her bedroom.

Just a few more days, and I would be gone. A new life, a new beginning.

"She wasn't happy in Newport," I murmured.

Tyler shook his head. "No one in that house was happy."

"Why not?"

He sighed. "When Skye was fifteen, her father divorced her mother. Terence was in his midfifties, and after twenty years of marriage, he tossed Alma out for a younger model. Literally. A thirty-year-old fashion model named Rochelle. It scandalized Newport, and believe me, it takes a lot to do that. Rochelle was a bombshell, magazine-cover body, tattoos and piercings—not exactly the woman for the upper-class social scene there. It created a huge rift in the family and the town. Savannah stood by her mother. She was bitter toward her father and refused to have anything to do with her new stepmother. Skye tried to be the peacemaker, but that was a losing battle."

I pictured someone outside the door of the ballroom while Andrew and Savannah argued. "There was another little girl in the house. Who was that?"

"Rochelle had a daughter. Vicky. I think she was about nine when Terence and Rochelle got married. Shitty situation for a kid to walk into. Really, the whole thing was ugly. Everyone was in different camps shooting barbs at each other. Savannah, her father, her stepmother, her stepsister, Alma living in a condo on the other side of town. It was nonstop conflict for the next few years. That took a big toll on Skye."

"But you fell in love with her?"

Tyler's face got a misty look. "Yes, by the time Skye was sixteen, I knew I wanted to marry her. She may as well have been twenty-five at that point. You could see she was growing up into this amazing girl.

173

Not that I was alone in feeling that way. Pretty much every teenage boy in Newport wanted to marry her, too."

"How did she feel about you?"

He laughed sadly. "Skye didn't know I was alive. Not back then. I'm not sure she knew any man was alive. She was too caught up in her piano, and her books, and her art. She was her own girl, and she lived by her own rules. But she had a magnetic personality. People were simply drawn to Skye. Men, women, young, old. Wherever she went, she was the center of attention."

"I can't believe that went down well with her sister."

"No. It didn't. There was a huge sibling rivalry there. Well, it was more of a one-sided rivalry. Skye was prettier than Savannah, better liked than Savannah, more talented than Savannah, and Savannah was incredibly jealous."

"When did you and Skye begin dating?" I asked.

"The summer after her first year in college. She went to Vassar. I was already in graduate school at MIT."

"You said she didn't know you were alive. What changed?"

He softened. "Skye changed. She was an extraordinarily empathetic person. She knew I was suffering as my grandparents drifted away, and she stayed at my side as I went through it. When I told her about my dreams for Hyppolex—about wanting to *do* something to make sure no one else had to watch a family member go through what I had—she said she wanted to help me. That's what brought us together. That's how she fell in love with me."

I was silent. He was still trying to convince himself that Skye had loved him, but I knew she hadn't. She had felt many things for Tyler— loyalty, devotion, sympathy, caring, pride—but she hadn't loved him. That was the kind of thing you could only pretend to yourself for so long.

"That's who Skye was," Tyler said. "Does that tell you what you want to know? She was a jewel. But if you can feel her inside you, then I'm sure you've already realized that."

I glanced out at the water. I saw a ferry on the horizon, navigating between the inner islands. That was the boat that would take me back to Boston. We didn't have much time.

"Thank you for the press release. I'm sure that looked good on the obituary page of the *Globe*. But now tell me the real story."

Tyler's brow furrowed. "What do you mean?"

"Skye killed herself," I said sharply. "Do you think I don't know that? She was carrying around something inside her that went back for years. Something she couldn't handle."

"Hallie, I don't—"

I cut off his protests. "Stop acting like you don't know what I'm talking about."

Tyler tossed more hash to the seagulls, and his voice grew quiet. "You mean Savannah."

"Yes, *Savannah*," I snapped. "When Skye went into Andrew's lab, she was thinking about her sister. That's the crux of everything. Tell me what happened to Savannah. Tell me about the murder."

23

"I don't know why you're so interested in Savannah's death," Tyler went on. "Yes, it was a terrible, tragic thing, but it had nothing to do with Skye. Skye was home in bed at the estate that night. Savannah went for a walk after midnight, and an intruder on the grounds killed her."

"Who?"

"His name was Elijah. He worked at the country club. He was a summer hire from Boston."

I closed my eyes. *Elijah.*

"When did it happen?" I asked.

"It was the Fourth of July," Tyler said. "Ten years ago."

Another July 4.

I thought about how ironic life could be. July 4 had changed Skye's life, and years later, it had changed mine.

"What was going on that day?"

Tyler shook his head. "Hallie, why are you asking about this? If Skye was thinking about Savannah when she was with Andrew, it was just regret over what happened to her sister. I'm sure she wished they'd been closer, and she never got the chance to change things between them. But there was no mystery about Savannah's murder."

"Tyler, please. Tell me about that day."

He ran his hands through his curly hair in frustration. "Fine. There was a big party on the grounds. Andrew's family always threw a party for the Fourth. There must have been a couple hundred people around. Upscale barbecue, lots of drinking. The weather was great, warm and sunny. Everyone enjoyed it. And then after dark, we watched the fireworks from the cliffside."

"Who was there?"

"The Seldens, the Edams, a lot of other Newport families. Friends, college kids. It was a big crowd."

"Savannah and Andrew were going to be married the next day, right? The ballroom was set up for the wedding and reception."

His eyes showed his surprise. "Yes, that's right."

"Was the wedding causing any family problems?"

He nodded. "Big problems. The family dynamics hadn't gotten any better over the years. Savannah wanted her mother there, but she *didn't* want Rochelle or Vicky to attend the wedding at all. Skye was trying to change her mind, but she wasn't having any luck. I'm not sure Savannah even wanted Skye there. I think she was afraid that Skye would upstage her. The rivalry between them was still strong."

"Skye wasn't her maid of honor?"

"No. Savannah didn't even ask her to be part of the wedding. She had other Newport friends standing up for her. Actually, Cara—Andrew's wife now—was Savannah's maid of honor. That hurt Skye a lot."

I tried to understand.

I tried to *remember* how the pieces of that July 4 night fit together. But the thoughts inside my head felt like jagged shards of glass.

"Did you know that Savannah broke up with Andrew that night?" I asked.

"What are you talking about?"

"Savannah and Andrew argued. She thought he was cheating on her with Skye."

"Andrew and Skye? That's ridiculous. There was nothing between them."

"Savannah was convinced there was. She was devastated. Furious. She called off the wedding."

"Well, I told you, Savannah felt inferior to Skye in just about everything. If she said some crazy things that night, it was probably the emotional jitters of being a bride. But she and Andrew never broke up. He would have told me. Besides, Savannah was madly in love with Andrew. She'd been picturing herself as Mrs. Andrew Edam since they were kids. There's no way she would have called it off."

I knew he was wrong.

Skye had seen the argument in the ballroom. Hadn't she?

Or was I misremembering things from that night? Maybe Skye's mind was protecting her. Or lying to *me*.

"What about the murder?" I asked. "Tell me about that. Who was Elijah?"

Tyler scowled at the name. "He was a golf instructor. He was living in Newport that summer and making money by giving lessons to the rich kids. Skye and Savannah were both getting lessons from him."

"And how did the murder happen?"

"Savannah went for a walk. It was late. She headed out toward the cliff. She probably couldn't sleep because of the wedding."

She couldn't sleep because she'd just broken up with her fiancé, I thought.

"Then what?"

"Well, nobody knows the exact details. Savannah must have come upon Elijah out by the cliff. He'd forgotten one of his golf clubs after the party. Obviously, something happened between them. The police assumed he tried to assault her, and she fought back. But in the end, he beat her to death with the golf club."

"Did the police find it?" I asked. "The golf club?"

"No. They figured Elijah took it with him and threw it in the water. But they found the rest of the set in his apartment, and they were able to match the type of club to the wounds in Savannah's skull."

"But how do they know it was him? How do they even know he was there?"

Tyler's jaw stiffened. "Because *I* saw him."

"What? You did?"

"Yes. I was in my car outside the grounds. I'd had too much to drink, and I was sleeping it off before I drove home. A noise woke me up, and I saw a black man climbing the fence into the estate. It was Elijah. I clicked on my headlights as he hopped the fence, and then he was gone. The next morning, when I heard about Savannah, I talked to the police and told them what I saw."

"But nobody actually saw him *with* her?"

"No. I drove home at that point, so I never saw Elijah leave the grounds. I only wish I'd stopped him from going over the fence. Or gone with him. If I had, Savannah would still be alive."

"Except you still can't be sure that *he* killed her."

"Hallie, there's more," Tyler insisted. "The police ran a background check on Elijah. He had a juvenile assault record. The country club didn't know about it when they hired him. He beat up his girlfriend when he was sixteen years old."

I shook my head. There had to be more to what had happened. I was missing something, not seeing something. Skye had been outside that night, not asleep in her bed. She'd been standing over Savannah's body, her hands covered in blood.

The way my own hands had been covered in blood, when they found me at Red Rock on the day my mother died.

Me and Skye. Like sisters. Like twins.

"What happened to Elijah? Did they arrest him? Is he in jail?"

"No. When the police named him as a suspect, he ran. He *ran*, Hallie. How many innocent people do that? The police caught up with him on I-95 not far from the Connecticut border. It turned into a high-speed chase, and Elijah lost control and rolled his car. He was killed in the accident."

"How long was that after the murder?"

"Not even a day. Less than twenty-four hours."

"And that was that? They closed the case?"

"What more did you want them to do?" Tyler asked. "It was open and shut. Elijah had a history of assault. He was at the scene at the exact time Savannah was murdered. The murder weapon belonged to him. He ran from the police when they tried to arrest him."

"You're sure it was him you saw?" I asked. "You couldn't have made a mistake?"

"Very sure."

"Did you see Skye? Was she out there, too?"

"No. I told you, Skye went to bed after the party. She didn't even know about the murder until that morning."

That was a lie. That wasn't what had happened.

I'd been there. I mean, *Skye* had been there.

"Who found the body?" I asked.

"Andrew did. He went for a run the next morning, and he found Savannah by the cliff. It was the worst day of his life. That was supposed to be his wedding day, and instead, he found his fiancée beaten to death and left there like garbage. It was horrific. The news spread like wildfire in Newport."

"Did you talk to Skye?"

Tyler nodded. "She was a wreck."

"Were you in her bedroom?"

"Yes, she barely left her room for days after the murder."

I hesitated. "When you went to her room . . . was she packing?"

"Packing? What do you mean?"

"Did you see a suitcase in her room?"

"Hallie, what are you talking about? Skye wasn't going anywhere."

"Yes, she was. I think she was leaving Newport."

"That's crazy. Why would she do that?"

"I don't know, but I remember her packing a suitcase. I remember her thinking that in a few days she'd be gone for good."

Tyler looked at me with a scientist's concern. His lab rat was behaving in an unexpected manner. "Hallie, nothing like that happened. There must be some mix-up in how your brain has processed Skye's memories. Or maybe your mind interpreted one of her dreams as an actual recollection. We can't be sure how the transfer worked inside you, because it's still in the experimental stage. You can't trust everything you remember."

Those words echoed in my head.

You can't trust everything you remember.

He was right. I didn't know what to believe. I didn't know where Hallie ended and Skye began. And yet everything I'd seen and dreamed felt *real*—and so far, it had all proven to be true. Skye had led me to Boston. She'd led me to her painting. And now she was guiding me toward the answers she wanted about her sister.

"What about Skye's family?" I asked. "A poster at Symphony Hall called her the last surviving Selden. What happened to her parents?"

"Savannah's death devastated all of them," he replied. "It ripped open the scars. Her mother, Alma, drank herself to death within a year. Skye's father, Terence, had a heart attack about five years ago. He and Rochelle never had kids of their own, so after he died, Rochelle and Vicky moved away. Rochelle opened up a retail boutique with some of the money Terence left her, and she's been very successful. But in terms of the Selden bloodline, Skye was the only one left at that point. I think it was a burden for her, being alone with the family legacy."

I saw the ferry docking at the pier. Passengers were already getting off. I stood up from the table because I needed to go, but I had one last question.

"Tyler, *why* did Skye kill herself?"

He exhaled a sad slow breath. "I'm not sure I can give you an answer to that. I'm not sure anyone can. Skye battled depression her whole life, and I guess it finally won. You can't see it in people's faces, you know. It hides behind their smiles."

I knew that was true. I knew it in my own life and in my mother's life. It didn't matter how accomplished or how happy someone looked on the outside. The inner reality could be very different. But I also knew that something was missing from Tyler's story.

Whatever happened to Skye on that cliff went back to the night of July 4.

"Was there anything going on before Skye's death that would have reminded her of Savannah?" I asked. "Anything that would have started her thinking about her sister's murder again?"

Tyler frowned, as if he didn't want to answer. As if he didn't want to feed my conspiracies. Then he slapped a hundred-dollar bill on the table for the waitress, and he got up and spoke softly.

"Yes, actually, the story was back in the news last fall."

"Why?"

"A group of Boston activists released a study on black men being falsely accused by the police," he told me. "It got a lot of media attention. They profiled a number of cases around New England where a black suspect in a crime had been killed before there was any trial. One of them was Elijah."

24

The ferry plowed through choppy water on my way back to Boston.

I found an empty stretch of railing on the upper deck and closed my eyes to the spray as we bounced over the waves. The motion felt natural, as if I'd grown up on the sea. I felt at home here, but I wasn't sure if it was my home or Skye's.

Islands surrounded us, dotting the water on both sides. In my head, I already knew their names. Rainsford Island. Georges Island. Gallops Island. Most looked undeveloped, just parkland and green hills, except for an occasional lighthouse or old fort. Distantly, on the horizon, I also spotted a small house nestled on its own among the trees. I thought about what it would be like to live in a place like that, with nothing but thousands of miles of ocean outside your front door. I could imagine myself living that way if I had the chance.

I found myself thinking a lot about Skye, too. The real woman, not just the visions she'd left in my head. She had money, confidence, grace, an ability to be instantly liked. I'd grown up with none of those things. We were as different as two people could be on the outside, and yet I was beginning to feel a kinship with her. Maybe it was just the intimacy of sharing someone else's most personal thoughts, but I felt sad that we'd never met. If we had, I think we might have become friends. In a strange way, I already felt closer to her than anyone else in my life.

The ferry journey to Boston wasn't a long trip, not even a half hour. A few dozen people were on the boat with me that afternoon. Most were clustered on the upper deck where I was, enjoying the sea air. A middle-aged woman wearing a raincoat was closest to me, and she had a wide-brimmed hat that she kept on with a hand on the top of her head. Two senior citizens held out pieces of bread for the gulls that followed the boat. Three young children chased each other from bow to stern while their father tried fruitlessly to contain them.

Then there was the man standing near the fluttering American flag.

I hadn't had the sensation of being followed since I'd arrived in Boston, but now that paranoid feeling was back. This same man had been drinking coffee and eating pancakes at Shipwreck'd a few tables away from me and Tyler. When I thought about it, I was also convinced that I'd seen him the previous day at the Area Four coffee shop near MIT, when I met Andrew.

The man was in his forties, of medium height, and a little over-weight. He had thick dark hair shot through with gray, long enough to cover his ears. He wore a sleeveless blue fleece vest over a dark tur-tleneck, along with jeans and Bean Boots. With one hand, he held his phone, and his thumb scrolled up the screen. He wasn't looking directly at me, and his eyes were glued to the phone. And yet I had the distinct impression that he was taking pictures of me.

He didn't stay there long. A couple of minutes later, he shoved his phone back in his pocket. He smoothed his hair against the wind and then took the stairs to the lower level of the ferry and disappeared without ever looking my way. Maybe I'd been wrong about him, but I didn't think so.

A few minutes later, we crossed into Boston's main channel, and the city skyline got larger in front of us. The runways of Logan Airport sprawled across Governors Island on my right. We docked at Long Wharf, and I lingered on the upper deck until most of the other people had left the boat. Finally, I went downstairs and took the gangway. Andrew had arranged for someone to move my car here from the parking lot at MIT. I was about to start looking for it when a man bumped hard into my shoulder from behind, nearly knocking me down. He continued past me without apologizing, and by the time I'd recovered my balance, he was well ahead of me in the crowd of passengers leaving the boat.

It was the man from the ferry.

He didn't look back, but I knew the collision hadn't been an accident.

I quickly made sure my wallet was still in my purse, which it was. Then I checked to see if he'd planted some kind of tracking device on me, but instead I found that a Visa debit card had been slipped into my rear pocket.

Clipped to the card was a small folded piece of heavy paper. The man on the ferry had been a messenger boy.

When I opened the paper, I found a handwritten note in neat script:

Ms. Evers,

I'd very much like to meet you and discuss your future. Shall we say dinner at Blu at 9pm?

The attached gift card is a little incentive to join me, but the money is yours regardless. It's ten thousand dollars.

Paul Temple

Well, well.

I had never met Paul Temple, but I certainly knew who he was by reputation. Everyone in the med-tech industry did. He was the founding partner of Temple Funds, a New York venture capital firm that invested in medical device start-ups. In fact, Temple Funds had sponsored the rooftop party in Las Vegas where I'd died and come back to life.

I was impressed that Temple wanted to meet me and was willing to pay so much money to get me to show up. But I didn't think that talking about my future had anything to do with my marketing career. Somehow he knew what Andrew Edam had done to me.

Like everyone else, Paul Temple was chasing what was in my head.

◆ ◆ ◆

Was I planning to meet him? Yes, I was.

But dinner at Blu was hours away, and in the meantime I was determined to find out as much as I could about the murder of Savannah Selden.

I decided to start with the activist group that had brought Elijah's death back into the headlines. They operated out of a storefront in the Hyde Square neighborhood, so after I found my car, I headed there from the downtown harbor. In addition to serving as headquarters for several community groups, the shabby little store sold used paperbacks, hemp T-shirts, and colorful posters about peace and justice. There was meeting space located at the back, and I could hear a speaker revving up the crowd with a blistering take on rent control.

A male volunteer with a gray ponytail staffed the cash register. There was also an orange store cat next to him that didn't wake up at my arrival. I figured I'd get more information by buying something, so I opted for a cannabis recipe book. Based on the smell in the place, I figured they were experts on that topic. When I asked the man about the crime survey that had gotten so much attention the previous year, he pointed me to a black girl tapping on a laptop on a tattered green sofa.

The girl didn't look old enough to be out of college, and she wasn't. After I said hello, she introduced herself as Whitney Bell, a UMass senior and social psychology major. Whitney was short and slim, with her legs stretched across the sofa. She wore ripped jeans and a No Justice, No Peace T-shirt, and had a rainbow-colored headscarf tied around her forehead under her afro. Her mouth bore a default frown, and her dark eyes studied me suspiciously when I mentioned the survey.

"Are you a reporter?" she asked. "Because press inquiries go through my Instagram account."

I squeezed onto the other end of the sofa next to her bare feet. Her toenails were neatly painted in red. "No, I'm not a reporter, but I am looking into one of the cases you mentioned in your report."

"Why?"

I thought about what to tell her. "Because I think you're right. The man the police said was the prime suspect didn't do it."

"And how does that concern you?"

"I had a relationship with a family member of the victim," I replied, which was at least partially true. "She killed herself last winter. I think the murder of her sister had something to do with that. So I'd like to find out what really happened."

Whitney's expression didn't change. "What's the case?"

"Savannah Selden. There was a golf instructor, Elijah—"

"Yeah, I know all about it," she said, cutting me off. She slapped down the laptop cover and planted her feet on the ground. "In less than a day, the cops pinned it on a black man and wiped their hands of the case. I'm sure it made all those rich people in Newport feel much safer not to look in their own circle to see who did it. Why unsettle their nice little Peyton Place?"

"I heard Elijah had an assault record."

"That was when he was sixteen. He was thirty-one when they killed him. Nothing in between."

"When they called him a suspect, he ran."

"He ran because he knew what the police do to black men. Look, the only evidence they had of Elijah being involved in the murder was one statement from one witness. A white boy woke up in his car and said he saw Elijah climbing the fence. That was it. No other witnesses, no nothing. Do you think the police even searched that white boy's car?

Ever checked on whether he had some kind of motive to kill that girl himself? I'll give you the answer. No."

"Are you saying you think *Tyler Reyes* killed Savannah?"

"I'm saying he was there, just like Elijah, but only one of them became a suspect. It's not hard to figure out why that is. You ask me, they should have looked in Tyler's trunk for the missing golf club."

I cocked my head. "How do you know all this?"

"Elijah told his brother what happened."

"His brother was in Newport, too?" I asked.

"Yeah. The two of them shared an apartment that summer. Elijah went to get his golf club and found that girl beaten to death by the cliff. With *his* club. He knew what was going to happen. So he panicked and got the hell out of there. Afterward, he told his brother that a shitstorm was about to land on his head. That's when he ran. His brother told all this to the police, but they didn't want to hear it. They already had the narrative they wanted. Black boy murders innocent white girl."

As I blinked, I saw the golf club on the ground.

I saw the blood on my hands.

"Did Elijah see anyone by the cliff? Did he have any idea who really did kill Savannah?"

Whitney shook her head. "You'd have to ask his brother about that. All he told me was that he knew Elijah didn't do it. Other than that, he didn't want to talk to me. It was like pulling teeth to get anything out of him."

"Why was that?" I asked.

"No idea, maybe he figures it's bad for business," the girl replied. "He's an artist now, does really well with the white Beacon Hill crowd. He's got a studio by the water. His name's Myron Glass."

25

"You change your mind about me painting you, Hallie Evers?" Myron asked when I returned to his studio on the fish pier.

He approached me in the dim light and stood so close to me that he was practically in my face. He wore a loose white smock, unbuttoned, and below it, nothing but boxers. His feet were bare, and his fingers were smeared with a rainbow of paint colors. The way he looked at me made me feel undressed, and I admit I didn't mind the idea of being naked for this man. His eyes told me that he knew that.

I struggled to keep my cool. "No, but you left out a few things when we talked."

"Yeah?" he asked. "What'd I leave out?"

"Elijah."

His eyes grew darker. "Not sure how Elijah is your business. Not sure how any of this is."

"My book," I said.

"Uh-huh. Your book about Skye. Except we both know there's no book, so what is this really about?"

I thought about telling him the truth, but I didn't think he would believe the truth, so I steamrolled over his question.

"Look, I came to talk to you because you painted Skye. You made it sound like that was the only way you knew her, but now I find out that your brother was accused of murdering Skye's sister."

Myron shook his head sourly. "Elijah didn't kill Savannah."

"Well, if that's true, I'd like to know who did."

"Why?"

"For my book," I repeated, but the lie hadn't gotten any more convincing.

Myron studied me with those penetrating eyes. I wondered if he'd kick me out, but instead, he walked over to one of the studio walls, where a set of Bose Bluetooth speakers sat on a wooden shelf. With a few taps of his phone, he started music playing, and I recognized it immediately. It was what I'd heard in my car on the way across the desert.

Rachmaninoff's Piano Concerto no. 3.

"You know this piece?" he asked me.

"Yeah," I whispered, my voice barely audible as the music thumped in my chest. "I know it."

"This was Skye's signature piece. Nobody played the Rachmaninoff Three like her. This dude on Pandora can play, but it ain't the same as Skye."

I found it hard to concentrate on what he was saying because of the *music*. The music consumed me. It wrapped itself around me like a cloud. My fingers twitched. I closed my eyes, and my body swayed sharply with the up and down of the melody. I could feel the keys, could feel my heart beating faster. It took all my willpower not to begin playing the notes in the air.

When I opened my eyes again, Myron was watching me even more closely than before, his eyes narrowed with curiosity. I bowed my head with a stab of embarrassment, and I walked over to the model's chair in the middle of the studio and sat down, my knees squeezed together awkwardly. Myron went and found a second chair and dragged it over in front of mine. He flipped it around and sat with his forearms on the back of the chair. We were only inches apart.

"What exactly do you want from me, Hallie Evers?"

"Tell me about Elijah," I said.

"I already told you. Elijah didn't kill anybody."

"But he was there that night."

Myron shrugged. "So?"

"What did he see?"

The musk of Myron's body drifted between us. "Nothing."

"He didn't see anything at all?" I paused. "Or anyone?"

"Elijah found the body. That's all. Savannah was lying near the cliff, beaten to a pulp with his own golf club. And Tyler Reyes saw him climbing the fence. My brother was no fool. He knew who the police would go after, and he was right. A lot of other people had motives, but the police didn't care."

"Like who?"

Myron shrugged. "Make a list. Tyler, for one."

"Why would Tyler want to harm Savannah?"

"You should talk to him about that, not me."

"Myron, please. If there's something about Tyler, I need to know what it is."

He exhaled, and his breath was like a breeze in my face. "Savannah knew a secret about him. Tyler was starting his company back then, and Andrew's father was going to be a big investor. You know who Andrew's daddy is?"

"I know his name is John David Edam, but that's all."

"Uh-huh. JDE's a judge on the First Circuit Court of Appeals. Except he was also up for a seat on the Supreme Court back then. Savannah heard Tyler mouthing off at the country club about a Halloween party where he saw Andrew's daddy in blackface. Somebody heard that story, passed it on to the press. The nomination got tanked. You think ol' JDE would still have plowed a few million into Tyler's company if he knew that Tyler was the one who'd sunk his chances for the court?"

"How did you hear about this?" I asked.

"Elijah worked at the club. He heard Savannah and Tyler arguing about it. She was threatening to tell Andrew."

191

"Did she?"

"Something got in the way before she did. Namely, a golf club to her head."

"Well, did you tell the police about it?"

Myron gave me a look that said I was a fool. "Sure. And how was I going to prove it if I did? You think they'd believe me? As far as they were concerned, anything I said was bullshit from a black kid trying to clear his brother."

I didn't know what to say. I just shook my head.

"Anyway, he wasn't the only one with a motive," Myron went on. "I told you, make a list."

"Who else?"

"There was Andrew Edam, too. He acts like he's always cool, always in control, but that guy has a roaring temper. When he snaps, you don't want to see it. He didn't like how close Elijah was to Savannah during one of their golf lessons, and he flipped out. Punched my brother in the jaw. Which was nuts, because Elijah could have leveled him, but Elijah kept his anger on a leash."

"Before she was killed, Savannah broke off her engagement with Andrew," I murmured.

"I know. That must have made Andy mad."

I leaned forward. "Wait, how do you know that? How do you know they broke up? Elijah wasn't there."

His full lips pushed together in a smile. "Neither were you."

"I—I talked to Andrew," I lied. "He told me."

"That's not very likely, Hallie Evers. I don't see Andrew admitting something like that. Seems like the only person who could have told you is the person who told me. But I don't see how that's possible."

"Skye told you," I said.

"That's right."

I went on softly. "What about Skye? Did *she* have a motive?"

"If you dig deep enough, everybody has a motive. What does it matter now? They're both dead."

"Tell me."

"Skye was in love," Myron said with a sigh. "And not with Tyler Reyes, either. If Savannah found out, she would have moved heaven and earth to make sure Skye stayed away from him."

"Who was it? Was it Andrew?"

"I told you, it doesn't matter anymore. You should let it go."

"Myron, who was it?" Then my eyes widened, and in my head, I saw hands covering mine on a golf club. "Oh, my God, it was *Elijah*. Skye was sleeping with your brother. She was going to run away with him, and Savannah tried to stop it. Was that what happened? Did they fight about it?"

Myron had a look of torture on his face. "You're wrong. It wasn't him."

"Then who?"

Confusion filled my face, but in the next instant, I knew. I knew because of what I felt in my own body, because of my desire for this man. It wasn't just my attraction that made it so strong. It was Skye's, too.

"*You*," I whispered. "Jesus! Skye was in love with *you*."

He didn't need to tell me I was right.

Without warning, he leaned across the chair, closing the distance between our faces. His lips met mine, softly and sensuously, moving them apart. My mouth responded to him hungrily. I reached out and ran my hands through his hair, and then I slid my fingertips down to his neck. I knew what he liked; I knew what he wanted. As we kissed, I played the piano gently on his skin.

Myron jerked away as he felt my touch. "Holy shit."

"I don't—"

"What did they do to you?" he hissed before I could say anything more.

"Who?"

"You know who. Tyler Reyes and Andrew Edam. What did they do to you, Hallie Evers? Do you think I can't tell? *You're Skye.*"

◆ ◆ ◆

We sat next to each other on the studio floor, our backs against the wall. Myron cracked the window, letting in the fishy, briny sea breeze and the noise of seagulls. He'd opened two bottles of Sam Adams Summer Ale, and we swigged them in unison. Our bodies were close enough that our hips were touching. He hadn't kissed me again, although a part of me wished he would. He didn't seem to want to look at me now, and I felt a new coolness in his manner.

I'd told him everything that had happened. To my surprise, he believed me. Skye had already told him what she'd done in Andrew's lab, so Myron had no trouble accepting that Skye's memories were in my head. But the revelation made it awkward between us. Now I was this half stranger, half lover, and neither of us knew how to deal with the other. We simply stared into the gloom of the studio as we drank our beer.

"Did Elijah see Skye at the cliff?" I asked him finally, my voice low and calm.

Myron looked at me. "Don't you remember?"

"Not that part. I don't remember Elijah, but I remember being there. I remember seeing Savannah's body, but not what actually happened to her."

Myron waited awhile to say anything. He kept drinking his beer. "Elijah told me he found you—I mean, he found *Skye*—standing over Savannah near the cliff. Skye was holding the golf club, and her hands were covered with blood. When Elijah came up to her, she gave him this empty look, like she didn't know what was going on. Then she said, 'It was me.'"

194

I heard those words in my head, too. *It was me.*

"So she did it?" I concluded.

"Maybe. I don't know. Elijah thought so. Skye said she couldn't remember. It was like she'd gone into some kind of fugue. She woke up on the grass, and there was Savannah, and there was the golf club. That was all she knew."

"She didn't remember anything that went on between them?"

"Not a thing."

"But why was Skye even out there?"

"The last thing she remembered was seeing Savannah and Andrew arguing in the ballroom. Savannah broke up with him and stormed out in a rage. Skye followed her to the cliff to try to talk to her. And then—well, she woke up, and her sister was dead. Not long after, Elijah found her there. Skye told him to get away from her, to run. She took the golf club with her."

"What did she do with it?" I asked.

"I don't know. She buried it somewhere. Elijah was just as happy to have it disappear. It was his club, so his fingerprints would have been on it. Not that it mattered in the end."

"Where were you?"

"In Elijah's apartment," he said. "Skye and I were planning to leave Newport in a few days. We were going to run away together. Instead, Elijah came back in the middle of the night and told me what had happened. He said the police would pin it on him, and he was right."

"But he had a witness. Skye saw him."

Myron's face darkened. "And he saw Skye."

I struggled with what he was saying, but then I understood. "He didn't want to implicate her, because you were in love with her."

"Yeah."

"But Skye said nothing? She let the police go after him?"

"I tried to talk to her, but she was holed up in her bedroom. She was out of touch for a whole day. I didn't see her. Nobody did. She told me later she didn't even know what was going on. She had no idea the police were focused on Elijah. And by the time she did, he was already dead."

I shook my head. "I'm so sorry."

He looked at me as if he was wondering who was apologizing. Me or Skye. "We split up after that. I blamed her for what happened to my brother. Honestly, she blamed herself, too. There was no future for us at that point. I didn't see her again for years. I had my world, and she had hers. It was probably naive to think we could ever have been together."

"She married Tyler," I said. "Why? She didn't love him."

"Maybe she was punishing herself. Or doing what she thought the world expected of her. She threw herself into music, too, like that was some kind of salvation for her. I read about her in the papers, people talking about what a star she was becoming. Every time she performed with the BSO, I got a ticket in the balcony so I could see her. But I never went backstage. I figured she didn't need me in her life."

"What about last year?" I asked. "What happened?"

Myron finished his bottle of beer, and he pushed himself off the floor. So did I. He went to the center of the studio, and he sat down in the model's chair himself, as if he were the one on display. "That report came out in the press last summer. Elijah's case turned up in the headlines again. Everyone was talking about it. If I'd known it would blow up the way it did, I never would have talked to that girl Whitney. I would have kept my mouth shut."

"Why?"

"Because no good comes of digging up skeletons," he snapped. "And I was right. Only bad shit came out of that."

"Skye came to see you?"

He nodded. "About a month later. She walked in that door just like you did—no call, no warning. She'd been out of my life for almost ten years, and suddenly there she was. She wasn't young anymore, not like we were then, but she was even more beautiful than I remembered. More mature. Deeper, too. She'd always been deep. But she was full of pain now."

"What did she say?"

"She was desperate to know what really happened that night. All that time had passed in between, and nothing had come back to her. She still didn't remember. It was driving her crazy."

"Had she done the experiment at Andrew's lab? Backing up her memories?"

Myron scowled. "No. She was thinking about it, though. I told her *not* to do it. I thought it was a bad idea. I didn't trust Andrew and Tyler, and I didn't like them playing with her head like that. But she thought it might open up something for her. Bring back whatever was hidden."

I sat down in the chair near him. "What about the two of you?"

"We were together again, at least for a while. It was like no time had passed. We were lovers—we were *in* love—just like that summer in Newport. But I knew it wouldn't last. She told me she was finally ready to get out of her marriage, but I never believed we'd be together after her divorce. There was just too much darkness in Skye for her to ever be happy. She kept running from it, but I guess she couldn't run fast enough."

He reached out to caress my face, and his touch made me melt. When he stared at me, I knew he was looking for Skye behind my eyes. I didn't know what came next between us. Would we kiss again? Would he lay me on the floor? If he did, I wouldn't say no. But after a poignant moment with our faces inches apart, he pushed the chair back and stood up. I checked my watch and realized I was late for my dinner with Paul Temple.

"I need to go," I said quietly.

"Yeah. You should go."

I turned toward the studio door, but he called after me.

"Hey, mind if I give you a little bit of advice, Hallie Evers?"

"Go ahead." I looked back at him and waited.

"Whatever happened out on that cliff, there's a reason Skye blocked it out," Myron said. "In the end, it killed her. Think about that, okay? I told you, no good comes from digging up skeletons."

26

The maître d' led me to the best table in the house, which was what I expected from Paul Temple. Blu was located on the fourth floor of the Equinox building, and the walls and ceiling of the restaurant were all made of glass. Outside, the lights of the downtown buildings glowed like thousands of small fires.

Temple was waiting for me when I got there. As I arrived at the window table, he stood up. I offered to shake his hand, but he leaned in slightly and kissed it instead. He had a very European way about him, which made sense, because he'd been born in Amsterdam before joining the venture capital crowd in New York. When he spoke, his voice still had the faint echo of a Dutch accent.

"Ms. Evers, what a pleasure. I'm so glad you decided to join me."

I sat down, and a waiter appeared out of nowhere to drape my napkin over my lap. The dim light above our heads gave the table a blue glow. Temple had opened a bottle of Silver Oak cabernet, and a full glass was already poured in front of me. He lifted his own glass, and we toasted with a clink.

"You definitely have me curious," I said. Then I pushed his $10,000 gift card across the table. "But you can keep your money, Mr. Temple."

One of his gray eyebrows arched. "Are you sure? I meant it when I said it was a gift. No strings attached."

He said it in a way that suggested he knew I didn't have tons of money in the bank, and $10,000 would go a long way toward keeping me solvent. So no, I wasn't sure at all about turning it down, but I also didn't trust him. At that moment in my life, I didn't trust anyone.

"I'm sure," I reiterated. "Keep it."

"As you wish."

Temple glanced out the window, admiring the view. He wasn't a big man, but he had presence, starting with his trim-fitted black suit. He was well into his sixties, with a poufy crown of curly white hair swept back over his forehead that made me think of a British barrister's wig. His face had sharp angles, including a square chin and a long, narrow nose that ended in a bulb. His skin was deeply lined and had a few splotchy blemishes. His pale eyes glittered behind oddly hairless eyelids.

"I took the liberty of ordering us the tapas platter," he went on with a take-charge confidence. "Also the diver scallops, which are amazing. I hope you're not allergic to shellfish, Ms. Evers."

"They sound delicious," I said. "And you can call me Hallie, by the way."

"Hallie. I like that name."

He didn't extend an offer for me to call him Paul, so I decided he was still Mr. Temple.

"I could spend time beating around the bush, but I don't want to waste your time nor mine," he went on. "Fair enough?"

"I prefer it that way."

"Excellent. All right, Hallie, let's be clear. I know something quite extraordinary happened to you in Las Vegas."

There was no point in denying it.

"Yes, that's true. But I'm curious, Mr. Temple, how *you* know that."

He smiled with only his lips, and he took a measured sip of cabernet. "I hope you won't think I'm being arrogant if I assume that you know who I am and what my company does."

"Yes, I do."

"Good. Then you know that the key to my investment success is the depth of intelligence I gather within the medical device community. It's fair to say that I'm familiar with the status of essentially all promising research projects throughout the industry. That includes the work being done by Tyler Reyes and Andrew Edam at Hyppolex and MIT. I've been keeping a close eye on their partnership for several years. I'm familiar with the kind of brain research they're pursuing."

He paused as the waiter reappeared at our table with an appetizer platter. Among the items were two neatly trimmed lamb chops in what appeared to be a pomegranate sauce. Temple took one of the chops, then used his knife and fork to cut a dainty bite for himself. I decided to be uncouth, so I took the other chop by the bone and ate it in two mouthfuls.

"No offense," I said, "but keeping tabs on their research doesn't explain how you know what happened to *me*."

His gray eyes shone. "Very true. Well, this isn't the kind of thing we typically say out loud, but corporate intelligence gathering often involves techniques that some may consider morally questionable."

"Spying," I concluded.

This time he laughed. "All right. Yes. I spy on companies, and I don't apologize for doing so. For example, we typically hire a contingent of people at conventions like MedX to do nothing but ride the elevators and hang out by the bars and pools to listen to conversations. Scientists are often terribly indiscreet in public. They don't think about who may be listening. We vacuum up quite a bit of useful intelligence that way. There's nothing illegal about it, although some might say it's not entirely ethical."

"And what about me?"

"Well, in fact, I was at the party myself on the rooftop that night. We sponsored it, as you'll recall. I saw what happened to you, and I saw Andrew Edam save your life. Good for him. However, not long after, my spies told me that something else rather amazing had also taken place."

I wondered if he was bluffing. I'd never been much of a poker player, but it occurred to me that he might *suspect* what had happened without actually knowing, and he was hoping I'd supply the details.

"What exactly do you think that was, Mr. Temple?" I asked.

Temple glanced at a man sitting at another restaurant table not far from us, and I saw a look pass between them.

"That's my chauffeur, Derek, over there," he explained. "Derek maintains a constant sweep for listening devices wherever I go. Just as I spy on other people, other people try to spy on me. I expect it. That's how the game is played. However, we're safe for now, so I can confirm what you already know. Andrew restored someone else's brain patterns—their stored memories—into your head. This is technology he's been working on for years—well, he and dozens of researchers at various companies and government facilities around the world. But obviously, Hyppolex has made a significant leap forward. Do I pass the test, Hallie?"

I shrugged. "You do."

"Since you're in Boston, I imagine Andrew and Tyler have admitted what they did to you," he went on. "I suppose they said it was an accident, too. Let me guess . . . Andrew grabbed the wrong phone or something like that."

I was surprised—but somehow not surprised—that Temple knew as much detail as he did. "You're right."

"Do you believe him?"

"No."

"You're smart. This wasn't an accident."

"How can you be sure?"

"My sources are confidential. However, I can tell you he admitted it."

"What did you do, bug his hotel room?" Then I added with a frown, "Did you bug mine? Were you watching me?"

Again Temple said nothing. I shook my head, because I was tired of feeling like a pawn in these industry games. "Let's fast-forward, okay? Is this where you finally tell me what you want?"

Temple appeared to be in no rush. "Well, let's enjoy our scallops first, shall we? We have plenty of time, but they won't wait."

So we did. They were as good as he'd promised. We finished the bottle of wine between us, and along the way, Temple asked a lot of questions about my life, my background, my career, my mother, and my physical health. As I'd expected, he was very well informed about me. He didn't have to check my wrist to know of my earlier suicide attempt, and he was suitably empathetic about my mother's schizophrenia. If I'd been stretched out on a couch, he could have been a shrink like Tori.

By the time we were enjoying bomboloni cups for dessert, he finally got to the point of the meeting.

"Hallie, you must realize by now that you have a uniquely valuable scientific resource inside your head."

"Andrew and Tyler said the same thing," I replied.

"No doubt. I'm sure they want to gather as much detail about the transfer as they can to assist in the next stages of their research. Particularly because—as I'm led to believe—the restore process was even more successful than they anticipated."

"So?"

"So I'm proposing you work with me instead of them."

"Why would I do that?"

"Many reasons," Temple replied. "But mainly because Hyppolex hasn't given you any reason to trust them. They subjected you to an invasive experiment without your consent or knowledge. They put your mental health in jeopardy, not knowing the potential outcomes of the procedure."

"Why should I trust you more than Andrew or Tyler?" I asked.

"You shouldn't. You should look after your own interests. In this case, start with your financial interests. I can outbid whatever Tyler Reyes wants to put in front of you. Plus, I can help you find lawyers to sue them on top of whatever my company will pay you. You will be a staggeringly wealthy woman, Hallie. And in return, I'd simply ask you to work with a couple of respectable research companies within my investment portfolio over the next few years."

"To examine what's going on in my brain?"

"Precisely."

I eased back in my chair and thought about it. He was right that I owed nothing to Andrew and Tyler, not after what they'd done to me. I admit I was also tempted by the money. It would give me a freedom in my life that I'd never had before. I wasn't ready to say yes to his offer, but I saw no reason to give him a hard no, either. Besides, he was a very charming man and hard to dislike.

Temple could see that he'd piqued my interest. "How about an after-dinner liqueur, Hallie?"

I smiled. "Why not?"

An hour later, when we were done with dinner, we left the Equinox building onto Avery Street. It was nearly midnight, with spitting rain in the air. Temple slipped a Burberry raincoat over his suit, and like a gentleman, he handed me his large umbrella. His chauffeur, Derek, hurried ahead of us to retrieve Temple's car, and the two of us strolled toward Boston Common a block away. At that hour, no one else was around on the narrow street. The drizzle awakened the city's dank smell.

In my heels, I was as tall as Temple was. Our shoes tapped loudly on the pavement. We reached Tremont, where there was a little more late-night traffic. On the other side of the street, the trees of the Common made silhouettes against the moonlit sky. Dampness from the rain shone in Temple's white hair.

"It was a pleasure talking to you, Hallie," he told me.

"I enjoyed it, too."

"Are you sure I can't change your mind about that gift card? Boston is a wonderful shopping town. Call it a down payment on our relationship."

"Thank you, but no."

"Very well. I appreciate your integrity."

From the north end of the one-way street, a sleek black town car slid smoothly to the curb beside us. I could see Derek behind the wheel, and he didn't even need to get out of the car. The rear door clicked open on its own.

"Think about my offer, Hallie," Temple said as he took hold of the door.

"I will."

"Can I drop you at your hotel?"

"No, it's only a few blocks. I think I'd like to walk."

I prepared to hand him back the umbrella, but he shook his head. "Keep it, my dear. I don't want you getting wet."

He smiled and turned toward the car.

Then all hell broke loose.

That moment on the street slowed down until it froze like ice in my memory. There was Paul Temple, standing by the limousine, stooping slightly to climb into the back seat. And there I was with the umbrella in my hand, rain dripping from its spokes.

In the next instant, Temple's head exploded. His forehead turned into a pink mass of blood and brain, and a loud crack rolled over me like thunder. Still smiling, but already dead, Temple pitched over and landed on my feet. My mouth opened, but I was too stunned to scream. I willed myself to move, but I simply stood where I was, lost in shocked disbelief.

I stared past the limousine door. There was a man standing on the sidewalk not even ten feet away. I *knew* him.

It was the man with the long blond hair from Las Vegas. The man who'd chased me down an alley and tried to stab me with a lethal hypodermic. He pointed his gun directly at me to fire again, but the driver's door of the limo flew open at the same moment, and the bullet pinged off the metal, sizzling by my head and ripping the umbrella out of my hands.

Breaking from my trance, I ran into the street. My heels slipped on the wet pavement, and I kicked them off. Cars barreling down Tremont squealed and swerved, barely missing me as I ran barefoot into the park. I glanced over my shoulder and saw the shooter weaving around the vehicles to follow me. Inside the Common, I sprinted through wet grass, zigzagging around the tree trunks. Two more shots exploded close to me, and I ducked, fell, got up, and ran again. He wasn't far behind me. The trees thinned, and I found myself on a swath of open lawn, easily tagged by moonlight. The noise of the rain and of my panicked breathing roared in my head. Another shot blew past my ear, so close that I was sure that I'd been hit, but I kept running.

Ahead of me was the fence at the border of the park and the traffic of Charles Street. I had no idea where to go next, but then I saw a car—a Ferrari convertible—squeal to a stop outside the gates.

It was Andrew Edam.

He shouted at me as he threw open the door. "Hallie, quick, get in!"

I took a look backward, hesitated only for a second, and then bolted through the gates of the park. I dived into the car, banging my head against the dashboard. The tires shrieked as Andrew accelerated, and the Ferrari leaped forward, the passenger door still hanging open as we peeled away.

One last shot echoed over our heads, and then we were gone.

27

Andrew kept the lights off in his house.

He owned a two-story redbrick home in a quiet area of West Cambridge. In the living room, he stood by the front windows, looking out at the neighborhood. He hadn't said anything since he'd pulled the Ferrari into the garage and led me inside. Instead, he kept a calm surveillance of the street, as if there were threats hiding in the suburban shadows.

Meanwhile, I was falling apart.

I paced frantically in the darkness, unable to stay still. My whole body trembled. I was wet and cold and dirty, and there was blood on my face and feet, and every time I closed my eyes, I could see Paul Temple's forehead erupting like lava from a volcano. The memory of it made me hyperventilate, my breathing so fast and deep I couldn't get air into my lungs. I finally stopped where I was, gasping.

Andrew noticed my distress. He came from the window and took hold of my hands and cupped them in front of my mouth. "Here, breathe into your hands. Do it slowly. When you inhale, hold it for a few seconds, and then let it out a little bit at a time."

I did.

After a while, I calmed enough to collapse into an armchair near the fireplace. The room was unlit, but I could make out the shapes of heavy furniture and oil paintings hung on the walls.

"They killed him," I managed to say.

"I know."

"They tried to kill me."

"Yes, I'm sorry."

"The police. We need to call the police."

Andrew returned to the window and kept his vigil on the street. "We will. Tomorrow. We'll see the police in the morning. First I need to talk to Tyler and consult with our lawyers."

My emotions boiled over, and I lost it.

"Your lawyers!" I screeched, my voice sounding loud in the quiet house. "Are you kidding? Call the police *now*! This is about *me*, not you, not Tyler, not Hyppolex. Do you not understand that? Do you not realize that I watched Paul Temple get shot to death right in front of me? Because of something *you* did to me? What part of that isn't sinking into your scientist's head?"

He remained on the other side of the room by the bay windows. His face looked emotionless, the way it always did. "Hallie, I know you're upset, and you have every reason to be."

"Upset? You think I'm upset? I am going—out—of—my—mind!"

"I understand that. I do."

I shook my head, then practically spat at him. "You don't have a clue."

"What you've gone through is horrific. I take full responsibility for that, and I want to help in any way I can."

"You can start by telling me the truth," I said.

"Name it. What do you want to know?"

"Did you have Paul Temple killed?"

His outraged voice burst from the darkness. "No! Of course not!"

"Really? You can rape me with your mind games, but murder is a bridge too far? Suddenly there are lines you won't cross?"

"Believe what you want, Hallie, but I didn't kill Paul."

"You were following me," I snapped. "It's not an accident that you showed up at the park."

He shrugged. "Yes, of course I was following you. For obvious reasons—I thought you were in danger, and I was right. That's why Tyler and I wanted you to stay out of the city."

"So who killed Temple? Who's trying to kill *me*?"

"I don't know. I told you, there are other companies pursuing very similar research regarding memory backup and restoration. The intellectual property rewards of getting there first are incalculable. Whoever it is may think that removing you would slow down our work and give them more time to dominate the space."

"How do they know where I am? How did they find out about me at all? Paul Temple knew what you did to me. He knew all about your brain research."

Andrew shook his head firmly. "Wherever I go, I screen for tracking devices. My hotel room in Las Vegas was clean. I don't see how Paul could possibly have known what happened."

"He said he's been spying on you for years. He also says you admitted that you knew what you were doing that night. It was deliberate."

Andrew's face twisted with concern. "He said that? He said I admitted it?"

"That's right. Is it true?"

He went to a sofa near the window and sat down. His face was in shadow. "Okay, yes, it's true. I chose to use Skye's memories when I revived you. I've been working on the transfer process for years, running tests in the lab. I knew what I was doing."

"Jesus. *Why?*"

He hesitated, as if he had to pick an answer he thought I'd believe. "Sometimes the urge to play God is too much for a scientist to resist. It was a grievous ethical lapse, and I regretted it the moment I did it."

Andrew went to a wet bar and poured himself a shot of whiskey. For the first time, he looked unsettled. "Look, Hallie, I never anticipated the consequences of this would go so far. That people would die over what I did. You're right, we need to talk to the police, and we *will*. But you're in no condition to do that now. You need rest. In the morning, we'll sort everything out."

"What about you? What are you going to do?"

"I need to get some questions answered," he replied.

"How? What questions?"

"I'll tell you about it tomorrow. I promise."

"Jesus, I'm so tired of you stringing me along. Giving me half truths."

"Hallie, I can't tell you what I don't know. When I learn more, I'll tell you everything. For now, go upstairs and sleep for a while. That's the best thing for you."

I got out of the armchair. Yes, I was tired, but I didn't think I would sleep. I was too wired. Too strung out. I stood in front of Andrew, who was little more than a ghost in the dark room.

"I talked to Myron Glass."

"Who?"

"Elijah's brother."

Andrew's face tightened as he sipped his whiskey. "Why talk to him?"

"To learn more about Savannah's death."

"Why does that matter to you?"

"Because it mattered to Skye. Because she won't be at peace until she knows the truth, and that means neither will I. Skye saw you and Savannah that night. She saw the argument. I saw it, too. So I know Savannah called off the wedding."

Andrew stared at me in the gloom. His personal conflict did battle with his scientist's excitement. "You can isolate a specific memory like that? With that level of detail? That's incredible."

"The point is, I remember it. Savannah accused you of sleeping with Skye."

"I wasn't."

"Maybe not, but she didn't believe you. She said the two of you were done."

"Yes, okay, Savannah broke it off. I don't see what difference it makes now."

"What did you do after that?" I asked.

"What are you suggesting?"

"You were angry. Did you follow her? Did you go out to the cliff?"

He exhaled in frustration. "You mean, was it me? Did I kill her? No, I didn't. I was devastated by her death. Savannah's murder nearly destroyed me. Think what you want about the kind of man I am, but I really did love her."

The darkness of his eyes betrayed everything he was feeling. Loss. Remorse. Doubt. Guilt. Maybe love, too, or whatever this man thought love was. Seeing those emotions, I realized he was being truthful about one thing.

He hadn't killed Savannah.

And then I understood the rest.

"Oh, my God," I exclaimed. "*That's* why you did it."

"What are you talking about?"

"That's why you put Skye's memories inside me. You risked everything, your whole career, your whole life, and it wasn't for science or for research. You wanted the truth, too. You wanted to know what really happened to Savannah. With Skye dead, your only hope of finding out was that *I'd* remember."

Andrew drained his whiskey and poured more. His voice was tired, and he no longer sounded like the king of the world. "We'll talk about it in the morning, Hallie. There's a lot to talk about."

Upstairs, I stripped off my clothes and took a scalding-hot shower. It didn't relax me. With my face tilted under the spray, a tidal wave of memories surged over me from the two lives I was leading. From tonight, watching Paul Temple die in front of me. From ten years ago by the cliff, with Savannah dead at Skye's feet. From fourteen years ago in that gloomy Las Vegas house, with my body under the water and my open wrist draining into the bathtub.

From that day when I was ten years old and I walked down that long horrible hallway and put my hand on the doorknob to go inside my mother's bedroom. The door that refused to open and show me what came next.

I could hear Skye asking me the question. The same question every shrink had been asking me ever since.

"What did you see, Hallie?"

But I couldn't answer her. All I could feel around me was blood and death.

Shivering, I got out of the shower. I'd left the lights off in the bathroom, but the window gave a glow from the street outside. In the mirror fronting the medicine cabinet, I stared at my naked torso, skinny and bony as a wet cat. An old instinct of self-harm overwhelmed me. I bent down to the toilet and sank to my knees. I leaned forward over the bowl, my finger trembling as I shoved it in my mouth. I needed to feel the acid burning my throat. That was my punishment. That had always been my punishment. Instead, I yanked my finger out and curled my hand into a fist and beat it hard against my forehead.

Purging wouldn't help me. This night was deeper and darker than that.

I stood up again. Tears streamed down my face. A headache pounded in my brain like a drum, driving away everything except Skye. She was right there with me, like a friend, but I couldn't handle her guilt and mine at the same time. I couldn't deal with the secrets we both kept.

The blood on both our hands.

My face stared back at me in the mirror.

I had a way out. An escape. It was the way I'd tried twice before.

I ripped open the bathroom cabinet. On the shelves inside, I pawed through bottles of mouthwash, and tubes of toothpaste, and cough medicine, and antacid, until I found what I wanted. A prescription bottle made out in the name of Cara Edam, Andrew's wife.

Trazodone. Dozens of little white pills. With those I could finally sleep, and I would have no more dreams.

I opened the bottle and poured the entire contents into my hand, some of them overflowing and falling into the sink. As I tried to hold them, my fingers quivered, and more fell. I opened my mouth wide. With my palm cupped around that little mountain of pills, I lifted my hand and shoved them all inside until I was gagging because there were so many.

My mouth closed.

I could feel them on my tongue, stuffed between my cheeks, beginning to melt at the warm moisture inside me.

Then I choked and spat them all into the sink. I turned on the faucet high and rinsed out my mouth until the sour taste was gone. The pills turned to paste and then to liquid and disappeared down the drain. My hands clutched the marble sides of the sink, my arms barely holding me up. My wet hair fell down my face.

Slowly, I closed the cabinet door.

I couldn't do it. She wouldn't let me go. In some strange way, she was there to save me. The mirror glass shone darkly, and just for a moment, the reflection staring back was not my own.

It was Skye's face I saw.

28

A noise awakened me in the middle of the night. The sound was a muffled crack, not far away. Or had I dreamed it?

I'd heard other noises as I drifted toward sleep. An angry, bitter voice downstairs. A shout, one half of a raging argument. It was Andrew talking on the phone. But was any of that real?

My mind tried to catch up with where I was. I had no recollection of putting on one of Cara's T-shirts or of slipping into a queen-size featherbed in Andrew's guest room. But when my eyes opened, I lay between soft sheets that smelled faintly of lavender. The house was still dark, almost pitch black. A clock's pale glow told me it was two in the morning. I threw the blankets back and felt a chill from somewhere, as if a door in the house was open to the night air.

Or was it fear making me cold?

Something was wrong. I knew something was wrong.

I slipped out of bed. When my bare feet landed on the hardwood floor, the beams creaked. I tried to walk softly, but it was an old house, its timbers giving me away with each step. I went to the bedroom door, which was closed, and opened it a crack. The hinges squealed. Outside in the hallway, I couldn't see anything, so I held my breath, listening.

Was someone there?

Was someone waiting to see what I would do?

I thought about calling Andrew's name, but I didn't want to make a sound. When my eyes adjusted to the darkness, I spotted the stairs to my right leading to the ground floor. There was an open bedroom door at the far end of the hallway. As quietly as I could, I tiptoed to that room, which was the master bedroom. I could see that the bed hadn't been used. Andrew hadn't come up here during the night. I went to the window and looked out at a wooded rear yard, which glowed with the blue light of a swimming pool. No one was there.

A footstep landed on the stairs, but the noise stopped quickly, as if whoever it was had paused to see if I'd heard them. I told myself it was Andrew. He was finally coming to bed, and he was trying to stay quiet to make sure he didn't wake me up. But I didn't believe that. Nothing about this felt right. My senses screamed at me that I was in danger again.

Another footstep.

Sweat gathered on my skin despite the chill. I skidded to the window and opened it silently. Cool wind flooded against me, and the whole house groaned with the change in air pressure. I leaned outside. A mature oak tree spread one of its thick limbs my way. I could probably make it to the tree without the branch breaking under me. Probably. I thought about jumping to the water of the pool below, but it was set back far enough that I didn't think I could make it.

Another footstep.

The person was taking his time on the stairs. He knew I was up here, and he was listening to see if he could figure out exactly where I was.

I stood frozen with indecision and terror. *Hide!* But where?

Next to the bed—this was Cara's side, based on the lotions and perfumes arranged on the nightstand—I saw a pair of slippers. I grabbed one and threw it out the window, aiming for the section of lawn between the tree trunk and the pool. It thumped to the ground, looking like a shoe that had been lost by someone running away. Then I grabbed a perfume bottle and tossed it toward the ribbon of concrete skirting the water. It smashed on the stone and glinted in tiny shards under the yard lights.

I heard footsteps accelerating. Whoever it was had heard the crash of glass. Instantly, I dropped to the floor and slithered under the bed. A few seconds later, the bedroom door slammed open on its hinges. The floorboards sagged as a man entered the room. I tried to hold my breath, which was almost impossible because of the beating of my heart. I needed air. When a gust of wind whistled through the room, I took the chance of silently exhaling and inhaling.

From under the bed, I could see the cuffs of jeans and dirty black boots, with camouflage laces. The man went to the window, looked out, and muttered a curse. He stood there for a long time, listening for someone running away, or climbing a fence, or screaming for help, and of course there was nothing like that. Then he turned around to study the bedroom. I didn't think I'd fooled him. When I stole another breath, I was sure he could hear me. Or he could smell my sweat.

The boots went to the bedroom door and closed it. Smart—that would slow me down if I ran.

"Hallie," he called. "Make this easy on yourself. Come on out, and let's talk. I won't hurt you."

A lie.

He was going to kill me.

The man began a methodical search. He went to the bathroom first, and while he was in there, I thought about scrambling out and taking my chances, but before I could move, he'd already returned to the bedroom. Next he checked the walk-in closet. I could still see his boots as he did that, and I had no chance to get away. When he came out of the closet, I knew he'd squat down to stare under the bed, and his eyes would meet mine. He'd pull me out. I'd be dead.

Then I heard something. The man heard it, too, because he left the closet and ran back to the open window. The sound of police sirens floated in on the wind, getting closer and louder.

Another loud curse.

The man gave up the hunt for me. His boots thudded to the bedroom door. He tore it open, and I heard his footsteps pounding back to the ground floor. He must have gone out the back, because a few seconds later, I heard boots slapping on concrete in the rear yard. He was running away.

I slipped out from under the bed and checked the window. In the next yard, I heard the gruff bark of a dog. Lights began to come on in the neighboring houses. The sirens couldn't be more than a couple of blocks away now. They seemed to be approaching from multiple directions.

Get out of here!

That was the only thought that made its way into my head. I panicked, trying to decide what to do. I was in a T-shirt with no pants; you can't escape with no pants. I grabbed jeans and shoes from Cara's side of the closet. There was no time to put them on. Instead, I ran down the stairs to the foyer.

The first thing I saw was the front door, wide open.

The next thing I saw was two police cars wheeling to a stop on the street directly in front of the house, and men getting out with guns in their hands.

The last thing I saw was Andrew Edam.

He lay on his back near the front door, his eyes open and lifeless, a bullet hole in the center of his forehead and blood running down his cheek onto the floor.

When I saw the body at my feet, my brain spun around. Then I was falling, falling, falling, speeding up as gravity took me down, like a woman throwing herself from a cliff.

PART III

29

I sat in the middle chair at the table in the police conference room. I was dressed in Cara's clothes. Tyler sat on my left, and the lawyer from Hyppolex's outside law firm sat on my right. She was in her fifties and had layered chestnut hair and wore a white blouse and gray skirt. Her eyes were steely and pale. She'd introduced herself as Susan, and I got the distinct impression that one did not mess with Susan.

The Cambridge detective on the other side of the table had apparently read too many Dennis Lehane novels. An unlit cigarette dripped from his mouth, and he periodically took it out and rolled it between his fingers. He wore a battered leather jacket over a blue button-down shirt that had grease stains on it. His face had the look of someone who'd taken too many punches in the gym, and his gray hair had mostly retreated to the back of his head.

He'd read me my rights. I didn't like the sound of that. But Susan the lawyer had told me that I was in no danger and to check with her before answering any of the detective's questions. I wasn't thrilled about putting my fate in the hands of the people who'd already messed with my head, but I'd also witnessed three murders in two cities over the past couple of weeks. As a rule, police detectives don't like that, so I was glad to have a lawyer with me.

"Hallie," the detective said, not bothering with the more respectful "Ms. Evers" approach. His name was Withers, no first name provided. "Gotta tell ya, Hallie, it seems like you're not having a really good summer."

"You could say that."

"I know about the shit in Las Vegas," he went on, the cigarette bobbing in his mouth as he talked. "So don't try to hide that. My Boston colleagues talked to Paul Temple's chauffeur. He had a lot to say about you, including the fact that you were part of a murder investigation in Vegas just last week. So I had a conversation with a Detective Angel out there."

Susan interrupted before I could reply. "If you talked to the police in Las Vegas, then you know that Ms. Evers was the *target* of an attempted murder and was interviewed by the police solely as a witness. Also, since the Boston police have a statement from Mr. Temple's chauffeur, I'm sure you know that Ms. Evers was a target and not the perpetrator with regard to Mr. Temple's death. The same thing is true here in Cambridge. There was no murder weapon found at the scene, and you tested Ms. Evers for gunshot residue, did you not? I'm sure the test showed that she did not fire the gun that killed Dr. Edam. She is completely innocent of any crime."

"She left the scene of a murder in Boston," Detective Withers pointed out.

"I was being chased by the killer!" I snapped, before Susan reached out and covered my hand, with a look that said, *Shut up*.

I did.

"Ms. Evers had every intention of contacting the police once she was safe, and she intended to offer her full cooperation," the lawyer went on. "After Dr. Edam rescued her, she was frightened and exhausted, and she was in no condition to tell you anything. Dr. Edam called me immediately, and I told him that I would accompany him and Ms. Evers to the Boston police first thing this morning in order to make a statement. Unfortunately, the killer struck again before we could do so. That's why we're here."

"Well, Dr. Edam might be alive if you'd called the police sooner," the detective commented.

"Dr. Edam was a friend and colleague," Susan reminded him angrily. "We are devastated by his death. We want to see his killer brought to justice, but the evidence is clear that Ms. Evers had nothing to do with this homicide or any of the others. I'd appreciate your acknowledging that fact, Detective."

He sighed loudly. "I haven't accused Hallie of killing anybody, Counselor, so how about you calm down? On the other hand, wherever she goes, she seems to drive up the murder rate. I'd like to know why that is and how the Hyppolex Corporation is mixed up in it."

"Hyppolex is not *mixed up* in any murders," Susan retorted.

Withers took his cigarette and tapped it on the table. His eyes shifted to Tyler. "Is that true, Mr. Reyes? Detective Angel said that the murder victim in Las Vegas was a private detective being paid by your company. Now we have a researcher with ties to you and Hyppolex shot to death on his Cambridge doorstep. That happened only a few hours after a man with financial ties to your industry—who'd just had dinner with Hallie here—was gunned down in Boston. That sounds pretty *mixed up* to me, Mr. Reyes, so maybe you can tell me what this is all about."

Tyler didn't take the bait. He simply nodded at Susan.

"If you want answers, address your questions to me, Detective," she reminded him. "And try to remember that Hallie and our colleague Dr. Edam are the victims here."

"Well, what is it about Hallie that people seem to want her dead?"

Susan delivered an answer that I suspected had been vetted at her law firm and rehearsed down to the word. "Ms. Evers is involved in a medical research project at Hyppolex. The proprietary technology at stake is of immense value. It's possible that rogue actors in the industry may believe that harming Ms. Evers would slow down or derail our research and therefore give them time to catch up."

"What the hell research project would be worth killing over?" Withers asked.

"As I said, the technology constitutes proprietary intellectual property. We're unable to disclose any details, and the fact is, the specifics of the project are not relevant to your investigation."

"Not relevant? Three murders, and the research isn't relevant? It sounds like your research is the motive for all of these crimes."

Susan didn't bother with an answer, which made Withers shake his head in frustration. He wasn't going to get more out of her. Instead, he took a photograph from the file folder in front of him, and he pushed it across the table to me. I recognized a blurry image from the alley behind the Las Vegas casino, where the man with the hypodermic had come after me.

"Detective Angel in Las Vegas sent me a copy of security video from the murder scene out there," Withers said. "This is a picture showing one of the men they consider a suspect in the homicide. I gather they think the other suspect is already dead. Do you recognize the scene, Hallie?"

I glanced at Susan, who nodded.

"Yes, I do."

"What about the man in the photo? Do you know him?"

"Well, I know he's the man who's been trying to kill me. Other than that, I have no idea who he is."

"Is this the man who murdered Paul Temple in Boston? Did you see him on the street?"

"Yes, I did. It was definitely him."

"What about Dr. Edam? Did this man shoot him, too?"

"I can't be sure. I was hiding under the bed, so all I saw was the man's legs. He wore black boots and jeans. For all I know, it was the same man, but I didn't see enough to recognize him."

Withers removed another photograph from the folder. This one was in sharp focus—a picture of several men outside a Chinese restaurant that I knew was on Desert Inn Road. Two of the men were Asian, but the others were white. In the background of the picture, I saw a taxi advertising the Cirque show at Bellagio.

"Do you recognize any of these men?" he asked.

I pointed at the man in the middle of the group, who had long blond hair. "That's the same man who tried to kill me. The man who shot Paul Temple."

Susan leaned forward to study the picture, too. "Do you know who this man is, Detective?"

"Yeah, we think his name is Chip Dutton. The Vegas police sent their pic to the feds, and they got a match on facial recognition. The FBI is after him, too. They think Dutton was responsible for the kidnapping and torture of a Chinese dissident who was abducted outside a casino in Primm. The dissident eventually turned up dead in the desert near Barstow, but what they did to him before they dumped his body wasn't pretty. Be very glad this man didn't get his hands on you, Hallie."

I swallowed hard, thinking about the hypodermic.

It occurred to me for the first time that maybe the plan had been to *abduct* me behind the casino, not kill me. Not right away. And I didn't like to think about what they would have done to me in between.

"A Chinese dissident," Tyler murmured, with a meaningful look at Susan.

"Does that mean something?" Withers asked.

"Some of the competing research in our field is coming out of China," Susan explained. "They may have an incentive to try to block the work that Hyppolex is doing."

"Any particular companies? Any names of people we need to talk to?"

Tyler shook his head and interjected on his own. "They're not likely to know anything. The companies and their people are legit. It's the operators in the shadows—the ones with government ties—who do the dirty work."

"Do you have any idea *where* Dutton is?" I asked. "I mean, I don't really care who he works for. He's still out there."

"We've got the word out around the metro area," the detective told me. "If he's anywhere around Boston, we'll find him."

"Hopefully before he finds me," I snapped.

"Yeah. You're right about that. Until we get him, you should watch your ass, Hallie. These people have tried to get at you multiple times. I don't see any reason to think they're going to quit until you're dead."

30

After the interview at the police station, Tyler and I drove to the Hyppolex headquarters in Waltham. He took me to his corner office on the second floor, where the windows looked out on the slow-moving river. He left me alone while he went to arrange lunch for us, and I took that opportunity to study the pictures on the credenza behind his desk. They were mostly of Skye: Skye at the piano, Skye on the beach, Skye asleep in a sun-splashed bed.

There was also a picture of Skye near the cliffs of what I assumed was her Newport home. I saw the statue of Poseidon looming behind her, his trident raised. The wind ruffled her long hair. Her face had a mournful quality to it, eyes looking away from the camera toward the ocean, lips turned downward in a frown. I could tell that this was an older photo, because she looked years younger.

"That was the last time Skye was home," Tyler said.

He'd reappeared behind me, and he shut the office door. "It was shortly after her father died. She never went back to Newport after that. Well, not until the very end."

"Did she sell the house?"

"No, it's sitting empty down there on the coast. Skye didn't want to live there, but she didn't want to get rid of it, either. It's been in the Selden family for generations."

I went over to the window. Tyler joined me and stood too close for comfort.

"I'll arrange security for you," he commented. "We'll get a body-guard to take you wherever you want to go."

"For how long?"

"For as long as it takes to make sure you're safe."

"You mean, until you don't need me anymore?" I asked. "Until you've taken as much information as you can out of my head?"

"This isn't about our research," Tyler said. He touched my shoulder, which made me cringe and shrug off his hand. "I'm concerned about you, Hallie. I want to make sure you're protected."

"I don't want your protection or your bodyguard," I replied sharply. "I don't want anything from you or your lawyers or Hyppolex. Most of all, I don't want you acting like I'm your wife. It creeps me out."

He backed away and raised his hands in surrender. "I'm sorry. You're right, I've been inappropriate. It's just hard knowing . . . well, knowing what's inside you."

Jesus.

Tyler talking with that erotic quiver in his voice about what was inside me didn't exactly dial down the creepy factor. My first instinct was to slap his face, but doing that wouldn't make the situation any better. "Look, I'm pissed, I'm scared, and I'm upset. I know you're upset, too."

"Yes, I am. Andrew was my best friend. I can't believe he's gone."

"Have you talked to his wife?"

"Cara's coming to Boston on the ferry this afternoon." He put a hand against the window glass. "I feel like this is my fault. Andrew is dead because of my obsession with this research. I wanted to change the world, but I never imagined the price would be so high."

"Well, it wasn't all your fault. Andrew knew what he was doing."

"What do you mean?"

"He lied about it being an accident. He gave me Skye's memories deliberately."

Tyler shook his head. "Andrew wouldn't do something like that."

228

"He admitted it to me last night."

"He *admitted* it? Seriously?"

"Are you saying you didn't know?"

Tyler went to the chair behind his desk and sat down. He leaned far back, rubbing his eyes with his hands. "No, I didn't know. I swear. I can't understand why Andrew would have taken such a risk. He put his whole career and the whole company in jeopardy. It makes no sense."

"He was hoping I'd remember something."

Tyler looked at me, his face screwed up with confusion. "What?"

"Savannah."

"What would Andrew want you to remember about her?"

"What Skye saw the night Savannah was killed."

He sat up, his feet banging down on the floor. His voice rose with frustration. "Hallie, I already told you, Skye wasn't there. She was in her bedroom."

"No, she was out on the cliff that night. She saw what really happened, but she blocked out the murder from her memories."

He looked ready to challenge me, to insist that I was wrong, but then he hesitated. "Even if that were true, what could Skye possibly have seen that would change anything?"

"I don't know. Maybe she saw you."

Tyler rose from his chair. He came up to me with a frown creasing his face. "Me? What are you implying?"

"You spread a rumor about Andrew's father that tanked his nomination to the Supreme Court. Savannah knew about it. Elijah overheard her threatening to expose you."

"How on earth do you know about that? Skye didn't even know that."

"It doesn't matter. But it gives you a motive to kill Savannah, doesn't it? Not to mention a reason to pin the murder on Elijah."

Briefly, Tyler closed his eyes. Then he reached out for my shoulder again but pulled his hand back when he saw the look on my face. "Did

I say something stupid about Andrew's father? Yes, I did. When it went public and he had to resign the nomination, I felt incredibly guilty. And yes, Savannah threatened to expose what I'd done. But she also shamed me into confessing. I went to Andrew's father and told him it was my fault. I assumed he'd yank the financing he'd promised for Hyppolex, but he didn't. He said the original mistake was his and that he took full responsibility for it. That was that. He never told anyone that it was me who'd accidentally leaked the story. Not even Andrew. That all happened two days *before* Savannah's death, Hallie. I had no reason to harm her, and I never would have."

"Well, Skye knew something about Savannah's death. She was hoping Andrew's treatment would help her remember what it was. Andrew was hoping the same thing about me."

Tyler sat down behind his desk again and buried his face in his hands. I went and sat in the chair on the other side.

"Except I don't understand one thing," I said.

"What's that?"

"Andrew told Skye he couldn't simply unlock her repressed memories. He said the technology didn't work that way. If that's true, *why* would he put her memories inside me? What did he hope to accomplish?"

Tyler glanced up, his sunken eyes focused on my face. I still felt he was trying to find his wife whenever he looked at me. "Things have changed since Skye worked with Andrew. We've had a breakthrough in our research in the last few months. It's still very primitive. But there may be a way."

◆ ◆ ◆

We were the only two people in the lab.

Tyler had asked the other researchers to leave. He put me in a chair very much like the one Andrew had used with Skye, and then he positioned a cap on my head that was studded with electrodes and cables connected to his computer. Once again I felt déjà vu. This was what I'd seen in my dream, but this time it really was *me* sitting in the chair. When I looked into the dark glass on one wall of the lab, I could see my own reflection.

Tell me who I am.

You're Hallie Evers.

Was I ready for this? I thought about Myron's warning that Skye had blocked out her memory of that night at the cliff for a reason. That maybe she—and I—weren't prepared to see what was behind the curtain. But Skye was leading me there, and all I could do was follow.

"How will it work?" I asked. Just like Skye had.

Tyler lifted his fingers from the keyboard. His chair swiveled. "The focus of our research has been on backing up and then restoring memories to a patient in the wake of disease or injury. But we've also been trying to translate stored memories into actual visual and sound imagery, just as the brain itself does."

"Is that even possible?"

"Well, the Russians got impressive results in image reconstruction a couple of years ago. You look at a photo, and the computer re-creates the picture as your brain perceives it. Our goal has been to take the process to the next level. Let the computer show us what you *remember*, not just what you see. Imagine children able to see actual images—even video—of memories from their parents who died years earlier. Or think about being able to see what goes through a person's head at the exact moment of death."

I thought there was something unsettling in all of this, like there were things in life you shouldn't want to know, even if you could.

"Why not just read Skye's memories directly? Why does it have to go through me?"

"Because at least for now, we still need the brain to do the translation," Tyler replied. "The challenge for us is to visualize and reproduce what the brain is interpreting from those memories."

"But I can't remember what Skye was blocking out."

"Yes, but it's possible the computer can get around that. Your brain is always doing plenty of unconscious work even though you're not aware of it. The fact that one part of your brain is 'protecting' you from a memory doesn't mean another part of the brain isn't processing it. In fact, one argument holds that the brain *has* to be processing it. Otherwise, there's nothing to protect you from."

"So what do I do?"

Tyler shrugged. "Just relax and allow yourself to think about Savannah. Remember whatever you can—or whatever Skye can. If there's something else out there, it may flow through to my screen even if it's not an active memory. And that in turn may allow your brain to see it more clearly. There's a symbiosis in the whole process."

"What does it look like?" I asked.

He pointed at a large flat-screen television mounted on the wall. With the push of a button, the black monitor bloomed to life. "Let me show you. Concentrate on something from your own life, and you'll see how it works."

"Like what?"

"Anything."

I let my mind drift. As I often did, I thought about my mother. I'd only been ten years old when she died, so most of my memories of her were lost in a kind of fog. But I could feel her presence, and I wondered if that was enough for the computer. I watched the oversize television screen on the wall, which at first showed nothing but a kind of Jackson Pollock painting of random colors and shapes. Then the images slowly aligned. Blues and whites drifted to the top of the screen, and below them, I saw irregular smudges of rusts, browns, and tans. The scene looked vaguely familiar, and all at once, I realized—

Red Rock Canyon. This was Red Rock Canyon.

Next to me, I saw a shape like a swirling amoeba, narrow streaks of black set against dots of peach and blue. With a rush, I realized that I was looking at my mother's hair, my mother's face. The image was barely clear enough to make out her smile, but seeing it supercharged my long-forgotten memories. What showed on the monitor was out of focus, but what flashed in my head was a brief, perfect image of my mother holding my hand as we stood on the canyon overlook.

Like a scratchy record, the computer speakers crackled to life, too. I hadn't expected that, but I was also remembering sounds from that day.

A song. "Soak Up the Sun." All I could hear were disconnected notes, but the singing was my mother's voice, like clips from a broken recording. I hadn't heard that voice in more than twenty years, but now it flooded back to me. I felt breathless with joy, and tears slipped down my cheeks.

Suddenly I understood the power of what Tyler was trying to do.

Then the images on the screen rearranged into something new. I didn't understand what I was seeing. The colors of the canyon disappeared, and all that was left was grayness and blackness. A gold circle took shape in the middle of the monitor, set against a dark background. I saw myself reaching for it, like a child on a merry-go-round grasping for the brass ring.

And then I heard music boom through the speakers. ABBA. "The Visitors."

My mother's screams rose over the song. Shrill. Panicked. Desperate.

I was reaching for the doorknob to my mother's bedroom. I was turning it, opening the door, going inside.

"Make it stop!" I shouted immediately, in a voice that didn't even sound like mine. *"Please make it stop!"*

Tyler switched off the monitor. The images on the screen vanished. Slowly, painfully, the memories in my head bled back into mist. I was breathing hard, my heart racing.

"I'm sorry," Tyler said. "I should have warned you. This can be very intense."

I couldn't even speak. I closed my eyes, trying not to see anything at all, trying to put the monster back in the box.

"Maybe we shouldn't do this," he said.

I shook my head firmly. "No. It's okay. I'll focus on Skye."

Tyler nodded. "All right. I'm going to leave the room. I'll turn off the lights but leave the monitor on. I'll still be able to see and record everything from the control room. If it becomes too much, just tell me, and I'll shut it down."

"Fine," I whispered.

He switched on the television screen again. His footsteps tapped on the floor, and the lab door opened and closed. The lights went out, leaving me in darkness with nothing but the rectangular blue glow of the monitor on the wall.

I didn't know exactly what to do. At first, I tried to hunt in my head for Skye's memories, but that wasn't how it worked. I didn't find Skye; she always found me. When I thought about the things I'd seen in my dreams, the screen took on a drab color like a kind of mud, but nothing materialized, either there or in my head. Her memories skittered away.

Skye, I whispered in my head.

Skye, talk to me.

Finally, I saw something on the screen—what was it?

It lasted only a moment before it vanished like sand between my fingers. Then it was there again, a bronze shape looming over me. The figure of a man. I knew what it was.

Poseidon.

I had a clear vision in my head for just a second or two, but I didn't understand what it was. I saw myself digging in the soft ground near the base of the statue with my fingers. Why? What was I doing?

As quickly as it had come to me, the image vanished.

Skye, are you there?

Next I saw piano keys under my fingers. Snippets of music burst from the speakers. Skye was playing, and whenever she was playing, she was happy. I tried to focus on that, tried to let out the memories she treasured. The safe ones. The music got louder, and I concentrated on the emotions I felt. Warmth. Laughter. Love.

The screen turned blue.

Was it water—the ocean? Or blue sky? I felt a wave of contentment wash over me. Yes, I was staring at the sky, and then I was looking down at a man below me. I could see bare brown skin and my own bare thighs. The images on the screen were only rough suggestions of what was happening, but in my head, I saw it clearly. I was outdoors, making love.

I knew who I was with.

Myron.

I'd never felt such exhilaration, both physical and emotional. My body merged with my soul. I loved this man.

Then darkness came again. That summer night, the Fourth of July, crept closer to me. Day became night. I ran barefoot through wet grass. I felt the wind swirling my hair and heard the roar of ocean waves below the cliff. The ocean burst from the speakers like booms of thunder.

I skidded to a stop and saw someone in front of me.

Savannah.

I was back there with her. I could see her face clearly. Voices overlapped, too many words crushed together like a language I couldn't understand. She screamed at me, her face twisted with hatred. She said something vile—did I hear that right?

Was that really what she said?

I took a step toward her, as if to slap her face, but when I lifted my arm, my wrist screamed with pain. I could barely move. And then—

Then the screen turned black. Deep black, no images at all.

There was still a wall between me and Skye. A wall I couldn't penetrate.

What happened? What did you see?

I begged her for more. Anything. A flicker of memory.

Finally, like a burst on the screen and in my head, one more vision came and went. I saw the golf club whipping straight up in the air like an axe, streaking through silvery moonlight. Then it plummeted down to land on Savannah's head with a sick crack of bone.

After that, nothing.

31

When we were done, Tyler asked in a monotone if I'd remembered anything more. I told him no, which was a lie. I'd gotten closer to the truth this time. I'd seen Savannah alive by the cliffside; I'd seen the two of us arguing. She'd said something that filled my heart with fury, and I'd felt a kind of raw, primal violence rise in my heart.

That memory was new.

So was the sight of the golf club landing on Savannah's skull. My dreams hadn't shown me any of that before. I couldn't think of any other explanation for what I'd seen, except that it was me.

I'd done it. I'd killed my sister.

No, not *me*! It was Skye, not Hallie! I had to keep the two of us apart, but I was finding it harder and harder to do that.

Tyler was pale. He looked shell shocked by the experience of watching me through the dark window. At first, I assumed that the blurry images on the screen had made it real for him—seeing his wife's memories alive inside another woman. Then I realized it was something else.

It was Myron.

He'd recognized enough of what was on the screen to know that he'd seen Skye making love to another man. Even though he couldn't *feel* it the way I could, he'd understood what that memory meant. His wife had been cheating on him. More than that, Skye was in love with Myron and had been for years. That was why she'd asked Tyler for a divorce that night at Saltie Girl. She was finally being honest with herself and with him.

When Tyler looked at me now, I felt a simmering rage at the hollowness of his marriage. There was jealousy in his eyes. And possessiveness. He wanted to scream at Skye, but all he had was me in front of him. I didn't like what I saw on his face.

"I need to get out of here," I said. "I need to go."

"Go where?"

"I don't know. I need to think. Process. Maybe more doors will open for me if I give it some time."

But that was another lie. I knew where I was going. Myron's presence was like a magnet—both to me and to Skye. I needed to see him and be with him.

"Do you want me to take you?" Tyler asked.

"No."

"Then I'll have someone go with you."

I shook my head. "I can take care of myself."

"It's not safe," Tyler said, his voice dull and flat. "The police think this Dutton character may still be out there."

"I don't care. I don't want your people anywhere near me. Don't you get that? None of you give a shit about me. I'm a commodity to you, to Andrew, to Paul Temple, even to the people who are trying to kill me. I'm sick of it."

"You're taking a big risk."

"Well, it's still my life. Isn't it?"

Tyler didn't answer.

I turned and left him in the office alone.

Outside, I called a taxi to take me back to the Copley Plaza, and when I retrieved my car, I sped toward the waterfront. I was in a hurry, feeling jittery and excited. My desire, Skye's desire, overwhelmed me. At the fish pier, I ran up the stairs to Myron's studio. Without even knocking, I let myself inside. I stood in the dim space, breathing heavily, not saying a word to announce myself.

Myron heard me arrive. His footsteps thudded from the back of the studio. There he was, a muscular shadow in the gray light. He didn't say anything when he saw me. He padded up to me, his skin a rainbow of paint colors, a sheen of sweat under his dreadlocks. He seemed to know why I was there. Heat burned between us. Electricity jumped between our nerve endings. He didn't move at all. He just waited to see what I would do. It had to be me; it had to be my choice. I closed the space between us and grabbed his face in my hands and kissed him. I kissed him everywhere, his mouth, his cheeks, his nose, his eyes, his neck. Then his arms engulfed my body, and I felt myself being lifted off the floor as if I weighed nothing at all. I clung to him, and we didn't stop kissing as he carried me to his bed.

An hour later, we lay naked on a mattress on the floor, the sheets tangled around us. A ceiling fan spun lazily high in the rafters of the loft. Our bodies were pressed side by side, and Myron's fingers idly caressed me from the peaks of my breasts to the wispy triangle between my legs. I was limp with satisfaction, my body used in a way I'd never experienced before.

This was sex the way it was supposed to be, and I wanted more of it.

The only cloud in my warm sunshine was suspecting that Myron had been making love to Skye in his heart, not me. Skye was the one he wanted. Skye was the one he loved. Just like Tyler. Everyone wanted Skye. I began to understand some of the jealousy Savannah had felt toward her sister, but at that blissful moment, I was content to live in her shadow. To *be* her.

"Tyler tried to read my memories today," I murmured after we'd been quiet for a while.

I didn't even call them *her* memories anymore. With every day, Skye and I seemed to be merging into one person. What's the line from the Keats poem? *Two souls with but a single thought . . .*

Myron's fingertips kept exploring me.

"What did you see?" he asked.

"You. Us. The two of us making love. That's why I came back."

"I've missed you," he murmured, but I knew he meant Skye. His eyes were closed, and he was thinking of her.

"I've missed you, too."

"It's like having you back in my life again."

"I know. I realized, seeing it from the outside, how much I loved you. Tyler saw the same thing. He was angry about it."

"You weren't trying to be cruel to him," Myron said.

"Well, I'm not sure Tyler ever loved me, either. I think he liked the idea of owning me. Collecting me like some kind of rare coin. But that's not the same as love. You and me, that's what love is. I've always known that. I'm sorry we were apart for so long."

Myron pulled his fingertips away from my body. He opened his eyes and propped himself on one elbow. "Stop it, Hallie."

"What?"

"You're *not* her."

I shrugged, as if that were a small thing. "I could be her, if that's what you want. It wouldn't be hard. I could just . . . let her take over."

"Skye's dead. She's gone."

"She isn't, though. She's still alive inside me." I turned on my side, and I reached for his face. "Don't you understand? We can be together again. You just have to look for me, Myron. I'm here."

He took my wrist and pushed it away. He climbed off the mattress and put his boxers back on, and then he sat down on a chair near the bed. Seeing the coldness in his eyes, I began to feel embarrassed, so I covered my body with the sheet.

"Is this a game to you?" he asked.

My cheeks grew hot with shame. "No. I'm sorry."

"Don't pretend to be someone you're not. My whole life is about seeing people for who they really are."

"You're right," I told him, as I sat up on the mattress. "I'm just confused by what I'm feeling."

He sighed. "Well, it's not just you. It's my fault, too. Part of me will always want her back. I can't deny that."

"Skye was so much stronger than me," I admitted. "On some level, I feel like it would be easier to live her life, not mine. An improvement on the original source material, you know?"

"Don't sell yourself short, Hallie Evers. Everything I've seen of you tells me you're pretty strong, too."

"I'm not in her league."

Myron slid down off the chair and joined me on the mattress again. His arms encircled my waist, and I liked the feel of him next to me. "Do you mind if I ask you a question?"

"What?"

He ran a smooth finger along the rough scar on my wrist. The scar that had been with me since I was fifteen years old and Uncle Jim had found me dying in the bathtub, my blood turning the water the color of sweetheart roses.

"Why did you do that?" he asked. "What happened?"

I tilted my head, staring up at the hypnotic turning of the ceiling fan. "There was this boy. Ronny."

"You don't seem like someone who would kill yourself because of a boy."

"Actually, I was the one who tried to kill him."

Myron said nothing, but his eyes looked at me curiously, encouraging me to go on.

"He was my next-door neighbor. He'd been abusing me for a year. I let him do it because I wanted to use his swimming pool. Stupid, huh?"

"Not stupid. And not your fault."

"Yeah, well, that day, I decided I was done with him. He sat on the edge of the pool and spread his legs for me and grabbed my hair.

The next thing I knew, I had him in the water, and I was holding him down."

"Sounds like the son of a bitch deserved a good scare."

"It wasn't just a scare. I wanted him dead. But afterward . . . I don't know, I felt this enormous, destructive wave of guilt come over me. Like my chest was being crushed, like I'd done something despicable, something I could never forgive myself for. I couldn't stop crying, and I didn't even know why. Later that night, I ran myself a bath and took one of my uncle's razor blades with me."

"You were a kid. He took advantage of you. It's absolutely wrong to blame yourself."

"Doesn't matter, that's how I feel." I shook my head, my eyes filling with tears. "It's always with me, this constant reminder of the things I've done. I look at my wrist and think, *That's who you really are, Hallie.*"

He seemed to know there was nothing he could say to change my mind. Instead, he went to kiss me again, but this time I pushed him away. I hugged my knees and balanced my chin on my arms. "Can I tell you something?"

"What?"

"The more I remember from that night, the more I think Skye killed Savannah."

Myron was quiet for a while, absorbing what I'd said. "Do you actually see that in your head?"

"No, the actual memory is still lost in the dark, but I've wondered about it from the beginning. And I think she didn't know how to forgive herself, either. Do you think it's possible? Do you think she could have done it?"

"Skye had fire in her. With the right spark, I guess she could have lost control. Just like you. It doesn't make either of you a bad person."

"But her sister?"

Myron shrugged. "Savannah had a very, very ugly side to her. She could push people's buttons. Especially Skye's."

"What do you mean?"

"I mean, Savannah was like her namesake city. She was the New England version of a Georgia belle. Gracious, attractive, well bred. But if you scratched the veneer from that pretty face, you'd find one of the most virulent racists I've ever met. I mean, in a place like Newport, you'll always find a current of racism. It runs like an underground river. But Savannah didn't even try to hide it."

I frowned, thinking about what I'd seen in the lab with Tyler.

"I remembered something that Savannah said to Skye. I didn't know if I'd heard it right. Honestly, I didn't want to believe it. It was just a fragment, but—"

"What did she say?"

"She was screaming about how awful it was . . . about sleeping with a filthy stinking . . ."

I let my voice trail off.

"That word?" Myron finished my thought.

"Yes."

"She was talking about me and Skye?"

"I think so. Right after that, that's when I saw the golf club crushing Savannah's skull."

"Well, Skye wasn't under any illusions about who Savannah was. That night on the cliff definitely wasn't the first time Skye heard her sister use the N-word."

"How can you be sure?"

Myron took my chin in his hand. "How much do you know about Skye's childhood?"

"Not a lot. Tyler said her father divorced her mother and married a fashion model named Rochelle. Sounds like it divided the family."

"Oh, this was more than division. This was war. I met Rochelle that summer. She told me about some of the poison Savannah heaped on her and her daughter. I don't know how they lived with the abuse."

"Why did Savannah hate them so much? Was it really just about the divorce?"

"You don't know about Rochelle?" he asked.

"What about her?"

Myron cocked his head with a world-weary smile. "Rochelle was black. A black stepmother for the lily-white Selden girls. Savannah treated that like the ultimate humiliation. So you can imagine what her reaction would have been if she found out that Skye was planning to run away with me."

32

Did I have the answer now?

Even if I couldn't *see* it in my memory, it seemed clear to me what had happened on that Fourth of July ten years earlier. Skye and Savannah had gotten into a fight over Myron, and Skye had done something she'd never intended to do. She lost control. She killed her sister in a wild moment of rage. When it was over, her brain had squeezed the horror of that event out of her mind until she didn't remember it at all. It simply stayed hidden, the monster behind the wall.

But ten years later, Savannah's murder—and Elijah's death—had made the news again. Everywhere Skye looked, there was Elijah's face, and there was her sister's face in the papers beside him. Jagged, unconnected details of that night began to creep back into Skye's head. She began to realize she was keeping a terrible secret, and that secret needed to come out.

So Skye went home to Newport. When she was by the cliffside again, in the shadow of Poseidon where the murder had taken place, she must have felt her memories roaring back. She saw it, heard it, touched it, lived it all over again. I could imagine her despair and guilt in that moment. The guilt of what she'd done to Savannah. The guilt of what had happened to Elijah.

In the end, the truth she'd been looking for had been more than she could bear. That was the last page in the mystery of Skye Selden.

And yet.

Despite everything, I was unsure of what I knew and didn't know. There was a missing piece in the puzzle, one open square I hadn't filled in. If I was going to move on, I needed to see for myself that moment when Skye had picked up the golf club and swung it at her sister.

There was only one way to do that. There was only one place where I could unlock her last memory.

I had to follow Skye to Newport.

So I drove back to the Copley Plaza to pack my bag. First thing in the morning, I'd go. When I got to the hotel, I hurried through the lobby, and I was so caught up in what I needed to do that I didn't pay any attention to the people around me. That was foolish. I was still being watched. Followed. The killer, Chip Dutton, was still out there, but I wasn't thinking about any of that.

Then a voice froze me in my tracks.

"You're Hallie Evers, aren't you?"

I turned around nervously. A woman got up from a patterned red sofa underneath the hotel skylight. She was a brunette with her hair pulled back into a severe bun, and she wore a navy-blue blouse over a black skirt. She was probably in her early thirties, but the stiff way she carried herself made her look older. Her face was pretty but heavily made up, and the whites of her eyes were ribboned with red.

She looked familiar—we'd met before—but I struggled to place her. Then, before she could introduce herself, I remembered.

Cara Edam. Andrew's wife.

Oh, shit. This wasn't going to be good.

When I'd seen Cara at Andrew's house on the water, she'd appraised me with the certainty of a wife who thought she was meeting her husband's lover. Now Andrew was dead. I'd been there, in her Cambridge home, when he was killed.

Just to add insult to injury, I was wearing *her* clothes, too.

"Yes, I'm Hallie. You're Cara?"

"That's right."

"I'm sorry about Andrew."

My sympathy didn't make an impression on her. She stared at me, her face a cold, sullen mask.

"I talked to Tyler," she went on, as if I hadn't said anything at all. "I talked to the police, too. But you were there. What happened to my husband?"

"I don't know if I should talk about this."

"You were there!" Cara repeated, her voice rising. "You were there when Andrew was killed. Everyone tells me he's dead because of *you*. I don't care whether you're supposed to say anything. I was his wife. You owe me answers."

I scanned the lobby. Some of the people around us had already noticed the uncomfortable conversation in their midst.

"Let's not talk here," I said. "Let's go outside."

Together, we left the hotel and crossed the street to the park. It was late evening, almost dark, and Copley Square was quiet. We found a bench on the cobblestones near the steps of Trinity Church. The church lights grew brighter as the daylight vanished. Cara sat beside me with her hands folded in her lap. Her back was rigid, and she barely moved, whereas I squirmed and finally tucked one leg underneath the other. My fingers drummed on the bench railing.

"First things first," Cara demanded. "Were the two of you sleeping together?"

"No."

Her head swiveled like a swan's atop her long, elegant neck. "You don't have to lie to spare my feelings. The Edams have always treated monogamy like the Kennedys. As long as you're trying to save the world, you can do whatever you want in your private life. I knew the arrangement when I married him."

"We were not sleeping together," I repeated. "I barely knew him."

She shrugged and pointed out the obvious. "You're wearing my clothes. You were alone in my house overnight with my husband. I know the kind of man he was. I find it hard to believe you didn't share a bed."

"You can believe what you want, but nothing happened. I slept in the guest room. I borrowed your clothes because I had nothing to wear. My own clothes were muddy because I fell trying to run away from someone who wanted to kill *me*."

"And all this was because of one of Andrew's research projects?" Cara asked with a dubious frown.

"That's right."

"What exactly was this research? Tyler was vague about it, and the police didn't know anything at all." She shot a look at me that didn't hide her condescension. "You certainly don't look like a scientist."

"I'm not."

"Then what was it?"

I knew she'd lost her husband, and she was upset. She was staring at life as a widowed mother, and she was scared. But I was getting tired of her insinuations. "You want to know about my relationship with Andrew, Cara? Okay, I'll tell you. My heart stopped at a party in Las Vegas during the MedX convention. Andrew revived me with a portable defibrillator. In doing so, he deliberately transferred data from one of his experiments to my brain. I woke up with a dead woman's memories in my head. Ever since then, people have been trying to kill me."

That took the wind out of her sails. She was momentarily speechless.

"Is that really true?"

"Yes, it is."

"A dead woman's memories?"

"Yes."

"Imagine that. I had no idea his research had gone so far. Andrew didn't talk about his work with me." Her eyes narrowed as she studied me. "Let me guess. The dead woman. Was it Skye Selden?"

248

"Why would you think that?" I asked, surprised that she'd made the leap so quickly.

Cara looked at me the way everyone did, as if she could *see* Skye if she stared at me hard enough. "Skye visited our beach house a couple of times last fall. She and Andrew had some long talks. Andrew said it was connected to his work, although I didn't know whether to believe him. And then, of course, Skye killed herself at Christmastime."

"Well, you're right. It was Skye."

"Congratulations. You must feel so lucky to be sharing headspace with the Sainted Ms. Selden."

"You don't sound like a fan."

"I'm not. But tell me about Andrew. Tell me what happened."

So I did.

I described my interactions with him, from the hospital in Las Vegas, to my finding him at MIT, to the violence of the previous night. None of it put Andrew in a good light, but Cara didn't look surprised by anything I told her. I got the feeling that she had an eyes-wide-open appreciation of her husband's faults. However, the story ended up with Andrew dead at my feet and me fainting on top of him. Cara showed a little bit of emotion at that point, when I told her about finding his body. Then she wiped away her tears, as if chastising herself for revealing any weakness.

"Thank you for your frankness," she told me stiffly. "You'll never hear this from Andrew or Tyler, but I'm appalled by the things they did to you. If it was without your permission, as you say, then it's a horrible violation, and I'm ashamed that Andrew did it. Honestly, I'd suggest you sue their asses, but the future of my children depends on the success of Hyppolex. I'd prefer not to see the company destroyed."

"I haven't decided what to do," I said. "Legally, that is."

Cara smoothed her skirt and took a look around the park, as if she had what she'd come for and was ready to leave. She began to stand up, but then she hesitated and settled back onto the bench. Her gaze traveled across me again, seemingly reassessing who I was.

"Do you mind if I ask you a personal question?"

"Go ahead."

"What is it like?"

I knew what she meant. What was it like to have Skye inside me? The Sainted Ms. Selden.

"I no longer know where I end and Skye begins."

"I'm not surprised. Skye had a very forceful personality."

"Did you know her well?"

Cara nodded. "I grew up in Newport, too. We were a tight-knit group in those days. Everyone knew everyone else."

"Including Savannah?" I asked.

She pursed her lips curiously at my question. "Yes, of course. I was Savannah's best friend. And her maid of honor. Until . . . well, you know what happened to her?"

I nodded.

"Andrew and I grieved together after Savannah was killed. We comforted each other. That was how things started between us." Again Cara looked momentarily sad, but then she pushed her emotions aside. "How much do you remember?"

"You mean about Savannah? About the murder?"

"I mean about everything. How much of Skye is there inside you?"

"Bits and pieces come back to me from different parts of her life. There's no real order to it. I find that I know certain things about her without really knowing why or how. I just feel them. She's always with me. It's gotten more intense since I came to Boston."

"Naturally. Skye owned this town. She was the star."

"Why didn't you like her?" I asked, hearing the edge in her voice again. "Did you think she was sleeping with Andrew?"

For the first time, Cara smiled. "No. I didn't like Skye because she thought she was so much better than the rest of us. She'd been that way since she was a girl. She was one of those women who pretended to be humble while feeding on everyone's attention. It drove Savannah crazy, too. But I didn't worry about Skye with Andrew. Skye only had eyes for one man, and it wasn't her husband."

"You knew about—"

"About Myron Glass? Yes, of course. Mind you, I understood the attraction. Myron is incredibly talented. And gorgeous. He painted me a couple of years ago, you know. He's painted a lot of the women in our circle."

"Did you know that Skye and Myron were involved back in Newport?"

"I heard gossip about it. Back then, I assumed that's all it was. I only found out later that it was true."

"What about Savannah?" I asked. "Did she know?"

"God, no! Savannah would have gone ballistic at the thought."

"Because Myron was black?"

Cara looked reluctant to say anything bad about her friend. "Life is complicated, Hallie. By and large, Savannah was a good person, but good people don't always live up to who they'd like to be."

"I heard it was more than that."

Cara sighed with a little whistle between her teeth. "I don't know why this matters now. It's ancient history. Yes, it's true—Savannah used to say things that I found very offensive. On the other hand, I knew where it all came from."

"The divorce? Her stepmother, Rochelle?"

"That's right. Savannah was devoted to her mother, and she despised Rochelle for breaking up their family. It wasn't really because she was black, but sometimes it came out that way. And let's be clear: Rochelle was no saint, either. Savannah told me she was cheating on her father with anyone she could find. Servants. Neighbors. Her daughter was the same way. Savannah caught Vicky screwing one of the local teenagers when the girl was only *thirteen*. The apple didn't fall far from the tree. So yes, Savannah used to say nasty things about them, and I won't deny that she treated them like shit, but she had good reasons for it, too."

I stood up from the bench and looked down at Cara. "Tell me something. Who do you think killed Savannah?"

"There's no mystery to that. Everybody knows who killed her. That golf coach, Elijah."

"I don't think that's true."

"What, did Myron tell you that? And you believed him? Look, I'm sorry, but Elijah was there. He found Savannah by the cliff. He tried to rape her, she fought back, and he bashed in her skull."

"Except there's no evidence of that."

"So what? Do you think it was someone else?"

"Yes, I think it was Skye."

Cara looked at me as if I'd landed from another planet. "*Skye?* No, I may not have been crazy about Skye personally, but she had nothing to do with Savannah's death."

"I think they argued about her affair with Myron. That's what set her off."

"I'm sorry, but you're wrong," Cara insisted without any doubt in her voice. "I don't know what you're remembering, but that never happened."

"How can you be sure?"

Cara stood up, too, and we were eye to eye in the glow of the church lights. "Because I was with Skye that whole evening. It's not just that she *didn't* kill Savannah. She *couldn't* have. She was physically incapable of it."

"I don't understand. What do you mean?"

"Skye was a pianist," Cara said. "One of the side effects of all that practicing and rehearsing was that she suffered from recurring bouts of severe carpal tunnel. That day, July 4, she'd been swinging a golf club with that son of a bitch, Elijah, and she'd hurt her wrists. By the evening, her carpal tunnel had flared in a bad way. I was with her throughout the party, Hallie. Skye was in so much pain she could barely hold on to a glass in her hand. I'm telling you, there is simply no way she swung a golf club into her sister's head that night. She didn't do it."

33

"Tori?"

My voice broke as I said her name. I was leaving a message on her phone, but I was rattled. My hand shook.

"Tori, it's Hallie. Can you call me back as soon as you get this? It doesn't matter what time it is. I need your help. I need a big favor."

I hung up.

The hotel room around me was dead quiet. I'd kept the lights off and shut the curtains to block out the glow of the city. My bag was already packed. I'd set an alarm to go off before dawn, and as soon as the sun rose, I'd take the highway south toward Newport. More than ever, I felt an urgent need to see it—to see Skye's home and the statue and the cliff—but I no longer had any idea what I would remember when I got there.

Ever since that first dream in the Las Vegas hospital, I'd been convinced that Skye was guilty. *She'd* killed Savannah, and the only real question, the only real mystery, was why. But if Cara was telling the truth, I'd been wrong from the beginning.

Skye was innocent.

She'd been the *witness* to her sister's murder. She'd seen a killer beat Savannah to death. When I thought about the golf club rising in the air, whipping down toward Savannah's skull, I realized something I'd misunderstood before. I was seeing it happen *through* Skye's eyes.

She wasn't holding the club. Someone else was.

Who'd been there with her? Who killed Savannah?

Tell me what you saw.

But Skye couldn't remember, and neither could I.

It was almost one in the morning. I tried to sleep, but my eyes stayed wide open. In frustration, I got out of bed and went to the windows and threw open the heavy drapes. Boston stretched out below me. Skye's Boston. I felt the ache of everything she missed from this city, the things she'd lost. Her memories rushed through me, but not the memories of ten years earlier. I was thinking about the deep depression of Christmastime. Skye's last Christmas. Splitting up with Tyler. Saying goodbye to Myron. Searching through her memories.

And then heading to Newport.

Had suicide been her plan all along?

Why?

If she was truly innocent, what could have driven her so far?

Behind me, my phone rang, and I ran to answer it. "Hello?"

"Hallie, it's Tori."

Her whiskey-smooth voice had never sounded so good. "Tori, thank God! Thank you for calling back. I'm sorry to bother you so late."

"I wasn't asleep," she replied. "What's going on?"

I couldn't talk fast enough to explain everything, so I jumped to the most important part. "I'm—I'm going to Newport in the morning."

"Newport?" Tori sounded instantly alarmed. "You mean where Skye killed herself? Why would you do something like that?"

"Because I'm convinced that her memories will come back to me if I do. Skye went there to find the answers. I have to do the same thing."

She took a long time to frame her response. "Hallie, I'll be very direct with you. I'm concerned about this plan. Do you understand that this isn't just about Skye? You've got your own issues to deal with. You're hiding secrets from yourself, just like she was. You are *fragile*, Hallie. Doing this may bring up a lot of things from your own life, your own past. Facing her memories may force you to face your own. Are you ready for that?"

I saw it again in my head. The brass doorknob. My hand reaching for it.

Was that what this was really all about? The urgency. The desperation. The need for peace. Was it Skye's—or was it mine? Was I using her to show me what was on the other side of that door?

Two of us.

Two secrets.

"I don't know. Maybe you're right. But I don't think I can stop. That's why I called. I want your help. Tori, please."

Her voice was cautious, tentative. "What do you need?"

"I know I have no right to ask this."

"Go ahead and ask."

"Come with me," I said.

"What?"

"Can you fly out here tomorrow? Meet me in Newport?"

"Hallie, I don't know—"

"I'm sure you have appointments, and you'll have to cancel on people. I get that. It means hopping on a plane and going across the country. Somehow I'll find a way to pay for your airfare. But I don't want to be alone."

"What do you think I can do for you?"

"You can help me—help *Skye*—remember once and for all. I'm so close. It's all there, it's all in my head, but I can't seem to break through. Being in Newport is part of it, but I don't know if I can do it on my own. I need something more. I backed out before when you wanted to do hypnosis. I'm ready to try now."

"That was for your own memory. Not a stranger's."

"Tori, I need to do this."

There was a long silence, and I waited for her to answer.

"All right," she said finally. "My mother's out on the East Coast, too, and she's been bugging me for a visit. This gives me an excuse. I'll clear my calendar for the next couple of days, and I'll check flights. I can probably get to Newport by early evening."

"Tori, thank you."

"*Do not* go anywhere near the estate where Skye lived. Wait for me. Do you understand?"

"Yes, okay."

"When you get there, text me a place where you want to meet."

"I will."

Tori didn't say anything more, but she also didn't hang up. I could hear her breathing.

"Tori?" I went on finally. "What is it? What's wrong?"

"Listen to me carefully," she replied softly. "I'm not sure who's making decisions in your head right now. You or Skye. You're letting her take you to the very place where she died, Hallie. If she wants to throw herself off that cliff again, will you be strong enough to stop her?"

Tori's warning kept me awake for several more hours. I sat by the hotel window and stared at the city lights. I knew she was right. I was following Skye's path, and that path had ended in her suicide. I'd been on the same path in my own life. I'd tried to kill myself twice and failed. But this time I was going to a place with a high cliff, and all it would take was one small step to succeed.

Eventually, I shut the curtains and stretched out on the bed again. I needed rest to calm my nerves, but I hadn't even closed my eyes when I was startled by a knocking on the door.

I bolted up with a start. I slipped out of bed and tiptoed across the floor. When I checked the hallway through the peephole, I recognized Detective I-Don't-Have-a-First-Name Withers from the Cambridge police.

I kept the chain on, and I pulled the door open a crack.

"You," I said. "What do you want?"

"Sorry to get you out of bed, Hallie," the detective told me. He still had an unlit cigarette clamped between his teeth. "I got a call about a crime scene in Boston. They asked me to come over and take a look. I'd like you to see it, too."

"Me? Now? In the middle of the night?"

"Well, we need to get there fast. They'll have the body processed before morning."

"Whose body? Who is it?"

"Let's leave that until we get there," he said.

I sighed with frustration. I didn't want to go with him, but I was already awake, and I wasn't going to sleep not knowing who had been killed. I nodded at Detective Withers, then closed the hotel door and got dressed. When I joined him in the hallway, I asked again whose body we were seeing and where we were going, but he simply chewed on his cigarette without answering my questions.

His car was waiting downstairs.

"Should I be calling the lawyer at Hyppolex?" I asked when we headed out on the empty downtown streets. "I don't think she'd want me talking to you."

"Call her if you'd like, but you're not a suspect."

"Oh?"

"No, my team has had you under surveillance since you left the Cambridge station," Withers explained. "We've been tracking your movements all day, so we know where you were. You didn't kill anyone."

"You've been following me? Why?"

"Partly to keep you safe, given that people have been trying to kill you. Partly to catch the killers if they made a move. And partly—"

"To see if I was caught up in something illegal?"

"Yeah, that too," he admitted.

Withers kept driving.

We crossed the river at Summer Street, and we had the city mostly to ourselves. He gave no hint of our destination, but when he turned toward the harbor, I began to get a sick feeling in my stomach. The queasiness turned to panic as we neared the twin buildings of the fish pier. I saw a riot of police lights swirling near the water.

Near Myron's studio.

"Oh, my God," I moaned. "Oh, my God, no! Myron!"

The detective interrupted and shot me an apologetic look. "Hang on, Hallie. The victim isn't Myron Glass. I should have told you that right away. I know you went to see him today."

"Myron's okay?"

"Yes. He found the body. He's the one who called the police."

I eased back against the passenger seat and closed my eyes with relief. "Then who is it? Come on, Detective."

Withers shrugged and finally told me. "Dutton."

"Chip Dutton? The killer? He's *dead*?"

"Yes."

"Well, who—"

I stopped. I didn't even know what to say.

I stayed quiet as Withers parked his car at the fish pier. There were several Boston police officers blocking access to the alley that led by the water, but Withers showed them his badge, and they let us through. I was so shaken that it wasn't easy for me to walk. The flashing lights made me dizzy, and the detective had to help me by taking my arm. The stench of fish made me even sicker.

We reached the end of the pier, where spray and foam sloshed onto the pavement in the high wind. I saw police tape cutting off the northwest corner, and inside the tape, I spotted a cluster of cops and medical personnel. I figured that's where the body was.

"Hallie!"

A deep smooth voice called to me from somewhere on my right. I saw Myron on the pier; he was standing outside the tape with a police officer next to him. He started to run to me, and I started to run to him, too, but Withers and the other cop stopped both of us.

"You can talk to him later," the detective said.

I mouthed an apology as Withers led me away. The detective and I headed toward the police tape, but I kept looking back at Myron, who tried to muscle away from the cop who held him in place. I realized that Myron didn't want me to see what I was about to see.

He'd found the body. He knew what was waiting for me.

The crowd of cops and docs parted as we got closer. I swallowed hard. The police let me get within a few feet of the man lying on the pavement, which was close enough to see that his neck was a mess of blood where his throat had been cut, making a grotesque smile under his chin. His long blond hair had turned red as it soaked in the blood under his head. There was splatter everywhere, making me think he'd flopped around like one of the fish pier mackerels as he died.

Nausea rose from my stomach, and I slapped my hand tightly over my mouth. I lurched away to the water's edge, then leaned over with my hands balanced on my knees. I swayed, trying to make sure I didn't fall. My breath heaved in and out, and my chest convulsed with spasms as I threw up in the water. Withers came up behind me and put a hand on my back.

"You okay there, Hallie?" he asked.

This was the third dead body I'd seen in two days, so no, I was not okay. I straightened up again and wiped my mouth with my sleeve.

"Jesus."

"Yeah, I know this shit is hard to take. But we think this is the guy who has been coming after you since Vegas, so we really needed you to see him and be able to answer some questions."

"Yes, I get it."

"Is that him?" Withers asked. "Can you confirm this is the guy?"

I steeled myself and returned to the body. This time I focused on nothing but his face. "That's him. That's the man who tried to kill me in Las Vegas. He's also the same man who shot Paul Temple."

Then I glanced at the black boots the dead man was wearing.

"I'm pretty sure he's the one who killed Andrew Edam, too. Or at least I think he's the man I saw from under the bed. The boots are the same, and so are the camouflage laces."

"Okay, that's good to know."

I backed away from the body. "How did it happen?"

"The Boston guys are still piecing that together. Your friend Myron Glass heard a commotion on the pier outside his studio about two hours ago. He found the body, but he didn't see anyone around. Whoever killed Dutton made tracks quickly and didn't leave anything behind. In, out—fast and smooth. Odds are it was another hit man like Dutton. If you want to take out a pro, then you better bring another pro to do it."

"But why was Dutton even here?"

Withers frowned. "My guess? He was looking for you. It doesn't seem like a coincidence that you were here just a few hours ago. Dutton must have figured you'd come back, and he'd take you out when you showed up."

I shook my head and went back to the water, which had a dank smell. Or maybe that was the foul taste in my mouth. "Somebody hired him to kill me, but then *he* gets killed? Why?"

Withers shoved a hand in his pocket and came out with a lighter. With a little sigh, he finally lit the cigarette that drooped from his lip, and he closed his eyes with satisfaction as he inhaled the smoke. He breathed out a gray cloud over the water. "Well, that's where things get interesting."

"How so?"

"Dutton got killed a couple of hours ago. Right around the same time, the Boston cops got a call from Paul Temple's chauffeur. The guy was drowning his sorrows with a late-night beer at the Tam. Apparently, somebody came up to him, bought him a drink, and said he had a message for the partners at Temple Funds."

"What message?" I asked.

"The guy said they had nothing to do with Temple's death."

"They? Who are they?"

"We're not sure. The chauffeur didn't know who this guy was. But the man was Chinese, and given what Tyler Reyes said earlier—"

"You think this was someone from the Chinese government."

"Right. I think the Chinese got word that one of their hired guns took out a big player in the industry. They wanted to make sure Temple's partners knew it *wasn't* them behind the hit. They also told the chauffeur the situation was being 'taken care of.' I assume they were talking about Dutton. That's why his body's over there."

"You mean the Chinese killed their own killer?" I asked.

"Looks that way to me. On one level, that's good news for you. Dutton's out of the picture. On the other hand, if the Chinese weren't involved, then Dutton must have been working for somebody else. Somebody hired him to take you out, Hallie. The question is *who*."

34

Myron kept his arm around my shoulder as we walked by the water. The police still had the fish pier closed, so we followed Seaport Boulevard to the adjacent pier, where the harbor walk bordered the channel. At that hour, we had the path to ourselves, but I could see a few lights blinking on in some of the waterfront condos. It would be dawn soon.

At the end of the pier, we stopped at a black fence by the water's edge. I could see early-morning boats heading out to sea. Myron inhaled the salty air and studied the dark horizon.

"Can you feel it? A storm's coming. A big one from the south. It should be here by tomorrow night."

"Well, I feel pretty rainy myself," I said.

He studied the darkness in my face, then put a hand under my chin and lifted it up. "So why didn't you tell me about the violence? About the danger you're in? I didn't even know Andrew Edam had been killed until one of the cops told me."

"There's nothing you could have done."

"Maybe not, but you should have told me."

"It's my problem. Why make it yours?"

He chuckled softly. "You need to figure out the whole idea of having a friend, Hallie Evers. That's the kind of thing friends do. The fact is, I like you."

I smiled and leaned a head against his shoulder. "I like you, too."

"Is all of this because of the experiment they did on you? Is that what's going on?"

"The police think so. Nothing else makes sense."

"What are you going to do?"

I answered unhappily. "I suppose I need to let Tyler and his people run their experiments on me. Poke and prod at all of my brain waves, try out their technology and see what they discover. Once they do that, once they've gotten what they want for the next phase of their research, there's no reason for anyone else to care about me. I won't be a valuable commodity at that point, just used scientific equipment."

"I hate the idea of those pricks pawing around inside that pretty head of yours."

"Yeah, me too. And thank you. For the pretty part."

"You don't need to thank me for that. That's not opinion. It's objective reality."

"Smooth talker."

Myron leaned in, and his lips molded against mine. For a few minutes, we kissed by the water like teenagers, our bodies pressed tightly together. When we finally came up for air, I blushed with a little embarrassment. We still didn't know each other that well, and I wasn't a girl for casual flings. But I really did like him. I wondered if, given time, it might be more than that.

But time was something I didn't have. On the horizon, I saw a pink glow, and I knew I needed to leave soon. Newport was waiting.

"Listen, I think I was wrong about Skye."

"You mean her and Savannah? Why the change of heart?"

I explained what Cara had told me about Skye's injury and her inability to swing a golf club that night.

"Well, she's right about Skye and carpal tunnel," Myron agreed. "When it came, it was usually bad. She had to back out of a couple of concerts when it flared up."

"Did she ever mention it with regard to that night? If she was in that kind of pain, she must have known she couldn't have killed Savannah."

"Well, maybe she did know. She and I never really talked about that night. We put it in a box, know what I mean? If we let it out, it would cause problems between us, and neither of us wanted that. I knew she'd blocked out what happened, and I knew how much she wanted to remember, but I wasn't going to ask her about it."

The two of us headed along the pier back toward the city. We held hands, and it felt romantic, the two of us strolling by the water in the moments before sunrise. But I knew I was about to ruin it.

"You're not going to like this," I murmured, "but are you really sure that Elijah didn't do it?"

Myron let go of my hand and turned to face me. "What?"

"Well, is it possible your brother did kill Savannah?"

His voice became a low rumble. "Seriously, Hallie? You, too?"

"I'm sorry, but I have to ask. Elijah told you he thought that Skye killed Savannah, but now we know that almost certainly wasn't true. It makes me wonder if he could have been lying about the rest."

Myron started walking away from me. I had to take long strides to keep up with him. He was upset, and I didn't blame him. He'd spent years defending his brother against everyone who thought he was guilty, and now the girl he'd slept with hours earlier was telling him she had doubts, too.

"Myron, stop," I said, because I couldn't keep up that pace. "Please."

He did. Then he folded his arms over his chest, and in the early light, his eyes froze into two dark orbs of ice. "Go on, Hallie, don't stop now. What do you want to know?"

"You told me if you dig down deep enough, everyone has a motive to kill. Did Elijah have a motive to kill Savannah?"

"No."

"They spent a lot of time together that summer."

"So what?"

"Isn't it possible he made a pass at her when he found out she'd broken up with Andrew? That she rejected him and called him—something vile? I can understand him exploding over that."

"My brother never exploded," Myron said. "That happened to him once in his life, and he learned his lesson."

"Okay." I held up my hands in surrender. "Okay. I'm sorry."

He sighed and turned back to the water. His fist pounded on the fence so hard that a ripple shuddered through the mesh. Then his chest swelled as he inhaled. He turned around again. "No, I'm the one who's sorry, Hallie. You're looking at life through a crazy lens right now. I'd be asking the same questions that you are. But you're wrong about Elijah. My brother was innocent."

"If you tell me that, then I believe you."

He took my face in his big hands, and he kissed me again. "Enough of the past. We should put it away for a while. Do you want to come back to my place?"

Yes, I did. There was nothing I wanted more. I wanted to go back to his place and let him hold me and make me feel safe until I forgot all about Skye. But I couldn't do that.

"No, I have somewhere to go."

His eyes narrowed with concern. "Where?"

I didn't answer, but I didn't need to. He read my mind.

"You're going to Newport, aren't you?"

"Yes."

His face took on a peculiar intensity. "Don't do that. Hallie, you are not Skye. She doesn't control you. Whatever happened in her life, whatever memories she put in your head, were *her* problem, not yours. You don't owe her anything."

"It's not that simple."

Myron shook his head. "It is. Go back to your own life. Or if you want, stay here with me for a while. Live in my studio until you figure out what you want to do next."

"Skye needs the truth."

"Skye's *dead*."

"Well, I need the truth, too."

He erupted in frustration. "You don't! Let it go! Hallie, when Skye went to Newport, she never came back. Do you have any idea how many times I wished I'd stopped her? That I'd told her what I'm telling you now? I let her tell me goodbye, and I never saw her again. Every day of my life since then, I've wished I could have that moment back so I could keep her from making that trip. Well, here we are. I've got my chance. Do *not* go to Newport."

A long silence stretched out between us. On the eastern horizon, the sky had turned a brilliant shade of rose. Myron was still holding my hands, as if he could stop me simply by holding me where I was. But when he looked in my eyes, he knew he'd lost. He turned away toward the water with a bitter sigh.

"If it's any consolation, I know one thing you don't," I told him.

"What's that?"

"It didn't matter what you said last December. Skye was always going to leave."

His shoulders slumped a little. His lips had turned downward, and his eyes were lost in the dawn. When he turned, I could see him in profile. He was so warm, so handsome, that I felt a stab of regret at leaving him. Skye had felt the same way. But she'd still said goodbye.

"I have to go," I said again.

"You do what you have to do. But I'm right, you know."

"About what?"

Myron nodded at the angry clouds gathering in the south. "You're driving into a storm, Hallie Evers."

◆　◆　◆

The two of us parted at the street, and I watched him walk away.

I promised myself that when this was over, I would return to Boston and let him paint me. I wanted to know what the Real Hallie Evers looked like—behind the mask, behind the abuse and the suicide attempts, behind the loneliness, behind the memories I was sharing with Skye.

Behind the closed door.

Somewhere out there was a life that was just me, for me. If I could find it.

I glanced up and down the street for a cab to take me back to the hotel. As I did, I spotted a sports car parked near the Hyatt. The car flashed its headlights at me, and I recognized the Tesla at the curb, because I'd ridden in it the day before. Seeing it made my anger flare.

Tyler was here.

I was getting very, very tired of people following me.

I crossed the street and threw open the passenger door. Inside, behind the wheel, Tyler looked like a nervous, guilty little boy, not a rich CEO and scientist. His curly hair was messy and unwashed. He pushed up his glasses on his sweaty nose, but they slipped right back down.

"What the hell are you doing here?" I demanded, leaning inside. "Are you stalking me?"

"No. I'm not, I swear. The police called Susan to tell her about the body. Susan called me."

"Then why aren't you with the police?"

His mouth made a tight unhappy line. "As I was driving down here, I saw you on the pier. With *him*."

"So what? That's none of your business."

His cheeks flushed. "None of my business? That son of a bitch destroyed my marriage. He slept with my wife. Skye wanted a divorce because of him. And now I have to see *you* with him, too? To see that you're obviously sleeping with him just like she was? I swear I had to stop myself from running over there and beating the shit out of him."

I let him stew for a minute, his fists clenching.

On one level, it was funny to think of Tyler trying to beat up Myron, who could have cracked him like an egg without breaking a sweat. On another level, it was disturbing to see a side of Tyler that burned with jealousy and humiliation. This was definitely a man who was capable of beating someone to death if his emotions overran him.

He'd told me he had no reason to harm Savannah. I wondered if that was true or just another lie.

"My relationship with Myron has nothing to do with you," I snapped. "And you and I have no relationship at all. Is that clear? Stay the hell away from me, and stay out of my life."

"Don't be naive," Tyler retorted sourly. "Do you think he'd be with you if it weren't for Skye? Do you think *you're* the one he wants? Every time he looks at you, he sees what's inside you, just like I do. The face is different, but nothing else. Do you think I can bear to lose her again? To the same man?"

"I'm leaving."

Tyler reached across the car and grabbed my wrist with a kind of desperation. Pleading filled his voice. "No, Hallie, wait."

"Let go of me!" I yelled, shaking free. "Keep your hands off me!"

"I'm sorry. Really, I'm sorry. But don't go. Give me a chance."

"A chance to do what? To fall in love with you? To let you dig through my brain to try to find your wife? That's not going to happen."

"I just want to be with you."

"No, you want to be with *her*, and she's dead." I leaned closer to his face to make sure he heard every word. "This sick little game is over, Tyler. You know what? I told Myron that I was thinking of letting you do your experiments on me, just to keep myself safe. But not now. No way. You're never getting your hands on me again. Are we clear about that? Don't follow me. Don't call me. Don't get anywhere near me. Skye was finished with you, and so am I."

I backed away from the car and slammed the door shut. I heard him shouting after me, but I walked away. I was done.

There was no more Tyler Reyes in my life and no more Hyppolex. For better or worse, I was on my own.

35

Myron was right about the storm. As I drove south, I saw a black ribbon of clouds pushing northward to meet me. There was talk on the radio news of punishing rain and wind, of near-continuous bursts of thunder and lightning. The storm had slashed its way through the Carolinas the previous day, and now it was aimed squarely at New England.

My anxiety increased the closer I got to Newport, because I couldn't rely on Skye's memories here. Her last trip had taken place after her sessions in Andrew's lab, so I had no way of knowing what she'd done during that final day of her life or what she'd thought about in those final moments. The only thing I knew was that, at the very end, she'd gone to the cliff, and with Poseidon watching, she'd thrown herself down to the rocks.

During most of the journey, I couldn't see the coast from the highway. Other than when I crossed the island bridge at Tiverton, all I saw were green fields, country cafés, little white houses with red shutters, and low walls built of hand-placed stones. The ocean felt far away, but I knew I was almost there. I took the road all the way to the wavy Newport harbor, where clouds made the water a deep dark blue and whitecaps dotted the surface. I pulled over near a little park just outside town and found a bench. Dozens of sailboats bobbed offshore, and a lighthouse marked the tip of a small island, which was where I'd booked my hotel room. Not far away, the arch of the Claiborne Pell Bridge rose in a steep angle on its way to Jamestown. I'd seen that scary silver bridge in one of my first dreams, glittering over the water in the

July 4 sunshine. Staring at it now, I realized that I'd seen it in Myron's painting, too, a shooting star that was unmistakably modeled after that high bridge span.

Right here, this was where Skye's story had begun.

I returned to my car and kept driving into the heart of Newport. I could feel the oldness of this town. The streets narrowed, made for horses and wagons, not cars. I could imagine the ghosts of soldiers and slaves among the colonial-style houses. But the echoes of the past didn't last long. When I got to the main waterfront street, the modern world crept back in. Hotels. Pubs. Shops. Tourists. Traffic. This was July, high season, and the town was crowded.

I'd never been here before, and yet I knew the layout of the streets, which seemed to come back to me from recollections of Skye growing up here. In the center of town, I passed Bowen's Wharf, then Bannister's Wharf, and I remembered being inside the galleries and bars there. Ahead of me, where the harbor road turned uphill at Memorial Boulevard, I saw a sculpture of two brass feet sticking out of an ocean wave. I had a vision of teenage Skye—drunk and giggling—adorning the feet with red stilettos.

Then there were the mansions. A century ago, Newport had been the playground of the Vanderbilts and the Astors. This was where the Gilded Age rich escaped from the heat of New York during turn-of-the-century summers. I had never seen mansions like these—European-style palaces of marble and stone behind wrought iron fences, sixty-room monuments to extravagance and greed. They were mostly museums now, places for tourists to marvel at what money could buy before income tax existed. But the money in town hadn't gone away. Today's rich families were hidden at the end of long driveways off Ocean Avenue and Brenton Road, where the houses stayed invisible behind high hedges and walls. The investment bankers wanted you to think that the robber baron days of the Vanderbilts were long gone.

I hugged the coastline and drove around the island's inlets. I knew I would reach Skye's estate eventually. Tori had told me not to go there. Not yet. Not alone. But I wanted to see where it was. I found the gated passage that led to her home off Ridge Road. Two numbers were mounted on a brick wall, marking two mansions inside. The Edam estate. The Selden estate. The iron gate leading inside was closed, but beyond the wall, I could see thick trees and wide green lawns leading to the cliff. The acreage was huge. There was plenty of room to wander, and hide, and have sex, and smoke weed, and commit murder.

The brick wall.

That was the dividing line between the outsiders and the insiders, between the haves and the have-nots. This was the wall that Elijah had climbed. I wondered exactly where he'd done it and where Tyler had been parked when he saw him.

I got out of the car and walked up to the gate. I pressed my face against the bars and closed my eyes, hoping to stir Skye's memories. I was *here*. I was *back*. The estate, the ballroom, the statue of Poseidon, the green grass, the cliffs, and the pounding ocean surf—they were all in front of me. I tried to let Skye drift back to that July 4 night ten years ago.

Remember.

But my mind took nothing away from this place. I didn't remember anything. I'd hoped that being close to where Savannah had been killed would trigger a flood of new memories, but I was wrong. The opposite was true. I felt further from that July 4 night being here than I had when I was in Boston.

This was not working.

I needed help if I was going to remember. Tori could help. Maybe, with hypnosis, she could guide me into the past, and I would find what I was looking for. Until then, I was just a stranger here.

So for now, I drove back into town and checked in at my hotel.

The atmosphere grew unsettled as the day wore on. The clouds darkened, and the wind kicked up. The first drops of rain began to spatter my face like advance soldiers of the storm. I walked through Newport as a tourist, going in and out of quirky shops. I had lunch near the water. Clam chowder. Some crusty bread. I found a little bar where a few jazz musicians jammed on the patio, and I sat and listened to them play. When I wandered past a seafood restaurant near the water called the Black Pearl, I texted the info to Tori and suggested we meet there in the evening.

Then, restlessly, I kept walking.

In Boston, I'd felt Skye leading me where she wanted me to go, but not here. In Newport, it didn't seem to matter where I went. I knew this place, and the area was familiar to me, but it didn't feel like home. Skye had left here long ago, and all I felt now were disconnected echoes of her childhood. Nothing on these streets seemed to have any special meaning to her.

Until I walked up to Bellevue Avenue.

Then something hit me like a rogue wave. It was as if someone had a hand on my chest, shoving me backward. I stood at the corner, looking at the green awnings of the Bellevue shops, but when I tried to cross the street, I felt as if Skye were standing in front of me, blocking my way.

There was something on that street that she didn't want me to see.

I didn't understand. All along, I'd felt this drive inside me to unearth Skye's secret, and yet now that I was so close, she seemed to be piling new defenses into keeping me away. Why?

Nothing looked unusual on the street itself. I noticed a breakfast restaurant. A card shop. A series of flags marked the entrance to the International Tennis Hall of Fame. I had no idea what I would find among the few upscale boutiques, but as I walked over there in the rain, I heard a voice in my head, just as I had near the Beacon Hill gallery.

Stop.

But I didn't.

Halfway down the block, I found what I was looking for. I stood outside a trendy clothing shop, which advertised its other locations in Aspen, Ibiza, Manhattan, and Saint Moritz. And Las Vegas, too. Yes, I remembered the boutique from the shops at the ARIA casino.

The green awning featured the name in antique lettering:

ROCHELLE

A window sign noted that private shopping times were available by reservation. Party dresses hung on jeweled mannequins, and if you added up all my paychecks for the past year, I doubted they would pay for any one of them. As I stood on the cobblestones, the door opened. A woman who was too beautiful to be real flowed out of the shop, tucking her Amex Black Card into her Hermès bag. A man followed, protecting her from the drizzle with an umbrella, and I saw her get into the back of a Rolls-Royce that had appeared as if by magic at the curb.

Skye begged me again. *Don't.*

But I went inside. It was cool and uncluttered, its merchandise chosen carefully. Party and business dresses. Blouses. Skirts. Swimwear. No price tags were on display anywhere. There was only a handful of other shoppers in the store, and none of them looked like me—the almost-thirty nearly bankrupt girl from Las Vegas. I felt out of place in my untucked orange blouse and jeans, but the staff had learned long ago that you couldn't measure money by what people were wearing. I got smiles. Offers of help. Compliments on my hair.

What was I doing here? What was I looking for? I didn't even know.

Then I saw a framed article from *Rhode Island Monthly* hung near the checkout area, and I saw the headline:

Rochelle Selden Brings Her Exclusive Boutique Home
to Newport

Below the headline was a half-page photograph of an extremely attractive black woman outside the shop on Bellevue Avenue. I knew that Rochelle was knocking on the door of fifty, but you wouldn't have guessed it from the picture. She still had the slim figure and cover girl looks of a *Vogue* model. She had long straight black hair parted in the middle, shaping her coffee-colored face like a diamond. She wore a knee-length dress in stripes of white, green, and red, with a gold belt tied around her tiny waist. Her eyes had the glittering confidence of someone who posed for cameras every day.

Rochelle Selden.

Skye's stepmother. The woman Savannah had hated.

I read some of the article framed on the wall, enough to learn that Rochelle had opened her chain of boutiques several years earlier with the first location at ARIA. The story mentioned her career in modeling as well as her marriage to Terence Selden of Newport. It also told me something I didn't know—that Rochelle still kept a condo in town at a multimillion-dollar resort near the yacht harbor.

"May I help you?"

When I turned around, I found a pencil-thin salesclerk standing near me. She had very pronounced cheekbones and a swirl of hair that looked like purple cotton candy. Her voice had a faint eastern European accent. She was polite, but she looked as if smiling might cause her face to crack.

"No, I'm just looking," I said.

"Stay right there. I have the perfect dress for you."

"Oh, you really don't—"

But Natasha was gone. I have no idea if that was her name, but I was calling her Natasha anyway. She returned moments later with a black dress on a hanger. It had square shoulders and a V for cleavage so sharp and deep that my belly button would probably have been visible. The length would barely clear my hips. A half dozen gold chains dripped from the left shoulder and hung from the sash in varying lengths. Natasha was right. I had no doubt it would look stunning on me.

"Would you like to try it on?" she asked.

"Oh, I don't think so."

She forced a smile onto her Botoxed lips. "Trying on is no obligation. What do you have to lose?"

I shrugged. "Okay. Why not?"

Why did I say that? There was no way I could afford this dress, and I didn't even dare ask how much it was. The words *how much* didn't cross anyone's lips in a place like this. But I had questions about Rochelle, and I was more likely to get answers if Natasha smelled a sale.

The two of us went into the back, where there was a large mirrored space behind a curtain. Natasha gestured for another clerk to join us. The second girl couldn't have been more than twenty; she had a pierced nose and wore a skintight white bodysuit on top and a frilly white skirt below. She looked like a pawn from a chess board.

"Champagne?" Natasha asked me. "Or wine, perhaps?"

"Well, champagne, sure."

She disappeared to get me a drink. To my horror, the second girl began to undress me. I put up my arms to stop her, but she pulled them away. She said something in a language that wasn't English. We battled for a couple of minutes, and then I finally surrendered as I realized that this was how things were done in Rochelle. The girl removed my clothes (I kept my underwear on after another brief struggle), and she folded them neatly on a glass table. Then she assisted me in pouring my body into the black dress. When she was done, she knelt and slipped high heels onto my feet. She used a brush to tame my hair.

By the time I was ready, Natasha had returned with a flute of champagne.

"You like?" she asked, nodding at the mirror.

I did like. I looked incredible. I had never looked so good in my life. If there had been a runway, I would have walked down it.

"It's stunning," I admitted. For the first time, I was tempted to ask, *How much?*

"This is one of Rochelle's own designs," Natasha told me. "For her creations, we do very limited runs. That way you don't have to worry about showing up at a party and seeing someone else wearing the same dress."

I sipped my champagne and tried not to laugh. "Yes, because who wants that."

"Exactly."

"Do you know Rochelle?"

"Of course. She's active in running all of the stores. Naturally, she travels around the world, but whenever she's in town, she comes here."

"And is she in town?"

Natasha gave me a puzzled look. "Why do you ask?"

"I have—well, I had—a relationship with a family member of hers."

"Oh? Who is that?"

"Skye Selden."

The clerk primped her purple hair and chose her words carefully. "Ah. Skye. Yes, we all knew Skye. So tragic."

"Very."

"How did you know her?"

"We were good friends. Some days it's like she's still with me."

"I see."

"So I was thinking, if Rochelle was in town, I would love to have a chance to talk to her about Skye."

Natasha assessed me with cool blue eyes. I could see her running through my possible motives in trying to meet Rochelle Selden. Maybe I was a reporter. Stalker. Celebrity fan. Or maybe I was who I said I was. Turning me away without knowing the truth was a risk. "Well, I don't know if Rochelle is here. She usually comes to Newport for the summer jazz festival."

I smiled, but I could tell that the woman was lying. She knew where her boss was, and I was sure that meant Rochelle was in town.

"Maybe I could leave her a note," I said. "If she comes into the store, you could give it to her."

The clerk considered the pros and cons of that proposal. "Yes, that would be fine. I'll get you a card and a pen."

"Thank you." Then I glanced in the mirror again. "I have to know. How much is this dress?"

Natasha told me. I kept a firm grip on my champagne glass to avoid dropping it. Let's just say there were five digits in the number, and the first was not a one. I thought about charging it to Tyler Reyes just for the hell of it—I was willing to bet he had an account here—but I decided against it. I had no interest in being in his debt.

Reluctantly, I let the girl with the pierced nose undress me again, and this time, I put my clothes back on myself.

When Natasha returned, she handed me a rose-colored note card and an envelope, along with a fountain pen. I thought about what to say and then began,

> Dear Rochelle,
> I need to talk to you about . . .

I almost wrote down "Skye." But I didn't. I changed my mind. When the card was done, it read like this:

> Dear Rochelle,
> I need to talk to you about the murder of Savannah Selden. It's urgent. Please call me.
> My name is Hallie Evers.

I wrote my cell phone number underneath my name. Then I put the card in the envelope, wrote Rochelle's name on the outside, and handed it to Natasha.

"You'll see that Rochelle gets this?"

"Of course I will."

I took one last longing look at that amazing dress, and then I headed back out to Bellevue Avenue.

36

When I got to the Black Pearl that night at seven o'clock, Tori was already waiting for me. The drizzle had turned to a steady downpour, so we sat inside. The restaurant had a nautical style, with black walls and a floor that resembled the weathered deck of a ship. Tori had gotten us a table near the window, and the glass was streaked with rain. The storm beat down on the roof over our heads.

She got up when I arrived and gave me a quick hug. Then we both sat down, and I had to laugh. She'd ordered a bottle of red wine and put it at my place setting, but she'd had them remove the glass. Obviously, she remembered my drinking straight from the bottle at the bar in Las Vegas.

"Cute," I said.

"Well, I wanted you to feel comfortable," Tori replied with a smile.

I played along and took a little swig from the bottle, and then I signaled the waiter to bring me a glass.

Tori sipped her own wine and studied me from the other side of the table. It was strange seeing her here rather than in her therapist's office in Las Vegas. She always looked so comfortable in her own skin, like a cat who knew how to find the perfect sunbeam. She was effortlessly pretty, with her auburn-brown corkscrew curls, pale-pink lips set against mocha skin, and a spray of freckles across her rounded nose. She wore an emerald-green spaghetti strap top that left her arms bare and black slacks. A gold chain hugged her neck. Her perfume, or maybe her shampoo, carried the flowery aroma of lavender.

"Thank you for coming all this way," I told her.

"Well, you needed help. And not to sound too clinical about it, but you're a very interesting case, Hallie, and you've only gotten more interesting lately."

"Dead woman's memories and all," I said, before drinking my wine.

"Yes, that's definitely a new twist. So how are you feeling? What's been happening to you in Newport?"

"It's not what I expected."

"How so?"

"I don't know. I thought maybe things would come pouring out when I got here, but it's not like that. Instead, it's like the wall in my head has gotten stronger. As if Skye is pushing back against me, keeping me away. Does that make any sense?"

"I think so."

"Can you help me?"

Tori eased back in her chair. The restaurant was noisy around us, and it had a damp smell from the rain. She glanced out at the storm and then across the table at me. Again I felt that cool analysis behind her eyes. "I don't know, Hallie. I'm not trying to give you therapist double-talk. From a physiological standpoint, I don't know what's really inside your head and what's not. If Skye were sitting there, I'd say we stand a reasonable chance of using hypnosis to get around the barricade her brain erected to protect her. But you're not Skye. With you, there may be nothing there. You may not be able to find that memory because it simply isn't in your head."

"Yes, I understand, but I don't think that's the problem. I know this sounds weird, but I feel like Skye is *scared* now that I'll learn the truth. It's almost as if she's trying to protect me from something. That may be my imagination, but that's how I feel. But I'm convinced I can remember."

"Well, I'll do what I can," Tori said.

"Thank you."

"One question, Hallie. Assume you find what you're looking for. Then what?"

"I don't—I don't know. I haven't really thought that far. I guess I'll feel free. Like Skye will finally be free, too."

"That's one possibility."

"What's the other?"

Tori shrugged, making her thick curls quiver. "People don't typically suppress *good* memories. You know that better than anyone. They suppress memories that their brains don't think they can handle. It can be cathartic to release them, or it can be deeply traumatic. It seems like Skye discovered that for herself. Maybe that's what she's trying to protect you from."

"Maybe."

My anxiety, which was already at a fever pitch, got worse.

We didn't talk for a while after that. The waiter brought a bowl of mussels and placed it between us. Tori squeezed lemon over them and then speared the meat from one of the shells with a tiny fork. She dipped it in the garlic wine sauce and placed it on her tongue. The gesture was sensual without her even meaning it to be. She had a natural magnetism about her movements, which was a quality I envied. Like Skye, Tori just seemed to have her shit together more than me.

I dug into the mussels, too. Then we split a Reuben sandwich between us, and Tori ordered another bottle of wine. That was fine, because I was really in no hurry to get to the final phase of the evening. I'd told her I needed to look into the memories hiding in the dark corners of my mind, but I was nervous about what I would find. So I drank more than I'd had since that night in Las Vegas.

It was dark when we finally finished dinner.

Outside, the rain had become a deluge. Tori had an umbrella—I didn't—so we shared hers. I clung to her a little drunkenly with my arm around her waist as we splashed for her car. By the time we got there, we were both soaked anyway as wind whipped the downpour against us. I got into the car, shivering. That was partly because of the cold and partly because of my fear of what came next.

"So where do we do this?" I asked.

"Wherever you like. My hotel. Your hotel. Someplace quiet."

"What about Skye's estate? Tyler says it's empty."

Tori hesitated. "We can do that if you like, but I would say it's a bad idea. You need some distance."

I thought about it. "My hotel."

"Okay."

She drove us to Goat Island, which was located on the end of a narrow half-mile-long bridge over the water. An inch of rain flooded the pavement and made me feel as if we were driving across the bay itself. We passed yachts that looked like something out of a James Bond movie. My room was at Gurney's Resort, with a water view that looked out on the Claiborne Pell Bridge. When we got there, I left the room dark. The rain gave the bridge lights a sinister fog. I cranked the heat in the room, then sat on the sofa by the window.

I felt another wave of apprehension. Suddenly, I began to think that Tori had been right all along. I should have let it go. I had to clutch the sofa cushions with my hands to stop myself from running.

"Now what?" I asked.

Tori sat down next to me. She reached behind her neck with both hands and unhooked the necklace she was wearing. She let it dangle from her fingers in front of my face, and I found myself oddly drawn to the glimmer of gold.

"Now I talk to Skye," she said.

◆ ◆ ◆

Was it another dream? I didn't know.

Was I Hallie or Skye? I didn't know.

284

I stood beneath the silhouette of Poseidon, who was framed by the night sky. Illicit fireworks from the July 4 holiday popped and sizzled through the postmidnight hours. A sting of smoke drifted in the air. Waves pounded against the rocks below me, a steady rolling thunder like the beating of my heart. The wind played with my sunflower dress, and when I looked down, I saw that I was barefoot. I ran to the cliff's edge and spread my arms wide, as if I could throw myself into the air and fly.

I was back where I needed to be.

Was this real? I didn't know. And yet somewhere in the fog, I was aware of Tori's voice, guiding me.

"You know what happened next. You have to let yourself see it."

I closed my eyes.

This was not real. My mind rebelled, trying to escape what was in front of me. If I didn't open my eyes, I couldn't see what was waiting for me. I needed to wake up from the dream. I needed to run away.

"You heard her scream. Listen for the scream."

No, don't make me listen to that.

But in the next moment, a wail rose above the wind. It was a cry for help that cut off sharply, silenced in the midst of its plea.

My own memories interrupted. *Mom? Is that you?*

No. It was Savannah's voice. My sister's voice. I was Skye. When I opened my eyes again, there I was by the edge of the cliff. My arms were wide, my dress blown backward by the gusts. If I jumped, if I let the wind take me, I wouldn't have to see anything more.

I could fly.

"Savannah needs you. Go to her."

No. This was a dream. None of this really happened. I looked down at the cliff below my feet, where the land fell away. White water surged among the rocks, rushing in, rushing out. Sharp, wet, jagged rocks. I knew what I had to do. What I always did. Punish myself. With a moan, I jumped, and there was no turning back. Gravity took hold of me.

My mind felt a dizzying sensation of speed. In another moment, there would be a microsecond of grotesque pain and then nothing.

But the impact never came. My body never reached the rocks.

I opened my eyes.

It started all over again.

I stood beneath the silhouette of Poseidon, who was framed by the night sky. Illicit fireworks from the July 4 holiday popped and sizzled through the postmidnight hours. A sting of smoke drifted in the air. Waves pounded against the rocks below me, a steady rolling thunder like the beating of my heart.

Time had rewound. I couldn't escape.

"You heard her scream. Listen for the scream."

Mom?

No. Savannah was screaming. I had to go to her. Like an angel in white, I ran through the wet grass. My dress billowed behind me. I was alone, the night sky huge over my head, the trees as ominous as soldiers, the waves pounding like the drums of a symphony.

Where are you, Savannah?

I was coming for my sister. I was coming to save her. All I had to do was take hold of the brass doorknob and go inside the bedroom. She was there. She needed me. I couldn't be afraid.

No—wait.

I stopped in the middle of the green grass and closed my eyes. Whose life was I leading? Who was I trying to save?

"Go on."

I can't.

"You have to save her."

This isn't real.

"She needs you, Skye."

I'm not Skye. I'm Hallie.

"Savannah is dying."

286

Oh, God. Yes, she was dying. I ran. My bare feet carried me, barely touching the ground because I was running so fast. All I could hear was the whistle of the wind in my ears. Tears ran down my face.

"Do you see her? Tell me what you see."

There she was. My sister. She lay below me in the grass, her limbs sprawled in strange directions, her eyes wide open but without any life. Fresh blood shone under her head like a ruby lake in the moonlight. Next to her, nearly floating in the blood, was a golf club. I knelt beside Savannah and called her name. She didn't answer. I lifted the club with two hands, stared at it with the horror of disbelief, and dropped it again. My hands were bloody. I turned them toward my eyes, palms upward, seeing nothing but crimson wine dripping from my fingers.

"You're so close."

No, this is a dream. None of this is real.

"Don't let go."

I don't remember anything else.

"Tell me what you saw."

This is not what happened.

"It is."

My eyes opened again. Tori forced me to see. Savannah, the golf club, the green grass, and the red blood. I was alone.

Except no, I wasn't.

Behind me, I felt a presence. Someone was there. I didn't want to turn around, I didn't want to see who it was, but she gave me no choice. I stood up and took a deep breath, and I turned around. A dark figure, darker than the night, stood by the cliff. He came toward me, arms outstretched, and his face came into the glow so I could see him very clearly.

I knew him. I knew him so well.

Myron.

His voice cracked as he told me what I didn't want to hear. *It was me.*

37

I broke free from the hypnosis, and for a while I didn't know where I was. I was still back at the cliff with *him*. Then, slowly, my breathing quieted as I looked around the hotel room, getting my bearings. I lay on my back on the sofa near the window. My clothes had dried, and the heat had gotten so intense that I was warm and sweating. The lights were off, making the room dark except for the outside glow.

Tori sat in a chair that she'd put next to the sofa. Her curls fell across her face as she leaned over me. The gold chain was around her neck again. "Welcome back."

"Jesus," I murmured, my mind still struggling to process what I'd seen. "How long did that take? How long was I under?"

"Three hours."

My eyes widened. "Three *hours*? Are you kidding? It felt like I was only there for a few minutes."

"Skye seemed to be adamant about keeping that night from you. Whenever you got to the edge of her memories, she backed away. We had to repeat it over and over and go a little further each time."

I got up from the sofa too quickly, then stopped and steadied myself on the table. My head felt light. I wandered to the window and balanced my hands on the ledge. Outside, the rain was still heavy, sheeting across the glass. A dense fog enveloped the span of the bridge.

"What did you see?" Tori asked me.

I was quiet.

"Hallie?"

I turned around and shook my head. "Nothing."

Her eyes narrowed with surprise. "Nothing? Really? It seemed to me that you finally broke through at the end. That's what brought you out of the hypnosis. You came back yourself, without my help. Usually, in my experience, that means you got to where you were trying to go."

"I didn't."

Tori frowned, and those damn eyes of hers shot through me like lasers. "It's okay, you know. You don't have to tell me anything. I get it."

"What did you do to me?" I asked.

"What do you mean?"

"This dream was different from the others. I could hear you talking to me, pushing me, telling me what to do. Your voice. Somehow it seemed like . . . like you were in there with me."

"Well, in a way I was," she said with a shrug. "Skye didn't want the truth, so I had to force her—and you—to go looking for it."

"Oh."

"You don't look happy with what you found."

I didn't answer her, but she was right. I wasn't happy at all. In fact, I was lost. Devastated. I couldn't admit the horror of what I'd seen. The only person who would understand was Skye, and she was already dead. All along, from the beginning, I'd wondered how this amazing woman could have killed herself. It made no sense to me. Now I knew why she'd gone off that cliff. We'd traveled a long twisting road to get here, but I finally had the answer I'd been looking for.

And I hated it.

"I have to go," I told Tori.

Her mellow face immediately grew concerned. "Where are you going?"

"I don't know. Out. To think. To walk around."

"It's pouring down rain."

"I don't care about that."

"I'll go with you," she said.

"No, I need to be alone with this."

"Hallie, that's the worst thing you can do right now."

"Look, Tori, I appreciate everything you did for me. You did more than I ever could have imagined, and I'm incredibly grateful. And you're right—I finally remembered. The wall came down. But it's—I don't know what to say—it's worse than I thought. I have to find a way to deal with this, but that's between me and Skye now. You can't help me."

"Do *not* go to her house. Do *not* go anywhere near that cliff."

"Yes, okay." But my voice didn't convince her, and Tori took my hand.

"Promise me. If you don't promise, I won't let you go."

"I promise."

She still didn't let go. She held on tight.

"I promise," I said again.

"If you're in pain, call me, text me, tell me where you are. I'll come to you."

"I will."

"This isn't just about Skye. Your mind is open now. Your own past may start bleeding through. You may see things you don't want to see."

"I understand."

"Nowhere near the cliff, Hallie."

"No."

I broke free from Tori and left the hotel. I couldn't stay any longer in that warm confined space, not for another minute. I found myself wishing that Skye was alive, that she was with me. I wanted to go back to that last day with her, that moment when she'd remembered the terrible truth. If only I could talk to her and we could share our pain together. Her memories, my memories. Somehow it would have been easier than carrying the burden by myself.

When I left Goat Island, I drove into a maelstrom. The storm mirrored the turbulence inside my head. I took my car across the causeway into town, and my windshield wipers struggled against the slashing downpour. The streets were empty. No one else was foolish enough to be outside in Newport on such a night. I drove, and I drove, and I drove. I drifted up and down the streets. Past the shops. Past the mansions. Somehow, after what felt like miles and hours, I ended up on Ocean Avenue on the coast. I parked near the sea and sat there in a kind of cocoon. The surf lashed the shoreline. The waves erupted like explosions and sent spray over my car. Ahead of me, on the eastern horizon, huge branches of lightning split the sky.

Myron.

Not Elijah. Not Tyler. Not Andrew. Not anyone else. It was Myron. I refused to believe it was true. And yet I'd *seen* it.

I took out my phone. For a long time, I simply held it in my hand, but then I punched the numbers and called him. The call dropped without connecting. The weather was interfering with the signal. I tried again, and finally I heard the staticky sounds of his voice as he answered.

"Hallie?"

Ever since I'd met him, that voice had brought me safety. Warmth. Desire. Not now. Not anymore.

"What's going on?" he asked me. "Where are you?"

"Newport."

There was a long, long pause, and I thought I'd lost him again. Then he said, "Did you find what you were looking for?"

"Yes."

"Are you going to tell me?"

My tears came immediately. "Tell you? Why? Why should I? You already know. You've known all along. For years, you let Skye suffer while she protected you. She protected you right to the bottom of the cliff."

"Hallie, what are you saying?"

"It was you, Myron. It was all *you.*"

"Me?" Urgency crept into his voice. "I have no idea what you're talking about."

"Liar! *You* were there, not Elijah. You went to get the golf club for him. You climbed the wall at the estate. You were the one Tyler saw. *You* killed Savannah. Skye found you on the cliff that night, and you told her what you'd done. And she's been keeping your secret ever since."

In the silence, all I heard was the drumbeat of rain.

"You're wrong," he said a moment later, the sound cutting in and out. "I can't say it any plainer than that, Hallie. You're wrong. It never happened. I wasn't there. I never hurt Savannah."

I exploded at him. "I remember it now! Don't you get it? I remember! I saw it! I saw you! That's what Skye was hiding from all these years. The man she loved more than anyone in this world was a killer! You took your brother's golf club, and you beat her sister to death!"

The louder my voice got, the quieter his voice became.

"I didn't."

"Myron, *I saw you!*"

"I don't know what you saw, or what's in your head, but it's not real. I did not kill Savannah. It was not me, Hallie Evers. Listen to the sound of my voice when I tell you this. *It. Was. Not. Me.*"

Tears and rain mixed on my face, and I felt myself going over the edge, losing my grip on reality. I wanted to believe him. God, how I wanted to believe him. But how could I? I'd seen the blood on his hands.

"I can't talk to you anymore. I can't even listen to you."

"Hallie, you're not thinking rationally. Don't you realize this is what I was afraid of? You're acting like Skye was in those last few days. I told you, I told you, *not* to go to Newport."

"And now I know why."

"No, you don't. You don't know anything. Whatever you saw is a lie."

"Myron, stop. Just stop."

But he rushed on, his words coming faster. "Stay where you are, Hallie. I don't know what's going on, but I'm worried about you. Don't move. I will drive down there right now."

"To kill me?"

"To *rescue* you. I'll come through the storm, I will find you, and we will figure this out together. Two hours. I can be there in two hours. But until then, I need you to be safe."

"Goodbye, Myron."

"Hallie, *wait!*"

I hung up the phone, cutting him off.

My car shuddered with the gusts of wind. Lightning blinked on and off like neon signs. The ocean surged, ten-foot waves rising up like huge sea creatures and crashing down over the windshield. And yet I felt no fear about what I had to do. All I felt was calm resignation now.

Even in my loneliness at the center of the storm, I didn't feel alone. When I glanced over at the passenger seat, I saw Skye sitting there next to me. The girl of my dreams.

Truly, she was the most beautiful woman I'd ever met. That blond hair, very long and straight, parted in the middle. The perfectly symmetrical face, pointed nose, golden skin. The arching eyebrows over tranquil blue eyes. The sad little smile playing on her lips. The fingers that could make the piano sing. She wore her pretty sunflower dress from years ago, and her long legs stretched into the shadows.

She leaned close to me across the seat. Her gaze held mine, eye to eye, face to face. I was under her spell, the way I'd been since that first day in the hospital. She stared at me with the same curiosity I had for her. It was as if she was trying to understand this quirky girl she was sharing her life with. For a single long moment, we studied each other with fascination, just inches apart. Hallie and Skye, two sisters, two opposites, the dark and the light, the yin and the yang, the inside girl and the people lover. Seeing her, I missed growing up with a sister. I would have liked having her in my life.

Her eyes were strangely desperate when she looked at me, but also strangely warm. Skye whispered to me. She reached into my head and told me what I had to do.

Kill me.

"What are you saying? I don't understand."

Kill me. I can't take it anymore.

"I can't do that."

Yes, you can. Please, Hallie, I need your help. You have to kill me.

I heard those words echoing in my head like a song. And then she was gone. In the end, there was just me in the car, surrounded by the rain and the ocean. I felt hollowed out, listening to an old familiar voice that said I had to be punished for the things I'd done. My own voice. My own guilt.

I reached for the key to turn on the engine.

My story was going to end the way it had been destined to end since I was ten years old. Like a mouse in a maze, I would follow Skye home. I would let her lead me to the statue of Poseidon and to the very edge of the cliff where the land fell away. I would stare down at the surf churning against the rocks.

And then?

What then?

I'll never know what I would have done.

Before I could go anywhere, my phone rang, and that broke the spell. I didn't recognize the number, but I answered the call, and I heard a woman's scared, nervous voice on the other end.

"Is this Hallie Evers?"

"Yes."

Crackling filled the line. Empty seconds passed in silence. The connection was bad because of the storm. Or maybe the woman I was talking to really didn't want to talk at all.

"This is Rochelle Selden," she said finally. "I got your note. You said you want to talk about Savannah's murder."

A shiver ran through me. "I do."

"Well, then you better come over here."

38

A dozen candles gave a flickering otherworldly glow to Rochelle Selden's waterside condominium. A burning stick of sandalwood incense scented the room. Outside the windows, I caught glimpses of the million-dollar view of the harbor with each flash of lightning. The decor here was ultramodern. I sat on a pale-blue sofa that resembled a stylized sleigh bed. On the wall was an abstract mural showing swirls of orange and azure that reminded me of ocean waves. A blond-wood sculpture of a leaping gazelle dominated the corner of the room.

Rochelle drank tea from a vividly colored crystal goblet, which caused strange reflections on the wall from the candlelight. She wore a silk African robe that reached to her ankles, and her feet were bare. She sat in a bucket chair near the window, and occasionally she reached out to stroke the flank of the gazelle. Her face looked drawn and older with no makeup and no smile. She was still an exceptionally striking woman, but right now she was without the show she put on for the world.

I wondered what I was doing here. After letting me in, she'd said nothing about my note or her phone call. Her eyes looked everywhere in the room except at me.

"I'm dripping on your furniture," I said apologetically.

She waved her hand dismissively. "Don't worry about that."

"This is a beautiful place."

"Is it?" she asked. Then she frowned. "I don't know. I keep fixing it up, but it never feels like home. One day I really need to sell it and get the hell out of Newport for good."

"You don't like it here?"

"Too many memories," she said.

File that comment under incredibly ironic things to say to Hallie Evers.

"I appreciate your talking to me," I went on. "My note must have been a surprise."

Rochelle shrugged. She got up and took her goblet to the wall of windows overlooking the harbor. Her back was to me. Rain fired at the glass like a nail gun. "Not really."

"No?"

"No. I've been expecting someone like you to show up for some time."

"I don't understand."

But Rochelle didn't explain. She stood at the window, not moving, her body proud and straight. She looked like a ship's masthead carved from a single block of wood. Even her face was rigid.

"Ms. Selden?" I said, when a couple of minutes passed in silence. "Are you okay?"

My voice seemed to wake her up. She turned around and stared at me. "So who are you? Police? FBI? A reporter? When I read about Andrew's death, I knew they'd be coming for me soon. I've been steeling myself for it."

"No, I'm none of those things."

"Then why do you want to talk about Savannah?"

I wasn't sure if the truth would help me here, and I tripped over myself trying to find an answer. "Because of Skye."

"Did you know Skye?"

"Well, it's difficult to explain. In a very unusual way, she's like a sister to me. She'd begun to believe that Savannah's death was not what the police made it out to be. So with Skye dead, I felt like I owed it to her to find out what really happened. Now I'm pretty sure she was right about that night."

"You mean, you think that Elijah was innocent?" Rochelle asked.

"Yes."

"Well, of course he was."

"You sound pretty sure."

"I am. I knew he was innocent back then."

"But you didn't say anything?"

Rochelle sighed and tightened her robe around her neck. "It was one night, and the consequences were already sealed. What could I do? But now it's gone too far."

"What do you mean?"

"There's been too much death. First Savannah. Then Skye. Now Andrew dead, as well. He may have brought it on himself, and I won't deny that I've detested him for years. Even so, he had children and a wife. They don't deserve this."

"I was there when Andrew was killed," I blurted out.

"*You* were?" she asked, her forehead crinkling with puzzlement. "Why?"

"The killer was after me, too."

Rochelle came and sat down next to me on the sofa. "I get the feeling that you're leaving out important parts of the story."

"I am, but I'm not sure you'll believe what I tell you."

"Hallie," she said. "Do you mind if I call you Hallie? You seem like an honest person. Believe me, in the worlds I live in, I've developed a good radar for falseness. If I thought you were playing me, I would have thrown you out. But if you expect the truth from me, then I expect the truth from you, too."

"All right. I'll tell you the whole story. But first I need to ask you something. Do you know anything at all about the research Andrew Edam was doing?"

"Actually, yes, I know quite a lot about it," Rochelle replied. "Backing up memories. Restoring memories. It's amazing stuff. For a singularly awful person, Andrew was quite the pioneer in his scientific work. I guess sometimes we have to accept the bad with the good."

"How do you know so much about it? The Hyppolex project is one of the biggest secrets in the medical device industry."

"The real question is, How does his research involve *you*?" she asked.

I told her. I expected her not to believe me, or to call me crazy, but she didn't blink at my story. She didn't even look surprised. Instead, she looked at me and said, "So you're the one."

"What?"

"Skye's memories. It's you. The mystery girl."

"You already know about this? How?"

Rochelle shook her head with a kind of wonder, but she still didn't explain. "That's a lot for anyone to take in, Hallie. What an experience. I can only imagine what it's been like for you. I'm sure you're scared and confused."

"You're right."

"It also explains everything," she went on. "Now it makes sense. You say you were with Andrew when he was killed?"

"Yes. In his house in Cambridge."

"Did you see who did it?"

"According to the police, it was a hired killer. Some kind of hit man. Tyler Reyes thinks a competitor wants to slow down the Hyppolex experiments by getting rid of me."

Rochelle shook her head. "No one is targeting you because of the Hyppolex research, Hallie."

"If you're saying I'm not in danger, you're wrong. It's real."

"Oh, I'm not saying you're not in danger," she replied. "Quite the opposite, in fact. The danger is very close to you. But it has nothing to do with Hyppolex."

"Then why would anyone want me dead?"

"You already know the answer. Because of Savannah. You have a secret in your head that someone is willing to kill to protect."

"Who?"

Rochelle stood up and wrapped her arms tightly around herself. The room was quiet except for the tumult of the storm.

"What did you hope to find in Newport, Hallie?" she asked softly. "Why did you come here?"

"I wanted to know what Skye was hiding. I was trying to unlock the memory of what really happened to Savannah. I asked my therapist to help me relive that night through hypnosis."

Rochelle nodded sadly. I could see in the candlelight that she was crying. Silver tears ran down her face. Then she took a breath and wiped her cheeks with both hands. She grew calm again.

"And what did you discover?"

"It was Myron. Elijah's brother. Myron killed Savannah."

"You saw it? You remembered that?"

"Yes."

Rochelle shook her head. "No. Myron didn't kill Savannah."

My heart skipped a little at those words. "Rochelle, I want to believe you, but I *saw* it. I saw Myron on the cliff through Skye's eyes. And really, it's the only thing that makes sense. I can't imagine Skye killing herself over anything less. The woman I feel inside me was too strong for that."

"I knew Skye, too. You're right. She was strong."

"Then I'm not sure I—"

I stopped, watching a shadow cross her face.

"Skye didn't kill herself," Rochelle told me. "She didn't throw herself off that cliff. Someone else was with her that night."

◆ ◆ ◆

The nearest candle flickered out, leaving Rochelle nearly invisible in the shadows. She seemed to prefer it that way. She drew her legs onto the sofa and curled up in the farthest corner, the way a child would.

Her eyes drifted to the window, and she shuddered with each clap of thunder.

"I met Terence—Skye's father—when I was thirty years old," she began. "I know how young that is now, but back then, it felt old to me. My modeling career was mostly over. Except for a few superstars, most models don't make it beyond their twenties. So I was in the market for financial planning and career advice. I needed to know how to make my nest egg last and what options I had for making money in the future. Terence advised me. And, well, soon it became more than that."

Her mouth formed a wistful smile.

"You probably think that Terence was my career plan. Marry him, and my money worries would go away. But it wasn't like that. I fell in love with him. He was much older than me, but incredibly smart, cultured, and mature. Yes, we were cheating, and I didn't like that, but his marriage had died long before he met me. Alma. What a truly bitter, unpleasant woman. Terence stayed with her as long as he did out of duty, but when he and I fell in love, he decided to face reality and break it off for good. Needless to say, Alma didn't take it well. Particularly given the color of my skin."

"Myron said Savannah didn't take it well, either."

Rochelle laughed without humor. "Myron has a gift for understatement. Savannah was cut from Alma's cloth. Yes, she hated me with a passion, and she made sure I knew it. I could have dealt with the way she treated *me*, if that's all it was. Children don't welcome stepmothers, particularly after a nasty divorce. But Savannah took it out on my daughter, too. I guess she realized I was too tough for her to take on, so she dumped her cruelty on my little girl instead."

"Vicky?" I asked.

"That's right. Vicky was only nine when I married Terence. I'd had her when I was at the peak of my modeling career. I was living the high life back then, making crazy amounts of money and using a crazy amount of drugs. Her father was a fashion photographer I'd worked with a few times. We went to a party together, and I took a lot of dope, and afterward he—he assaulted me. That's how I became pregnant. I didn't press charges. My career didn't need the scandal. Honestly, I blamed myself for a long time, as if it was somehow my fault."

"But you kept the baby."

"Oh, yes. For me, there was never a question of that."

"Did anyone else know about the rape?"

"There were rumors that followed me for years. I didn't say a word about it publicly. But after I married Terence, someone mentioned the story to Alma. Alma in turn told Savannah."

I closed my eyes. "And Savannah told Vicky."

"Yes. I'd kept the truth about her father from Vicky all that time, but when she was ten years old, Savannah began taunting her with the fact that she was a child of rape. So I had to tell her what happened. I think that's when her problems began. Something about that secret derailed her. She was never the same after that. She began acting out, going wild. Most of all, she began looking for ways to torment Savannah the same way Savannah tormented her. It became an ugly, ugly battle between them."

"And Skye? How did she fit into the mix?"

Rochelle smiled. "Skye was sweet. I liked her. She and I became very close, despite Alma. Skye hated what was going on between Vicky and Savannah, but she had no way to stop it. Neither did I, and neither did Terence. I was hoping the feud would run its course as the girls got older. Savannah went away to college, and when she was gone, Vicky seemed almost normal. But then Savannah would come home on breaks, and the war would start up again. Later, when Savannah got engaged to Andrew, I thought the end was near. I figured Savannah would be out of the house soon, and she and Vicky wouldn't be at each other's throats anymore."

"How old was Vicky then?" I asked.

"Fifteen."

I could see the girl in my dream, outside the ballroom door. The smirk on her face, almost like pride. *They're really going at it this time.*

And I knew.

I knew what had happened.

"Savannah thought Andrew was having an affair," I murmured. "She was sure it was Skye, but it wasn't, was it? It was Vicky."

Rochelle nodded. "Vicky was uncontrollable back then. Jealous. Violent. Sexually voracious. I couldn't make her stop. She was desperate to humiliate Savannah, and what better way than to seduce her fiancé? And Andrew, that son of a bitch, allowed it to happen. Vicky was *fifteen*, and regardless, he began an affair with her. When you have that kind of money, you think you can do anything. That's why I've always despised him."

I got up and went to the window, and I tried to make sense of this. It should have been a relief. I'd been wrong about Myron. The answer to this mystery was all about a girl I didn't even know.

So why did my horror increase?

"*Vicky* killed Savannah," I said.

"Yes."

"You knew that all along."

Rochelle's voice became broken and soft. "Later that night, she came to my room, and she had blood all over her. She told me what she'd done. I should have called the police, but instead, I helped her clean herself up. She said Skye had been there, too, so I assumed the truth would come out the next day. But the morning came, and Skye didn't remember a thing. She didn't even remember being out there on the cliff. It was like . . . like she couldn't bear to face what had happened between her sisters. So as strange as it sounds, Vicky was out of danger at that point. Fate had made the decision for me. I couldn't turn her in."

"And Elijah?"

Her voice hardened. I heard no repentance. "We all make difficult choices, Hallie. I love my daughter. I protected her. If I had to do it over again, I would do the same thing."

I could feel the memory of it coming back to me now. I saw it all. The curtain parted in my mind, and as it did, I realized that this was not simply about a murder from ten years earlier. The violence hadn't ended that night. This was not just about Savannah.

This was about Skye.

This was about Andrew.

This was about *me*.

I came to Rochelle and stood over her. I felt cold. Cold on my skin. Cold in my heart. There was a question I had to ask. The most important question of all. But I had to drag it from my lips, because I was scared of the answer.

"What happened to Vicky?"

She looked at me with a kind of stiff reluctance, and I saw the story in her eyes. When I looked in Rochelle's face, I could finally see the resemblance.

"I thought she'd put it behind her," Rochelle told me. "After that night, she grew so much *calmer*. It was like Savannah's death became a way for her to finally bury her demons. Or at least, that was what I thought until last year. When Skye began to search her memories for the truth, I realized it wasn't over. I swear to you, I tried to stop her. I tried to get her to turn herself in. I did everything I could."

"Where is she *now*?" I asked, but I already knew what she was going to say.

"She went home. Back to where we grew up."

"Where was home?"

"Las Vegas."

I closed my eyes. I'd been such a fool. Right from the beginning, I'd been a fool.

"I was certain that Vicky had turned the page on the girl she was," Rochelle hurried on, as if she needed to convince me. "She left everything about Newport behind her. She became a different person. She even—"

Rochelle stopped, and I finished the thought for her.

"She even changed her name."

"Yes. I'd always called her Vicky, but one day out of nowhere she told me she was done with that. She wasn't Vicky anymore. She wasn't Victoria."

"She was *Tori*," I said. "She became Tori."

39

The iron gate leading into Skye's home, which had been closed earlier in the day, was open now. I drove inside, and at the end of a long driveway, the estate rose in front of us. There were no lights on, but when the lightning flashed, I could see the house, which was like a castle built of gray stone. Sharp gables adorned the three-story facade, and white columns marked the entryway. I could see a widow's walk high on the roof, and I knew from my memories that Skye had spent time there as a child, staring out at the sea like a tiny pirate.

I got out of the car, and Rochelle got out on the other side. It was hard to stand because of the intensity of the wind. I felt as if the epicenter of the storm was directly over our heads. Squinting, bent over, we made our way to the massive front door. Like the outer gate, the house door was open, too, letting the rain pour inside.

"Vicky's here," Rochelle murmured, seeing the open door. "I knew she'd come here. She's waiting for me."

That was only partly true. I knew Tori was actually waiting for *me*. And for Skye. She knew we'd come, knew that neither one of us could stay away. Our fates converged right here, in this house, on that high cliff. I couldn't walk away and not see the end. To be free, I had to finally stand where it had all happened and watch the past unfold in my mind.

We walked inside and shut the door behind us, giving the interior a deathly quiet. A high angled ceiling loomed over the foyer. Marble stairs wound to the upper floors. The house was empty, stripped of furniture, with no art left on the walls. I coughed as dust got in my throat. Seeing this sterile, imposing mansion, I understood the complexity of Skye's feelings for it. She'd never wanted to live here again, but she also couldn't imagine it in the hands of strangers. This was the Selden estate. So the house stayed as it was, desolate and populated by no one but ghosts.

"Tori?" Rochelle called loudly, her voice sounding hollow in the empty space. "Tori, where are you? It's Mama."

There was no answer and no movement in the darkness.

"We should call the police," I said, but Rochelle refused to hear me.

"And risk them shooting her like a dog?" she snapped with rage and fear. "I won't let that happen to my daughter. I can *talk* to her. We both can. We can persuade her to turn herself in. You're not just Hallie to her. You're Skye, too. It wasn't like her and Savannah. She loved Skye."

"Tori *killed* Skye."

"It was an accident!" Rochelle insisted. "They argued; they struggled. Tori never meant for it to happen like that."

I didn't believe that was true. I didn't think Rochelle believed it, either, but she was determined to live with a lie.

"Where would she go?" I asked. "Where would she be hiding?"

"Her old bedroom, maybe."

So we climbed the stone steps to the estate's top floor. The darkness inside the house was almost impenetrable, but I knew the layout by instinct, just as I'd known the streets of Boston and the streets of Newport. Skye was still in my head. Her presence, her memories, were strong here. At the end of the third-floor hallway, a tall chambered window looked out on the sea, and as lightning flashed outside, I spotted large walnut doors opening to bedrooms on either side. I chose the door on the right, because I knew that was Skye's room. Rochelle opened the opposite door. We each went inside.

Like the rest of the house, there was no furniture left here now. Even so, I could picture what it had looked like in my head. I thought about Skye's excitement that night, her plans to run away with Myron, her suitcase half-packed. By morning, those plans would be gone, and her sister would be dead, and her relationship with Myron would be in ruins. I went to the bay windows that looked out on the gardens and the water. Rain blurred the glass. With the next burst of lightning, I caught one fleeting glimpse of the statue near the cliff.

Poseidon. The bronze god on his pedestal.

I was back where it had all started, for Skye and for me.

I returned to the hallway. Rochelle met me there, and she shook her head. There was no sign of Tori upstairs. We returned to the ground floor, and this time we followed a wide corridor that led to the rear of the house. On our right was a wall of windows. At the far end, glass doors led toward a multilevel terrace above the gardens and the lawn. On our left was the ballroom wing.

I remembered my dream, seeing Vicky spy on Andrew and Savannah as they argued. And then me—Skye—taking her place. The door where Skye had watched them was open by a few inches. I went inside the ballroom, but Rochelle stayed in the corridor. I wandered in amazement across the inlaid floor, between white stone walls decorated with gold sconces and beneath a ceiling mural of angels in the sky. Elaborate brass chandeliers dangled over my head, but I could see cobwebs hanging between them. The north end of the ballroom opened onto the terrace through high doors. The lightning outside was almost continuous now.

I could see them in my head. Andrew and Savannah on the night before their wedding. Savannah screaming at her fiancé in rage and despair.

I had the strange idea that you should actually love me! Because I've never loved anyone else.

I couldn't decide how I felt about that scene. I knew now that Savannah had been a terrible person. Vindictive. Cruel. And yet I also found some sympathy for her. I could hear in her voice that she'd really loved Andrew, even while he was cheating on her. She had imagined her charmed life going one way, and instead, she'd watched her parents divorce, watched strangers come into her house, watched her fairy-tale dreams dissolve into nightmares.

Is it her? My sister. It's always her. Do you think I haven't seen her sneaking out at night? Do you think I don't know where she was going?

Savannah had been right about everything, but also wrong. Yes, Skye had been slipping out of the house all summer, but she'd been seeing Myron, not Andrew. Yes, her fiancé had been cheating on her, but the sister Andrew was sleeping with was actually a fifteen-year-old girl bent on paying Savannah back for every slight and humiliation she'd endured.

I saw that night finally taking shape in my mind now. The rest of the memories began to fall into place like the last pieces of the puzzle. No more shadows. No more closed door keeping me from the truth. I saw what Skye had seen: Savannah slapping Andrew hard across the face as she broke up with him, and then, in tears, running across the ballroom to the far doors and out onto the terrace.

To the gardens and the green grass.

To the cliff.

In the hallway outside the ballroom, Skye had followed her. She couldn't let the accusation go unanswered. She needed to tell Savannah that no matter what her sister thought of her, no matter what conflict and rivalry had always existed between them, she would never have betrayed her with Andrew. There were some lines she would never cross. It was not her.

I stood in the middle of the ballroom and closed my eyes as Skye's memories flooded through me.

Then I heard something else, not in the past, but in the present. I was back in the real world. A woman's cry, sharp and high pitched, rose from the corridor. It began like a scream, and then I heard the heavy thump of someone falling and the noise of running footsteps.

Seconds later, the wind screeched like a witch through the far doors.

When I returned to the hallway, I found Rochelle on the floor. She tried to get up, then moaned and fell back. She put her hand to the back of her head, and it came away with a smear of blood. I helped her to her feet, and she balanced herself against the tall window.

"Tori?" I asked.

Rochelle nodded. "She's going to the cliff."

"Call the police. You have to call the police now."

"Yes, yes, okay. But you need to find her. You need to keep her safe. I don't want them to kill her."

At the back of the house, one of the doors to the terrace was wide open now, quivering in the wind.

"Stay here," I told her.

I headed down the hallway alone. I could see my reflection in the windows with each flash of lightning. In my mind, in my memory, I saw Skye heading for the garden to catch up with Savannah ten years earlier. After a few steps, I began to run, the way she had. I got to the door and plunged outside into the teeth of the storm. The gales twisted around me, and the storm seemed to lift up the ocean and pour it over the clifftop along with the rain.

Ahead of me, steps led to the green grass. I hurried down from the terrace, searching for Tori in the bursts of lightning, but I didn't see her. All I saw, when the night sky momentarily turned to day, was Poseidon. I stood at his feet, the naked god towering above me, ready to toss his trident toward the sea. I looked down and saw the wet ground disrupted. Someone had been digging at the base of the monument, turning over grass and mud.

More memories.

Skye had the golf club as she ran from the murder scene. She needed to hide it. She needed to protect Elijah. So she'd buried it right here between the soft wet grass and the base of the statue. All these years, the murder weapon had been in the ground, guarded by Poseidon.

But not anymore. Now Tori had it again. How had she found it?

Then I knew: Me. I'd told her under hypnosis what I'd done. Where was she?

I made my way to the cliff. The ground fell away, weeds growing over the edge. Below me, white surf swirled and crashed on the wet black rocks. The lightning spiked closer, so close now that I could feel my body tingling with each hot crack. The blasts of thunder made me cover my ears. I ran along the edge, my feet slipping. One wrong step, and I'd follow Skye to the bottom of the cliff.

I didn't have to go far. There. Right there.

I saw where it had all happened.

Trees and brush made a grove at the precipice, near the huge field of green lawn. I ran to the spot, and I remembered it all clearly now. I saw Savannah on her knees in the grass, beating her forehead with her fists. She screamed at Skye, her face wild with fury and tears.

You ruined everything! You ruined my life! How could you?

And Skye told her she was wrong, she had it all wrong; over and over, she begged Savannah to believe her. She'd never betrayed her with Andrew. She'd never slept with him.

Two sisters.

I didn't have to close my eyes to see it play out. Like a movie in my mind, I watched Savannah rise to her feet and stalk toward Skye and then shout at her in disbelief.

If it wasn't you, then who? Who was it?

I heard the answer.

The answer came from the cliff. Not in my memory. In real life.

"It was me."

40

Tori emerged from the trees with the golf club clutched in her hands. Even in the rain, I could still see dark stains of blood on the shaft. The shock of being jolted from the past froze me where I was, and that split second was all Tori needed. She whipped the club head at me like a bat, so hard and fast I didn't have a chance to jump away. It collided squarely with my shoulder.

My arm broke. I heard the crack of bone.

In the instant it took for the agony to register in my mind, Tori struck again. She swung a second time, and the club head slammed into the side of my left knee. I wailed as the joint came uncoupled and my leg buckled beneath me. I crumpled to the ground, staring up from the wet grass at streaks of rain and watching lightning paint the sky orange and yellow. All I felt was shock after shock of pain.

Tori squatted over me as I writhed. Her wet curls were pasted to her face.

"Hallie, Hallie, Hallie. What did I tell you? Don't go to Skye's house. But you didn't listen. You couldn't stop yourself, could you?"

I tried not to cry out. My left arm was useless, virtually immobile. My left leg burned like an open flame.

"I tried to save you," Tori went on. "I really did. Honestly, I thought it was such an elegant solution, planting the idea in your head that Myron was guilty. You kept resisting during the hypnosis, but I just kept pushing until you gave in. If you'd let it end that way, none of this would have happened. It all would have been over. But no, no, you had to keep going."

"Police," I managed to say. "The police are coming."

Tori smiled at me as rain poured down her face. She didn't look crazy, or angry, or sadistic. She looked as unflappable as she had during every one of our sessions in Las Vegas. That was the scariest part of all. She showed no emotions about what she was doing.

"No, they're not. My mother talks a good game, but she'll never turn me in. She feels too guilty about what I went through as a child. She won't call anyone. Once you're at the bottom of the cliff, I'll tell her how sorry I am, how it's over now, how it will never happen again. She'll forgive me and keep her mouth shut the way she has for ten years. As for you, well, everyone will assume that Skye's memories drove you mad. You couldn't take it anymore, so you followed in her footsteps by throwing yourself down to the rocks."

I let her keep talking.

As long as she kept talking, I had a chance.

"Don't feel sorry for Savannah. She deserved what she got. Do you know what she called me? Did that make it into Skye's memories? When I showed up here and told her I was the one sleeping with Andrew, she dished out all the racist slurs she'd been hurling at me for years. I didn't come out here to kill her, you know. I just wanted to brag about fucking her fiancé. But she started in on me, and all those years of abuse went off like a bomb. I picked up the club and swung it into her head. Direct hit. Skye tried to stop me, so I hit her, too. I knocked her out. That's why she didn't remember anything, I guess. I could have left it at that, but when I looked at Savannah in the grass, I realized how good it felt to hit her, so I hit her again. And again. And again. And again. I kept hitting her until she was nothing but pulp. I paid it all back, everything she'd put me through since I was nine years old. Then I dropped the club and ran."

I eyed the club, which thudded up and down as she beat it on the ground.

"What about Skye?" I asked.

Keep talking.

Give me a chance.

Tori stiffened at the sound of the name. The self-satisfied smile bled from her face. "I feel bad about Skye. She was decent to me. Not like Savannah. When she said she didn't remember anything, I wondered if that was a lie. If she'd actually decided to protect me. I mean, she hid the golf club. It had my prints on it. If she'd left it there, the police would have found me. But I guess she really did block it all out. You're the proof of that. Either way, ten years went by, and she never said a thing about that night. I thought I was safe. Then at Christmastime last year, she called me in Las Vegas. She asked me to meet her here. She said she was having flashbacks of the murder, that she thought she'd been at the cliff when Savannah was killed. She figured I could help her see what she'd forgotten. Twist of fate, huh? Just like you did. So I met her here."

"She remembered," I said.

"Yes. Being out here with me, she finally remembered. She wanted me to admit everything. Go to the police. So I had to get rid of her. She never saw it coming. Right to the end, she was too trusting. To the rest of the world, it was suicide. No one questioned it. Skye was dead, and the whole thing was finally over. After all those years looking over my shoulder, I was free."

Tori's fists clenched around the leather grip of the golf club. With a flash of anger, she got to her feet and swung it down hard, the oversize head landing inches from the left side of my skull. My broken arm couldn't grab it.

"Except Skye wasn't really dead. Not really. Thanks to Andrew. And thanks to *you.*"

Again she whipped the club over my face, so close I could feel the rush of air. And then it was gone before I could yank it away from her.

"Andrew. That impossible fool. He never could let go of me. The next night, after Savannah was dead, we were already in bed again. He never suspected what I'd done. He swallowed the story about Elijah, because that was easier than thinking he was partly to blame for what happened. We've been lovers ever since. I've been the rock in his life more than anyone else, more than Tyler, more than his wife. Whenever he had a breakthrough in his work, he told *me*. He wanted to impress *me*. He said his research was worth billions, and he was right. When I heard about it, I approached Paul Temple, and Temple paid me a fortune to spy on Andrew and pass along information. That night in Las Vegas? The party at the casino? I was there to meet Andrew. But of all things, he was late. Another twist of fate. When he finally got there, I was ready to leave, but someone got in our way."

I closed my eyes. "Me."

"You, Hallie. My skinny, drunk, bulimic, suicidal patient. You died, and Andrew just had to be the hero."

Tori knelt beside me again. The golf club was close to me, but I didn't know if I had the strength to jerk it out of her hands. I only had one chance. If I tried and failed, she wouldn't let me near it. She'd swing it into my head and then push my body off the cliff. Like Skye.

"Later that night, Andrew admitted what he did to you. He told me about putting memories inside you. But he was cagey about who it was. I think he'd begun to have doubts about me. Anyway, alarm bells went off in my head. In the hospital, when you talked about your sister being murdered—and you didn't even realize you'd said it—I knew it was *Skye* inside you. That meant my secret was in there, too. So I had to do something fast."

"You hired someone to kill me."

Tori shrugged. "You meet interesting people in Vegas. Especially in my line of work."

"Dutton."

"Yeah. I paid him to track you down. When you went to Boston, I had him follow you there, too. It was a bonus that he'd done some of his 'assignments' for the Chinese. The things people will tell you in therapy, huh? I figured it would look like you were being targeted for what was in your head. That's why I told him to take out Paul Temple when he was going after you. It added to the lie. Besides, I didn't need Temple giving anybody my name as his spy."

"What about Andrew? Why him?"

Tori sighed. She stood up and began swinging the club. She was on my other side now. My right side, where I was uninjured. The club head swished through the air only inches from my hand.

"Andrew finally figured it out. You told him that Paul Temple had a spy, that Paul knew what Andrew had done to you. There was only one way Temple could have found out so quickly. Me. So Andrew called me that night. He was starting to unravel everything. Not just the spying. Skye, too. And Savannah. He realized it was all me. I said I would come to Boston and explain, but instead, I sent Dutton to take care of both of you."

Tori stared down at me, and I stared up at her.

She was almost done with her story. I was running out of time.

The golf club swung back and forth over my body like a pendulum. Behind her, lightning cracked, lighting up the sky and silhouetting her in shadows. For an instant, just an instant, she glanced away from me and looked up at the rain and the storm.

I had my one chance, and I took it.

My fingers snapped around the shaft right above the club head, and I yanked the golf club out of her hand. I jabbed it with all my strength into her stomach, as if I were impaling her with a spear. The impact punched the air from her lungs, and she gagged and staggered backward, losing her balance.

The cliff's edge was right behind her.

Inches away.

I watched Tori teeter over the high drop like a marionette, struggling to land her feet on solid ground. Another flash of lightning exploded, closer than ever, then another bomb of thunder.

I willed her to fall backward. I watched her leg slip in the wet grass and dance in midair. Her other leg bent, and her mouth fell open in panic. She threw her torso forward as the lower half of her body spilled off the cliff. Her fingers clutched for traction in the mud, but she slid down. All I could see were her head and shoulders as she disappeared over the cliff.

Then her momentum stopped. Her face was still above the weeds, her eyes locked on mine. She didn't fall.

I'd lost.

With a groan, Tori dug her hands into the grass and pulled herself back onto solid ground. Covered in dirt, like a fresh body unburied from the earth, she swayed as she got to her feet. Her chest heaved with the effort. I tried to skitter away, but when I pushed myself up on one hand, I crashed back to the ground.

Tori marched toward me and wrenched the golf club out of my grasp. Her fingers clutched the wet grip. Her dark eyes were two electric bulbs reflecting the dazzle of lightning. Her face had no expression. When she looked down at me, I didn't think she saw Hallie or Skye. She was a girl lost in the past ten years ago. I was Savannah, and she was going to kill me again.

Like a lumberjack wielding an axe, Tori drew the golf club back high over her head. Her chest swelled as she began to send the club head hurtling toward my skull. I saw it move. It became a streak of silver, a shooting star. I wondered how much pain there would be.

Beneath me, in that same millisecond, the ground tingled.

I felt the oddest sensation, as if millions of bugs were crawling over my skin.

Then the world detonated with fire and noise as a blast of lightning exploded around us. Right on top of us. Rising from the ground,

317

shot straight up from hell. The head of the golf club spat out a column of flame, and a kind of x-ray image flashed in my brain as I saw Tori launched into the sky like a rocket.

My skin burned. My eyes went blind. My ears bled.

A concussion wave roared over my skull, and I was gone.

41

Dreams.

They're such strange things, taking us places we don't want to go, showing us things we don't want to see. There I was in the grass, unconscious after the lightning strike, but my dreams took me somewhere else entirely. They took me back to the place I'd been avoiding since I was ten years old.

My mother's house.

Skye was waiting for me there. She smiled at me and put her arm around my shoulder. Her long blond hair brushed my face. I knew why she'd brought me to this place, and I wasn't afraid of it anymore.

"We can't block out our past," she told me. "All we can do is live with it."

"I know."

"Do you remember what happened now?" she asked me.

"Yes."

"Show me," Skye said.

So I did. We weren't alone in the house. There was also a little girl with us, standing in the shadows of the hallway that led to my mother's room. Tall for ten years old. Messy black hair. Pale skin. Pretty. She held both hands over her ears, trying to block out "The Visitors" and trying to block out the screams from the bedroom. My mother's desperate voice cut through the closed door, calling to her and begging her for help.

Begging me.

"Make it stop! Please make it stop!"

Oh, Mom. Oh, the horror you were going through.

I watched ten-year-old Hallie squeeze her hands hard against her head, but she couldn't stop what she heard. I knew that. The world was just too loud for a little girl to keep it out forever.

"Help me! Oh, God, Hallie, help me, you have to help me!"

"What does she want you to do?" Skye asked softly.

I told her, because I remembered now what my mother needed from me. I was finally ready to see it again.

"She wants me to kill her," I said.

The little girl began to walk down the hallway, step by gangly step. She knew—we both knew—what was on the other side of the door. And what she would have to do in that room. Together, Skye and I watched the tableau play out like a horror movie. I saw the girl go to the door and take hold of that brass doorknob, shiny in the shadows.

That door had stayed closed in my head for nineteen years.

Now I watched myself open it and go inside.

"Look at you," Skye said with a kind of reverence. "I think that's the most courageous thing I've ever seen."

We followed the young girl through the open door, and we could see her in the bedroom now. She was there with the monsters on the walls and the duct tape over the windows and the broken glass on the floor from shattered mirrors. And my mother. She was there, too. My mother, her clothes dirty and torn, her hair unwashed for days, her face bloody where she'd beaten her head against the walls to drive out the demons.

There was a gun in her hand.

She wailed with grief and terror and exhaustion and madness. Her eyes were wide and wild.

"Make it stop, make it stop, help me please. Oh, Hallie, make it stop. I can't take it anymore. I can't."

The little girl spoke for the first time. She was so calm. *I was so calm.*

"I love you, Mom."

"I can't live with it. I've tried, you know I've tried, but I can't do it. It's too much."

"Yes, I know."

My mother sank to her knees. Tears ran down her face. Then reality fled from her again; it happened that fast; it turned in a moment. She thumped a fist against the wall and howled like a wolf. Her teeth bared. A growl roared from her throat. She came away from the wall and jammed the gun into the girl's face. The barrel was so close it pushed into my forehead. But the little girl didn't move or flinch or show any fear at all at the prospect of death.

"He sent you, didn't he? The demon sent you! He sent you to torture me! He's here!"

"No, Mom, it's just me."

My mother bellowed toward the sky.

"I shall drink his blood and be reborn! I am the goddess Andromeda! I come from the stars! You are nothing at my feet, you shall die, Devil, die!"

"It's me, Mom. It's Hallie."

"Hallie . . ."

The fit passed like a cloud from the sun. My mother sank slowly to her knees, her whole body trembling. She closed her eyes and opened them, closed them and opened them. In an instant of clarity, she saw her daughter and saw what she'd been about to do. She turned the gun around and pressed the grip into my hands and curled my little index finger around the trigger.

"Quickly, sweetheart. Quickly, you have to do it. You have to do it before she comes back. There's no time."

Her hands clasped over my hands, and she drew the gun forward to her breast. Her heart.

"Kill me. Please, Hallie, I need your help. You have to kill me."

"I don't think I can."

"Oh, Hallie, please, I can't live with it. You have to set me free. Please— oh, Hallie, please, please, please."

"Mom. Mom, I can't."

"She's coming! Oh, God, no, Hallie, Hallie, she's coming! I can't stop her! Do it now, do it now, please, I can't hold her back. If she takes me again—"

My mother's face dissolved into a red, cruel mask as the wolf came back.

ABBA sang about the visitors.

Ten-year-old Hallie closed her eyes and squeezed the trigger.

One loud shot.

And then it was done. Over. The house around me was gone, my mother was dead, the girl I'd once been had vanished. Somewhere in my past, that girl was running through the empty streets of Las Vegas toward Red Rock Canyon as her mind painted over those moments in the bedroom with dense black paint to make sure she would never see what was underneath.

Skye and I stood together. Two sisters in a white room, empty and so silent I could hear the beating of my heart. I looked down at my hands, which were covered in my mother's blood.

"I killed her," I said.

Skye rested her forehead against mine and told me the truth. "No, Hallie, you saved her."

42

Someone shook me.

A hand touched my arm, then my face, but I was only vaguely aware of it. Rain continued to fall, a light drizzle that slowly brought me out of unconsciousness. I felt wet and cold, and my head buzzed with a ringing that wouldn't go away. There was a metallic taste on my tongue. My eyes blinked open, but at first I saw nothing except strange orange fireworks. I closed my eyes, then opened them again. Darkness crept in at the edges and squeezed out the lights. It was still night around me.

I murmured something, but I couldn't hear my voice. In fact, I could barely hear anything other than that annoying ringing, like a phone that no one was bothering to answer. The rest of the world had become muffled, as if I were on one end of a long tunnel. Distantly, far away, someone shouted at me, but the voice sounded like a whisper wrapped up in an echo. Even so, I thought I heard my name.

"Hallie."

My eyes opened again. When the flashbulbs in my brain settled down, I was able to make out Myron kneeling beside me. His mouth moved, but I couldn't make out what he was saying. When I touched my right hand to my ear, my fingers came away with blood.

He called to me again. I heard him from the far end of the tunnel.

"Hallie, are you okay?"

I think I swore loudly in reply. Whatever I said made him smile, and he eased back on the wet grass and looked relieved. He reached out and held my hand. I could feel him squeezing it, and I could see his face more clearly now, and that told me that I was still alive.

However, the pain soon caught up with me. When I put pressure on the ground to push myself up, my shoulder reacted like a child with a hand on a hot stove. I collapsed. My knee throbbed, and I couldn't bend it or move my leg. I made another futile attempt to get up from the ground and fell backward.

Myron leaned closer and spoke in my ear, loud enough that I could hear him. "Don't move. I called an ambulance. They'll be here soon. The police, too."

I craned my head to see what was around me. I tried to make sense of what was going on, but my mind was scrambled. Inside me was nothing but a blank slate, a white space, no memory of where I was or how I'd gotten here. I looked for any kind of hook to remember what had happened, and finally, a far-off spark of lightning revealed the outline of Poseidon towering over the gardens.

Everything rushed back. The present. The past. Skye's memories. And my own.

"Tori," I said suddenly. "Where's Tori?"

Myron shook his head. "I didn't see her."

"What happened? Where did she go?"

"I don't know. I found you out here, but that's all I know. I could see that you were injured, so I called for help."

I remembered the tingling. The bugs on my skin.

"Lightning," I said, trying to hear myself say the word. "We were hit by lightning."

"You're lucky to be alive."

But I didn't feel lucky.

"The golf club," I said. "Do you see the golf club?"

Myron nodded. "It's near the cliff."

"Tori," I said again.

"She must have escaped. She's not here."

"What about you? How did you get here?"

"I told you I was driving down to find you. I figured you'd come here, so I went straight to the estate. I found Tori's mother inside. She admitted what was going on with her daughter. I came out to the cliff and found you lying in the grass."

"You drove here to save me."

"Of course I did."

"Even after the things I said to you."

"No matter what you said, I don't think you believed any of it was true."

I settled back into the grass with a sigh and closed my eyes again. At that moment, the only thing I wanted was to make the pain go away. I began to moan as the numbness wore off. Myron held my hand tightly, and I shuddered as the memories came back to me.

Tori swinging the club into me.

Tori clawing her way back from the cliff's edge.

Tori whipping the club over her head, getting ready to crush my skull.

Tori exploding into the air with the lightning.

My eyes flew open, because suddenly I knew where Tori was. I tried to get to my feet again and screamed when I couldn't. "Get me up, get me up, get me up," I begged Myron.

"Why? Hallie, wait for the ambulance. You're hurt."

"No, no, I need to get up! Take me to the cliff!"

I slung my good arm around his neck and held on. Reluctantly, Myron slid his hand and forearm under my thighs. As he pushed himself to his feet, he lifted me effortlessly with him. My left arm dangled uselessly, and the pain in my knee scorched me to the point of passing out.

"The cliff," I said again. "Take me there."

Myron balanced my weight in his arms. We crossed the short distance to the cliff's edge. The wind had diminished as the storm moved out, but the waves at the bottom still landed fiercely on the rocks. Myron leaned over as far as he could, and I held on tightly. We stared down below us, where black water surged and swirled. At first, the base of the cliff seemed invisible, and I couldn't make out any details.

Then the water shone from the glow of far-off lightning, and I saw her.

Tori lay draped over the rocks. Tendrils of seaweed dripped from her skin. Her limbs were bent in odd angles, and her head was tilted sideways where her neck had snapped. The waves came and went in crashes of spray over her body. I didn't know if the lightning or the fall had killed her, but regardless, she was dead.

I was free.

Free of everything. Free of guilt and punishment and regret.

"It's okay," I said to Myron. "You can put me down now."

"Let me take you to the house. It'll be warmer there."

He carried me across the wide stretch of grass. My body bounced along the way, and the tremors stung me, but I felt safe in his arms. As we neared the gardens, we passed beside the statue of Poseidon. From the beginning, Poseidon had been Skye, the towering symbol of who she was to me, and so I was surprised to feel nothing as I saw it. It elicited no emotions in my heart as I stared at this bronze god who'd been a fixture of my memories for days. I didn't understand why that was, but the emptiness gave me a strange sense of loss.

We climbed the terrace steps. The entire estate glowed above us because someone had turned the interior lights on. The door was still open, and we went inside. I squinted at the brightness, feeling a headache behind my eyes, but for the first time I could see the mansion in all its glory. Its elaborately carved sculptures. Its multicolored marble columns. Its hand-painted ceilings. Even empty, Skye's home was a Gilded Age museum.

And still I felt—nothing. The void puzzled me and left me afraid.

"Take me inside the ballroom," I said urgently.

"Hallie, you should rest."

"Please. I need to see it."

He carried me through the doors to the ballroom. I heard the damp squish of his shoes on the varnished wooden floor. I looked overhead at the soaring angels in the mural. I saw dust through the lights of the chandeliers and gold paint on the walls. But that was all. It was just a beautiful empty room. Melancholy filled me, a tidal wave of sadness and goodbyes.

"What is it?" Myron asked me, reading the look on my face.

"Something's wrong. Something's missing."

Here I was in the ballroom where I'd remembered so much, and yet I was adrift. My emotions had drained away, leaving me hollow. But I wasn't just coming down from an adrenaline high. I realized that I no longer felt *crowded*. That sensation of too many memories squeezing my head had vanished. I knew what had happened here, but I couldn't *see* any of it the way I had before. The images and sensations weren't alive inside me anymore. They existed, but they were dead.

The lightning strike.

It had to be the lightning rocketing through the ground and through my body. The memories that had been planted inside my head had somehow short-circuited. Electricity giveth, and electricity taketh away.

"She's gone," I murmured.

Myron didn't understand. "What do you mean?"

"Skye's gone. She's not there."

"You mean her memories?"

I shook my head. "No, I remember everything I did before, but it's two dimensional now. Flat. The memories aren't real. I don't feel *her* now. Skye's not with me anymore."

He tried to read how I felt. "Well, this is what you wanted, isn't it?"

"I guess—I guess it is."

"Now you have your life back."

"Yes, I do."

Myron stared at me, and his face changed. I knew he could see the difference in me, too. The ghost of Skye didn't look back at him. For good or bad, I wasn't the girl of his dreams anymore. I was Hallie Evers and no one else. I was someone he would have to meet all over again, and learn about, and discover.

My shoulders shook, and my face was wet, but not from the rain. I didn't know what was happening to me, but then I realized I was crying. Sobbing. Hopelessly sobbing, unable to stop. I shook my head in wonder as tears poured down my face. Myron held me cradled in his arms in the middle of the ballroom, and all I could do was cry and cry.

I cried for my mother. I cried for Skye. I cried for the emptiness I felt.

I'd found and lost a best friend in the space of a few days. A soul mate, a sister I'd never met. We'd come together to find our own truths, and now we were on separate paths again. I suppose that's the way it had to be.

But I was going to miss her.

43

There is a painting on my wall.

It hangs above my fireplace, a spectrum of bright colors showing an abstract rendering of bare skin, pink lips, naked limbs, and black hair. It's me, the real Hallie Evers, seen through Myron's eyes. Around me is a sky filled with lightning bolts and tridents, and in the background, like an angel retreating into bloodred clouds, is the faintest image of a girl with long blond hair. You have to look very closely to see her.

Myron calls the painting *Independence Day*.

A year has passed since the events at the cliff in Newport. A new summer is underway, warm and calm. I haven't put the experience of last July completely behind me. I still walk with the slightest limp, and my left arm doesn't have the full mobility it once did. I get headaches, and my hearing is only at 30 percent in my right ear. But those are small things in exchange for being alive.

I never went back to Las Vegas. As I told you, I'm a water girl, and I'd found a new home thanks to Skye. Not in Boston, though. Without her inside me, Boston didn't have a hold on me in the same way. Instead, I found a house an hour north of the city, in the little town of Gloucester. It's small, but I don't need much space, and it literally sits on the coastline, so I can watch the ocean waves and storms from my front window. There is a swimming pool in the back. I swim every summer day.

The location made the house *extremely* expensive. I'm not staggeringly wealthy, not the way Paul Temple told me I'd be, but I found a lawyer who negotiated a very lucrative settlement with Hyppolex for what they did to me. In exchange, I agreed not to sue them or drag their name through the media mud. So Tyler's money bought me my oceanside Gloucester home, with enough to spare that I don't feel the need to write websites for medical device companies anymore. I can do what I want with my life, but I'm still in the early days of figuring out what that is.

Yes, I'm alone most of the time. I'm at peace being alone. Myron comes to see me sometimes, and sometimes I drive into the city to see him. He's a good friend, occasionally a lover, but neither of us seems to want more than that. Otherwise, this place works for the solitary me. When I want to shop, or eat lobster, or visit the library, I go into Gloucester. The locals have begun to recognize me, greet me by name, and ask about my day. It's a simple life. No alcohol—well, okay, a glass of wine now and then. No drugs. No purging. No yearning for things I don't have. I've discovered that I'm happy being simple.

I'm also learning to forgive myself for the things I've done in my life. All of them—my mistakes and my sins. Even what I did in that bedroom when I was ten years old. I think my mother would be proud of me.

And Skye—well, Skye is just a memory now. The more time that passes, the further she recedes into my shadows. Of course, she's still here in small ways. I'm taking piano lessons, and the instructor is astonished at how quickly I'm picking it up. She says she can't believe I've never played before, which makes me smile. I won't be soloing on Rachmaninoff for the BSO, not with the stiffness in my arm that never goes away, but Skye is close to me whenever I play.

That's Hallie today. That's who I am.

It's funny. When I was a girl, the only thing I wanted to do was write books that would take me around the world. I guess when the place where you are doesn't feel like home, you always want to be somewhere else. Now I *am* home, and I find I never want to leave. I've stopped running.

Oh, I still write. That's part of me, and it hasn't changed. But if Skye taught me anything, it's that there are endless stories locked away inside my own head. I just have to look in the mirror to find them. So in the evenings, I've begun to take out my laptop and tap away at the keys.

Myron says I should begin with a memoir. I like that idea. The strange true story of Hallie Evers and Skye Selden, two girls who were both dead and both reborn. Two girls who—at least for a little while—lived the same life.

I know just how it starts.

How bad was that July 4? Let me count the ways.

ACKNOWLEDGMENTS

Back in 2015, my father passed away while I was writing my novel *The Night Bird*. This past year, I lost my mother two days after I turned in the manuscript for *I Remember You*. My parents knew that I'd dreamed of a career writing books since I was a boy, and they were cheerleaders for that dream throughout my life. I'm very glad they both lived to see me break through as an author and that they were there for many of the amazing highlights I've seen in the book world for the past eighteen years. But I miss them.

No author is an island. We may put the words on the page ourselves, but getting the book in your hands (and living the author's life) takes a whole lot of support from family, friends, agents, publishers, booksellers, librarians, and readers. For me, I'm exceptionally lucky to have the best partner in love, life, and the book business that anyone could ever have—my wife, Marcia. She gets the first read on each new book, and her feedback makes each book better. So if you enjoy my novels, a big part of the thanks goes to her. I also want to thank Ann Sullivan for her editorial feedback on all of my manuscripts; together, she and Marcia make sure I've accomplished what I want to do with my stories and characters.

I've had an amazing agent throughout my career: Deborah Schneider has seen me through this crazy business since the very beginning! And she works with terrific teams, including Josie Freedman of ICM in Los Angeles, Cathy Gleason and Penelope Burns in New York, and Alice Lutyens and Claire Nozieres in London. I wouldn't have this writing job without their hard work!

The folks at Thomas & Mercer do an incredible job from the editorial side all the way to copy editing, cover design, marketing, publicity, and production. I'm honored to work with all of them. Jessica Tribble Wells has an amazing eye as an editor, as does developmental editor Charlotte Herscher—and they both made invaluable suggestions on this book. The whole T&M team is a treat for authors.

If this book is in your hands (or on your Kindle), I'm also thankful for YOU! My readers have been supportive of me from the beginning all the way back in 2005 and have stayed with me on this wide-ranging creative journey from series books to stand-alones. I'm very grateful, and I hope to keep introducing you to new characters for a long time to come.

ABOUT THE AUTHOR

Photo by Malyssa Woodward

Brian Freeman is an Amazon Charts and *New York Times* bestselling author of psychological thrillers, including the Frost Easton and Jonathan Stride series. His books have been sold in forty-six countries and translated into twenty-four languages. His stand-alone thriller *Spilled Blood* was named Best Hardcover Novel in the International Thriller Writers Awards, and his novel *The Deep, Deep Snow* was a finalist for the Edgar Award. *The Night Bird*, the first book in the Frost Easton series, was one of the top twenty Kindle bestsellers of 2017. Brian is widely acclaimed for his vivid "you are there" settings and for his complex, engaging characters and twist-filled plots. He lives in Minnesota with his wife, Marcia. For more information on the author and his books, visit bfreemanbooks.com.